To CC
Felle

X

SHARON WRIGHT:
BUTTERFLY
JOHN LYNCH

Published by Mandrill Press www.mandrillpress.com

Penguin Random House is committed to a sustainable future for our business, our readers and our planet. This book is made from Forest Stewardship Council® certified paper.

Printed and bound in Great Britain by Clays Ltd, St Ives plc

ISBN 978-1-910194-10-2

Also by this author

Zappa's Mam's a Slapper by John Lynch
A Just and Upright Man by RJ Lynch
You can follow John's books on his blog at
http://jlynchblog.com/
Writing is a solitary business and John is always happy to hear from readers. His email address is
rjl@mandrillpress.com

CHAPTER 1

The outside tables would have given a better view, but sitting outside in the growing dark would attract attention, and not attracting attention was one of the things that kept Carver out of jail. He watched the girl as she walked down the road. Tart. Look at the length of that skirt. Asking for it.

She turned between the stone pillars. There would have been a gate once, a handsome gate for this had been a moneyed people's street in the days before they turned the houses into flats. She fumbled for her keys. Carver hadn't needed a key to get into her flat. A tart's flat. Cupboards full of drink. It wasn't womanly. Carver's mother had drunk Cyprus sherry, and that only on special occasions.

Carver's mother hadn't lived alone, either. Not at that age. It wouldn't have been proper. She'd lived with her family, been a wife and mother, enduring. She'd stayed with her husband till he died, and she'd gone on looking after Carver until he went south, looking for a place where people would pay for good service, properly executed. Properly executed! It still made him smile. There were people who thought he wasn't the full shilling, he knew that, but he'd dreamed up his own slogan, good as FCUK any day.

She'd still been a young woman when the old man's liver packed up, but she'd continued to show the proper respect. Carver's mother wouldn't have disgraced her dead husband's bed by bringing another man into it. She wouldn't have draped underwear all over the place, either, even if she'd owned the kind of underwear this tart wore, which she wouldn't have.

3

As was his way, Carver had pocketed a pair of the bitch's knickers. Not out of the laundry basket or off the bedroom floor, he wasn't stupid, she'd notice that and she'd know someone had been in the place. She'd be on her guard. No, he'd taken them out of a drawer, and from the bottom of the drawer at that.

They'd still smelt of the tart's perfume, though.

Don't put them on guard. He'd learned that in Twickenham when he'd written that message on the dressing room mirror. *TART,* he'd written, using her reddest lipstick. He'd put her on guard all right. She'd known something was going on, been waiting for him, half waiting at any rate, subconsciously aware at the very least and Carver hadn't been able to talk sense to her, get his warnings out while she still had enough self-possession to take any notice. He hadn't even had time to get the tape on her mouth, and so he'd had to put his hands round her throat to shut her up.

And even then she hadn't had the sense to be still. Bitch. He didn't want to go through that again.

The door closed; the little whore was out of sight. She'd reappear in a minute or two, moving behind the windows of her flat. Carver sipped his coffee. He wanted a cigarette, that was a real drawback to the inside tables, you couldn't smoke there. In another place, under different circumstances, Carver might have lit up anyway, to hell with them, but that would have drawn attention. If she told the police what had happened, they didn't always, often they didn't, usually in fact, it was shame and the certainty that they'd been asking for it, but if she did the police were going to be asking around. Had anyone seen someone acting suspiciously? And of course they'd remember a man who got into an argument over a smoke.

They might even ask Carver. He'd been coming to this café for a while, that was how he'd seen the girl in the first place. A regular now whenever he was in London, he'd used it ever since he'd done that guy coming out of the Richmond Rugby Club's ground a short walk away, the one he'd followed from the club house and shot just below Mick Jagger's place up on the hill.

He wasn't worried. The waitresses liked him here, he was quiet, nicely spoken, a good tipper. He had a certain charm, a lot of people had told him so. A nice voice that people who didn't know the real thing thought was public school. A way with words. Properly executed! You had to laugh.

No-one was going to think he'd do something like that, even to a piece wiggling her arse in a skirt that was far too short, asking for it. Not as long as he obeyed the rules, and why wouldn't he? They were his rules.

But the police wouldn't question Carver, because Carver wouldn't be here. The police kept records of everyone they interviewed. You got yourself on one of those lists and then you could get yourself on another list when some other girl in some other place complained about getting what she'd been begging for. Then someone put the lists together and spotted the coincidence. Policemen don't believe in coincidences, so Carver didn't believe in them, either. Before he left, he'd plant his alibi in the waitress's mind. Tell her he was going to France the following day and probably wouldn't be back for a while. He didn't want to be remembered as the man who stopped coming in right after that little whore got what was coming to her.

Carver twisted slightly on the stool. The girl's panties were a bit tight for him, a bit constricting, and he loved the feeling when they rubbed against him, got off on it in fact. He had to be just a little careful, he didn't want to anticipate his own pleasure, he'd done that with that little tart in Barnes and had to put the operation off for a couple of days until he felt ready again. He'd liked it, the feel of it, walking around in a pair of tight nylon panties glued to him by his own outpouring, but liking it wasn't the point.

It was four o'clock and the lights were going on. What a climate. Carver would be glad to get the job over and be on his way home. The job he'd come from Burgundy to do, not this little interlude with the short-skirted tart—this was pleasure but that was strictly business. The tunnel had changed his life, he enjoyed the service in first class on the train to Paris, but he wouldn't really be at ease until the TGV pulled out of the Gare de Lyon and he was on his way home to Auxerre. His first night back, he'd have dinner at one of the outside tables at *Le Quai*. No-one there would object when he lit up.

The little tart was moving around in her lighted flat. Carver went to the counter and settled his bill.

'As people remember it, the Beat movement was a male preserve. Kerouac, Ginsberg, the little catamite Neal Cassady. Women didn't count, except to cook and sleep with. Joyce Johnson's a woman, and if we think of her today at all, it's as Kerouac's lover. But Joyce Johnson could write the arse off the lot of them.'

The speaker, a young bearded man with better clothes than students usually wore, looked round the table. It had been a prepared utterance, all of them knew that, but worth a smile nonetheless. The bearded man drained his coffee and stood up. 'Shall we go?'

Sharon Wright watched the little group gather their things together and leave. What must it be like to be able to say things like that? What must it be like even to be the sort of person people said things like that to?

Turning an unlit cigarette over and over in her hands, lost in a dream world of knowledge and café conversation, Sharon became aware that someone beyond the now empty table was smiling at her. With an effort she brought the face into focus. 'Yoxer!'

"Lo, Sharon.' He stood up and shambled over to her table, carrying his coffee. 'Mind if I join you?'

It had often amused Sharon, back in the days when she and Yoxer were a secret, illicit item, to think how they might appear to other people. Anyone looking at the pair of them would have thought: father and daughter; uncle and niece; older and younger neighbours. She, short skirt, heels, dyed hair, knowing eyes. He, thirty years older, give or take a decade, the pasty complexion that came from a life lived indoors in smoky halls and bars, a touch of resignation. What would be would be. Anyone looking at the pair of them would have been wrong.

'How's it going, girl?'

'Mustn't grumble, Yoxer. How about you?'

He shrugged. 'Same. Buggy keeping you happy?'

She smiled, but didn't answer.

'You deserve better, girl.'

'I know, Yoxer. I know. Thought I had it, once.' She turned her soft gaze on him. 'When you were champion of the world. And I was your naughty little girl.'

'I was always too old for you, Sharon.'

'A naughty little girl needs an older man to keep her in order.'

'You haven't got Buggy playing, then?'

'Buggy's a meat and potatoes man when it comes to sex, Yoxer.'

'Slam, Bam, thank you, ma'am? Roll over, fart and fall asleep?'

'Something like that.'

'We had some good times.'

'We did, Yoxer. You opened a whole world for me.' She put the cigarette back in the packet. 'Wish I could light one of these. What's a catamite?'

'Dunno, girl. Bet it isn't a nice thing to be, though.'

'What happened to all the money, Yoxer?'

'Beats me. I had it, I spent it. Pissed it up against the wall, I suppose. Pissed off the Inland Revenue, too.'

'I'll never forget that day. Pitching up and finding you gone.'

She'd been fifteen when it started. Spotted him, driving around in his Bentley. And he'd spotted her, coming out of a corner shop where she'd been buying cigarettes. All the kids knew Yoxer. Local boy made good. Face all over the telly. One or two of the older girls would smirk quietly when his name came up, but no-one ever said why. He'd never taken much notice of Sharon. Ignored her, in fact.

But not that day.

He'd stopped the car and stared, pretended not to notice the fuck-you look of disdain she gave anyone who wasn't Buggy, or maybe Jackie Gough. He held up a twenty pound note. Seeing a slight reaction, but no movement, he added a second twenty to it. Sharon crossed the pavement and slipped into the passenger seat. Simple as that.

Looking back, she knew she must have been mad, but the kind fairies had been looking after her. Yoxer was a funny bugger, but he didn't hurt people.

He had a big house out towards Ashford. She knew it would take a while to get home and she'd have some explaining to do, but she had the forty pounds in her hand and, frankly, she didn't give a toss. It wasn't as though she had parents like Veronica Payne's. Parents who cared.

She was no stranger to sex. Her mother knew all about early sexual activity, having had Sharon when she herself was seventeen. She put Sharon on the pill when Sharon and Buggy became an item.

But Buggy had never put her over his knee and ripped off her knickers. Buggy had never spanked her till her bottom was as red as his bulging-eyeballed face.

What first stopped her from protesting, throwing Yoxer off and telling him to get lost, disgusting pervert that he was, was the thought of the money she was earning. What stopped her after that was more basic. She was enjoying herself as she had never enjoyed herself in her life before.

He picked her up every week after that. When her mother asked where she went every Saturday, Sharon told her she was earning ten pounds a week for tidying in the People's Theatre. She handed over a fiver—half her earnings, as her mother proudly told everyone. What a good girl Sharon was, so generous to her mother. Not like some of these stuck-up little madams. That Payne girl, for example, nose always in a book, never think of a Saturday job, earn the money to buy her mother a packet of fags. Not that the stuck-up Mrs Payne smoked, of course. Her husband used a pipe, which was all right because Prince Philip had smoked one, too, when he was a naval officer. But smoking wasn't something ladies did.

Any other venue—a fast food place, Woolworth's, a supermarket—her mother might have dropped in to see her. But a theatre? Never.

Apart from which, Sharon had had a sneaking unadmitted interest in the theatre ever since they'd read *What the Butler Saw* in school, and then been to the People's to see it performed. Sharon had walked home from there in a daze wishing Buggy would, just this once, stop feeling her up and let her *think*. Wishing there was someone she could discuss the play with without looking like a swot.

Jackie Gough would have been just the person, of course. But Buggy would have gone berserk if she'd talked to Jackie about a stupid play instead of letting him inflict horrible great love bites on her throat. And Jackie knew that, so he was never going to oblige.

It went on for three months and then, suddenly, Yoxer failed to arrive at the pick-up point. Sharon went home and told her mother the theatre was closed for renovation. He wasn't there the next week, either.

With some difficulty, Sharon worked out how to get to Yoxer's house by bus. Three busses, in fact. And three back, which was why she felt so unhappy knocking on the door of an obviously empty house with a For Sale sign at the end of the drive.

CHAPTER 2

Inside the flat, Stacy Teasdale kicked off her shoes and slipped into the padded moccasins with the little Piglet heads on the front. She thought they were Piglet, anyway—Mark said they looked more like rats. She took a Coke out of the fridge, popped a straw into the neck of the bottle and checked for messages on the portable telephone handset. There was only one, telling her that Mark hoped to finish early in Birmingham and might get back before the weekend; that she should think of something nice he could cook for her; and that he loved her even more today than he had loved her yesterday.

She danced away from the phone, effervescing more than her Coke, then danced back. Time for the weekly call home.

Stacy's parents liked Mark. They liked his safe job, they liked his politeness, they liked the way he cared for Stacy. But most of all, she knew, they liked the fact that he didn't live with Stacy and wouldn't until they were married. She smiled. She, too, liked Mark for the way he cared for her. But she liked him even more for having a bigger cock than any man she had known, and for being better able to hold back his own climax till she had reached hers.

Would her mother be shocked? Don't tell her, then, was Stacy's view.

She picked up the phone and dialled the number.

When the girl approached him, Doyle was window shopping. On one side of the window, a silk jacket with a £500 price tag. On the other, thrown away pizza boxes, hamburger wrappers and coke tins.

'Can you spare fifty pence?'

'Holy shit, I hope so,' he said. 'I'd be in a mess if I couldn't spare fifty pence.'

She was studying him carefully. Normally, a professional hit man in town to do a job might not like that, but there was something about this girl. 'But you don't intend to,' she said at last.

A nice face. Intelligent. And she had, at least, a better approach than "Spare some change?" which he heard whined at every mainline station. Fifty pence was such a specific sum; a clear request with some hope of being met.

'No,' he said. 'I don't.'

She held eye contact a little longer. Showing she wasn't afraid of him. Then she turned away. The back view as nice as the front. Tight jeans, swelling where they were supposed to.

'Hey.'

She turned back and looked at the ten pound note he held out. 'What do you expect for that?'

'What are you offering?'

Thin, freckled nose. Tanned cheeks. A touch of pink on the lips; of blue on the eyelids. Brown hair that had caught the sun, hanging around her face but clean. Blue T-shirt, also clean. 'Nothing,' she said.

He shrugged. 'Take it for nothing, then.'

She stepped closer, looking for the catch. 'Who are you?'

He took a pen from his pocket and wrote on the note. 'That's who I am. And that's where I'm staying. You want another four of those, come up and see me.'

A smile touched the edge of her mouth. 'And how long will you be staying at the Hilton, Mr. Brown?'

'I'll be there tonight. After six. Don't ask for me at Reception. Just take the lift and come straight up.'

She nodded. 'The other forty. Do I get that for nothing, too?'

'What do you think?'

She tucked the note into the back pocket of her jeans. 'Well, thanks for this. But don't hold your breath tonight.'

'If you're not there by six thirty, don't come.'

She walked away, hips swaying. He saw her stop at the lights and look back. Then she went down the filthy steps into the tube station and was gone.

He went into the shop and tried on the jacket. Five hundred wasn't much. Not against the five thousand he was getting for this job. Plus expenses. Never forget the expenses. And there was something very chic to a Boston boy about a red silk jacket bought in London. But he didn't have enough cash to buy it and still pay his hotel bill, and he used only cash when he was working. Cash couldn't be traced like plastic or cheques. He admired the jacket's perfect fit and opulent feel. What the hell. No-one was going to tie him to this shop. He handed the assistant his platinum American Express card and the sport coat he had worn when he came in. 'Put that in a bag for me.'

The assistant looked at the name on the Amex card. 'Of course, Mr. Doyle.'

'I hate the thought of you doing this.'

The small flat was clean and tidy. Old furniture, worn but well looked after. A large glazed pot, full of white lilies. And books. A lot of books.

'I know you do. But forty pounds is food for a week. And it could lead to a lot more.'

Melanie Cantrell threw herself onto the sofa beside Caroline. 'You got ten for nothing. For forty he's going to want sex.'

'Melanie, we need the money.'

'We should be able to provide for ourselves without men.'

'And we can't. Look, we agreed. I have to do this. It isn't the first time. I took Stapleford's money for six months. You were happy to eat the food he put on the table.'

'Money is about power. *Sex* is about power.'

Caroline smiled, and pressed a hand to Melanie's thigh. 'Except when we do it?'

'You know nothing about this man. He might be dangerous.'

Caroline shrugged. 'He has a nice smile.'

Melanie shook her head. 'A nice smile. Hitler had a nice smile. Tony Blair has a nice smile. I bet Jack the Ripper had a nice smile.'

Caroline intensified the pressure on Melanie's thigh. 'Shall we take our clothes off and be horizontal for a while? Before I go?'

The room smelt bad, of cigarette smoke and fear. Buggy lit another cigarette and filled his glass from a bottle of Scotch. This was his third cigarette and his third Scotch. The meeting had so far lasted forty minutes.

'All I did,' he said, 'was what you asked me to do. You wanted a man who handled a certain kind of work. I found him for you. You wanted someone who didn't have a record and wouldn't talk afterwards, or come back for more money. I gave you that.'

'You gave us a loony.' Jim Cameron was the least unappealing of the three men. His strong chin was clean-shaven; his light grey suit expensive and carefully pressed; his pale blue shirt freshly ironed. He alone did not smoke; he alone had taken only one glass of Scotch, which stood half tasted before him.

Carefully, Buggy said, 'Jim. You wanted a killer. You wanted a man who'd walk up to someone he'd never met and blow him away. You think sane people do that for a living? You know what happens when you say to a man in the street, "Here. You see that guy over there? Someone you never even saw before? I want you to take this gun and walk over there and shoot him. Dead." You know what happens when you do that? The guy gives the gun back to you, and he says, "You do it." And you know what he does next? He calls the police, and he tells them about this interesting conversation he's just had. That's what he does, Jim.

'You asked me to find you a killer. That's the same thing as saying, "Find me a nutter, Buggy. Find me someone who likes killing people".'

Johnnie Walker pushed a cigarette between purple lips. 'I think we knew the Pope wasn't going to pull the trigger, Buggy. What we hoped was that your man would only like killing people he was paid to kill.'

'And you got someone who makes his hobby his work.'

Cameron sipped from his glass. 'We're not getting anywhere,' he said. 'It's too late to get a new hit man now. Look at it from our point of view, Buggy. We come to you to get a job done. The job's going to be done. Fine. You tell us this guy doesn't know who we are. We believe you. He knows you, and you do know who we are. But that doesn't worry us, because you aren't going to grass.' The eyes fixed on Buggy. 'You aren't going to grass,' Cameron repeated carefully. 'But you get this guy for us, and we give you the go-ahead, and we pay you right up front, and then we find out—and not from you, Buggy. Not from you—we find out that this man Doyle likes to kill people for fun. At random. He doesn't work in the States anymore, where he was born and brought up and people know him, because he likes to kill people for fun. And he got caught, Buggy'.

Cameron looked around the room as though looking at something he did not quite believe. 'A man who does a nice clean job for a price on someone he never saw in his life isn't going to get caught. But a man who kills people because he feels like it? He got caught once, Buggy, and he's going to get caught again. And that might not be good for other people.'

Watch the eyes was Buggy's rule. It's the eyes that give them away. Your true psycho, you can see it in his eyes. There's nothing there. He looked at Cameron. 'Doyle has killed seven men in this country, that I know of. He's never been caught yet.'

'He was caught in the States.'

'Yes,' Buggy said. 'And you know how much time he did?'

No-one spoke.

'He didn't do any time,' Buggy said. 'He was not guilty.'

Cameron laughed. 'Not guilty,' he said. 'That's a good one, Buggy. Listen, what would you say if we wanted him hit after he does the job?'

Buggy licked dry lips. 'Doyle's never been caught yet,' he said again. 'I can vouch for him.'

'With your life?'

Jeez, Buggy thought. How did I get mixed up in this? 'That won't be necessary', he said.

'No,' Cameron said, 'it won't. Because we're doing it our way.' He took a piece of paper from his wallet. 'The name Carver mean anything to you? Donald Carver?'

People in Yoxer's road didn't have neighbours in quite the way people in Sharon's block of flats did, but someone must have seen her walk up the drive.

A police car arrived, with two uniformed policemen in it.

'Am I in trouble?' asked Sharon in the back of the car.

'I don't know, love. Are you?' He looked back at her over the top of his passenger seat.

She ran her tongue along her lower lip. It was a trick she had learned with Buggy and perfected with Yoxer, and she could see it was working here. 'I might be,' she said. 'If I don't have forty quid to give my mother.'

A conversation ensued between the two policemen. Sharon didn't follow all of it. She didn't need to—she knew it was going her way. "It's Yoxer, for God's sake," was the argument that clinched it. "We *know* what she's here for." That and "Don't be ridiculous. She's begging for it."

They drove to a wooded lane outside town where the two policemen took turns guarding the approach while the other gave Sharon a seeing to in the back seat of the car. When it was over, Sharon hadn't minded it, quite enjoyed it in fact, better than with Buggy if she was honest. As Yoxer was fulfilled by his particular kink and never consummated the relationship afterwards, this was her first penetration by a grown man. Size, she discovered, really did matter.

And the coppers were decent enough fellers. They put their cash together and gave her the forty pounds for her mother "and ten for yourself, love." Then they took her to the station and bought a ticket for a train that would get her home far faster, but much more expensively, than the three busses. One of them pressed a fiver into her hand. 'Take a taxi from Waterloo, love.' He patted her on the bottom. 'You've got a gift, sweetheart. A real gift.'

When she got home, Sharon told her mother there was an economy drive at the People's Theatre and she wouldn't be needed till further notice.

CHAPTER 3

Carver turned left out of the café and walked three hundred yards to the big roundabout. Over the dual carriageway, crossing with the green light, never drawing attention even by jaywalking, taking his time. Right to where the road forked, then slowly back, this time across three roads. All the time looking casually around. No-one was watching. As he walked, he slipped on a pair of surgical rubber gloves.

Steadily now, back along the other side of the road from the café towards the flat where the girl waited. He let himself feel the rub of silk (was it really silk? Probably not. Silk, satin, some man-made fabric—Carver couldn't tell) on his hard penis. Not long now.

A glance across the road as he came level with the café. The outside tables were still empty. No waitress looked towards him, even for a moment. He passed the café, turned in through the stone pillars, took the thin piece of plastic from his pocket and opened the street door. The exhilaration was physical, now; it was all he felt. There had been a time when playing cricket gave him all the excitement he needed, or rugby league. Now, the only times he was fully alive were when he was doing this. He moved lightly, almost dancing towards the stairs. His skin was flushed; his eyes shone.

Letters and old free newspapers lay here and there in the entrance hall. The carpet was worn, to the backing in some places. The house was London in microcosm—no-one cared about the public areas. What a selfish country this had become. He was glad he was out of it.

18

On the second floor, he pulled the stocking over his head, took the gun from his pocket and banged loudly on the door.

Inside, Stacy's voice was raised. 'Mum, I'm not saying I'm going to go. I'm not saying that. It's just, the door's still open, okay? I told them I couldn't go now, they said fine, but don't say never. If I change my mind, all I have to do is call them. Okay?'

'Oh, but Stacy. Croupier on a cruise ship. You know nothing about being a croupier.'

'Vanessa knew nothing about it when she started. Now she's making a pile of money and having a good time.'

There was another loud bang on the door.

'What does Mark think? Would he wait for you?'

'Mum, I'm twenty-five. You know? I'm not ready to settle down yet. Mark can wait or not wait. Listen, there's someone at the door.'

'And what kind of people would you meet in a job like that?'

'Ah. Now we're getting to it.'

The hammering on the door seemed likely to bring it down. 'Listen, Mum, I'm just going to lay the phone down, okay? I'm not hanging up on you, you understand? I'll just get rid of whoever this is and we'll carry on talking. Okay, Mum?'

She laid the handset carefully on the table and went to the door. Her face was pink, her expression cross. Whoever was making that noise was going to wish they hadn't.

When Caroline had showered, Melanie lay on the bed and watched her dress. 'Do you have to wear those?'

'Those?'

'Stockings. Suspenders. Don't play dumb.'

Caroline sat down and took the young woman's face in her hands. 'It's a game, Melanie. You know—like you and I play?

19

Men like to play them, too.'

Melanie sat up, brushing her lover's hands away. 'Where are you going to put the tape recorder?'

'No tape recorder, Mel.'

'But ...'

'I'm not going to a restaurant, I'm going to his room. Suppose he goes through my bag? What do you think he's going to say if he catches me recording our conversation?' She stood up and finished dressing. 'Wish me luck.'

The two women held each other tight. Then Caroline broke away. She pulled on a denim jacket, blew a kiss across the bed and left. Alone, Melanie wandered slowly into the living room. 'Good luck,' she murmured to the closed door.

In one smooth movement Carver pressed the gun to the girl's throat, put his other hand over her mouth and pushed her back inside the flat. His foot kicked the door closed behind him. He pressed his nylon covered face close to hers. 'Not a word,' he hissed. 'Not a word or I'll blow your head off.'

This was the time, he knew that. Get it under control now and it's all over. The girl's head was pressed against the wall, his gun against her throat, his hand still over her mouth. Carver didn't move. He listened to her whimpering, watched the terror in her eyes, waited for it to change to something else. Waiting for her brain to kick in was how he described it to himself. Dirty little cow.

At last he said, 'I'm going to take my hand away. Make a sound, I'll kill you. Do you understand?'

She couldn't nod. Her eyelids fluttered up and down.

Slowly, Carver moved his hand until it was two inches from her face. 'What do you want?', she whispered.

'You'll find out.' He moved away from her, the gun pointed at her face. They stared at each other.

'Money?', she asked. 'Do you want money?'

'When I tell you,' Carver said, 'You're going to move over to the window. You're going to close the curtains. You're going to do it quickly. You're not going to look at anyone out there and you're not going to make a signal. Do you understand?'

'I've got money,' the girl said. 'It's in my bag.'

'You don't strike me as stupid. Are you stupid?'

The girl shook her head.

'I didn't think so. Now you're going to close the curtains. Do I have to go through it all again?'

Another shake of the head.

'Good. Get it wrong and I'll kill you. Do you understand?'

The girl nodded.

'Say it. Say it out loud.'

She obliged with a voice that was much louder than it had been. 'I won't do anything silly. I understand you'll kill me if I do.'

'That's good.' Carver liked it when they got over their initial shock. It meant they were more aware and he liked them to be aware. He waved the gun. The girl moved towards the curtains.

Sharon took in the state of Yoxer's slacks and casual jacket. Old, but obvious quality, and well cared for. 'Do you live on your own?'

'Mostly.'

'Right now?'

'Yes, right now I'm on my own.'

'So who looks after you?'

He laughed. 'I do. I can work a washing machine as well as a woman. I can iron. And I'm a pretty good cook. You think it needs a woman's touch? You saying you look after Buggy?'

She ignored that. 'My Dad said you went bankrupt.'

'Oh, yeah. It was the only way. The Revenue did a number on me. Took everything I had left.'

'And you came back here.'

'Eventually.'

'How do you manage?'

'I do all right. My old agent gets me a few gigs. Sportsman's dinners. Speeches. The odd exhibition. I get by. And the agent deducts the tax before he pays me and sends it to the Revenue himself. Sends them too much, as a matter of fact. I got a refund last year.'

'And they paid it?'

'Course they paid it.'

'You didn't still owe them money?'

'That's what being bankrupt means, Sharon. They take your car, they take your house, they take everything they can find. But in return your debts are cancelled. You don't owe anyone anything.'

'Didn't you see it coming?'

'Funny thing, Shazza. You always think you've got one more year in you. One more year to earn the big money, pay everyone off, get a nest egg, set yourself up. Then, one day, you find out you haven't.'

'Don't you feel sad?'

'Why should I? I used to be world champion. Now I couldn't even win a qualifier. But people round here, they know what I was. And I've always got enough to keep myself clean, buy a paper, packet of ciggies, come in here for a coffee. If it all turns to rat shit tomorrow, what the hell? I've had a few laughs.'

Sharon pulled her jacket around her, picked up her cigarettes, dropped them into her handbag. 'You want me to come back to your place?'

'I haven't got forty quid, Sharon.'

'That's okay, Yoxer. I'll stand you one. For old time's sake.'

Buggy sat at the back, out of the way. He had chosen an empty table in a pub where no-one knew him. He couldn't go home, couldn't face Sharon, until he had stopped shaking.

France. He'd stand out a mile. He didn't speak a word of the language. He'd never been there. Never wanted to.

Cameron thought he was such a wit. 'Leave that to the train driver, Buggy. He knows where to go. And he has those track things to help him.' Walker had laughed and Buggy had smiled too, being a sport.

'You'll be met at the Gare du Nord, Buggy. That means Station of the North. It's where the train stops in Paris. It doesn't go any further, so you'll know you're there.' He wagged his finger. 'Remember not to get off in Lille. Wait till journey's end.'

The moron Walker had had the cheek to laugh. 'You should take Shazza to Paris some time, Buggy. Show her a good time. Maybe she'll stop playing around.'

Buggy had ignored him. 'Who's going to meet me?'

'You'll find out when you get there.' Cameron had pushed some cash across the table. 'That's a grand, Buggy. Buy yourself some euros and a ticket. You've got a credit card?'

'In my own name, you mean?'

Cameron sighed. 'Don't use one to buy your ticket and don't use one over there. Under any circumstances. Not even to buy the lovely Sharon some new lingerie.' He pronounced the word in an overstated French drawl. 'Let me know when you've booked your seat. Make it the day after tomorrow, Buggy. Your minder has to come up from Spain.'

'Why can't he contact Carver?'

'Because whoever sees Carver now has to see him again in England.' Cameron grinned. 'Coming to England is problematic for our man in Spain.'

Buggy lit a cigarette.

The barman was at his side in seconds. 'You're breaking the law. Put that out or I'll put you out.'

Buggy dropped the cigarette on the floor and stood on it. No point causing a scene in here. He was in enough trouble already. 'Sorry, mate. I forgot. Dunno what came over me.'

The barman relaxed. 'You're okay, son. I'm a smoker myself. But you have to take it outside. Okay?'

Buggy nodded. He stared at his beer. Seven o'clock. Sharon would be sitting in front of the dressing table, pulling faces in the mirror, making up. Wearing the underwear she wore when she went out without him. Pouting her beautiful mouth as she painted it red. If he'd been there she'd have smiled at him as she pencilled in the line where her eyebrow should have been. She'd probably have let him kiss her on the back of the neck, rub her shoulders, maybe even hold her firm breasts in the shiny golden brassiere, but nothing would deflect her from what she meant to do. She'd tell Buggy, if he was stupid enough to ask her, that she was going up west with some girlfriends, but Buggy knew what she was up to. She was going to give some other man what she had promised to reserve to Buggy alone till death them did part, and nothing was going to change that.

He wouldn't mind quite so much if she shared the money with him. But she never did.

She'd respected him once. She didn't respect him now. The memory was like a tape he could switch on at will. "You're a messenger boy, Buggy. I didn't set out to marry a messenger boy, but that's what you are. People tell you what to do and you do it. You're a nice guy and I like you, but you've no class."

Well, he couldn't argue with that. When Cameron had wanted a hit man, he had told Buggy to find one and Buggy had found Doyle for him. Okay, he'd needed Jackie Gough to tell him where to find Doyle, but Cameron didn't need to know that. Now Cameron wanted Buggy to go to France, find another hit man called Carver who lived in some garlic-smelling shithole called Auxerre—didn't they have a football team? Hadn't they knocked out Forest back when Forest were good enough to play in Europe?—and tell him to kill Doyle. Buggy liked Doyle and he didn't like Cameron, but that's what Cameron wanted and Buggy was going to do it. No style was right.

CHAPTER 4

Carver lay naked in the girl's bed, his surgical gloves on the table beside him with his stocking mask, clothes folded neatly on a chair. A used condom was knotted and wrapped in a tissue together with its foil packet; a similar, unopened packet lay beside it. Not leaving DNA samples was one of the rules. The rules were what kept him out of jail. Whatever else he might imagine, Carver couldn't bear the thought of going to jail.

The girl beside him was nude but for the tape that bound her hands behind her and covered her eyes. When Carver put a hand on her shoulder, pressing her onto her back, she whimpered. Carver would have liked to see her eyes, but that would have meant letting her see him. Being seen was against the rules. She shuddered when his hands pressed her knees apart. His face was close to hers; he would have liked to kiss her but that, too, was against the rules. Kisses left DNA. He contented himself with nuzzling his nose against her throat.

Her voice was no more than a whisper. 'Are you going to kill me?'

Carver smiled. 'Why on earth would I kill you?' He felt her recoil as his thumb rasped against the pink nipple. He reached over for the unopened condom. 'I want this to stay with you all your life. I want you to think about the man who did what he wanted with you. I want you to remember how it felt to be this helpless.'

'Why are you doing this to me?'

His hand rested for a moment against her cheek. 'As a lesson.'

'But what have I done?'

'It isn't what you've done, darling. It's what you are.'

'I don't understand.'

'You're a tart. A dirty little scrubber. People like you, walking around in your short skirts, showing your knickers, you're asking for it. And then some man takes you at your word and it's "Oh, no, that wasn't what I wanted at all." Well, this time it's what you're going to get.'

Carver sat upright on his heels and rolled the condom into position.

Stacy's voice was quiet and sad. 'I'm sorry you've been hurt.'

'Nobody's hurt me, darling. Don't you worry about me.'

She felt him moving forward and said very quickly, 'Would you do something for me?'

Carver smiled. 'I intend to, darling.'

'Please. It hurt so much having my arms underneath when you were on top of me. I thought you were going to tear them off. If you did it from behind?'

Carver could feel himself going soft. He couldn't let her arouse his sympathy. Sympathy made you do terrible things. Stupid things. 'You must think I'm very stupid.'

'No. I don't think that. I think someone's hurt you and I feel very sad for you but I don't think you're stupid.'

She flinched at the feel of his hands around her throat.

'I told you. Nobody's hurt me.'

'Okay. I'm sorry.' Carver could feel the pulse in her throat, pounding in her fear. He took his hands away. 'Shit.'

'What's the matter?'

'Never mind what's the matter.'

'If you're having a problem ...'

'I told you ...'

27

'But if you were having a problem, I could do something to help you.'

'Why should you want to help me?'

'So you won't hurt me.'

He liked that. If she'd pretended he was turning her on he'd have laughed in her face, well, not her face exactly, she couldn't see him, but he'd have laughed all right, he'd have known she was trying to trick him. But trying not to get hurt, that was something he understood. His fingertips played lightly over her cheek. 'I've still got the gun. If I cut the tape and you try to run, I'll kill you. Do you understand?'

'I won't try to run.'

A shadow caused Buggy to look up from his beer. His fourth? Fifth? He had lost count. It was after nine. He'd been here for hours. Then there had been the scotches at the meeting with Cameron. Buggy thought about the old rhyme: beer after whisky makes you feel frisky; whisky after beer makes you feel queer. He didn't feel particularly frisky. Even less so when he looked at the grinning face of Jackie Gough.

'Buggy. I didn't think you came in here.'

'That's right. I don't.'

'I was over your place, looking for you. Sharon didn't know where you were. Why don't you answer your mobile?'

'Didn't hear it ring.' Buggy jerked the phone awkwardly out of his pocket. Bought in a pub from a petty thief, it took videos as well as still photographs and offered every conceivable form of connectivity. Gough took it out of his hand and pushed buttons till he had the Missed Calls screen. 'There,' he said. 'Three from me. And one from Sharon. Did you really want to miss that?'

'Shit,' sighed Buggy.

'Why do you have to have such a dickhead phone? See this?' He held up a neat little handset. 'Fifty quid. Does everything I want. Makes calls. Lets people call me. Sends text messages and receives them. You want to take pictures? Get yourself a camera.' He picked up Buggy's glass. 'Another pint? Something else? Little scotchy-poo?'

Buggy fished in his pocket for a cigarette and then, remembering, pushed the packet back. 'Scotch.'

'Well mannered as ever, Buggy.'

Gough returned from the bar with two glasses.

'Sharon was at home?' asked Buggy.

The slightest hint of embarrassment passed across Gough's face. 'Not at home, Buggy, no. I found her in whatsername. That place behind the Post Office. You know it.'

Buggy nodded. He knew the place behind the Post Office all right. He suppressed the savage urge to ask who his wife had been with. 'What's that you're drinking?', he asked.

'Sparkling mineral water.'

'Poof's drink. What you drinking that for?'

Gough leaned forward. 'Are you pissed? I have a proposition to put to you, but I don't want a business meeting with a drunk.'

Sitting back in his chair, Buggy found it difficult to bring Gough's face into focus. He could get the nose and the mouth, but the bits closer to the edge seemed to want to split, amoeba-like, and drift away from each other. 'Shouldn't go in pubs, then. What sort of proposition?'

'Keep your voice down. Do you know how many grasses get in here? A business proposition. A little fetch and carry job.'

'Fetch and carry. A messenger boy. That's all you think I am.'

'It'll be well paid.'

Buggy leaned back and thrust a hand into his inside jacket pocket. With difficulty, he extracted Cameron's wad of twenty pound notes and waved it under Gough's nose. Three men at the bar had turned on their stools to watch. 'Everything I do is well paid,' Buggy said. He fanned the notes. 'A thousand quid,' he said. 'For two days of my time.'

Gough stood up, placed his empty glass carefully on the table and ran a hand through his hair, brushing it flat. Very quietly, he said, 'You're a menace, Buggy. A danger to yourself and a menace to other people.'

'What about this business proposition?', Buggy asked without lowering his voice.

'I'll see you tomorrow. When you're sober. Or maybe I'll find somebody else.'

Buggy watched him go. Shoulders back, a half-smile on his lips, arms bent at the elbows so that his hands were raised. Buggy knew the walk. Gough would have used it to impress the other plonkers in the exercise yard at Pentonville or wherever it was he'd done his time. The way he used his education. Buggy couldn't understand why a man with a degree in whatever it was Gough had a degree in should bother with crime. Gough could have done anything, for God's sake. He could have been a teacher, even.

Buggy waited until Gough had reached the door. Then he raised his voice and said, 'I may be pissed, Gough. But I've never been in prison.'

There was not the slightest change in Gough's posture to show whether he had heard.

Caroline came out of the bathroom. 'How would you feel about taking a shower?'

Doyle stood up and put down his bottled Heineken. 'You saying I smell?' He began to remove the belt from the hoops around his waist.

'No. But I think a shower would make life nicer.'

Doyle looked at her. 'OK,' he said at last. 'I'll take a shower. You want to join me?'

Caroline laughed. 'Have you seen the size of that shower cabinet? I'll wait in the bed for you.' She lay down.

Looking straight at Caroline, he removed his trousers. 'Are you up to something?'

'Isn't that your job?'

He threw his T shirt onto the floor. Through the tangled, curly hair that matted his chest ran a thin line where no hair grew. It was an old line, but the lividity had not faded. It ran in a jagged arc from just below his collar bone to just above his navel. 'I'm not the sort of person people should cross.'

Caroline stared at the scar, licked her lips. 'I'm not the sort of person who crosses people. This is supposed to be fun, isn't it?'

Doyle took her ankle and raised it over his shoulder. She made no attempt to stop her skirt from falling back to her waist. She did attempt to make her smile casual and fearless. It was not a successful attempt.

'Very sexy,' Doyle said. 'The garter belt's a nice touch. Keep it on. And the stockings. Everything else off when I get out of the shower. He picked up her shoes. Then he opened her handbag, took out her purse and her keys and waved them at her. 'These will be in the bathroom with me. In case you get any ideas about leaving.'

Caroline listened to the click of the lock on the bathroom door. She lay and waited for the sound of the shower, and for the beating of her heart to slow. Standing, she took off skirt, knickers, blouse, brassiere. She was as he wanted her.

There was no wallet in view—no notecase, nothing to tell her where he lived. She opened the wardrobe door as silently as possible. Two jackets hung there. She recognised one as the red silk he had been admiring when she had first approached him. She went through the pockets. Nothing. Reaching out a hand to the other jacket, she realised with a sudden shock that the sounds in the room were different now. The shower had stopped.

She pushed the wardrobe door closed and jumped onto the bed. There was just time to put her hands behind her head and arrange a smile on her lips when the bathroom door opened. Doyle came into the room, his towel doing little to mask his excitement.

'Very nice,' he said. 'How about a little deep throat, to get things started?'

It took twenty-five minutes for the police to arrive. Twenty-five minutes of pacing the floor, kicking the walls, screaming silently inside her head, sobbing, wanting to throw up but determined not to. Determined not to take a glass of water, either, however desperately she needed one. And then, when they did arrive, the first thing they wanted to do was to make her a cup of tea.

'Don't you think I've wanted a drink?', she spat at them. 'I haven't had so much as a glass of water since he left.' The young police constable looked blankly at the WPC.

'Don't you understand?', she wailed. 'I've got his sperm in my mouth. His *sperm*. His DNA. Ah,' she said as the PC's face lit up in understanding. 'The light comes on.'

'You want to be tested for his DNA. To identify him.'

'As a start,' she said. 'Then I want to be the one who cuts his filthy cock off and shoves it down his throat.'

The constable winced.

'Then,' she went on, 'I want him boiled in oil. And then I want to sit on his face and piss on him till he drowns. But, yes. Right now I want my mouth tested for that bastard's DNA.' She unrolled her clenched right hand and held up a condom. 'And this. I took it off him before I blew him. He didn't come in it, but he put it on after he'd come in another one and the inside is smeared.'

The constable held out his hand.

'I'll keep hold of it,' she said. 'You just get me to the hospital. And ring my mother. Find out why the hell she didn't call the police when she heard what was happening to me.'

From an estate agent's doorway, Carver watched the three of them emerge from her building and get into the patrol car. He had stood here to check whether she would call the police, although he had known that she would not. And she had.

He had freed her hands. He had allowed her to take him in her mouth, just to bring him back to readiness, but she had used such sweetness, such affection, such tenderness that he had let her finish him. He had given her what she seemed to want more than anything in the world. And she had betrayed him.

He had broken the rules. Deep in his memory, a little boy looked at the ground. His father was unbuckling his belt. 'Why do you think I tell you what to do?', the boy's father was saying. 'You think we have rules for fun?' He raised the belt above his head. 'We don't have rules for fun.' Later, there would be hours in the cold and dark of the unlit cellar. But now there was the boy's father, and the strap, and the boy's mother who could have stopped his father but wouldn't because it wasn't her place. The woman's place was to endure. Inflicting pain was the man's job.

Without the coloured contact lenses, Carver might have been unaware of the tear that pricked his eye. He had trusted her. The bitch. He scowled at a couple strolling arm in arm past the doorway. Well, he knew her name now. And he certainly knew where to find her. She'd get what was coming to her, and when she did she wouldn't be able to complain. She'd asked for it, all right.

He took the half-smoked Disque Bleu from his mouth and trod on it. When the patrol car was gone, he turned up his collar and began the walk to Richmond station. Revenge would have to wait. He still had a job to do.

CHAPTER 5

Sharon had not come home last night. Or so Buggy assumed—he had not got in himself until after midnight and it was quite possible that Sharon had come home before then, found the place empty and gone out again. That happened sometimes.

Today, though, it was a nuisance. He wanted to tell her he wouldn't be around for a while. "Going to France—back in a couple of days." No, he couldn't see himself leaving that on a note on the kitchen table. For a start, she knew he'd never been to France in his life—would never go, left to himself. And, anyway, she'd talk about it all over the place. People would find out where he'd gone and they'd start asking questions. Cameron would not be pleased.

He wasn't going till tomorrow, so why was he so keen to tell Sharon today?

Buggy knew why. He didn't like it much, but he knew. He wanted to show her Cameron's money. Tell her he had to go away for a day or two, set up a deal. Not as a messenger boy; as a player. And not in Dagenham or New Addington. He was going to France.

Bloody hell. Anxiety went straight to Buggy's stomach. Surely Cameron would have said something if...

Buggy picked up the phone. He dialled 192. 'What town, please?' said the operator.

'I want to get the train to Paris,' Buggy said. 'Through the tunnel.'

'You want the Eurostar train enquiries number?'

'Yes,' said Buggy. 'Yes, that's it. But I've got a question I've got to ask them.'

'The number is 0990 186186, caller.'

Buggy started to say thank you, but the line was dead. He dialled the number she had given him. 'I want to go to Paris,' he said. 'Tomorrow.'

'What time do you want to travel?'

'In the morning, sometime. I don't know. But, listen...'

'We have plenty of availability on the morning trains, sir. Except the first three. Can you go at 9.20 or later?'

'Yes. Yes, I can.'

'Do you want to pay by credit card, sir?'

'Eh?' Buggy remembered Cameron's instructions. It was just the kind of thing Cameron would check. 'No. No, I need to pay cash.'

'You'll have to go to a travel agent, then, sir. Or you could come to Waterloo and buy your ticket when you're ready to travel, if that's more convenient.'

Shut up. Just shut up. 'Do I need a passport?'

'A passport, sir? Yes, I'm afraid you do. Paris is in France, you know.'

Shit. Buggy put the phone down. Shit shit shit. 'Paris is in France, you know,' he imitated. 'Paris is in France, you know. Stupid cow.'

But what the hell was he going to do about a passport? He looked at his watch. Nearly twelve. Bloody hell. He found a piece of paper and a pencil. "Sharon," he wrote. "I need to talk to you. If you come in, wait for me."

He left the note in the middle of the table, under the sugar bowl. Then he picked it up again and wrote, "Or say where you'll be." No point in asking the impossible.

His hand was on the door knob when the phone rang. He was going to ignore the ring until he realised that it could be Sharon. He went back into the kitchen and picked up the receiver.

'Buggy!'

'Who's that?'

'It's Jackie, Buggy. Jackie Gough. I want to talk to you, remember? Or is last night just a blur?'

Gough. He was an educated man, Jackie, and a traveller, he'd know how to get around this mess. 'Jackie,' he said, 'I need help.'

'I'm not surprised, the way you were flashing that roll last night. Were you mugged?'

'Can you get over here?'

'I want to see you, remember? I'll be there in about twenty minutes. Don't go wandering off, will you?'

'Twenty minutes. Right. Listen, I've had nothing to eat for hours. You know the Macdonald's in the High Street? I'll see you there.'

He hung up. Relief flooded through him. He wasn't out of the woods yet, but if it could be done, Gough would know how. He really didn't want to go back to Cameron and explain that he, the fixer's fixer, couldn't go to France tomorrow because he'd forgotten to mention that he didn't have a passport.

Buggy bought a Big Mac, large fries and a coke. He squeezed ketchup all over the fries. He thought about last night, and the state he'd got into.

Sharon would see him in a different light now. Buggy bit into his Big Mac. His father had laughed when Buggy had said he was marrying Sharon. Buggy had often remembered that laugh. His mother had told him not to do it. And sometimes Buggy hated Sharon. But there were still times...

He couldn't remember when she had last looked at him in public without laughing. Smiling, at least—that special, private, inward smile. But sometimes, when no-one else was about, she'd turn to him and give him that full blast of concentration he remembered from when they were at school together.

He'd been the one people looked up to then, the one they feared—the one who knew the pushers, the one who could win any fight, the one the teachers didn't bother with. Not that they'd really bothered with anyone, the tossers. What kind of education had they given him? What was it worth?

Sharon had had eyes for no-one else in those days, and sometimes—not often—it was like that again. She'd put her face close to his, stare unblinking into his eyes, laugh at his jokes, run her tongue along her lower lip in that way that drove him crazy. Kiss him. Use her hands or her lips to bring him to the brink. Then, when she took him into herself, her eyes would get that far off, trance-like look and he'd know she was away somewhere, on her own—somewhere no-one else could reach.

It had been the same when she was thirteen and pretending she didn't know why he was taking her into the old air raid shelter. Even lying there with her knickers round one ankle and her parted knees bent, she managed to look as though all this were really happening to someone else and she—the real Sharon—floated somewhere in the grey half darkness above.

'You're still the best, Buggy,' she whispered to him one evening as they floated lazily back to earth.

'I could be a lot better with a bit more practice,' Buggy said.

She laughed. 'We'll have to get you fixed up with someone, Buggy.'

And, next day, she'd introduced him to a fat, pasty girl with a bad eye. Even when she built him up, she had to knock him down again.

Gough brought a mineral water to Buggy's table.

'Is that all you're having?'

'Buggy, I wouldn't eat in one of these places if I was starving.' He surveyed the other tables. 'Tell me about your problem.'

Scraping up ketchup with his fries, Buggy told Gough about the desperate need for a passport. Gough stared at him. 'You don't have a passport?'

'No.'

'Not even an expired one? You've never had one?'

'What the hell would I need a passport for?'

'School trips?'

'I never went.'

Gough raised his voice. 'Well, why do you need one now?'

Buggy looked away. 'I have to go to France.'

'France? You? Why?'

'It's business, Jackie.'

'Well, it's no big deal. You get a couple of pictures out of one of those machines. You get a form from the Post Office. Then you go and stand in line in the Passport Office at Petty France.'

Buggy stared at him.

'I think you have to make an appointment these days.' Gough laughed. 'And you need to get some pillar of the community to sign the form and say he knows you. A vicar would do. Or a bank manager. Or a copper.' He finished his water. 'Better be the copper for you, eh?'

'Jackie. I'm going to France on a job for Cameron. I don't think I want a passport with my name in it.'

In the silence that followed, Buggy finished his meal. He belched quietly.

Gough stood up. 'Let's go, Buggy.'

'Where we going?'

'Well, *maybe* we're going to get you a passport. As soon as I know I'm not getting into more trouble than I need by helping you.

'Jackie, I need that passport. I need it for tomorrow morning.'

'I know, Buggy. You said. But why?' He backed away and began to sing. 'What's it all about, Buggy?'

The park had been a place where rich people's nannies pushed rich people's babies in rich people's baby carriages. There had been flower beds, shrubberies, grass, gravel walks, a lake, a bandstand. That was a long time ago. By the time Buggy's parents arrived, the rich had left and the lake, flower beds and bandstand were gone, too. Weeds had grown through the gravel. What benches remained were carved and broken. Buggy and Gough sat on the end of one.

'So, Buggy,' Gough said. 'Tell me the story.'

Buggy lit a cigarette. 'Do you have to do that?', Gough said. 'First you fill your stomach with filth, and now your lungs.'

'I have to go to Paris. I have to meet a man there. He'll take me somewhere else.'

'Where?'

'When we're there, he'll introduce me to another guy. This guy lives in that place. I have to ask him to come back here to do a job.'

'Names, Buggy. Places. Who are these people you're going to meet? Where do they live? What's the job?'

'I can't tell you. I've already told you who the job is for, and you'd better keep that to yourself.'

Gough nodded. 'Like I'm going to stick my nose in Jim Cameron's business.' He was silent for a while. Then he said, 'Yes, well, if Cameron's involved I can see why you don't want anything to go wrong. OK. We'd better get you a passport.' He took a mobile phone from his pocket.

'Can you do it in a day?'

'Buggy, you can do anything in a day if you're prepared to pay the price. You have still got the money?'

'Thanks, Jackie. I don't know what I'd do without you.'

'Yes, you do. You'd fail. You'd fester in the nick. If Cameron didn't off you first. Oh, don't do that, Buggy. I can't stand men crying.'

'I'm supposed to be a fixer.'

Gough watched as tears of relief rolled down Buggy's cheeks. 'You only think you're a fixer, Buggy. What you are is a messenger who a few people happen to feel sorry for. But not as sorry as you feel for yourself. Look. When you needed a killer, who told you where to find Doyle?'

Buggy sighed. 'You did.'

'When Mad Dan Ablett thought you'd grassed him up, which by the way I suspect you had, who told Sharon what to say to get him off your case?'

'All right, Jackie.'

'Who was it, Buggy?'

'It was you. Don't rub it in.'

'That's not what I'm doing. What I'm trying to do, I'm trying to help you see yourself straight. Keep you out of trouble. Again.' He placed a hand on Buggy's arm. 'Last night, you took the piss out of me because I'd been inside. Prison was better than university, Buggy. It's where I learned the really useful stuff. And met the really useful people. Before I went in there, I was just another bum going nowhere fast.'

'Like me.'

'I didn't say that.'

'It's what you think.'

'I said I had a job for you,' said Gough. 'You'll earn more than you did all last year. You interested?'

Buggy sniffed.

'Let me put it another way, Buggy. If I get this passport for you, you owe me. Understand?'

Buggy nodded.

'Good. And I will expect you to deliver.'

CHAPTER 6

The dressing gown was worn—how many women had hugged it to themselves as Stacy Teasdale did now? The police had insisted on her giving up her own clothes for examination. Why, she didn't know, she'd worn nothing when that...that... She couldn't find a word that described what she felt about him. And the clothes she'd put on while she waited for the police were not the clothes she'd been wearing. Not the clothes he'd made her take off.

So WPC Maitland had gone back to Stacy's flat to collect something for her to wear and she was left with this well-meaning but absolutely hopeless replacement to whom she'd had to explain everything that had happened, all over again. A doctor had examined her, and after swabs had been taken from her mouth, Stacy had drunk hot sweet tea, one cup after another. And yes, the doctor had said, intercourse had taken place, but there didn't seem to have been unusual force? The question, unspoken, had hung in the air. Except that it wasn't a question but an accusation.

They weren't happy with her other answers, either. No, she didn't have family who could come for her and no, she certainly didn't want her parents in Norfolk told what had happened. No, she had no friend she was prepared to spend the night with. No, she didn't have a boyfriend, she had a chap, a man, and no, she didn't want the police telling him, either, and, in fact, no, she didn't want to tell them her feller's name. Staring unbelievingly at WPC Brown's face she said that, no, he couldn't have had anything to do with it because he was away. On business. In Birmingham. What kind of lives did these people lead?

It was Maitland who drove her home and insisted, against not much resistance, on coming in and making sure no-one was in the flat. 'You'd better get the lock changed,' she said.

'Why? He didn't take a key.'

'You were blindfolded. How do you know what he took?'

Stacy checked the drawer where she kept the only spare key. It was still there.

Maitland shrugged. 'He could have taken an impression? Look, I'm trying to help. You need a secure lock on that door.'

'Your colleague doesn't think so. Your colleague doesn't believe I was raped.'

'Oh, I know you were raped, all right.'

'How?'

'Shall I help you put new sheets on the bed?'

'I don't understand why you took the others away.'

'We won't find anything. He doesn't leave stains—you know why. And there won't be any hairs. Either he shaves his body beforehand or we're dealing with an exceptionally hairless man.'

Stacy stared at her. 'What are you telling me?'

WPC Maitland paused before answering. 'You're not the first, Stacy. That's how I know you weren't lying.'

Stacy had begun to shake. 'How...how many...?'

'How many times has he struck?' She shrugged. 'Who knows? For every one who comes to us, how many don't report it? How many lock their doors and hide under the bedclothes and try to get on with their ruined lives? I don't know. But there was a woman in Sheen and another in Twickenham. Tomorrow I'm going to ask you to talk to the DI handling those investigations.'

Stacy sat down. The room had begun to swirl around her.

'The woman in Twickenham seems to have resisted, Stacy. So he killed her. About four months ago.'

Stacy seemed unaware that her hands were over her mouth. 'It was in the paper. I read about it. It didn't say he'd done it before.'

'I'm telling you this in confidence, Stacy. Publicise a thing like this, you get copycats. And panic.'

'Panic? *Panic?* This man's killed someone. He might have killed *me*.'

'Yes, Stacy, he might. And he could kill someone else. That's why we have to catch him. You were very brave. You've given us our first real clue. If he's ever had his DNA taken—anywhere—we'll find him.

'That may not be quite our only clue,' she added after a moment.

Stacy looked up.

'Have you noticed anything missing?' Maitland coughed. 'From your underwear drawer?'

'What?'

'Take a look, would you?'

Slowly, Stacy stood up and moved to the chest of drawers near her bed. She opened the second drawer and began a methodical search. When she had finished, the look on her face had turned from fear to anger. 'Pale grey,' she said. 'Satin. A present.' She held up a lace-edged slip. 'Went with this.'

WPC Maitland took the slip. 'I'll need to hold on to this. You hadn't noticed them missing before?'

'No, but I don't wear them often. They're special. Anyway, it was today he was here.'

'Stacy. We're pretty certain he comes on a recce—a preliminary visit. And that's when he takes the knickers.'

'Oh, no.' Stacy had begun to tremble uncontrollably.

'Will you see about changing the lock?'

Caroline took the four ten pound notes from Doyle's hand. 'Thank you, kind sir. I hope you found the service satisfactory?'

Doyle grinned. 'You're a pro, honey.' He began to pull on his black Calvin Klein undershorts. 'You want to eat?'

'I thought I just did.'

'Funny. I need a meal. Want to join me?'

'Sure. What did you have in mind?'

'Well, there's a restaurant downstairs. Or, in the bar, they do real burgers—best I've had in this country. There's a Benihana next door. Or we could go downtown?'

'Up town.'

'Eh?'

'In London you don't go down to the centre—you go up. Up town.'

'Whatever you say.'

'You choose.'

'OK. Up town it is.'

Caroline reached up to touch the curly hair that, she had discovered, ran all the way down. 'There is an alternative.'

'Which is?'

'We could stay here and have one of those burgers sent up?'

Doyle laughed. He had a nice laugh, Caroline had decided, just as he had a nice smile. He was probably a very nice person. She wished she did not have to deceive him. He fell forward, using his arms to avoid squashing her. 'Honey,' he said, 'You have yourself a deal.'

Sharon felt out of place in Waterstone's. She didn't know when she'd last been in a bookshop. Wasn't even sure when she'd last read a book. For sure there were no books in the flat she shared with Buggy.

She didn't want to ask for help, but in the end she had to.

'Joyce Johnson,' said the young man. 'I'm sure we must have. Let's take a look.'

As they walked to the shelves he said, 'She was the most interesting of the Beats in many ways.'

'She could write the arse off the rest of them,' said Sharon.

The young man laughed.

'She didn't count,' Sharon went on, 'because she was a woman.'

'Yes. They had strange attitudes in those days.'

'Oh. That was in those days, was it?'

'There only seems to be this one,' he said. 'We could order something if you wanted?'

Sharon saw him snatching a surreptitious look at her ring finger. 'My husband and I have split up,' she said.

He didn't seem to have heard. Was she losing her touch? 'In the Night Café,' he said. 'This is her best known, of course.' Still looking at the book, he said, 'Would you like to have coffee?'

'What? Can you?'

'I'm due a break. Wait here.'

He walked away and was back moments later. 'Sam's going to cover for me. Let's go over the road.'

'Sam?'

'She works here.'

As they walked out through the glass doors, Sharon said, 'Waterstone's has its own coffee shop, hasn't it?'

'I'm not going in there with you.'

It stopped Sharon in her tracks. 'What are you saying? You're ashamed to be seen with me?'

He looked at her in astonishment. 'Ashamed? Quite the opposite, I assure you.'

Buggy sat in the booth, staring at the red spot and concentrating on keeping all trace of expression from his face. Before they went in, Gough had bought a packet of Wet Wipes and told Buggy to remove any trace of tears from his face. 'It's a passport photo. A *dodgy* passport photo. You don't want anyone to look twice at it.'

Then they stood outside the booth while the automatic developing and printing process went on. Buggy looked around the post office. 'My granddad used to knock these places over,' he said.

'Did he get much?'

'Fifteen years all told.' They stared at each other. Then Buggy smiled and in a moment the two of them were doubled up, giggling.

The row of four pictures dropped into the chrome pocket near the base of the machine. Gough picked it up and led the way to the counter that ran along the outside wall. He handed Buggy a pen. 'Your name's Jim Patterson.'

'Why that?'

'Because it's Jim Patterson's passport you're buying. Sign it on the back of each photo.' When that was done, he produced a sheet of paper. 'Sign this. Give me three of Jim Patterson's signatures, in case they have trouble.'

'Who are you getting it from?'

'Buggy, you don't need to know that.'

As they left the post office, Buggy took the cigarettes from his pocket and lit one. The question that had been nagging at his mind for fourteen hours had crystallised.

'Why did you go into that pub?'

'What?'

'The Black Bear. Why did you go in there? I never drink in

there. I don't think I've been there in my life before. How did you know I'd be in there?'

'I wasn't looking for you.'

Buggy strolled on. 'Yes you were. You said you were. You'd been to my place, you'd seen Sharon, you had a proposition for me. A piece of business. Sharon didn't know where I was. Far as I know, *no-one* knew where I was. How'd you find me, Jackie?'

Gough looked exasperated. 'I wasn't looking for you, OK? I'd been looking for you, but I'd stopped. I just wanted a drink. And there you were.'

'Often go in the Black Bear, do you?'

'I've been in. Sure.'

'You want to watch yourself, mate. Lot of grasses get in there. A guy told me.'

'I can look after myself,' Gough said levelly.

'So,' Buggy said. 'What is it?'

'What is what?'

'This proposition. This job. Well paid, you said. What is it?'

'Wait till you get back from France.'

'What's the job, Jackie?'

'Buggy, I'll tell you what the job is when you get back from France, all right? If you get back. Look at it my way. If you do this job for Cameron and it all turns to rat-shit, do I want you knowing what I've got going?'

'Are you calling me a grass?'

'I'm saying you can't tell the Bill what you don't know. Now you can take out that roll you were flashing last night and give me five hundred quid.'

'Five hundred...*how much?*'

'The passport, Buggy. Jim Patterson, remember? It has to be paid for.'

Buggy came to a halt in the middle of the pavement. 'I've got to buy Euros with that, Jackie. I've got to get a ticket. I've got to live while I'm in France.'

'France is a lot cheaper than here, Buggy.'

'Listen, I don't...'

'Tell you what, Buggy. I'll lend you the five hundred, OK? You come back from France, do my job, I'll take it out of your fee. It'll still be a nice earner for you.'

CHAPTER 7

After breakfast, Carver checked his shiny aluminium briefcase, set the combination locks and walked out of the three star hotel off Queensway. He had chosen it because of another of the rules—if you did something you shouldn't in one part of town, you stayed in another. And because the staff, whose first language English was not, took almost no interest in their largely tourist clientele.

Bayswater to Paddington was a single stop on the Circle Line but it was a nice morning, there was plenty of time and the Tube was filthy so he walked instead. On Craven Hill, three youths larked about in front of him. When one dropped an empty cigarette packet, Carver suppressed a savage desire to make him pick it up. This was no time to be conspicuous.

He paid cash for a first class return ticket to Cardiff. In England, Carver travelled first whenever it was available. Standard was filled with riffraff, young people who drank the awful British lager at ten in the morning and played dreadful music loudly on ghetto-blasters. They reeled around the carriages, swearing and ignoring other travellers. Carver would have to tell them to stop and he couldn't afford any trouble that might see the police called. He wasn't carrying a photo of his mark—although he didn't know what the man looked like, the job was set up so that he didn't need one—but he didn't relish the thought of explaining the gun in his briefcase.

He carried on board a waxed paper cup of coffee and two newspapers. There were no smoking carriages. Carver sighed.

The seats were in pairs on one side of the aisle; in fours on the other. Choosing one of the pairs, Carver placed his briefcase

51

on the rack and his jacket on the seat opposite, discouraging visitors. He put the papers and coffee on the table. Then he went outside and stood on the platform so that he could smoke till his departure was signalled. An officious railway employee was there immediately, telling him smoking was not allowed anywhere on the station. Carver would have loved to deal with the man the way the man deserved; instead he smiled, said he hadn't known, threw his cigarette under the carriage and got back onto the train. Someone was going to pay for all this suppression of his own self.

The train moved slowly through Royal Oak, across the scruffy edge of North Kensington and then past Acton before coming to a halt at Ealing. Carver watched the shoppers in the Waitrose car park. The carriage had filled a little, but no-one had asked him to move his jacket. When the train moved off it began to pick up speed, moving smoothly through Hanwell and Southall as it headed for the more affluent towns to the west. Carver finished his coffee and returned to the Times. He was filled with a feeling of contentment. Get this job done, execute whatever nameless mark had been set up for him and make his way home to France. Drink a proper coffee. Someone had told him the Italians made the best coffee in the world. He'd have to try it some time. Until then, he'd settle for a Café Crème in the French style.

The train took on more passengers at Reading, but still Carver had the table to himself. He had reached the sports pages, or what were supposed to be the sports pages. There was a story about Beckham—wasn't he retired now?—and the only purpose seemed to be to resurrect the old story his pop-star wife had told. No wonder he'd gone to Spain, and then LA. The most gifted

English player of his generation and all people could do was take the piss out of him for wearing his wife's knickers. Carver smiled. That was two things they had in common. Maybe that's what you needed to be the best—a liking for the feel of women's undergarments.

And he was the best, whatever Doyle might imagine. A strange meeting, that. When he came to Britain, Doyle had been amazed at the state of contract killing here. Butchers found in pubs by strangers, botching the job with half bricks, driving over people, blasting with shotguns in busy streets. Those who commissioned them ending, as often as not, in the Old Bailey. Eventually the American had heard of Carver, contacted him, suggested a meeting. Two pros in an amateur world.

They had met in Amsterdam, neutral ground, circling at first like wary dogs. But they had liked each other and the evening had ended after a good meal with a walk among the canals until Doyle went off with a tart. Carver never paid for sex. Bullied for it, yes, took it by force, occasionally killed for it, but never paid.

They had an agreement, Carver and Doyle. There was always the possibility of sub-contracting, of course—but, most of all, they agreed to watch each other's backs. They practised a dangerous trade. And their paymasters could be treacherous.

When the trolley arrived, Carver selected a ham and cream cheese sandwich, coffee and a bottle of mineral water. He picked up the *Telegraph* but found his attention drifting to Stacy Teasdale. Her tenderness had seemed so genuine. Could it really have been assumed, a way to stay alive? Assumed or not, she had betrayed him and she was going to die. Not now, the police would surely be watching her place, should be if they weren't, a disgraceful dereliction of duty, but anyway he wasn't going to take that chance. He'd give it a few months, do her next time he came to England, maybe even the time after if next time was too soon. But do her he would.

Carver remembered the soft country burr in her voice, the bloom on her flawless skin. It might be possible to let yourself love a woman like that. He heard again the fear in her hesitant pleading. He imagined her tied face down on a bed, screaming silently into an unforgiving gag, the alabaster flesh turning pink, then red as his belt rained down blows she could not turn aside. His stiffness became uncomfortable. How he wished he had put on the satin panties this morning. He would take her like that— that would be his revenge for her betrayal.

He came back to the present with a start. There were the rambling mud-flats at the mouth of the Usk. The train was slowing for Newport. Another thirty minutes and his journey would be over.

At Cardiff, he took his briefcase from the rack, left the station and headed north-west, crossing the road to the Empire Pool. They wouldn't be able to call it that if they were building it now. There were no more Empire Games, and Empire wasn't something the British liked to talk about any more. Not that Carver thought of himself as British. He was English, and proud of it.

Right along Park Street, moving quickly, a fast right into Westgate Street and stop almost immediately, swing round and light a cigarette while watching the gap he had just emerged from. No-one followed him out.

He finished his cigarette, then dawdled up Westgate Street to the very end and turned right into a broad, light thoroughfare, shops on one side and on the other the grassy approaches to Cardiff Castle. Castle Street. Sitting on a bench, he smoked another cigarette, his eyes methodically checking every passer-by, lingering on newspaper readers and a man who paused to retie a shoelace. Did Commonwealth Pool have the same ring? Not to Carver it didn't. Satisfied no-one was watching him, he picked up the briefcase and crossed the road again, this time turning down High Street. Two minutes later, he arrived at the Marriott.

Carver ate an omelette with a wholemeal roll and a bottle of water and drank two cups of coffee. His aluminium briefcase beside him, he was one more businessman in a room full of businessmen. He paid the bill in cash, adding an unremarkable tip. In a men's room cubicle he relieved himself, then opened the briefcase, took out the gun and checked it before slipping it into his inside jacket pocket. He also extracted a pair of gloves. Walking without haste to the car park, he found a royal blue Mondeo where it was supposed to be: third bay from the end.

He slipped on the gloves. The door was unlocked, as promised. Taking his time, he removed his jacket and hung it from the hook beside the offside passenger door. He strolled to the back of the car, looking round casually. No-one was watching him. He placed the briefcase inside the carpeted boot. One last check of the hotel windows and he opened the driver's door and slid behind the wheel.

The key was in the parcel box at the foot of the driver's door. Without removing his gloves, Carver extracted it and placed it in the ignition. Casually, he reached out to the large card on the passenger seat and turned it over. On it, in large letters, was written the name *Julie Been*.

Carver quickly turned the card face down. His heart was pounding; inside the gloves his palms were sticky with sweat.

He thought back over the conversations he'd had. "The mark will be carrying a brief case. We want it." "The mark's name will be on a card in the car." Always "the mark;" never "he." They hadn't lied to him, except by omission.

He rolled down the window, slipped off his right glove and lit a Disque Bleu. He checked his watch. The train was due in thirty-five minutes. He didn't kill women. Only that one, the stupid bitch in Twickenham who wouldn't stop screaming, and he had hated himself for it. Doyle had done it, he knew, the American had told him so. If ever there had been a job he would willingly have sub-contracted, this was it. But there was no time for that.

Carver replaced the glove, rolled up the window and started the engine. A deep sadness possessed him as he turned out of the hotel car park, heading back towards the station. Parking the car, he checked his watch again. Twenty minutes. He got out of the car, put on his jacket and smoked a cigarette. After fifteen minutes, he took the card from the passenger seat and went to stand at the station exit. When people began to stream out of the station, he held the card high.

Her briefcase was much larger than Carver's. She was surprisingly young to have got herself in this much trouble. Mostly, marks were forty or more. Carver would not have put Julie Been's age at much more than twenty. While she wasn't really pretty, she had that youthful sweetness that Carver often went for. And she wore a skirt as short as the one that had angered him on Stacy Teasdale, though her legs were just a touch too thick to carry it off.

She smiled. 'You're here. They said I'd be met.'

'You didn't believe them?'

'Something always goes wrong. My Dad says I'm the one Murphy wrote his law for.'

'Well, that's one worry you can strike off the list.'

They walked towards the short stay car park. She asked, 'Is it far?'

'You don't know Abercynon?'

'I don't know Wales.'

'Half an hour, maybe. This is mine.'

She opened the front passenger door and placed her handbag on the floor.

'Do you want me to put that in the boot?'

'I'd rather keep it with me.'

Carver held up his hand, palm forward. 'No problem.' He got behind the wheel and started the engine. This was the dangerous bit; if they were being watched now, he wouldn't know—wouldn't pick up a follower, most likely, until they were on the outskirts of Cardiff. He edged the car into the traffic. The fact that she'd never been to Abercynon was a blessing. The sensible route was dual carriageway all the way, and busy. That wasn't the way Carver planned to go.

He picked up the Caerphilly road and headed north. The traffic thinned out after he crossed the M4. Carver was confident now that no-one was following. They made small talk about Wales, trains and the weather. He could tell that Julie Been was excited. She was no courier; this was an adventure she'd been sent on, probably by someone who cared about her and needed a person they could trust. An adventure that was going to cost her life.

He left Caerphilly on the road signposted Abertridwr. It was like every valley road in South Wales. Grey slate houses, doors giving straight onto the street, no front gardens. Space was precious on the valley floors, because most of the valley was walls—mountain walls. The houses went on and on; a visitor would have been forgiven for thinking it the most densely populated place on earth had it not been for the empty hills looming on each side, running down to the backs of the houses themselves. They reached Senghenydd, climbing all the way, and suddenly the houses stopped. One moment a long drawn out village, the next sheep, the occasional wind-bent tree, but no people. Only stone walls kept the hills from swamping the narrow, winding road.

'Is it much further to Abercynon?' She pronounced it in the English way.

'Cunon', he corrected her. 'Abercunon. The Welsh don't pronounce letters like we do.'

She smiled. 'I've noticed. But is it far?'

'Five miles if we could go over the top,' he answered. 'But there aren't any roads so we have to go the long way round.' A bend, then another and there was the gate he was looking for. Slowing, he removed the glove from his right hand and reached into his pocket. 'Unfortunately, that's not what I'm planning to do.'

She looked uncertainly at him, then saw the gun. 'What...what are you doing?'

The wall veered away from the road to provide space to park a tractor. Carver brought the car to a halt. He turned off the ignition and rolled down his window. The silence was broken only by the wind and occasional sheep.

'What are you doing?' she asked again. 'Who are you?' She clasped the briefcase close to her chest. 'I'm not giving you this.' She was trying to make her voice firm, but not succeeding.

'You'll give me anything I ask for.' He stared into her face. Tears were standing in her eyes, ready to spill onto her lightly made-up cheeks. Carver silently cursed whoever had sent him here. He was a professional killer, not a murderer of children. Female children.

Through the open window came the sound of a car approaching from behind. Carver saw the look of sudden hope in the girl's eyes. He pressed the gun into her side. 'If you do anything to attract their attention, you'll die and so will they.'

As the advancing car turned the bend, Carver seized the girl's head in his left hand and pressed her face to his. Her lips were closed tight. He kept the gun firmly pressed to her ribs. The car passed with three blasts of the horn; Carver turned one eye to see two young men in the back seat grinning back at him and gesturing obscenely. The car disappeared around the next bend and silence descended once more. Carver released his hold on the girl's head.

There was no need for her to know she was going to die. He wasn't a sadist. He said, 'If you do everything I tell you, you'll get to Abercynon with your bag. That isn't what I want.'

The tears had begun to fall, turning what little mascara she wore to thin black rivulets. 'What *do* you want?'

She flinched when his hand touched her cheek. 'You,' he said. His hand dropped to her thigh, touched the hem of her short skirt. 'We'll have a little fun together. Then I'll leave you here.' He pointed up the road. 'Three or four miles up there is a place called Nelson. It's on a main road. Turn left, you'll see the sign for Abercynon.'

'You promise?' Her voice was a hoarse whisper. 'If I do what you want, you'll let me go?'

'I promise.' He leaned forward and kissed her. This time, when he pressed his tongue against her lips, they parted but her body remained rigid. Carver broke the kiss.

He lit a cigarette. Gently, he said, 'Put your bag behind the seat. Then take off your knickers.'

She had to struggle in the confined space. Carver watched greedily as she kicked off her shoes and raised herself in the seat, reaching under her skirt for the waistband of her tights. The pressure on his hard erection was almost unbearable.

'Do you want me to lie down in the back?', she whispered.

'Wait.' Carver got out of the car, flicked his half-smoked cigarette away and went round to open her door. When she was on her feet he took her arm. 'Let's get over the wall,' he said.

He had to help her climb the gate. Once over, he told her to kneel. 'Rest your head on the ground. Now reach back and pull your skirt up.'

Intense lust possessed Carver as he stared at the waiting girl. Kneeling beside her, he placed a hand gently on her upraised bottom. She had begun to sob. Carver put the gun into the hollow behind her ear and pulled the trigger.

He went back to the car and picked up the discarded pants. Virginal white cotton, he saw with disappointment. He pushed them into his pocket, took her tights back to the wall and dropped them beside the dead girl. Then he put on his gloves, placed the girl's briefcase in the Mondeo's boot and opened her handbag. He examined the contents with care, then closed it and threw it over the wall. He leaned against the wall and lit a cigarette. When you've just done what he had done the only thing that make sense is to leave. Self-preservation demands it. And yet, he couldn't do it. He'd killed a woman. Not by accident or unavoidably; he'd killed her because he'd been hired to kill her. He hated the person who had paid his fee. He hated himself even more. He lit another cigarette. Car after car went by, even on this lonely road, and all the drivers must have seen him and he didn't care. A dreadful line had been crossed.

It was late when he left the Mondeo outside the Marriott, the girl's briefcase still in the boot. Walking swiftly to the station, he boarded the Paddington train. He went to the buffet car, bought two miniatures of scotch, a plastic glass and a coffee and carried them to an empty seat with no-one opposite. Picking up a discarded *Sun*, he sat down and poured the first scotch.

He wanted to be home. As soon as he reached London he would collect his bag, check out and make his way to Waterloo where he would take the first available Eurostar to Paris. It would be too late to travel on to Auxerre, but at least he could pass the night in a civilised country.

He stared out of the window. It was warm in the train. Carver shivered.

CHAPTER 8

The young man settled Sharon at a table. 'Latte okay?'

'Mhm. I'm Sharon.'

He smiled. 'Adrian.' Awkwardly, he put out his hand. Awkwardly, she shook it.

'Want anything to eat with your coffee?'

'No, thanks, Adrian.' She'd never known an Adrian. It wasn't the sort of name people in the flats gave their children.

When he came back from the counter with two fair-sized cups, Sharon was glancing round the room.

'What are you looking for?'

'Oh, nothing. I'm wishing I could smoke, that's all.'

'There are tables outside?'

'Too cold. I'll be all right.'

'You'll get by without your nicotine hit?'

'For now.' She looked up at him and did the thing with her tongue and her lower lip. 'Thanks for the coffee.'

'You're welcome.' Most of the men Sharon knew felt the need to pose. The way they sat, stood, walked was meant to project an image, show them in the way they wanted to be seen. Not to be messed with was the image of choice. Someone who'd always give better than he got.

Until they got older, her father's age, say, when suddenly the truculent self-confidence gave way to bewilderment and defeat.

Adrian sat as though at ease with himself. Comfortable with who he was. Not posing.

Sharon was quite pleased with that insight. She'd need to notice things like that if she hoped to be a writer like Joyce Johnson.

And where the hell had that thought come from?

'Sam must be very kind,' said Sharon.

'You think so? I'll tell her.'

'Do you like working with her?'

'She's the head of my department. She's also my cousin. She got me the job.' When he smiled it wasn't like smiles she was used to. Not making a point, being clever, showing toughness, calling someone's bluff. Just smiling. 'I think she's under orders from my mother to fix me up with a girl.'

What kind of man would admit something like that? No-one Sharon knew, that was for sure. 'That's why she was ready to cover for you?'

'I guess.' He opened the book. 'Have you read this?'

'No. That's why I want to buy it.'

'Listen. "Missing persons don't die. Time congeals around them. They remain as young, as unfinished as when they went away." Isn't that wonderful?'

'Fantastic.'

'You don't look certain.'

'No, it is. Really. Amazing.'

'She writes like an angel. What have you read of hers?'

'Nothing, yet.'

'So how do you know she could write the arse off the other Beats?'

He wasn't different after all. Softer, maybe, but he still had to put you down, show he was better than you. 'Thanks for the coffee.'

'What?'

These couldn't be tears, could they? 'I need to go.'

'Sharon, I... Look, I'm sorry. I've upset you. I don't know how and I know I didn't mean to. Forgive me?'

She couldn't believe this. A man apologising to her. Now she really was going to cry.

He put his hand on hers. 'Sharon? What is it?'

'Nothing. It doesn't matter.'

'Of course it matters. Tell me.'

Sharon glanced towards the next table where two middle aged women were ostentatiously not looking at her. She could just imagine what they were thinking. Young man's bit of rough has got herself up the stick to trap him into marriage. Bastards.

And all the time, somewhere in some unlocated crevice of her mind, the thought that this is good, this is what a writer needs. Was Joyce Johnson the kind of person who stole her friends' lives? Is that what writers do? Does she qualify?

Aloud, she says, 'You haven't upset me. I'm trying to be somebody I'm not and it isn't working.'

'Who do you want to be?'

'What?'

'Only act yourself if that's the self you want to be.'

'Age. Only act your age if that's the age you want to be. Tell me on a Sunday.'

'It works my way, too.'

'I need a cigarette.'

'Let's sit outside.' Had Buggy ever stood back to allow her to go first? Ever? He picked up the two coffees and followed her.

At the outside table, she offered him a cigarette. He shook his head. She lit one for herself. 'What's a catamite?'

'Eh? Sharon! Why do you want to know that?'

'I need to improve my education. What is it?'

'Well. It's a boy who...well...he takes the female part in a sexual relationship. With an older man.'

'Oh.'

'Does that explain anything?'

'Was Neal Cassady one?'

'Cassady? Who knows?'

'So he was?'

'Listen. Cassady married a number of women. I don't know how many. And he had a few kids.'

'So he wasn't?'

'Well. He did it with Alan Ginsberg. I don't think anyone doubts that.'

'So he was.'

'Sharon. Does it matter? He's been dead nearly forty years. The question is: Who do *you* want to be? And what did I say to upset you?'

Moment of truth. She'd heard the expression but never known the fact. Relationships in her experience didn't involve truth, merely degrees of deception. But a moment of truth it was. She could take it, embrace it, see where it led. Or she could go away.

'You don't want to tell me, do you?'

No, she really didn't.

'Have you heard of Abe Wagner?'

She shook her head.

'He's involved with neurolinguistic programming.'

'What's that when it's at home?'

'It doesn't matter. Abe Wagner said, always ask for what you want and expect the other guy to do the same. If you ask for what you want and don't get it, you broke even. Because you weren't getting it before.'

Slowly, Sharon nodded her head. It made sense. She said, 'I want to be educated. I want to know about books.'

'Books are life. Good books, at any rate.'

'They're not my books. Haven't been.'

'You want to tell me about your life?'

'Huh. How much time have you got?'

He looked at his watch, taking the question seriously. 'I have to be back at work soon.'

'That's what I thought.'

'We could meet later? Tonight? I could cook you a meal?'

No man had ever cooked her a meal. She couldn't imagine that any man ever would. 'I don't know, Adrian.'

'Where do you live?'

'I don't want to tell you that. Not yet.'

'You want to know where I live?'

'Eh? Okay. Yes.'

He took a small notebook from his pocket, tore out a page, wrote on it. 'My address, my phone number, my mobile.'

'Thank you.'

'You'll call me?'

'Maybe.'

'Doesn't have to be tonight, Sharon. When you're ready.'

'You know what, Adrian? If you want a girl, it doesn't pay to be desperate.'

'Is that what I seem?'

'Aren't you?'

'No. What I am is interested. I've met a girl who fascinates me, her mind that is, and she's beautiful as well. I want to know her better.'

'You think I'm beautiful?'

'Don't you?'

She stood abruptly. He said, 'Will you call me?'

'I don't know. Maybe.'

'Is that a real I don't know? Or are you humouring me?'

'I mean I don't know. You're not like any man I've known.'

'Is that bad?'

She laughed. 'No. Probably not.'

'So will you call me?'

'I'm not going to tell you again.'

'Okay. Don't forget your book.'

'It isn't my book. I haven't paid for it.'

'Take it. It's my treat.'

She folded the book into her arms like a baby. 'Thank you.'

He watched her go, waited for her to look back. He waited in vain.

Stacy Teasdale had passed a dreadful night. At two in the morning, she had given in and telephoned Mark. Less than two hours later, he was in Richmond with her.

'What about work?', she asked.

'Bugger work. I'll say I need a few days off.'

'You won't tell them what's happened?'

'No, darling. If you don't want me to, of course I won't.'

'I don't, Mark. I don't want anyone to know. Oh, I don't, I don't, I don't.'

She fell, sobbing, against his shoulder. Mark put his arms around her, holding her tight. 'Do you think you can sleep a little?'

It felt so much safer when Mark was here. 'I think so. I might. If you're here. Mark...' She turned a tear-stained face towards him.

'Darling?'

'Mark, I want you to hold me tight. In bed. But you won't mind if I don't...if I don't want to...'

'For goodness sake, Stacy.' He hugged her close.

'It isn't because I don't love you,' she sobbed. 'And I'm sure I will want to again. And it really isn't because I don't know the difference between you and him.'

He kissed her gently. 'Darling. Whatever you want is fine with me.'

Tears were streaming down her face. 'I mean, I'm really not going to let that bastard ruin my life. It's just for now.'

'Stacy. Get into bed. I'm going to ablute.'

He went to the bathroom. When he returned, she was fast asleep.

She woke groggily at eight. Mark brought coffee and opened the curtains. 'How are you feeling?'

'Glad you're here.' She folded her arms across her front. 'Am I being a ninny?'

'I think you're being amazing. But then, you are amazing.' He took her hand. 'When do you have to see this Inspector?'

'The police woman is coming for me at ten.'

'Not long, then. Do you want me to come with you?'

She nodded. 'And would you see about getting the lock changed?'

'Of course.'

'They have ones you can get with special keys burglars can't get copies of.'

'I'll get the best there is. Now I'm going to make you breakfast.'

'I can't eat anything.'

'Yes, you can. You can eat an oeuf boilé et du pain toasté.'

'Don't do that.'

'What?'

'That stupid cod-French thing. Do you have any idea how often you do that? Oh, for God's sake, don't look so hurt.'

'I thought you liked it.'

'I know you think that. It drives me round the bend.'

'I'm sorry.'

'I was humouring you. I'm sick of humouring people. My humouring days are over.'

'No more silly French, then. Is there anything else I should get rid of, while you're in the mood to tell me?'

'Plenty. It can wait. Yes, I'll have some breakfast. You can make it while I shower.'

There was a clattering sound from the front door. She said, 'If you say that's the homme de poste, you're history.'

When Jackie Gough arrived with the passport in the name of Jim Patterson, Buggy and Sharon were both at home. 'Do you know what's going on?' Sharon asked him.

Gough raised an eyebrow in mute question.

'Buggy's being the mystery man,' Sharon said. 'He's got some big deal job on and he won't tell me what it is. Do you know?'

'No, and I don't want to. If someone grasses him up, I don't want anybody thinking it was me.'

He handed Buggy an envelope. Sharon removed it from Buggy's hand and opened it. She leafed through the passport pages in silence. Then, she said, 'OK, Buggy, three questions. Who's James Robert Patterson? Why has his passport got your picture in it? And what do you need a passport for, anyway? You never go further than Dagenham.'

'You don't need me here,' Gough said. 'I'll be off, Buggy. Good luck with the trip.'

Sharon stopped him with a hand on his chest. 'Trip? So you do know about it?'

'Sharon, I know Buggy has to go to France for Jim Cameron. That's all I know and, believe me, it's all I want to know. If you have any sense, you won't want to know any more, either.'

He pressed her hand aside. 'I'll see you.'

When Gough had gone, Buggy took the passport from Sharon. 'He's right, Sharon. It's better you don't know.'

Sharon sat down at the kitchen table. 'Just tell me this. Is what you're doing dangerous?'

Buggy shrugged. 'You didn't want me to be a messenger. Did you? OK, so now I'm not a messenger. I'm a player, Sharon. I'm setting up a deal. For Cameron.' He picked up his jacket and extracted Cameron's money. 'With this.'

'*Jim* Cameron?'

Buggy nodded.

With a sigh, Sharon reached for her handbag and took out a pack of cigarettes. She placed one between bright red lips and stared at Buggy until he lit it for her. She inhaled deeply before pushing out her lower lip and blowing the smoke straight upwards.

'Buggy,' she said. 'Are you doing something stupid to impress me? Because you needn't.'

'It's what you wanted.'

'Oh, Buggy, don't look so hurt. You are what you are.' She reached out a hand to him. 'We still have a good time, don't we, Buggy?'

'Oh, sure,' Buggy said. 'Sometimes. When you're here. When you remember I exist.'

Sharon shook her head. 'Listen, Buggy, you make problems for yourself. You've told me you're in on a deal for Jim Cameron. Well, if it's a deal, and you're setting it up, there'll be a payoff. Won't there? You'll get some money. Real money. 'So if, in a couple of months, you haven't got a nice big roll to spend on me, I'll know it wasn't a deal, Buggy. Won't I? I'll know you were just carrying messages. Again.'

Buggy kicked savagely at the table leg. 'There'll be a roll. You'll see. You'll be able to have anything you want.'

Sharon stubbed out her cigarette. She stared at him in silence. Then she said, 'Anything I want. You're sure of that? You don't want to back out?'

'I told you...'

'Last chance, Buggy.'

'I'll be loaded. All right?'

'OK, Buggy. As long as you're sure. Well, here's what I want. I want to go up west. To Harrods. And I want to drop two grand in there. On anything I want. Then I want to go to Harvey Nicols, and I want to spend another two grand in there. And I want to have lunch there. Not dinner—lunch. The way people like that do. Anything I want. Then, at night, I want to have dinner in some place where the chef's always on telly, I don't care who as long as it's expensive and it isn't Delia bloody Smith. That's what I want, Buggy. And afterwards I want to stay in a hotel, a posh one, the Ritz or the Savoy, some place like that. And when we're in that bed, Buggy, I will give you the time of your life. I'll do things to you, you'll wonder where I learned how to do them.' She held up her hand. 'But you won't ask, Buggy, because that would spoil things. And then I'll know you're a wheeler-dealer, Buggy, because you'll have dropped the thick end of five thousand quid without crying for your mother. But if you can't give me that in two months time I'll know you're not a wheeler-dealer after all. I'll know you're still a messenger boy. And you know what I'll do then, Buggy? I'll find someone you really don't like, someone who knows all your pals and never learned to keep his mouth shut and those things I was going to do to you in that bed in the Savoy? I'll do them to him instead.'

She placed another cigarette between her lips and held it up to be lit.

'Two months, Buggy. Eight weeks. Better piss off to France and set up that deal.'

When Buggy turned away, Sharon held up her hand. 'And remember, Buggy. This was your idea. I didn't want it.'

CHAPTER 9

'So. How was it?'

When Caroline looked at her partner, she felt the same sort of frisson as when she had stared at Doyle's scar. Melanie had had the whole evening to stoke her rage. She was an inch or so shorter than Caroline, but stockier. Her hair was cropped short, her face un-made up, her shirt and jeans studiedly masculine. The contrast with Caroline's long blond hair, knee-length skirt and flowing blouse was sharp. Caroline experienced an intense thrill of anticipation. 'It was fine.' Walking into Melanie's range, she said, 'He fucks like a champ.'

The slap sent her reeling. Following up, Melanie caught her again on the other cheek. Caroline fell onto the sofa. 'Mel, don't.' Her arms came up to protect herself. Melanie wrenched the handbag from Caroline's hand and reached inside for the purse.

'There's sixty pounds in here.'

'He gave me a bonus.' She leaned back as the furious woman lifted a hand to hit her again. 'Mel, please, please, no.'

Panting heavily, Melanie dropped her hands to her sides. 'You're a filthy little whore.'

'I'm sorry, Mel.' Caroline tried to keep the excitement from her voice. It was a convention between them, part of the half-conscious game they played, that Melanie's discipline was unwelcome, was not what had brought them together in the first place, did not keep them together now.

'A tart.'

'I'm sorry, Melanie.'

'Dirty little trollops have to be punished.'

Caroline made a little play of peeping imploringly from behind her hands.

'It's no good looking at me like that. You know what you deserve.'

Caroline stared beseechingly as though she thought the woman's mind might be changed. Then, with a little whimper, she turned onto her front, shuffling forward until she lay over the sofa's rounded arm-rest. She reached back and pulled up her skirt.

Melanie stood beside her, looking down. 'Lower them, you dirty little scrubber.' She watched as Caroline, with every show of unwillingness, obeyed her. Then she raised her hand. Caroline cried out as the first blow fell.

When the spanking was over, Melanie slumped into an armchair. Caroline, breast heaving, remained where she was. After what she thought a decent interval she stood up, smoothed down her skirt and crossed the floor to Melanie. She moved the other woman's hands gently out of the way and sat down in her denim lap. She rested her head on Melanie's shoulder and softly kissed the flushed, moist cheek. 'I'm sorry, Mel.'

When Melanie turned to her, Caroline took her face in both hands and kissed her tenderly on the open mouth. 'We have to eat, my love.'

Melanie nodded. 'Did I hurt you?'

'No more than I deserve.' She stood up and went into the bedroom. Returning, she carried on up-turned hands a pink plastic penis with a harness resembling the jockstrap her athlete brother had once worn. She placed it in Melanie's lap.

'I'm going to bed,' she murmured, kissing the other woman on the trembling forehead. 'Don't be long, will you?'

CHAPTER 10

The DI's name was Martin Hiden. Unlike WPC Maitland, he did not look doubtful when Stacy introduced Mark. Stacy had stood her ground with the WPC. 'If I go, so does Mark,' she had said. 'Anyway, you should be pleased. Your colleague thought he might have been involved.'

Hiden shook hands with both of them. 'We're very grateful to you for coming in.'

'We want this man locked up,' Mark said.

'All his victims want him locked up. Not many are ready to come forward and help.'

'All his victims?', said Stacy. 'How many are there?'

Hiden spread his hands in a gesture of helplessness. 'We don't know. That's the point—many rape victims don't report the attack. Most, possibly. That's why your courage is so valuable.'

'Have you traced his DNA?', Stacy asked.

'Not yet. It takes a while, I'm afraid. Like an AIDS test. You've thought of that, of course?'

Stacy shook her head. 'He used a condom.'

'Not in your mouth, Stacy.' He waited while it sank in. 'You get HIV from an exchange of fluids. Not just from intercourse. I'm sorry.'

He moved to sit behind his desk. 'I'm sure it will be all right. Our test will help us find our man and yours will show you're in the clear. Of course, until it does you probably shouldn't...' He looked from one of them to the other.

Mark's face reddened. 'I think you can safely leave our relationship to us, Inspector.'

'Of course. Now. Just a few questions, if I may, Stacy. Did you get a clear look at him?'

'No. I was blindfolded.'

'All the time? What about when you...'

'He freed my wrists. He didn't remove the blindfold. And before he blindfolded me, he had a mask over his face. A nylon stocking, I think.'

Hiden looked at Maitland. 'Whatever it was, guv, he took it away with him.'

'Pity. Think very hard, Stacy. Is there anything you can tell us that might help find him? Anything at all?'

'He hates women. Somebody hurt him sometime and he hates us all because of it.'

Maitland's pen hovered over a pad but she had not begun to write. Hiden looked slightly irritated. 'We do sometimes use profilers to help us get inside the villain's head. I'm not a great fan. Anything else?'

'He's not a fashion freak, I'm afraid. It was my short skirt that got to him. He said I showed my knickers. I was a scrubber. I walked around asking for it.'

'Anything *physical*, Stacy?'

'He was bigger than me. About six inches. So that would make him—what? Six foot one, I suppose. I'm not short.'

She took heart at the sight of Maitland at last scribbling in her notebook. 'He wore a tweed jacket. Pale brown. Not one of those like teachers wear—this was stylish. It had an almost foreign look. Trousers, not jeans, slightly paler than the jacket. Turn-ups. That's unusual, isn't it? Smart brown shoes.'

'Can you describe them?', asked Maitland.

'Give me a piece of paper and I'll draw them.' She sketched a quick likeness on the pad Hiden pushed across the table.

'You draw well, Stacy.'

'I trained to teach art.'

'You don't do it now?'

She shook her head. 'Not enough money in it, I'm afraid. And the children depressed me. I wasn't cut out to be a teacher. But I do have good visual sense, Inspector. You can have faith in my descriptions.'

'I'm sure. Anything else you remember?'

'Yes. He smelled.'

'Smelled?'

'Cigarettes. He reeked of them. Not ordinary cigarettes, either.'

'Cigars?'

'If I meant cigars I'd say cigars. No, these were cigarettes, but not the kind...actually, they *are* a kind you get here. When I was a student teacher, we had a French teacher who chain-smoked in the staff room. It drove me mad. He smelled like this.'

'Was there ever trouble between you?'

'Inspector, he's not your man. He was three inches shorter than I am. But he smoked French cigarettes and I'm ready to bet the man last night smoked the same ones.'

'Can you remember what they were? *Gitanes?*'

'No, not that. Disk something.'

'*Disque Bleu?*', asked Maitland.

Stacy snapped her fingers. 'That's it. *Disque Bleu*. I'd swear to it.'

'So,' Hiden said, 'let's get this straight. He wore a jacket that could have been foreign. Those shoes you've drawn have a stylish, continental look. And he smoked French cigarettes. But he was English?'

'Oh, yes. Nicely spoken, in fact.' She shuddered.

The centre of Auxerre was a model of what London could have been and wasn't. The paved banks of the River Yonne were not only tidy and unlittered but also open. Unlike the English capital, where walkways were ugly or obstructed or both, Carver could walk as far as he liked in either direction. To the north, the road would turn into a footpath through the woods of Chemilly and Beaumont; to the south, family walks behind the football ground (a football ground from which—unless a side from Britain, Germany or Holland was in town—no drunken thugs ever spilled in open riot) and onto the landscaped parkland of Chamos.

Carver turned towards the bar by the Cathedral in the Place St Etienne. Coffee and a fine, and then he would make his way home.

The booking clerk had offered Buggy a special deal on a first class ticket. Only twenty pounds more than the standard fare he was on and that included lunch, wine and coffee. 'No chance,' Buggy had said. Lunch might be French and they he wasn't eating French food any earlier than he had to. In any case, how would he order it? He had gone to the main line StPancras station and bought a burger and chips, several chocolate bars, two cartons of cigarettes and four cans of lager.

He had eaten the burger before the train entered the tunnel and drunk the beer before it emerged beyond the Channel. Now, with an hour to go before Paris, he would have liked a coffee. Other people had coffee; they walked away from their seats and came back with little bags containing coffee, sandwiches, beer. The coffee smelled good. Clearly, there was a buffet car not far away—but would whoever served there speak English? And, if they didn't—or even if they did—would they choose to embarrass Buggy?

The other passenger at Buggy's table was a Frenchman of about twenty-five. He gestured out of the window. 'You come to France often?'

Buggy shook his head.

'No? This is your first time?'

'Yes.' Buggy was astounded to find this young man, so clearly foreign, speaking English as well as he spoke it himself—if with a strange intonation. Sharon would have liked this man's accent. Sharon, in fact, would already have been giving those little signs she did so well. The signs that said, 'I will if you will.' Sharon found accents exotic. Buggy's father claimed that Sharon thought Alan Shearer the sexiest man in England.

'I am in England a month.'

Buggy stared at the Frenchman. Surely he was having Buggy on? 'But you speak good English.'

The man shrugged. 'I learn in school. Vouz avez étudié français?' He watched blankness spread across Buggy's face, then shrugged again. 'I think French schools are better than English, no? I fetch coffee from the buffet car. You want one?'

When he returned, he placed before Buggy coffee, cream and a bottle of beer with a glass. Buggy picked up the bottle. '1664', he read. 'I've had this.'

'Excuse me,' the Frenchman said. 'What you have had was in a can, yes?'

Buggy nodded. 'I think it was.'

'And did you like it?'

Buggy shrugged. 'Not a lot.' He poured the cream into his coffee and sipped. It tasted as good as it smelled.

'In cans, the *soixante-quatre* is made in England. Somewhere horrible—Swindon, I think—and the beer also is horrible. They make it under license. I think they employ men to stand in a row, pissing into the cans. Kronenbourg in bottles is French, from Strasbourg. Not the same thing. When you finish your coffee, try it.'

Buggy drank his coffee. 'How do you know so much about England?'

'Hein?'

'I never heard of Stras ... where?'

'Strasbourg.' The Frenchman smiled. 'It's in Alsace. Half German, half French.'

'Strasbourg. But you know Swindon. I don't know Swindon. I know they have a football team. But I don't know where it is.'

'The home of the English Marilyn Monroe.'

'What?'

'Diana Dors. Mavis Fluck. The English Marilyn Monroe.'

'I don't know her.'

'You never saw the Weak and the Wicked?'

'Never heard of it.'

The Frenchman shook his head. 'To the English, movies means Hollywood. She could act, your Diana Dors. And she had...' He gestured with his hands.

'Big tits?'

'C'est ça. Exactement.'

Buggy picked up the bottle of Kronenbourg and looked around for an opener.

'Excusez-moi, monsieur.' Taking the bottle from him, the Frenchman twisted the cap with his hands, then handed it back. Buggy poured it into his glass and began to drink. The Frenchman watched him.

'So?'

Buggy put down the glass. He smiled. 'Not bad.'

'Not bad?'

'It's very good,' Buggy said.

'Very good.' The Frenchman waved a hand towards Buggy. 'You thought only the English know about beer, yes? I tell you— the English know nothing about beer. What the English know about is getting drunk. No offence.'

He picked up the bottle and poured the remaining drops into Buggy's glass. 'If you want this beer in France, ask for *soixante-quatre*. Not *soixante-neuf*—I think that is one French expression you do know, yes?

'We have Kronenbourg also on draft,' he went on. 'We call draft pression.'

'Pression,' repeated Buggy.

'Just so. But regular draft Kronenbourg is not so good. If you want this, in the bottle, you could ask for la Kro-col-blanc. You can say that?'

'La Kro-col-blanc.'

'Ah, monsieur, soon you will be taken for a Frenchman!'

Buggy grinned.

'That means, you see, the Kronenbourg with the white collar.'

And so, as the train pulled into the Gare du Nord, Buggy had reached the conclusion that the French might not all be bastards, after all.

Buggy's departure had left Sharon feeling restless. She might ignore him for long periods when he was there, but that didn't mean she had to like it when he wasn't. He was the one who had failed to deliver on the promise of their teenage years, so he was the one who had to be around to take his punishment. When he'd been cock of the walk, she'd been queen bee. She'd never have gone with him otherwise. (Would Joyce Johnson have mixed metaphors like that? She'd have to find a way to ask

Adrian, without actually asking him. If she saw him again, that is). So, when he'd slipped, she'd slipped. The girls who had envied her possession of Buggy could now snigger at her expense. She didn't see them do it, because by and large they'd moved away, but their mothers were still there to put the knife in at every opportunity.

There was fat Mrs Henderson, for a start, she of the swollen ankles and the hairy wart on the side of her nose. 'Hello, Sharon. Sonia was asking after you. Bill came in his company car to take me down to Brighton to spend the weekend with them. Who'd ever have thought he'd do so well? And how's Buggy?' That's right, Mrs H. When you've got me down, stamp on me.

And how on earth had Veronica Payne got where she had? Obvious enough now, of course, that the name was aspirational. Her parents had wanted something better for her than they'd enjoyed themselves, and they'd got right behind her. But marriage to a television presenter! Sharon had laughed, and so had plenty of others, when Veronica went to college to study IT skills. Hadn't they all had enough schooling? Wasn't sixteen too old to be sitting in a classroom being lectured at by old farts? And Veronica's first job showed they were right. She was nothing but a glorified post girl and coffee fetcher.

Not now, though.

And the Paynes never missed a chance to rub Sharon's nose in it. What new projects Veronica's husband was working on. Where they took their holidays. Which celebrities invited them to parties and exclusive dinners in famous restaurants. The private schools their children were educated at. The size of the house they lived in, the extent of the gravelled drive, the rarity of the fish in the pond, the decor of the heated indoor pool, the luxury of the toiletries in the special bathroom that was just for guests.

What had these girls known that Sharon hadn't? How had they come out on top, when she at thirteen had been boss bitch? What a bastard life was. How it came at you from behind when you thought you had it on the floor in a headlock.

Oh, sure, there were plenty of girls for Sharon to look down on. The ones who'd got themselves pregnant at sixteen, seventeen, eighteen, pushing snotty brats around the mucky streets, the fathers long gone, their lives over before they'd had time to start. If there was one thing Sharon knew, it was that she wasn't going to having children. Not now, not ever.

But these no-hopers weren't the ones Sharon cared about. She had grown up thinking of herself as pack leader, and it was against the leaders that she measured herself.

She knew who dragged her down. Buggy. What on earth had she been thinking about when she said "Yes" to his marriage proposal? And it was even worse than that, because Buggy never had proposed marriage. She had. What sublime idiocy!

Sharon had been first to puberty, and Sharon had grown the biggest breasts, the roundest hips. Sharon's mother let her wear her skirts shorter, her blouses lower and her hair blonder than any other girl. As it happened, she had also grown one of the best brains the school had ever seen, but brains didn't win men. Sharon didn't want them, didn't acknowledge them, didn't cultivate them.

Jackie Gough had had the hots for her, but he wouldn't make a move while Buggy was on the scene. All right, Jackie hadn't done as much with himself as he could have, a small time pusher and grass (though she didn't let on that she knew about that, and she certainly didn't tell Buggy. How she'd laughed to herself when Jackie had rehearsed her in what she had to say to Mad Dan Ablett to clear Buggy of suspicion of grassing. She knew who'd turned Mad Dan in). But what might Gough have achieved with someone like Sharon to push him?

And maybe it wasn't too late. Sharon knew stuff about Buggy's work for Cameron, the lock-ups and what was in them, where the keys were. Stuff Buggy didn't know she knew. All she needed was for Buggy to go away for long enough to let her get Gough involved in liberating the cash, then leave Gough to face the music and be gone by the time Buggy came back. Typical of Buggy that now, when for the first time he *had* gone away, he wasn't going to be gone for long enough.

There was something there, some hope of escape from this miserable life. Maybe she could find a way to get Buggy away for longer. In the meantime . . .

In the meantime she had to have consolation. She had said she wasn't sure about meeting Adrian, not because she didn't want to, but because of Buggy. And Buggy wasn't here.

She opened her handbag and took out the piece of paper Adrian had scribbled his number on.

She picked up the phone.

CHAPTER 11

All Buggy's fear of the unknown returned when he stood in the huge and bustling station concourse. The jabbering all around him was assuredly not English. He leaned against a pillar and lit a cigarette. He was to be met—but by whom? And how would they know each other?

He had smoked the cigarette down to the filter when he became aware that someone was standing beside him. 'Buggy,' a deep voice said. 'It's been a while since I had the pleasure.'

Buggy stared up into an unwelcome face. 'Sergeant Mitchell! I haven't done anything.'

'That's not what I hear, Buggy. And it's plain Mr Mitchell now.'

'You're not a copper?'

'Not any more, Buggy. I've become a nursemaid. Shall we go?'

'Go?'

Mitchell sighed. 'The train to Auxerre doesn't leave from here, Buggy. We have to take the Metro to the Gare de Lyon. Come on, son. Pick up your bag.'

'Auxerre?'

'That's where you're going, isn't it? So Cameron says, anyway.'

'You're working for Cameron?'

'Are you planning to repeat everything I say? I always worked for Cameron, Buggy. In a manner of speaking. I'm retired now.'

'In Spain?' Buggy felt stupid as he said the words.

'You sure you want to know the ins and outs? Knowledge

85

can be a dangerous thing, Buggy. Especially to the intellectually challenged.' He leaned forward to bridge the six inch height difference between them. 'You can't tell people what you don't know, can you?'

Buggy remembered Jackie Gough talking to Sharon: "If someone grasses him up, I don't want anybody thinking it was me." And there had been Cameron: "He knows you, and you do know who we are. But that doesn't worry us, because you aren't going to grass." Not being a grass—being *known* for not being a grass—was important to Buggy. It was one of the few things of value he possessed. But everyone had a price. No-one was ever safe.

'It's people grassing *me* up I need to worry about,' he said.

The Metro was clean, you had to give it that. Mitchell had bought the tickets and it was Mitchell who followed the map, getting them out of one train and managing the long walk through Bastille station to another platform. For a man who must be fifty, Mitchell was in good shape. 'You were a bit young to retire?', Buggy said as he hurried to keep up.

'It wasn't that kind of retirement, Buggy. They don't pay me a pension or anything. Fortunately, I'd made my own arrangements.'

The Gare de Lyon was as big and as busy as the Gare du Nord. Buggy was struck by the cleanness of the stonework and the general airiness. What grated was the confidence of the people. Only the English were entitled to quite that degree of self-regard. That was why it was sometimes necessary for followers of English football to give foreigners a good kicking—to remind them of their slightly inferior place in the world.

Mitchell led the way into the lofty booking hall. He took a

timetable from one of the holders screwed to the wall and studied it.

'Give me seventy Euros, Buggy.'

'How much?' Buggy's voice had risen in panic.

'It's about forty quid, Buggy. That gets us two first class tickets to Auxerre. Come on. I know how much Cameron gave you.'

Buggy took the roll of strange coloured notes from his pocket and looked helplessly at them. Mitchell grabbed them and removed four twenty Euro notes, handing the rest back. 'Thank you. Now stand right there while I get the tickets. The train leaves in fifteen minutes.'

'Get smokers.'

'There aren't any, Buggy. Just like England.'

'Bloody hell.'

The train was immensely comfortable. Mitchell took a book from his bag and placed the bag on the rack. He sat down. 'This is a TGV, Buggy. A Train Grande Vitesse. A high speed train. It takes us to Laroche-Migennes and then we change to the local puffer for Auxerre.' He leaned forward and lowered his voice. 'We are not the only people in this carriage, Buggy. Just because you don't speak French doesn't mean they won't understand English. Do you follow me?'

Buggy nodded. Mitchell picked up his book. 'Good,' he said. 'So don't irritate me with a lot of noise. Now look out of the window and enjoy the scenery. You're abroad, Buggy. They do things differently here.'

Carver poured coffee into a large mug. He liked his coffee this way—whitened with more hot milk than most people would think usual but made double strength from Colombian beans so that the sharp edge cut through. He was going to follow up that Italian recommendation some time soon.

Carver's home was as he liked it, too—neat, clean and private. Privacy was something you could rely on the French for. Like those on each side, Carver's house looked inward, offering the street only shuttered windows, a door and grey painted walls. Many people here, as Carver knew, had money; but money was traditionally guarded from public view. What the State didn't know about, the State couldn't tax. At the back of the house, an expanse of plate glass gave onto a terrace leading to a walled garden. Carver's Renault was parked behind a trellis of climbing roses at the far end.

Burgundy had suited Carver from the moment he arrived. He liked the rural French way of concealing indifference behind formal politesse. If you walked into a shop you greeted everyone there with "Bonjour messieurs/dames" and they replied "Bonjour monsieur". Failure to do so marked you as a rude ignoramus and incurred the shopkeeper's contempt—but the politeness itself meant nothing. For all of the eight years he had lived here, Madame Poitou had cleaned for him two days a week and Monsieur Grabet had worked the garden but they remained "Madame" and "Monsieur" to him, and he "Monsieur" to them.

Not that he didn't know how Madame Poitou scanned his belongings for clues to her employer's mysterious life. But that didn't matter, as long as he kept the special box in his sitting room locked and ensured that nothing that should not be seen was left on view.

Carver took his coffee onto the terrace and watched Grabet weeding by hand in the flower beds. No vegetables were grown here; the old boy raised them on his own land and, by arrangement, brought salads and beans in season. The rest

Carver bought in the market. A charcuterie and a boulangerie were within walking distance. And there was no shortage of good restaurants and bars.

He sat on a wicker chair beside a large stone pot filled with bedding plants. For all the contentment of home, he could not get Stacy Teasdale's treachery out of his mind. It had been her idea, not his, to do what she had done. To do that and then call the police was simply beyond Carver's understanding. There would have to be a settling of accounts. He would have her, and this time there would be no pity, no mercy. Stacy Teasdale would never forget what was going to happen to her.

Carver took his cup back into the kitchen. He needed exercise. He would ride his bike up to Sommeville and then cycle back down the bank of the Yonne right into the centre of town. It would take about two hours. Then he would be ready for lunch at *Le Quai*.

He would allow himself a little extra excitement—something that would help him to relish the coming settlement with the Teasdale tart. Normally, he didn't do this. Normally, he reserved this frisson for the times immediately before a strike. But then, what was normal? Normal was for others. Normal was for people who tied themselves into tedious jobs and boring marriages. Normal was for men who could make love without anger. Normal was not for Carver. He carefully unlocked the heavy wooden box with the key that stayed always on his key ring.

A collection of laundered and folded women's underwear lay on top of the sort of books and videos that would cause a customs official to ring the bell for assistance. Carver took out the satin knickers he had placed there the previous night and removed the piece of paper tucked inside. He relocked the box and went into the bathroom, locking the door behind him.

Before re-emerging, he dropped his own underpants into the laundry basket.

The train from Laroche-Migennes was somewhat different from the TGV. Grey and old-fashioned, it looked like something pre-war—a relic from the days when France was beginning to emerge from its peasant past.

They took a cab from Auxerre station, crossing the Yonne by the Pont de la Tournelle and driving along the broad and tree-lined Boulevard de la Chainette to the Hotel Normandie on the Boulevard Vauban.

'Hotel Normandie,' Buggy spelled out. 'Is this Normandy, then?'

Mitchell shook his head. 'No, Buggy, this is not Normandy. Normandy is bloody miles away. This is Burgundy. The home of good food and good wine.'

The Normandie serves breakfast, but not lunch or dinner. 'That's how it is in France, Buggy,' Mitchell explained. 'Lots of hotels don't do meals. They don't need to. You go to a hotel for a bed. For a meal, you use a restaurant.'

And so, after a beer at a table in the hotel's front garden followed by a shower, Mitchell and Buggy strolled through the town towards the Yonne and its quayside. The streets were narrow and the pavements wide enough for only one person at a time. The sun shone on honeyed grey stone.

'When will we see Carver?', Buggy asked.

'We'll look for him tomorrow.'

'Look for him? You don't know where he is?'

'I know he lives here. I know an Englishman in a town like this won't have gone un-noticed. Especially an Englishman as peculiar as Carver.'

The centre of Auxerre is small. The boulevards, including the Boulevard Vauban, form a sort of inner ring road around a compact old town. They had crossed the central Rue de Paris, passed the cathedral and now found themselves in an open square with the great church to the east and the quayside opposite. To the south was the Hôtel du Département; to the north, a restaurant calling itself simply *Le Quai*. A large fountain stood in the cobbled square, and tables with sun umbrellas were arranged outside the restaurant.

Mitchell took a seat at one of the tables and motioned Buggy to do the same.

'What did you mean,' Buggy said, 'about Carver being peculiar?'

Mitchell stared across the table. 'You're right,' he said. 'The man kills people for a living. Nothing strange about that. Just your loveable English eccentric.'

'I'll tell you what I don't understand,' said Buggy.

'We're only here for a couple of days, Buggy. I'm not sure we have time for all the things you don't understand.'

'Very funny. When Cameron wanted someone killed, he asked me to find someone and I got Doyle for him.'

'Buggy!' Mitchell's response was explosive. 'Will you keep your mouth shut! And what are you telling me for? I don't want to know what you've been up to for Cameron.'

Buggy, beetroot-red, stared away from the table. He fumbled for his cigarettes.

'Don't go huffy on me, Buggy. You can't do the tight-lipped thing and smoke at the same time. It's a physiological impossibility.' Mitchell leaned forward. 'You were going to say, why did Cameron need you to find a killer if he knew Carver. Right?'

Still peeved, Buggy nodded.

'Cameron doesn't know Carver, Buggy. All right? When Cameron decided he wasn't happy about your man, he asked me for help. *I'm* the one who knows Carver. OK? Carver has his regular clients and he won't work for just anyone. It's one of his rules. He's a big rules man, is Carver.'

The waiter arrived to take their order. Mitchell waved him away. 'Deux minutes, monsieur.'

'There's something else you need to know, Buggy. Carver and I go back a long way. I did him a service when I was in the Job. I kept him out of trouble. So Carver owes me, and Carver won't forget. See, Carver isn't your usual poxy little chancer. When Carver's your friend, Buggy, you need no other. Loyal to the end, our boy. And when he's your enemy...well, Buggy, just don't let that happen to you. Know what I mean? If you upset Carver, Carver will do you. And I won't stop him, Buggy. Cameron or no Cameron.

'And one last thing. I'm here to introduce you to Carver. Nothing else. As far as he's concerned, I don't know what you want him to do. When you ask him, you make sure I'm not around. Understand?'

Mitchell looked up suddenly. His forefinger, which had been jabbing vigorously towards Buggy's chest, was arrested in mid-air. Buggy turned to follow his gaze and saw a man of indeterminate age, could be thirties, could be forties, a shade over six feet, resting a bike against the stone rim of the fountain. The most striking thing about the man was his eyes. Buggy had never seen green eyes before, but this man's eyes were green. And they were fixed unblinkingly on Mitchell.

Without haste, the newcomer advanced across the cobbles. 'Mitch,' he said. His voice was soft and well-modulated. 'Is this coincidence? Or are you looking for me?'

CHAPTER 12

He'd suggested meeting after work outside Waterstone's, but Sharon wasn't going to risk being seen walking through the streets with an Adrian. She arrived at his flat twenty minutes after the agreed time. Late enough to show who was in charge; not so late that Adrian might have decided she'd changed her mind and gone out.

It was a bigger flat in a nicer street than a Waterstone's assistant could afford on his own, and Adrian shared it with three others. Only one of them was there when she arrived, and he was just going out.

Adrian said, 'This is Charlie.'

Charlie stuck out his hand and Sharon took it. It seemed these people had a thing about shaking hands.

'And I'm Lizzie.' A firm handshake and a firm stare. Lizzie wasn't the kind of girl Sharon met very often. Tall, slim and oh, what an outfit, from the gold wedge espadrilles to the flowing golden hair. A pale pink cropped cardigan over a gold silk vest. Cropped brown linen trousers. Almost no makeup; almost no jewellery.

'I love your vest,' breathed Sharon.

Was Lizzie's puzzled look genuine? Or assumed as a way of putting the other woman down? Sharon thought she knew. 'Is that chiffon?' she asked. 'On the cardy?'

'Oh, God,' said Lizzie. 'We're not going to do the clothes thing, are we? So boring. And what could I possibly find to say about yours?'

There was a sharp intake of breath. From Charlie, from

Adrian—who could tell? Charlie said, 'Lizzie and I are just going out.'

Lizzie said, 'We hear you're interested in the Beats.'

Sharon said, 'Is that right?'

Lizzie said, 'It was all sixty years ago, and in another country. What can they possibly have to tell us now?'

Charlie said, 'Lizzie, we really do have to go.'

Sharon said, 'Don't let me keep you.'

Lizzie said, 'It's all right. We don't really have anywhere we have to be.'

Charlie said, 'But we do have a deal.'

'Ah, yes,' Lizzie said. 'The deal that says flat sharers who bring someone new home get to have the place to themselves. And let's be fair. Up to now, it's always been Adrian going out. This is a new experience for all of us. But especially for Adrian.'

Sharon moved closer to the blushing Adrian and took his hand in hers. Charlie moved towards the door. 'I'm going, Lizzie. If you want to come along, you're welcome. But you can't stay here.'

'Does she live here?' asked Sharon when they were alone.

'No. She's engaged to Charlie, and Charlie lives here, so she spends a lot of time here.'

'Poor you.'

'Oh, Lizzie's all right.'

'She's a cow.'

'Sharon!'

'I know a bitch when I see one. So. What are you going to cook for me?'

'You like pasta?'

'I like anything I don't have to cook myself.'

'Are you hungry?'

'I could eat a scabby cat.'

'Don't think I've got one of those. Would you settle for tagliatelle with flaked salmon and cream?'

'Sounds lovely.'

'I thought fish because I didn't know whether you'd be vegetarian.'

Sharon laughed. 'Me? No, love, I'm not vegetarian.'

'Charlie doesn't eat meat. Nor does Lizzie.'

'You could have fooled me.'

'There's a bottle of wine in the fridge.' He handed her a corkscrew. 'Glasses in that cupboard. Would you pour us both a glass?'

He filled a pan with water and placed it on top of the stove. When he turned round, Sharon was eyeing the corkscrew. 'What's up?'

'I've never done this before.'

'Never opened a wine bottle?'

'No,' she snapped. 'I've never opened a fucking wine bottle. Does that make me too cheap to bother with? Shall I go home now?'

He stepped across the kitchen floor and held out his arms. She came into them without a word. He pressed her close, patting her gently on the back. 'What's up, darling?'

'I don't belong here.'

'Of course you do.'

'I don't. I'm a failure. I haven't done anything. I haven't got anything.' She stepped back and stared into Adrian's face. She could have been utterly sincere. She could have been checking for signs that he had clocked her mendacity, if mendacious is what she was. What she knew for certain was that Adrian would never know the difference. 'Nothing someone like you would want, anyway.'

He turned her round so that her back was pressed against him. Reaching around her, he guided her to pick up the corkscrew and place it in position. Sharon allowed her hands to be manipulated. His cheek was very close to hers. 'What is someone like me?' he murmured into her ear. With a smooth pop, the cork came out of the bottle.

She pressed back against him. 'Someone educated,' she said. 'Someone with a future.'

'Your future's over, is it? How old are you, Sharon?'

'Mind your own business.'

'Did you ever hear of Yogi Berra?'

'The little bear in the park? The friend of the Ranger?'

'No. Yogi Bear was named after him. At least, I suppose he was. Yogi Berra was an American baseball player. He said, "It ain't over till it's over."'

'He didn't live where I live.'

'And there was another American who said, "The opera ain't over till the fat lady sings."'

'What's this got to do with anything?'

'You want a future. We've all got a future, Sharon.'

'For some of us, it's shit.'

'It's what we make it. You want to be educated? Go to university.'

Sharon laughed. 'Just like that? Your water's boiling.'

He stepped away, picked up a couple of large handfuls of tagliatelle and dropped them into the water.

Sharon said, 'I haven't got a single GCSE.'

'Why not. Are you stupid?'

'I must be.'

'No, you're not, Sharon.' He wheeled around. 'Are you?'

'Maybe not.'

'Why didn't you get any GCSEs?'

'Didn't do any work.'

'Why not?'

'Didn't see the point. No-one did any. No-one I wanted to be friends with.'

'But now you do? See the point? Now you want to go to university?'

'If only.'

'So do an access course.'

'I don't...what's an access course?'

'I'll tell you over dinner. Which if I don't see to it now we won't be eating.' He held up his glass. 'To Sharon. May the butterfly emerge from the chrysalis and soar close to the sun.'

Sharon touched glasses with him. 'That's lovely.'

She watched, fascinated, as he prepared the salad and made the dressing for it using the juice of a freshly squeezed lemon, olive oil, Dijon mustard, salt and Tabasco.

'It's just a salad dressing,' he said. 'What would you use?'

'I don't eat salads. But if I did, I'd probably use salad cream. That's what my Mum used if she ever made a salad. Which she didn't.'

He'd bought rolls, which he warmed in the oven. They were just off white, and the surface powdery with flour. 'The French would call them artisan rolls,' he said. 'They're very fond of their traditional baking skills, the Froggies.'

'I'd love to go to France,' Sharon said.

'We'll go together.'

'Maybe. Let's not get ahead of ourselves. Is it nice there?'

'The food certainly is. Speaking of which, this is ready. Shall we sit down?'

Over dinner, Sharon asked him to explain access courses, which he did.

'So anyone can go to university?'

'Anyone with a brain,' he said. 'Which you have.'

'And people there won't look down on me?'

'You're joking. The government wants people like you there. So do the unis.'

'Why?'

'Inclusion, for a start. Not everyone goes to a good school...'

'...you can say that again...'

'...and the government makes a big thing of helping people catch up. And the unis know that someone whose done an access course really wants to be there. Why do you, by the way?'

'Want to go to university?'

He nodded.

'I don't know. Growing up, I only knew one person who went. Jackie Gough, his name is. And he's still a small time crook, which is what he would have been if he'd never gone. But he's a different kind of small time crook, if you know what I mean. He's cleverer. He says smarter things. He's better to be with.'

'Better than your husband?'

'Oh. Anyone's better to be with than Buggy.'

'So why did you marry him?'

'I haven't finished saying why I want to go to university.'

'Sorry.'

'Oh, I don't know. I'm sick of my life, Adrian. And sometimes I see people...No, *listen* to people. And I think, that's how I want to be. That's how I want to talk. That's how I want people to talk to me. I want to talk about clever things without putting my foot in it. I want to talk to clever people without them thinking I'm stupid. Do you understand?'

'I think so. What subject do you want to read?'

'Eh? I don't know. If I want to learn about Joyce Johnson, what subject would that be?'

'Well, it could be English, could be American studies, could be American literature.'

'Oh. Do I have to decide now?'

'Of course not. There'll be lots of time. While you're doing the access course.'

'Where will I do that?'

'There are hundreds of them. Thousands. I can get some addresses, if you like?'

She put her hand on his arm. 'Yes, I'd *really* like.'

'I'll do it tomorrow. We have directories at work.'

'Fantastic. Will I have to pay?'

'I don't know. Probably. Can you?'

'I'll get the money. And I'd like to do it somewhere away from where I live.'

'Then you've got living costs on top.'

'I told you, I'll get the money. I don't want people like Buggy finding out where I am and spoiling things. The old Sharon's just going to fade away and leave the new one that no-one can ever know was a failure. Like your butterfly.'

'How's the pasta?'

'Lovely. Beautiful. It's not like anything I ever ate before, which is great because it feels like it's the first meal of my new life. You're very clever.'

'Thank you. So. The other question. Why did you marry Buggy?'

Stacy Teasdale sat by the window in her flat, staring into the road. An untasted cup of coffee grew cold on the table beside her. It was no good. This was going to have to be done.

'Mark.' There was no answer. She raised her voice. 'Mark!'

'Darling?' His head appeared round the kitchen door.

Her voice shook. 'Come and sit with me for a while.'

He came into the sitting room. 'You feeling down?'

She nodded. 'Yes, Mark. I'm feeling down.'

'Stacy, you heard what the doctor said. It's very difficult to get HIV from...from...'

'Oral sex, Mark. It's all right to say it. I sucked another man's cock. Yes, I did hear her say that. It's difficult. And it isn't impossible.' She took a deep breath. 'But that isn't it. Or it isn't all of it.'

'You want to tell me, angel?'

'No. No I don't want to tell you. But I'm going to have to.'

He sat down beside her. 'You're going to send me away, aren't you?'

She didn't speak.

'Stacy, I'm prepared to wait. I mean, I know how hard it must have been for you...'

'No, you don't.'

'No? Well, I know how hard it's been for me.'

'Mark, I really don't give a shit how it's been for you. I was raped and you weren't there. You're supposed to be my man, you're supposed to be there for me, look after me, protect me *and you weren't there.*'

'Honestly, darling, I think that's a bit...'

'Will you stop telling me what you think? When I needed you, you were in bloody Birmingham. You're not entitled to think, after that.'

'Look, darling, you're overwrought. It's not surprising, is it? Given what you've been through? Why don't I take you up to stay with your parents for a few days?'

'My *parents?* Hah! Do you know what I was doing when that creep came knocking on my door?'

'You were on the phone to your mother.'

'I was on the phone to my mother. I put the phone down on the table. Not on the hook, on the table.'

'Stacy, please don't shout.'

'On the fucking table. Where my fucking mother could hear everything that went on. My own mother heard a man telling me to take my fucking clothes off. And she did nothing! *Nothing!* She thought she was listening to a fucking TV show. Even when I didn't come back on the line. She waited, and when I didn't come back, you know what she did? She went and made jam.'

'She's a little hard of hearing, Stace. You know that.'

'Don't call me Stace. She's offered me some of the jam. You believe that? She's offered to send me some of the fucking jam!'

'So she's out of your life too, is she?'

'You're all out of my fucking life.' She walked into the kitchen, Mark following, and emptied her cold coffee into the sink. She poured water from the filter into the kettle and pressed the switch. 'And don't tell me you're not secretly relieved. Because I know better.'

'What will you do?'

'What I should have done weeks ago. Take the job Vanessa got me.'

'On a cruise ship?'

'Why should that surprise you? It's my Dad whose the vicar. Not me.'

On the melamine counter was a wooden knife block from

which several black knife handles protruded. One of them was attached to a long, thin blade of great sharpness. Mark used it, rarely, to bone joints. Stacy had never touched it. She pulled it out now and stared at Jim. 'I'd kill that bastard, you know. If I had the chance, I'd kill him.'

Later that day, when Mark had left her life permanently, Stacy would tell herself the conversation hadn't gone at all badly. She'd needed to rid herself of this man whom she had so recently loved and who had become superfluous in her life, and she had done it—and made it his fault, into the bargain.

And now the cruise ships awaited her. Cruise ships full of men. Who would pay for what that bastard had done to her.

"Why did you marry Buggy?" It was such a simple question, with such a simple answer. 'I married Buggy for the same reason as I didn't get any GCSEs or go to university,' she said. 'Because no-one told me I could do something different.'

She drained her wine glass and Adrian refilled it. She placed her knife and fork on the plate as she had watched him place his. 'That was delicious, Adrian. Really lovely.'

'I've got some blueberries and cream for pudding.'

'Not for me, my love.'

'Cheese?'

She shook her head. 'I couldn't eat another thing.'

'You're not still in the market for a scabby cat?'

She turned her head to face him. Her eyes locked with his. Calmly, she said, 'No. But I'm hoping you might want to eat a little pussy?'

Stunned silence.

She put her hand over her mouth. 'Oh, my God, I've shocked you.'

'No. No, you haven't...'

'Adrian, you've gone scarlet. Oh, I'm so sorry.'

'Honestly, I'm...'

She leaned forward, kissed him full on the lips. 'Put it down to the drink, my sweet.' She stood up, took his hand in hers. 'There's only two things we can do after that,' she said.

He looked at her, mute.

She said, 'The first is for me to leave, now, and go home, and never see you again. You can find a nice, clean, quiet girl and forget you ever met a filthy slut called Sharon.'

'What's the second?' he whispered, holding firmly on to her hand.

'You can show me your bedroom and let's test the springs.'

Sharon surveyed Adrian's bed doubtfully.

'My mother bought it for me,' he said.

'I thought she wanted you to get off with a girl? Is it wide enough for two people?'

'I don't know. I've never tried.'

For someone who rarely approached men with tenderness, Sharon surprised herself. With the utmost gentleness, she put her arms round him and kissed him gently on the lips. She lay back on the pale coverlet. 'Would you like to undress me?'

He nodded, speechless.

She lay on her back and smiled at him. 'Good. I'd like that, too.'

She'd had to show him everything. She should have hated it, but she'd loved it. He'd undressed her like a child unwrapping a Christmas present he'd longed for but never thought he'd get. His first attempt had ended in fiasco when he emptied himself on her thigh before she'd even got him safe inside her.

She'd wrapped her arms tightly round him, refusing to let him move. He was close to tears, but she kissed him again and again, on the forehead, the cheek, the throat, the lips. 'There's lots of time, darling,' she murmured.

'I'm useless.'

'You're excited. Do you think you can get excited again? I think you can.'

'What use is that if I can't even...'

'...but you can. You'll see. Now that the fever's passed.'

And he had.

Detective Sergeant Anne Milton had been on leave when Maitland had brought Stacy Teasdale in. Now she was back at work.

'What have we got?', Hiden said. He pointed towards the whiteboards on the incident room wall. 'Write this up, Anne, will you?'

'Start on the left with the man. Six foot one. Dresses quietly but stylishly. The style may be continental. He's English. Well spoken. Smokes French cigarettes. May hate women; may have been hurt by a woman; may have some kind of fetish about women's underwear. Is there anything else we know about him?'

'He has a gun,' Milton said, writing it below the other information. 'His body appears to be hairless...'

'May be hairless, Anne. Make that clear—it's only a possibility.'

'Body may be hairless. And we have a DNA sample that doesn't match any on record. Still,' she said, 'it means we'll almost certainly get him sometime or other.'

'By which time...'

'...he may have raped or killed who knows how many more women. Yes, guv.'

'Did we ever get a description of that gun? Is it always the same one?'

'I haven't found one.'

'Ask the Teasdale woman. She's got a good eye and she had her wits about her. Get her to draw it. What else do we know? He's a psychopath.'

'I don't think so, guv.'

'How's that?'

'He's capable of showing compassion.'

'Compassion? How do you work that out?'

'According to Stacy Teasdale's statement, he untied her wrists when she asked him not to hurt her.'

'You call that compassion?'

'What do you call it?'

Hiden was thoughtful for a while. 'All right, then. Don't put psychopath. What else?'

'He's organised.'

'Because...?'

'He brought his mask with him. He brought gloves. The condoms weren't to keep her from getting pregnant—they were to stop us collecting his semen.'

'OK, so he's organised. Is that worth knowing? Except that it might make him harder to catch?'

'I've got my notes from the profiling course here.'

'Oh, please, no.'

'Let's see. Yes. An organised attacker is likely to be socially skilled and smarter than the average. He's probably married or has a partner. He works himself up before the crime, but while he's committing it he's calm and methodical. Listen to this bit, guv: he fantasises about the crime and may take mementoes.'

'Anne, this guy takes the girls' knickers *before* he attacks them. Possibly days before.'

'Organised attackers are more likely to target strangers. They look for the right kind of target for them...'

'Anne, this is bullshit.'

'How so? It fits.'

'Yes, it fits, but what does it tell us that we couldn't work out anyway? The man's a fantasist who targets young women with short skirts. We know that.'

'So you don't want to know that he's probably the first born son?'

Hiden snorted.

'How about the fact that he probably doesn't find his job fulfilling?'

'Anne. Put that tripe away and let's get back to work.' He gestured towards the board. 'If it makes you feel better, you can write "organised" up there. But none of that other stuff.

'Let's go on to the next board. Head it "Locations". He killed a woman in Twickenham, but didn't rape her. He raped a woman in Sheen but didn't kill her. And now he's raped another in Richmond.'

'Those are the ones we know about. The stats say, if we know about three, there are five more that haven't been reported.'

'Anne, we can only deal with what we know.'

'How about a call for other victims to come forward?'

'And announce the existence of a serial rapist and occasional killer? The Commissioner won't go for that.'

'Well, can we at least look for other cases that have been reported but we don't know about?'

Hiden looked thoughtful. 'Sure,' he said. 'Circulate every collator in the country. Ask if they've had any cases that match this MO. But spell out that we don't want to start a public scare. Until we get replies—*if* we get replies—we have three cases. Twickenham, Richmond and Sheen.'

'Three miles apart at the most. Less than ten square miles.'

'Heavily populated square miles. Any conclusions?'

'The obvious one is that he lives somewhere close by.'

'Obvious, yes. Not necessarily correct. What about the French connection?'

'You're not suggesting he comes from France to Richmond when he wants a shag? Guv, Richmond has the highest concentration of second degrees in the country. It's a cosmopolitan sort of place. French clothes, French cigarettes, French style—there's plenty of those things in Richmond. The best Lebanese I ever ate was in Richmond.'

'I didn't know you went for Arabs.'

'I'm talking about a meal, Guv. Mick Jagger has a house there, for Heaven's sake.'

'I suppose you're right. You don't suppose...'

'No, guv. Jagger has his hands full dealing with the mott that throws itself at him. He doesn't need to use a gun to get more.'

'You're a bit salty this morning, Anne. Is there a new man on the scene?'

'That's my business. What's next?'

'Didn't mean to pry. Why did he kill the one in Twickenham?'

'Something went wrong. Most likely she didn't co-operate the way Stacy Teasdale did. But how can we know? Rape can always lead to murder. Rape by a stranger, anyway. Maybe she simply refused to be cowed.'

'You think that's what he wants?'

'Guv, he's a rapist. He isn't looking for love. He likes to make women frightened. And he likes to make an indelible mark.

Remember what he told Stacy Teasdale: "I want this to stay with you all your life."'

'OK. Last board, for the moment. The women. What do we know about them?'

'Stacy Teasdale. University educated. Gutsy but sensible. Lives in Richmond, a flat—one of several in an old house. Been there three years. Blonde, twenty-five years old, wears short skirts. Long term boyfriend. On the face of it, not promiscuous. Comes from Norfolk, father a vicar there, both parents still alive and together. Trained as a teacher, works up west as a graphic artist.

'Ingrid Torton. University educated. Lived in Twickenham. A flat—one of several in an old house. Had been there six months. Described by friends as excitable and nervous. Hair mousy. Twenty-two years old, wore short skirts. No known boyfriend, no known indicators of promiscuity. Came from Fulham. Parents divorced, mother re-married and living in Leeds, which is where she came from, father living alone in Fulham. Worked in personnel with software company.

'Margaret Bolan, known to her friends as Peggy. Thirty-two years old. Left school at sixteen. Steady personality. Redhead. Almost always wears trousers. Divorced three years ago, ex-husband re-married and has custody of their two children, lives in Hitchin. Broke up with boy-friend of six months standing three months before she was attacked. Boy-friend's alibi apparently watertight. Ex-husband ditto. No male interest at time of rape. Came from Sunderland. Father dead, mother in Australia with Margaret's brother and his family. Runs own business providing office services. Employs eight people and earned more than a hundred thousand last year. Lives in Sheen in Victorian villa.'

She finished writing and put down the magic marker.

'Bolan,' said Hiden. 'Why did the husband get the kids?'

'She didn't want them. She gives him ten grand a year to look after them. Sees them every couple of weeks—she goes to Hitchin; never has them to her place. She's supposed to take them on holiday every year but hasn't yet. Kids bore her.'

'How did she respond to the attack?'

'Took it in her stride, guv. Some women say they do, but almost none mean it. Bolan did. Said if she ever had the chance she'd kill him without a second thought but she wasn't letting him ruin her life.'

'Mmm. OK; so what are the similarities between them? Serial offenders are looking for victims who conform to a type. Why did he pick these three and not some other women?'

'Well, it isn't for showing their knickers, whatever he told Stacy. Peggy Bolan almost never wears skirts and certainly not short ones.'

'It's success,' Hiden said. 'Or the appearance of success. Confidence, let's say. He doesn't like women he thinks are too big for their boots. This is a man who likes women subservient. That's why he picked these three and that's why he wants them to remember him for the rest of their lives. What would your profilers make of that?'

'Women frighten him.'

'OK. You and I are going to have to frighten him a bit more.'

The lobby of the Kensington Hilton is a good place for surveillance, being overlooked by a lounge area where snacks and drinks are served and, at appropriate times, a pianist plays. Caroline and Melanie sat in the corner. Caroline wore a wig, her face was heavily made up and the cotton wool she had pushed into her cheeks made her feel as though she might be sick at any moment.

'There he is,' she said when the lift door opened.

'The blue shirt?'

'That's him.'

'He's going for breakfast. Wait till he's out of sight, then get out of here.'

'You will be careful, Mel?'

'I'll be careful. Now—go!'

CHAPTER *13*

Grinning, Mitchell stuck out his hand. 'Don,' he said. 'You haven't met Buggy.'

Buggy felt the green eyes turn to him. He put out a hand, which Carver ignored. 'Do I want to?' He dropped into a seat, his eyes still fixed on Buggy.

Mitchell turned to Buggy. 'Why don't you give Don and me a few minutes, Buggy? Take a walk up and down the quay?'

Buggy did his best to stare Carver out. It didn't work. Contempt might have sparked some kind of defiance in him, but the green eyes conveyed only indifference. He stood up sharply, scraping his iron chair on the cobbles, and walked away.

He heard soft laughter behind him. Looking down, he realised he had adopted the stance he had sneered at when Jackie Gough walked out of the Black Bear. The same high shoulders, the same half-smile, arms bent and hands raised in the same way. The jail yard walk. He was conscious that his face was bright red. This humiliation was what Cameron had sent him to. Who the hell did Mitchell think he was, a bent copper kicked off the force, treating him like this? He lit a cigarette and stared at the waters of the Yonne, then turned to his right and began to walk.

Melanie saw "Mr Brown" come back into the lobby after fifteen minutes. His breakfast had not been a leisurely affair. She watched him go into the lift. A few minutes later he returned, wearing a corduroy jacket and carrying a newspaper. He walked briskly through the lobby and out into Holland Park Avenue. As Melanie reached the door she saw him get into the front

111

passenger seat of an illegally parked white Ford Mondeo.

Three taxis waited in the tarmac half-moon in front of the hotel entrance. Melanie got into the first.

'Where to, love?'

Melanie smothered her revulsion at being called "love" by this fat middle-aged male. 'Follow that car. Don't lose it.'

The driver turned to look at her. He smiled, a smile not for her. 'Whatever you say, love.'

He pulled the car right, pushing through three lanes to take a right turn at the roundabout where they were held up by the lights. When they were again in motion, the Mondeo was four hundred yards in front.

'Is he heading for the M40?', the driver asked. Melanie said nothing.

The Mondeo swung left onto the flyover. Melanie's heart sank. She had thirty pounds in her purse, half the money Caroline had brought home. If Brown was indeed heading out of town, she would be unable to follow for long.

She felt a flicker of relief as the Mondeo turned left onto the slip road, then signalled a right turn into Wood Lane. 'Are you a cop?,' asked the driver. 'Is he visiting someone in the Scrubs?'

'Just drive the car,' Melanie snapped.

The Mondeo drove past the entrance to Du Cane Road. 'Not the Scrubs, then,' said the driver.

The white car turned right into North Pole Road, the taxi following two hundred yards behind. A right turn into Latimer Road followed almost immediately.

'He's spotted us,' said the driver. 'He's doubling back.'

Melanie stared forward at the Mondeo. No-one was looking back. Without confidence she said, 'He's just being cautious. Keep after him.'

'Are these people dangerous? I'm not getting into anything. You should have your own people doing this.' The taxi followed the Mondeo down Latimer Road, under the Westway and left in busy traffic into Darfield Road. Another left turn took them back under the raised motorway where they caught a glimpse of the tail of the Mondeo disappearing into Crowther Road. The rest of the traffic carried straight on.

The towering concrete pillars were oppressive. This was a land of concrete and litter, of closed buildings and closed eyes. The taxi stopped.

'I don't like this,' the driver said.

'We'll lose them.'

'We can't lose them. That's what I'm worried about. This goes nowhere. There's no way out at that end. You're going to have to call for back-up. I'm not going down there.'

Melanie said, 'They must have gone somewhere.'

'I don't care where they've gone. I want to stay out of trouble. Haven't you got a radio with you?'

Melanie opened the door. 'How much do I owe you?'

'Forget it. I always help the police. Do you want me to wait?'

Melanie considered. 'No. You go. I'll be all right.'

'D'you want me to radio your station? Ask for help?'

'I'll do what has to be done.'

'On your own head be it.'

'I can look after myself.'

The taxi drove off. Full of foreboding, Melanie let her eyes wander ahead through the dirty brick labyrinth. No more than two hundred yards away, Crowther Road bent sharply to the right. Whatever was down there was out of sight.

Perhaps she should give up. She hadn't wanted to do this in the first place. She could tell Caroline she'd lost him. But

Caroline would have a moody, and Caroline's moodies could last for weeks, during all of which Melanie would be reminded about who brought in the money. And that lovely body, for which she longed, would be withheld from her.

As she pondered the options, she became aware that someone had come up behind her. Startled, she turned to see Mister Brown smiling mockingly. The folded newspaper was in his hand.

He raised an eyebrow. 'You want to explain what you're doing?'

'What...what do you mean?'

'You've been following me.'

'You're mad.' She moved as if to go round him. He eased the folds of the newspaper so that she could see the gun concealed there. She came to a halt. He stepped forward, keeping the newspaper in his right hand and linking his left arm through hers. 'Let's go.'

She tried to wrest her arm free, but it was held tight. 'Let go of me!'

'Look, honey. If the taxi driver had stayed with you, I'd have shot him. It wouldn't have troubled me.' He spoke these words as someone might have remarked on the clemency of the weather. 'And if you attract anyone's attention, I'll shoot them. I won't even think about it. But if I do that, I'll have to shoot you, too. So make up your mind. Start walking. Or start dying.'

Reluctantly, Melanie moved with him. After the right bend, Crowther Road became Bramley Street. As the cabbie had said, Bramley Street went nowhere. It was a dead end.

The white Mondeo had turned to face them. It was drawn up against the pavement, cigarette smoke floating out of the driver's open window. When they came into view, the car eased forward and drew up beside them.

Doyle opened the rear door. 'Get in.'

Melanie hesitated. She looked around. There was no-one about.

'I meant what I said, honey.'

Melanie bent her head and got into the car.

'Move over.'

She did so, and Doyle got in beside her.

'Is she the law?', asked the driver.

'We haven't established that yet.' Doyle looked at her. 'What kind of woman doesn't carry a handbag?'

'A dyke, by the look of her,' said the driver.

Doyle surveyed Melanie's cropped hair and unmade-up face. 'You could be right. Put your hands on the seat in front, honey.'

Melanie did so. She shuddered when Doyle's hands patted her down. 'She's not carrying a wire,' he said. He reached into her pocket. 'There's a purse in there. That's English purse. Little bitty thing. Start the car.'

The Mondeo moved forward. 'Where to?', the driver asked.

'Have you got somewhere we can go? Where we won't be disturbed?'

Melanie bit her lower lip. A soft touch? Caroline must have been blinded by lust.

'There's a lock-up.'

'What the hell's a lock-up?', asked the American. What struck Melanie was that he was conducting this conversation as—well, as a conversation. A routine encounter among acquaintances; something that really didn't matter.

'A garage. Rented. People keep stuff there.' The driver laughed. 'Stuff people don't want people to know about.'

'Take us there. And pass me the gloves.' The driver passed back a pair of yellow rubber gloves. Doyle put them on. To

Melanie he said, 'Always wear gloves when you're cleaning up. It stops you getting in a mess. Now, honey, let's have the purse.'

Melanie weighed the possibility of defiance. She knew it was useless. This man got what he wanted.

Doyle opened the purse and extracted the contents one by one, placing them on the seat between them.

'Look for a warrant card,' the driver said.

'There's nothing like that. She's no copper.' He laid down two currency notes—a twenty and a ten. A handful of change. Paper tissues. A pen and a small notepad. A library card with the name Melanie Cantrell and an address. And a photograph.

Doyle picked up the photograph and stared at it. 'Will you look at that,' he said.

'What is it?'

'It's a picture of our friend here. Miss Melanie Cantrell— allow me to introduce you. And another young lady. Who is already known to me.'

The car was passing Euston heading towards King's Cross. Melanie was filled with the dull ache of disaster. Tears began to trickle down her cheeks. 'Are you going to turn us in?', she asked.

'For what?'

'Blackmail, of course. What do you think?'

'That's your game, is it?'

'You didn't think Caroline fancied *you*, did you?' She sneered at him. 'Dream on.'

'That's what you do? How you live? Pick up men and blackmail them?'

'Sometimes we don't have to—they fall in love with her and they want to look after her. Caroline's good at spotting money.'

'You never do the picking up?

The girl shuddered. 'Let a man put his hands on me? There isn't that much money in the world.'

'Does no-one ever say no?'

'Course they do. Most of them, probably. But Caroline's out there every day. How many men do you think we need, to live like we do?'

King's Cross was on their left. The driver went straight on down Pentonville Road, a ragged array of shops, fast-food outlets, bars and flats.

'In the US,' said Doyle, 'they'd call this underclass territory.'

'It's no different here,' said the driver.

The occasional flashy front of a bookmaker lit up the down-at-heel stores. Advertisements for political meetings and bands Doyle had never heard of were fly-posted on every available space. At the Angel, they veered right into City Road. The East End was where Melanie had been raised. She hated it. 'Where are we going?' she asked.

'So, Melanie Cantrell, what were you planning to do?'

'Nothing. Follow you, that's all. Try to find out who you are. Where you live.'

'That's pretty dumb, isn't it? I'm an American. I'm staying in a hotel. Would you expect me to come out of the Kensington Hilton and go home?'

Melanie's voice was breaking. 'That's what I said. But Caroline insisted there was something funny about you. She said we should see what you did.'

'Do you always do what Caroline says?'

Tears rolled down her face. 'I was horrid to her last night.'

'Oh. I see. A lovers' tiff. Because she'd been with me?'

'You don't know what she's like if she doesn't get her way,' the girl sobbed. 'Please tell me where we're going?'

Doyle looked out of the window. 'I was brought up in a blue collar part of Philadelphia,' he said. 'Very blue collar. Fishtown. I don't suppose you ever heard of it?'

'No,' whispered Melanie.

'Strangely enough, Fishtown is part of lower Kensington. But Kensington in Philadelphia is nothing like the Kensington I'm staying in here. It's a big Irish Catholic area, Fishtown.'

'Is that what you are?' asked the driver.

'You got it. We were, as I say, blue collar. But we were never underclass. We had no underclass. You want to know what makes an underclass?' He looked at Melanie.

'Being poor?'

'Nah. We were poor. What makes an underclass is when every child a woman has has a different father. Which none of them was married to the mother. And you want to know what makes that possible?'

Melanie shook her head.

'Government money,' said Doyle. 'Sucking on the state's tit. You want to get rid of the underclass, get rid of benefits and housing for single parent families.'

'Never happen,' said the driver.

'Your choice,' said Doyle. He patted Melanie on the thigh. 'Your choice. It's always choice in the end, honey. Even when it doesn't look that way.'

At the end of City Road the car turned right, then left into Old Street and right again into Great Eastern Street. If King's Cross had been tacky, this was worse.

'Please let me out,' the girl said. 'I won't tell anyone.'

Doyle laughed. 'Tell them what? You don't know anything.'

'You've got a gun. You kidnapped me at gun-point.'

'Oh, my. You mean I could be in trouble with the law? Dearie, dearie me.'

'Please, Mr Brown.'

'Get on the floor.'

'What?'

'A cop's going to see you crying. Get on the floor.'

Melanie was at the end of her resources. There was no resistance left in her. 'Please, Mr Brown, please, just stop the car and let me go. I've learned my lesson. I'll never do anything like this again. Please, Mr Brown, let me go.'

Doyle put his hand on her back and pressed forward. 'Get on the floor.'

Melanie sank to her knees in the well behind the front seats. She leaned forward, then lay on the floor. Doyle rested his feet on her. He looked out at the fetid landscape. 'Where the hell are we?'

'We're making for Shadwell. You'll like it.'

CHAPTER 14

Buggy had not enjoyed his stroll along the Yonne. Most people ignored him, for which he was thankful, but some casual strollers had nodded and asked if he was English. 'Anglais?' Struggling to understand the question, unable to put together an answer, Buggy did his bit for Anglo-French incomprehension and distrust.

When he got back to *Le Quai*, he could scarcely believe his eyes. They were eating! The pair of them sitting there, laughing, Carver with a white napkin the size of a small tablecloth tucked into his collar. Did they not know he was starving?

Buggy was uncomfortable if he got as far from home as Slough. It incensed him that these two could settle so happily into this alien environment. He approached the table. Carver, joshing in French with someone who had stopped to speak, ignored his arrival. Mitchell grinned up at him. 'Buggy! Sit down and let's get you something to eat.'

He poured red wine into an empty glass and pushed it towards Buggy. 'Don, will you get your man to bring another bottle?'

Buggy looked at the menu. It was, of course, in French. 'I saw somebody with a pizza', he said.

Mitchell laughed. 'This is Burgundy, Buggy. The home of Coq au Vin and Boeuf à la Bourgignonne. You'll eat no pizza here. Not while you're with me.'

Carver's attention had returned to the table. He called over the waiter, pointed at Buggy and spoke rapidly a message Buggy could not understand. The waiter looked down his nose, grunted and walked off.

'Don't worry about him,' Carver said. 'He's a French waiter. They learn disdain in college.'

'He went to college just to learn to be a waiter?'

Carver sighed. 'Ah, monsieur Buggy. You just summed up all the reasons I choose to live in France.'

'Drink your wine, Buggy,' Mitchell said. 'Enjoy the sunshine. Eat a good meal. You're on holiday.'

'I'm here on business,' said Buggy. "Monsieur Buggy"! The man was as English as he was himself.

Carver lowered his voice. 'You're not on business till we say you are. And Mitch here tells me that won't be until he's somewhere else. He's vouched for you. I'll hear what you've got to say. Later. I promise no more than that. Now enjoy yourself or go back to your hotel and leave us in peace.'

The waiter returned and put a plate before Buggy. For all the fancy talk, it was nothing but beef stew. The waiter picked up the basket in the middle of the table and replaced it with another containing a sliced up French stick. He put down another bottle of red wine.

Buggy started on his meal. The vegetables were not cooked properly, but he was ravenous. Carver lit a foul-smelling cigarette and belched softly.

Eating the stew wasn't hard. Mitchell watched him, grinning. 'So, Buggy. What do you think of your meal?'

'The stew? It's not bad.'

'Use the bread to soak up your gravy. It's allowed in France.'

Buggy's attention was now focused solely on the plate before him. The vegetables may not have been cooked long enough, but they were surprisingly good. There was something about the gravy, something he couldn't place...but it wasn't bad. Not like the stews his mother had made, but not bad. He took a gulp from the wine glass Mitchell kept filling. He reached for more bread to wipe his plate. Sharon, of course, never cooked. Buggy became aware that a feeling was creeping over him, one he hadn't known since childhood and not often, even then. He didn't think of it as happiness, because he didn't expect to be happy. But that was what it was.

When there was nothing left on his plate, he pushed it away. He began to suppress a little burp, then let it go. What the hell. He was on his holidays. He, John Wright, was abroad and he was hacking it. He was doing OK.

Mitchell was still wearing the stupid grin. He topped up Buggy's glass. 'So, Buggy,' he said. 'You want to try a little French cheese?'

Buggy beamed. 'Sure,' he said. 'Why the hell not?'

Doyle had been entirely happy with the Shadwell lock-up. As well as boxes of stolen electronic goods, bootleg tobacco and liquor, there were chairs, a table and a radio. The driver explained that it was often necessary to spend some time here and there was no reason not to be comfortable. The walls were soundproofed, so as not to attract the attention of nosy passers-by.

'The police don't know about it?'

'We've never had a raid yet.'

'And we won't be interrupted by any of your friends?'

'I've been paid to look after you. Trust me to do my job.'

'Fine. This one's got to write a note to her girlfriend. Then you can help me get her tied up. The sooner you get going, the sooner you'll be back. You couldn't fetch me something to eat before you go? Sub? Burger and fries? Pizza?'

'Sure. You want something for her?'

'I don't think so. I might feed her a bit of prime meat I happen to have about my person. Other than that, she can go hungry. You know we've still got a job to do? Are you available again tomorrow?'

'No sweat. Our man will be in the same place.'

Caroline was already tense with worry when the driver knocked on her door. Melanie should have made contact hours before. She looked at the note.

```
Caroline
You can trust the person who brings
this. Please come to me. Say nothing to
anyone or we may never see each other
again
Love
Mel
```

It stank, she knew that, but the driver would say nothing except, 'She needs you. Let's go. We have to be quick.' The driver didn't smell too good, either.

'Let me get my handbag.'

Conscious of the driver listening near the bedroom door, she reluctantly left the phone alone. She took Mel's note and laid it squarely in the middle of the bed, where any visitor would be sure to see it.

They drove for forty minutes in silence, the driver blowing cigarette smoke through a half-opened window. By the time they reached Sidney Street, Caroline was filled with the deepest foreboding. Whatever she had got her beloved Mel into, it wasn't good.

The car turned twice, then a third time, before picking a service road behind high walls. There were five garages at the end. The driver parked, signalled Caroline to get out and knocked in a rhythmic pattern on the garage door. The door opened. The driver put a hand in the middle of Caroline's back and propelled her hard into the darkness.

She stumbled, scraping her hands on concrete as she broke her fall. Someone whimpered in the darkness. The door closed behind her. Close by was the sound of unlaboured breathing. 'Who's there?' she cried out. No-one answered.

Suddenly there were hands in her hair, wrenching her to her feet. She cried out in pain and alarm. Then the light came on. The man she knew as Mr Brown stared into her face from only inches away. He smiled at her and touched her gently on the chin. Then his forehead smashed viciously forward and Caroline went down, consciousness sliding away from her.

When she came to, she was lying on her side. Her limbs were bent and immovable. The floor under her face was cold and metallic. It took her a few moments to realise that she was in the boot of a car, her hands tied behind her. She could see a wall against which were stacked cases of Johnnie Walker Red Label. Then the light was cut off as Melanie, sobbing and wearing only a torn and twisted brassiere and ankle socks, was lifted into the boot. Her jeans and pants were thrown on top of them. Caroline was conscious that she could scarcely breathe and that Melanie's shoulder was jammed agonisingly into her rib cage. Then the boot lid came down and all was darkness.

CHAPTER 15

Sharon stretched, cat-like. She sat up in bed and picked up the mug of tea Gough had placed by her head. Sharon liked being looked after. She watched Gough hang his dressing gown on the hook behind the door and come back to bed. He had a nice body, Jackie, and a nice way with him. Strange to think he had grown up with the rest of them—he could be such a gentleman.

It was going to college, of course, and the people he met there. Bound to rub off. But he was still from the same streets as her and Buggy. She wanted some of that.

'So what was the emergency, Jackie?'

'Eh?'

'I was out last night. I was having a good time. And you sent me three text messages. The last one, you sounded so frantic, I left who I was with and I came here. It seemed like there was an emergency. I'm waiting to hear what it was.'

'Oh. Sorry if I broke up a date.'

'You haven't answered.'

'Who was he?'

'Jackie, can we answer my question first?'

'Only I feel like I know him. You know? The taste of him.'

'Don't be disgusting.'

'I wouldn't have gone down there if I'd known what you'd been up to.'

'Jackie...'

'Sorry. There wasn't an emergency. I just wanted to see you is all. I knew Buggy was away.'

'You're supposed to be his mate.'

'Come on, Sharon. You know how I feel about you. We have a hell of a job getting together while he's home. I wasn't going to pass up the chance while he was away. If I'd known you were otherwise engaged, I wouldn't have texted you. Why did you come, anyway?'

Why indeed? It had been lovely with Adrian, sweetness itself, but not exactly fulfilling. Leading an innocent young virgin down the path of love was fun for a while, but there came a time when what you needed was a good rodding. She wasn't going to tell Gough that, though. Men were bad enough. Tell them you'd left someone else's bed to be with them, they'd think they were God's gift. And, if she was honest, she hadn't wanted to be there when the rest of his flatmates turned up. Not if they all had girlfriends like Lizzie.

'Why did you never get married, Jackie?' she asked.

Gough ran his hand across her stomach, moving gently up to the soft swell of her breast. 'You'll make me spill my tea,' she said.

He smiled and kissed her on the cheek.

'So why didn't you?', she insisted.

Gough shrugged. 'You were spoken for,' he said. 'And if I couldn't have you, who else would I want?'

'You don't mean that.' She drained the mug and reached over to put it down on the bedside table. Jackie had a nice flat. He'd spent money on it. You'd think, really, he'd have preferred to spend it in a district with a future.

'And why did you come back here?'

'Here?'

'You could have gone anywhere after college. You could have got a job. You could have been living in a nice house somewhere with a garden and children at a posh school. Why did you come back here?'

Gough drew her down into the bed and put his arms round her. She could feel his excitement. It was fun with Jackie—he knew how to make her feel good and he made it last. Maybe he was the man, the one she could relive the excitement of Yoxer with. It would have to be soon, though. Her plans for Jackie Gough did not involve the long term. But... The idea moved within her, and she could never have said afterwards how it came. She needed money...to move away, take an access course, go to university. There had to be a way to that money. Maybe Gough was it. Feeling him over her, trailing kisses as he moved down, Sharon gasped, arranged her legs, put her hands on his head.

When they were done, Sharon was suffused with warmth and well-being. She laughed, that throaty laugh that she knew her lovers liked. 'I hope Buggy's all right.'

'Do we have to talk about him?'

'Jackie! He's never been out of the country before. If they don't have MacDonald's, he'll starve.'

'He'll be all right. It'll do him good.'

'When is he coming back?'

'He's your husband, Sharon. How should I know when he's coming back?'

'I thought you might know what he's doing there.'

Gough sat up. 'Sharon. It's no good pumping me. I didn't ask what he was doing there because I didn't want to know. Still don't.'

'All right, cross-patch. Anyway, pumping's your job.' She looked sideways at him. 'I've always wanted to go to France.'

'Have you told Buggy?'

'My fantasies don't carry much weight with him.'

'Come on. He can't refuse you anything.'

'Maybe not. There are some things too private to ask for.'

'Oh? Tell me more.'

'Some day. Maybe.'

'Sharon! You've gone pink.'

'Stop it, Jackie. You're embarrassing me.'

The cab driver flicked ash over the scuffed vinyl floor. 'All I'm asking is whether your policewoman got back safely. I've worried about her ever since I dropped her off.'

'And I'm telling you I don't know who you're talking about. And pout that cigarette out before I nick you.' The young constable glanced at a colleague for support. He hated desk duty. 'You don't know the officer's name. To be honest, you don't even know she is a police officer.'

'Well, will you make a note of it? In case someone goes missing.'

'I've made a mental note, sir.'

'Write it down. Please.'

The constable leaned across the counter. 'Look, mate. I'll make a deal with you. I won't sit in the back of your cab and tell you how to drive. And you don't come in here and tell me how to do my job. All right?'

CHAPTER 16

DS Milton knocked on Hiden's door and entered without waiting. Hiden looked up enquiringly.

'Guv, you remember I put out that request for information on offences like our rapes?'

'You've had a result?'

'A fax from Cardiff. Here, read for yourself.'

Hiden read the proffered sheet. 'This is a killing, Anne. An execution, by the sound of it. In Wales. What's it got to do with us?'

'Since when does an executioner go off with his victim's knickers?'

'That's a bit far-fetched, Anne.'

'Have we got anything better? Follow up every lead, no matter how apparently small or irrelevant. The essence of good detective work. Who was it told me that?'

'Yes, yes. And you fancy a trip to the land of the leek and the sheep disturber, do you?'

'Wouldn't mind.'

'Try to be back tonight, Anne.'

'Have a heart, Guv.'

'All right, tomorrow. Before lunch.'

For the second morning in a row, Doyle ate an efficiently rapid breakfast and was met in the lobby of the Kensington Hilton. Once again, he got into the passenger seat of a car (in this case a dark blue Vauxhall) but this time no-one followed them.

'Where do you get these cars?', Doyle asked.

'Why do you want to know?'

'You're a pro. Like me. You're good at what you do. Like me. I'm interested.'

'Okay. Well, there's a couple of airport car parks I use. I watch someone drive in. I choose long stay, so I know they won't be back for a while. No-one knows this car's been stolen, so who's going to be looking for it? Usually, I get the car back and the owner doesn't even know it's been nicked. I couldn't do that yesterday, obviously.'

'How do you get it out of the park?'

'See, here's what I do. Last night, after you and me were finished, I nicked a car on the street two miles from the airport. I drove it straight there and parked in the long stay. I was in it half an hour, tops. No-one's going to report it lost and get the number to the cops in that time. Then, this morning, I used that ticket to get this one out. I had to pay, but so what? The same person as pays your expenses pays mine.'

'That's neat.'

'Yeah. When I take this one back, if I wanted I could get the one I drove in there last night. Take it back where it came from, you know? But why would I want to? It'll be hot by now. So, it sits there until somebody spots it. Could take weeks. Then, see, the Bill thinks what's happened, some geezer nicked a car and drove it two miles to the airport? Lazy bugger could've walked.'

'And you've got a spare ticket in case you need another car in a hurry.'

'Exactly. My sister married this guy, he works in the City, he talks about risk management. Well, that's what I do. I mean, there's no way you can nick a car and guarantee you're not going to be seen. But the only car I'm going to be spotted in that's been reported stolen is one I'm driving two miles to the airport. It's a very long shot, matter of fact I never have been stopped, but if I was—*if* I was—what am I going to get? A slap on the wrist? A fine? Community service?

'But I get stopped in a stolen car and linked to what you're gonna do today, what kind of trouble's that? That's mega, right? I mean, I'm going away and I'm not coming out for a while, am I right? So you manage the risks, see?

'What you did last night to those two dykes, I was in favour of that and that's why. OK, it's a risk, topping someone is always a risk, but the big risk is letting them walk so they can go and tell the police about these nasty people with a gun who took them away, shagged one of them as a matter of fact when she didn't want to be shagged, gave the other a beating. See what I mean?'

'You approved of that?'

'Sure I did. Approved of the shagging and the beating, too, if you want to know. You did fuck the dyke? While I was collecting the other one?'

'Certainly did.'

'Nice?'

'It left a bit to be desired, if I'm honest. She was a less than whole-hearted participant.'

'Anyway, topping them, you did the right thing. Although, I've got to say, for me it was like I say, risk management, and for you I think there was something else in it, too.'

'Something else?'

'Sure. You mind me talking to you like this?'

'Well, if we're going to get personal, there's something I might want to mention.'

'I could shower more?'

'You know about it.'

'Of course I know about it. You think you're the first person to tell me I smell a bit ripe?'

'You ever think of doing something about it?'

'Not particularly. Think of my smell as a personal protest if it makes you feel better.'

'Against what?'

'Against my upbringing. Against my parents. I went to a good school, you believe that?'

'I believe anything you tell me. I also believe it's not too pleasant to sit in a car beside you for a few hours.'

'Okay, so maybe I'll shower tonight.'

'And put some clean clothes on.'

'And put some clean clothes on. But now you've got personal with me and I still don't know whether it's okay for me to get personal with you. I mean, you're not gonna get upset and decide to top me, too? Because there's people know I'm with you, you know?'

Doyle smiled. 'You're as safe as can be. So what's this something else?'

'Well, I think, when you were topping those two, I mean I know, as I say, risk management, it's something you've got to take care of. But I think, as well as that, there was a bit of pleasure there, too. Know what I mean? Quite a lot of pleasure, matter of fact. Set fire to a car, two dykes locked in the boot, *both* of whom you'd shagged at one time or another, I think you enjoyed that more than somewhat. But don't answer if you don't want to. And I'm gonna have to go quiet for a while, because we're approaching the place and I need to concentrate.'

'You think a man shouldn't take pleasure in his work?'

'Listen, whatever makes you good, do it. And you are a top man, I know that. Now, please, let me watch these roads.'

'You should get SatNav.'

'Maybe. But I haven't.'

'I'm going to buy you one before I leave.'

'Thank you. That's very kind.'

The car skirted the south end of Weald Park.

'What is it with this place?', Doyle said. 'We've passed three golf courses in the last ten miles.'

'It's a funny area. It used to be a nice place, outside London but close enough for people who needed to be there. Ford executives have lived here for years. There's a lot of footballers around here. The wives like the big houses and the men have plenty of time on their hands.' The car turned north on Sandpit Lane. 'In the seventies, you started getting criminals moving in. Blaggers, successful ones. Had money to retire and didn't need to go to Spain. No coppers looking for them with warrants. They play a lot of golf, too.'

'Including our man?'

'Every morning, long as it isn't pissing down. He's bored, see. And now he's thinking of going back into business.'

'And someone doesn't want him to?'

'The world moves on. You step out for a while, someone takes your place. Doesn't necessarily want to give it up when you feel like coming back.' The driver turned briefly from the road and grinned at him.

'A toothbrush. I'm gonna get you a toothbrush, too. See that stuff on top of the wall? Grey, green? What do you call that?'

'Those are lichens.'

'You've got stuff on your teeth looks like that.'

Set back in the wall was a gate that looked as though it hadn't been used for a while. Pushing into last year's tall, whitened grass, the driver brought the car to a halt and took a pair of binoculars from the back seat. A group of four golfers was emerging from behind a little spinney outlined against the sky at the top of a rise.

'Is he there?'

'Not yet. He doesn't usually start his round until ten. Should be coming by here in about thirty minutes. Gets him back in the clubhouse for lunch.'

Except when a car passed, it was very quiet. There was a springlike lift to the warm air. Birds sang to each other from the trees. Some kind of finch—Doyle didn't know English birds— sat at the top of a grass stem, snapping out what seeds were left after winter. Doyle watched the first of the golfers get set to drive his ball. It rose in an arc against the pale blue sky, coming their way. The green was less than a hundred yards to their left. Two bunkers guarded the direct approach; four well furnished conifers stood between the car and the green. The driver rolled down the window and lit a cigarette. 'See, the glory of this spot, the golfers have to pass close by. All we have to do is wait. And the trees and the wall let you get up nice and close. Our man will be in a pair. What you gonna do about his partner?'

'I've got no contract on him.'

'Don't want him chasing you, though. You could put one in his leg.'

Doyle nodded. 'That'd do it.'

The driver lit another cigarette. Cars passed on the road behind them. The foursome finished its business at this hole and moved on.

'What brought you into this line of work?,' Doyle said.

'Family tradition, I suppose.'

Doyle grinned. 'You come from a long line of criminals?'

The driver was watching the spinney. 'Long line of coppers, actually.'

'What?'

'Both my parents are coppers. My grandfather was a copper. I didn't fancy being the third generation, so I thought I'd try out for the other side.'

'Your parents are in the police?'

'Sure are. Matter of fact, my Dad'll probably get to hear about this job we're pulling here today.'

'No shit? Do they know what you do?'

'You're having a laugh. We only talk through my sister. They think I'm on the dole. That's what they want to think, so they think it. Which suits me fine.'

Two golfers were walking down towards the hole. One of them had hit his drive so far off the fairway they could see the pattern on his tie. 'Be handy if our man does that,' the driver said, then stiffened. Two men had come out from the shelter of the spinney and were looking down, waiting for the pair in front to finish. The driver focused the binoculars, then handed them to Doyle. 'The one in the yellow windcheater.'

Doyle stared hard at the magnified view of his mark. His heart began to beat with the excitement of an impending kill. The man looked to be in his late fifties, solidly built, a face reddened by the wind and good living but without fat or puffiness. Well groomed grey hair. An air of authority. A hard man, probably—not in the scrapper's sense, though Doyle felt he could probably hold his own, but the hardness of the man accustomed to being obeyed. Given another birth, another upbringing, a successful captain of industry. Beneath the unzipped yellow jacket, a white shirt covered a flat stomach. Doyle focused hard on pockets and armpits. He was prepared to bet the man wasn't carrying.

He handed back the binoculars. Waiting till a passing car had moved safely out of sight, he removed his gun from the folded newspaper, took the silencer from his inside pocket and screwed it into position. He checked the magazine. There was a new stillness in the car as they waited their moment. Only birdsong disturbed the silence.

The golfers at the nearby hole moved away. Doyle watched his mark take up his stance over the ball. The shot was strong and true, the ball curving high before coming down in the centre of the fairway and bouncing on to stop thirty yards short of the green. His partner's shot was less assured, swinging left to fall twenty yards short of the mark's and much closer to the car.

They watched the two men chatting as they walked down the sloping ground towards them. When they were fifty yards away, Doyle took a stocking mask from his pocket and pulled it over his head. He opened the door and slipped out, staying low until he reached the gate. He watched the two men drawing nearer.

When the mark had reached his ball, Doyle went noiselessly over the gate. Keeping the gun behind his back, he walked towards the mark's partner. Arriving at his ball, the man looked up at him, curiosity changing to shock as Doyle brought up the gun in one fluid motion and shot him just below the knee. The man folded to the ground without a sound, but the mark had heard the dull thunk of the silenced gun. He turned to look at Doyle, now only twenty yards from him.

Still advancing, Doyle brought the gun up to shoulder level and aimed at the mark's chest. Staring at him, the mark put his hands on his hips and stood with his feet slightly apart, facing Doyle full on. He made no attempt to run. The expression on his face was one of open contempt.

'Hey! Hey, you!' The shouts came from someone freshly emerged from the edge of the spinney. Doyle kept his eyes on the mark, now only eight yards distant. He pulled the trigger. The mark went over backwards, a red stain spreading across his chest. Doyle kept walking forwards. Coming up to the prostrate mark, he placed a second bullet squarely in his forehead.

Then he was running for the gate. Behind him, he could hear yelling from the top of the rise and an agonised sobbing from the mark's partner. Ahead, the sound of a car's engine. Doyle went over the gate as easily as before, slid into the passenger seat and slammed the door. The driver set off the way they had come, driving without haste. Even with mobile phones, no-one could get a roadblock in place before they were safely back in the London streets.

'Nice job,' the driver said. Doyle removed the stocking mask and placed it, with the gun, in a carrier bag.

The driver dropped Doyle at Woodford underground station. 'I'm not likely to be stopped, but if I am I don't want you with me.'

'I like your style,' Doyle said. 'Tell me. Do you trust the guy who gave you this job?'

'I don't trust anyone.'

'You do right. Give me your phone number, in case I want to get in touch.'

'You weren't listening. I said I don't trust anyone. But I'll tell you how you can contact me.'

CHAPTER 17

They ordered coffee and Buggy lit a cigarette. Two women, obviously English and equally obviously monoglot, sat at another table and tried to make the waiter understand what they wanted. They were not getting very far.

The waiter looked towards Carver. Without troubling to lower his voice, he shouted, 'Eh, monsieur! Pourriez-vous demander fissa ces deux grognasses qui n'entravent que dalle au français ce qu'elles veulent tortorer? Je n'ai pas que foutre, moi!' The diners at other tables sniggered. Carver dropped his napkin and strolled off to interpret.

'Tsk,' said Mitchell. 'The English abroad. Not like us, eh, Buggy?'

'How much have you told Carver about me?'

'Relax, Buggy. He knows you work for Cameron and he knows who Cameron is. I've built you up a bit, told him you're a big man. I might even have exaggerated Cameron's importance. You'll get to make your play.'

'Yes, but when? Will I be able to go back tonight?'

Mitchell laughed. 'Only if you want to blow it, Buggy. Is that what you want?'

Buggy was losing the sense of warmth he had been enjoying since he began to eat. Blowing it was something he hadn't considered. Sharon's last words were never far from his mind. Eight weeks to raise five grand or she'd humiliate him. No, blowing this assignment wasn't a possibility. And even if it worked out, he'd still have to go back and take on Gough's job—whatever it entailed.

Mitchell stood up. 'But I'll let you get started. Tell Carver I've gone for a walk. Think you can find your way back to the hotel?'

The feeling of being out of his depth returned. He pushed a paper napkin across the table. 'Write down the name. And the address. Just in case.'

When Carver came back, he didn't seem surprised to find Mitchell gone. 'So, Buggy,' he said. 'This is your moment. Make your pitch.'

Buggy drew a deep breath. 'I'm an associate of a man called Jim Cameron.'

'Mitch told me.'

'We need a man killed. In England.'

Carver grinned. It wasn't the nicest grin Buggy had ever seen. 'You've come to the right place, Buggy. Carver's the name, killing's the game.'

'Five grand. Two when you take on the job and three when it's done.'

'Plus expenses, Buggy. And I always go first class.'

'Plus expenses, sure.'

'Five hundred up front on account. That's two and a half grand before I set foot out of Auxerre.'

'OK.'

'Have you got the cash with you?'

Buggy shook his head. 'It'll be wired wherever you want whenever you say.'

'And who do I have to waste?'

'You'll be led to him when you come over.'

Carver smiled again. 'No dice, Buggy.'

'That's how we always do it.'

'So get someone you always get.'

Buggy looked uncertainly at Carver. The pitiless green eyes focused on him. 'Let me tell you how it is, Buggy. I don't know you and I don't know Cameron. I do know Mitchell, which is what buys you the right to talk to me, but that's all it buys you. I need to know what I'm going into. You want me to do a job for someone I never heard of till today, I need information. All the information.'

Buggy tried to form words in his dry mouth. Sharon's message was clear in his head: "I'll know you're a wheeler-dealer because you'll have dropped the thick end of five thousand quid without crying for your mother." The threat was clear in his head, too.

'Buggy, a couple of days ago, I did a job for someone I've known for years. I've regretted doing that job. It was beneath me. Doing it hurt me. Made me feel dirty. Now, who is it you want me to top?'

Buggy's silence continued.

'Buggy,' Carver said. 'Are you an "associate" or an errand boy? This is an executive decision. Make it.'

Tears were not far away. Buggy stared into the green eyes. 'Cameron can't know I've told you.'

Carver inclined his head slightly.

'We want you to kill a man called Doyle.'

Not the slightest flicker crossed Carver's face. 'Doyle. And he is...what?'

'He's a professional hit-man. Like you.'

Carver raised his eyebrows. 'Like me, eh? I think maybe the price just went up. Why do you want him killed?'

'I can't agree any more money.'

'Why do you want him killed?'

Buggy held his breath, then exhaled. He'd gone this far, he might as well go to the end. 'We hired him to do a job. I hired him.'

'To kill someone.'

'Yes.'

'And he didn't do it.'

'No, he did it. I mean, he's doing it.'

'So why do you want him wasted?'

'Cameron wasn't happy about him. Doyle kills for fun as well as for money. Cameron thinks he's a risk.'

Carver lit a cigarette and fell silent. The silence stretched itself out. Uneasy, Buggy lit a cigarette of his own. The two English women went by on their way towards the Cathedral. They called a giggling thank you to Carver, who scarcely acknowledged their going.

'So, Buggy,' Carver said. 'Let's get this clear. You,' he pointed his finger at Buggy's chest, 'you, personally, made a deal with this man Doyle to kill someone. You've got no problems with the job he's doing. But now you want to hire someone else to kill him. Have I got that right?'

Buggy nodded.

'You're not a nice person, Buggy. You know that? Have you never heard of loyalty?'

Buggy licked his lips.

'Who did you hire Doyle to kill?'

'I can't tell you that.'

Carver stared at him in silence.

'It was a man called Burns,' Buggy said. 'Matt Burns. Cameron used to work for him, years ago. Burns retired.'

'And he wanted to come back?'

Buggy nodded.

'And for that Cameron decided to waste him? For wanting to come back?'

Buggy nodded.

'He killed a man who'd brought him on? Shown him the ropes? Been a mentor to him? A father figure?'

Buggy didn't know what a mentor was, but he got the general idea. He nodded. Carver leaned back and flicked his half-smoked cigarette away. Then he changed his mind and lit another. Anyone who knew him well would have told Buggy that this indecision was not good. But few people knew him well. The smile on his lips was almost admiring. 'You're rude boys, Buggy. All of you. Rude.'

'So. Will you take the job?'

Carver blew smoke down his nose. 'I don't know, Buggy. I'll think about it.'

'When will you know?'

'Let me give you a tip, Buggy. When you're anxious, never let it show. It makes a very bad negotiator. Two days, three days. When I know, I'll tell you.'

He stood up. 'Where are you staying?'

Buggy looked at the paper napkin. 'The Hotel Normandie. On the Boulevard Vauban.'

'I know where the Normandie is. And it's Voe-ban, not Vorbin. I'll be in touch, Buggy.' He turned to walk away.

'Excuse me?'

'What now?'

'You couldn't show me the way back?'

Carver took the handlebars of his bike and, silently, gestured to Buggy to follow him.

DS John Cooper of South Glamorgan CID met Anne Milton off the train at Cardiff and took her into the station coffee bar.

'I need to be away from my desk,' he said. My boss is chasing me for paperwork.'

Anne screwed up her nose in sympathy.

'The dead woman's name was Julie Been,' Cooper said when they were sitting down.

'Local?'

'No. Interestingly enough, she's from your neck of the woods. London. We're working with a DS called Moran. You know him?'

She shook her head.

'No, well, I suppose the Met's a big place. And he's drugs—you're what? Serious crime? Know everybody down here, we do. I don't think I'd swap.'

'It's not for everyone, the Met.'

'Julie Been has no form. Had no form,' he corrected himself. 'Hasn't got anything now, has she? But the people round her, they've got plenty.'

'Really?'

'Her father did time for armed robbery. Moran says he's been under observation for a while. The old man and Julie's brother went into drug distribution a couple of years ago. Coke, heroin.'

'Nasty.'

'Been's wife is Welsh. A Jones from Port Talbot. There's thousands of Joneses in Port Talbot, most of them law-abiding.' He grinned. 'Well, by Welsh standards they are. But Clive Jones is Julie Been's cousin and he's an old friend of ours. Until a year ago, it was nothing big. Bit of assault, bit of thieving. But he's been looking to expand his interests.'

DS Milton let herself be caught up in the lilting Welsh flow. Cooper was a big man in his thirties, with dark curly hair and carrying no spare weight. He used his voice like an instrument of seduction. Anne could imagine him coaxing confessions. She could imagine him coaxing other things, too. The hair on her neck was beginning to tingle in a way she knew well.

143

'Moran's been talking to his snouts. The word is, Been had found new outlets outside London.'

'Here?'

'It would seem so. Don't know why, we've got more than enough of our own. There's no shortage of ports in Wales, and plenty of other places a boat can come ashore. People in London assume we're country boys, is it? A soft touch for city slickers.' He smiled his easy smile.

'Clearly a mistake.' She smiled back at him.

'So Moran thinks Julie was sent out here with a consignment for her cousin. And she was bumped off.'

'Have any drugs turned up?'

'No. There were none with her and we've seen no sign of extra supplies on the street. And we've been looking, believe me. But the ticket inspector on the train remembers her and she was carrying a sizeable briefcase. We've no idea what happened to it.'

'Who would have known she was coming out here?'

'Interesting question. We have informants of our own...'

'...I'm sure you do...'

'...and no-one here knows anything. No-one up here seems to have been aware that Clive Jones was expecting a shipment. And perhaps he wasn't.'

'How do you mean?'

'As we see it, Julie Been was met at the station, driven into the hills and killed. Now, if you were Clive Jones and you were expecting your cousin to arrive with a case full of heroin, let's say, what would you do?'

'I'd meet her at the station.'

'Of course you would. So would I. And so would Clive Jones. So, either the man who met her was paid by her cousin to collect her, blow her away and steal what she was carrying...'

'...or Clive didn't know she was coming. What does he say about it?'

'He isn't talking. But when we first told him his cousin had been murdered, here, he was stunned. Shattered, he was, and he wasn't pretending. I'd stake a ticket to the Wales-England game he didn't know she was coming.'

'Has Moran asked her father?'

'Well, what can he say? "Yes, I sent her to Wales with a bag full of heroin"? I don't think so. Anyway, isn't it the knickers you're interested in?' As with all two syllable words, he pronounced it in the Welsh way as two words—"knick ers", with the accent heavily on the first syllable and the second turning upwards. Anne had noticed that "ticket" became "tick ett" in his mouth.

'Or the lack of them.'

'What's going on in London?'

'I'm not supposed to spread alarm and despondency, so keep this to yourself, but it looks as though we've got a serial rapist with a knicker fetish. As far as we can tell, he breaks in to his victim's home beforehand and steals a pair of her pants. Then he comes back later and attacks her.'

'Wearing them, is it?'

'What?'

'Well, I'm no psychiatrist, but I think I know why a man is stealing a woman's panties like that. He's wearing them. Wearing them when he rapes the woman, like as not.' He laughed. 'Disgusting, some people are. Gets him in the mood, I shouldn't wonder. It takes all sorts to make a world, you know.'

Anne laughed too. 'It's not really funny,' she said. 'He's killed at least one woman. You're quite sure the knickers weren't there? They hadn't been thrown away in the heat of passion?'

'This was a professional hit, Anne. Not a hobbyist. It doesn't sound like your man. Anyway, there was no passion. She was kneeling on all fours with her skirt up but she hadn't been touched. Well, he might have touched her up, but if he'd shagged her the autopsy would have shown it. And we did a thorough search. We even found a half-smoked cigarette.'

'Not a Disque Bleu?'

'How did you know that? Anne? What is it?'

'Have you still got the fag end?'

'Eh? Yes, I should think so. Yes, I'm sure we have.'

'Has anyone tested it for DNA?'

'DNA? No, of course not.'

'John. Can we get it done? Now? I promise you, my guvnor will pay.'

Carver made coffee and placed it on a low table in his sitting room. He turned the key in his wooden box. He wasn't in the mood this evening for a video or a book. After the conversation with Buggy he felt curiously rested, at peace. Villainous treachery was loose in the world and he, Carver, was the man to root it out.

He fingered his way through the little stock of underwear. One pair of pants was a little smaller than the others, and a lot older. This was the only pair that didn't have a slip of paper with a name on it. Carver didn't need help in remembering who had worn these knickers. He pressed them against his cheek. Jenny's scent was long gone, but Carver could still call it up across the years.

He folded the knickers gently in his hand and carried them to where his coffee waited. He sat down and lit a cigarette. Jenny. His first real girlfriend. He had been fifteen, she a year younger. Slim, pretty, not the cleverest person he would ever meet but she had a wit and humour that drew people to her. And she had chosen him.

He had kept it from his parents. Not for any special reason; by then he kept everything from his parents. Told them nothing. His father had not beaten him for years because Carver had given him no cause. He obeyed, respected, was polite, followed the rules, but told them nothing. A wall had come into being between him and them.

They had gone to the pictures, walked, played records in her room. She kissed him. He held her tight. Raging hormones fed his desires but he never transgressed against her innocence. She was entitled to respect, as his mother was. Carver scarcely dared think about the future. He barely knew that something was missing from his life at home, or that he found it with Jenny.

A more worldly-wise boy might have known that these things come to an end. Three months wasn't a bad innings at fifteen. But Carver wasn't worldly-wise. And he had given his heart.

She transferred her attentions to another youth called Graham Miller. Now it was Miller who took her to the pictures, Miller who sat in her room listening to Queen.

Rumours began to reach him—snippets of overheard conversations that stopped or changed direction when he arrived. "Miller's knobbed her." "Can't get enough." "A nympho. Donny-boy was useless, apparently."

Carver never let the hurt show. That was one of the rules his father had thrashed into him. Never show you're hurt. He had been betrayed, utterly betrayed, but nothing of the rage he felt at Jenny's disloyalty ever appeared on his face or in his conversation. He took other girls to the pictures. And he learned his lesson. Respect was forgotten. He lost his virginity on a fourteen year old's bed while her parents watched Bruce Forsyth downstairs. Word began to get around. Apparently Donny-boy wasn't useless at all.

And he bided his time.

And he watched.

Three months went by and, inevitably, Miller and Jenny fell apart. She was alone. He knew her parents went out together on Tuesday evenings.

'Don,' she said. 'Come in, gorgeous.' She lowered her lashes flirtatiously. 'I've been hearing things about you.'

He pushed her back into the house. 'Get upstairs.'

'Don!'

He grabbed her arm, twisted her round. 'Upstairs. Now.'

All the time they were doing it, Carver was staring at her face. Jenny's fear exhilarated him. Carver had never felt this potent—this good—with any other girl.

When it was over, he took her face in his hands. 'If you ever tell a soul about this, I'll kill you. Do you understand?'

She lay absolutely still.

'Do you understand?', he repeated.

Jenny nodded.

'You'll never forget me. Will you?'

She shook her head.

Carver dressed without haste. He bent down, picked her pink cotton knickers from the floor and slipped them into his pocket. He couldn't have said why. Going downstairs, he heard her begin to sob.

Later that night, preparing for bed, Carver had taken Jenny's knickers from his pocket. On an impulse he had slipped them on before getting into bed. They had been tight, but not too tight. It had felt good to be held like that. A feeling of peace had settled over Carver as he drifted off to sleep.

Now, twenty years later, Carver pressed the soft cotton again to his cheek. He could see his whole life since that evening as an attempt, sometimes successful, to recover those emotions—that potency, that power to intimidate, that peace.

Jenny had betrayed him. Carver hated disloyalty. Betrayal wrecked the foundations the world stood on. If you couldn't trust, where were you?

That bitch Teasdale had betrayed him when she called the police. And Buggy was disloyal. Worse, Buggy was betraying a man to whom Carver was bound by an oath of brotherhood.

Well, Carver didn't forget his obligations. Carver had never betrayed a friend, and he never would. Stacy Teasdale would have to wait, certainly for months, probably for a year or more. It wouldn't be safe to go near her before that. But Buggy. Buggy was here, now.

He lit another cigarette and walked out onto the terrace, cool in the still evening air. Jenny's face, framed in soft brown curls, stared at him from the Gloire de Dijon rose climbing against the old brick wall. A single tear left Carver's eye and travelled slowly down his cheek. Absently, he raised the knickers to his face and patted it dry.

Sharon hadn't been sure what she was going to do about Adrian. Perhaps she'd get in touch; perhaps she wouldn't. And it was her choice, because she hadn't given him her number.

She had, of course. When she'd called him to say yes, she would come to his flat, would let him cook for her, her phone number had been attached to the call.

Thank God she'd called on her mobile and not on the home phone she shared with Buggy.

It was a surprise when she got his call. But not completely unwelcome.

'I've got those access course details you wanted.'

'Oh, fantastic.'

'So what do you want to do?'

'Can I come to the shop and get them?'

She could hear the disappointment in his voice. 'You wouldn't rather come to the flat this evening?'

Oh, God. 'Who'll be there, Adrian?'

There was a short pause. 'I knew Lizzie had upset you. Charlie was furious with her.'

'That's very nice of Charlie.'

'But she probably will be there tonight.'

Sharon let the silence run. Adrian broke it, as she'd known he would. 'I could come to your place?'

'No, Adrian, you couldn't.'

'No. Well. We could meet for a drink?'

'Okay. Let's do that.'

'And maybe a meal?'

'Only if you let me pay.'

'We could go halves?'

'Okay.'

'There's a little Italian near my place. Three doors down from the tube station?'

'I'll find it.'

'Half seven?'

'I'll be there.'

'Sharon...'

'Half past seven, Adrian.'

'Oh. Okay. I'll see you then.'

She wasn't sure about Adrian, wasn't sure at all. Or, if she was, she was sure he was wrong for her.

So why was she smiling?

She tucked the phone away in her handbag. She put the kettle on, made a cup of instant coffee. She sat down at the kitchen table with the coffee, lit a cigarette and opened *In the Night Café*. The opening sentence struck her with stunning force.

It's a good name, you once said, for a vanishing act.

A vanishing act. Wasn't that exactly what she needed? Her life was a complete mess. What better than to walk away from it and start over somewhere else?

Sometimes, when Buggy wasn't around, she'd switch the radio to Radio 4. It was at Jackie Gough's that she'd first heard it and it had blown her away that first time, the thought that there was a radio station where people just talked to each other. About ideas, or things, or little bits of history. And they had plays, sometimes, and stories. And that meant there must be other people who liked listening to those things as much as she did.

She needed to find those people.

But what had made her think of Radio 4 was the quote she remembered hearing, although who'd said it or where it came from she had no idea. "If you don't like your life, you can change it."

Fatuous, she'd thought at the time. That was a Radio 4 word, she'd just heard it, wasn't one hundred per cent sure what it meant if she was going to be honest and she certainly wouldn't use it in conversation, but the thought was fatuous.

If you were married to someone you no longer wanted to be married to, yes, you could probably change that. But if the person you no longer wanted to be married to was mixed up with people like Jim Cameron and Johnnie Walker, maybe trying to change your life might be a bit risky.

But look at this. Tom Murphy steps back into a doorway, takes a ride towards some fresh start, some different identity in uncountable locations. Anyone with the slightest hope of finding him would have to know where he'd gone to, at least roughly. Or have amazing luck, unthinkable persistence.

That was it, all right. That was what she had to do. Disappear into a new identity, a new location.

That couldn't be so difficult, could it?

Two cups of coffee and two cigarettes later, Sharon had reached the end of the third chapter. She was entranced. Absorbed.

Was this what university would be like? Reading a book you enjoyed over coffee and a ciggie in the comfort of your own quiet room? No-one bothering you? No-one worrying over where to hide stolen goods, or whether Johnny Walker had looked funny at him that morning, or trying to cop a feel when she really wasn't in the mood.

And then going out and talking to other people who'd read books they'd enjoyed over their own coffee in their own quiet rooms?

Was that what it would be like?

And, in the evening, going out for a meal with someone you really liked, who knew about books and stuff? Going Dutch?

Oh, that was a thought.

She put the book down and took the purse from her handbag. She counted her money. Counted it again.

Then she picked up the phone and dialled.

'Wayne,' she said when her call was answered. 'Have you got any business for me?'

'Sharon. I thought you didn't want to do any more.'

'I said I wanted to be a bit fussier. I didn't say I'd never do it again.'

'Well, actually you did, Sharon.'

'You must have got it wrong. Anyway, have you got anything? Not tonight, though.'

'I've got plenty. Not all of it to suit your delicate tastes. Couple of Greeks on Thursday.'

'No threesomes, Wayne. You know how they end up.'

'They're interested in an exhibition.'

'Two girls? Forget it. They'll want the suspenders and the fishnets and all the rest of it. I can't do that shit any more. I just want to lie on my back and make nice noises and tell some dickhead what a big man he is.'

'Okay. Hey, there's that American you did in February? Calls himself Gene Kusten?'

'Nope. Not him.'

'What's the matter with him? Is there something I should know?'

'Not him, Wayne. Okay?'

'Hey, okay. Well, there's a man from Dubai on Friday.'

'An Arab?'

'Yeah, I guess. By the sound of his name.'

'He'll do.'

'That's right. You like Arabs, don't you?'

'They're clean and they're polite, Wayne. And they tip nicely. What more can a girl ask?'

'Okay. I'll put you down for Kafteem. Friday night, eight o'clock, Claridge's.'

'You know they won't let me walk in there on my own.'

'I'll be there to escort you in and hand you over.'

'Okay. Wayne...'

'How did I know this was coming?'

'Any chance of an advance? Today? If I come round?'

'If you weren't my cousin...'

'But I am, Wayne. Please?'

'How much do you need?'

'A hundred would be good.'

He sighed. 'All right. I'm going out in a minute. I'll see you about six.'

'You're a prince, Wayne.'

She hung up. One day she'd stop all this shit, but it was better than working. Paid better, too. Buggy was generous enough when he had it, but he didn't always have it.

There'd be no more Gene Kustens, though. Filthy pig. She'd heard about that stuff, but never been asked to do it before. Okay, there'd been the extra two hundred Wayne knew nothing about, but even so. He'd had the gel and he'd promised her it wouldn't hurt. And it had. It had hurt like hell.

She'd been worried enough afterwards, she'd gone to get herself seen to. The doctor had been quite cross with her. He'd brushed away the explanation she'd dreamed up. He knew exactly what had caused what he was looking at.

'There's a muscle there, Mrs Wright. It's called the sphincter. It's like a valve and it's designed to go one way only. It's for things coming out, not things going in. You can get away once or twice with what you've done, but if you go on doing it you'll end up incontinent. You'll go through old age wearing a nappy. You understand?'

She understood, all right. And she wouldn't be doing it again, with Gene Kusten or anyone else.

All the time the doctor had been lecturing her, though, he'd had his hand resting on her thigh. The fleshy bit at the back, just below her bottom.

The bit that tingled.

Speaking of tingling, it was time she heard from Buggy. Maybe she should go and see Cameron, find out what he knew. If she dropped lucky, flashed her knickers, did the thing with her tongue along the bottom lip, he might give her a few quid. Take it out of Buggy's wages.

CHAPTER 18

Doyle went back to the Hilton and settled his bill in cash. He hailed a black cab to take him to Euston. Three hours later, he was home. He dialled 1571 on his telephone. 'BT Call Minder. Thank you for calling. You have one message.'

Doyle pressed "1" to hear his message and Carver's voice said, 'Would you please get Janet to call me. Sooner rather than later.' Doyle pressed "3" to delete the message. He made a pot of coffee and drank it. He thumbed through his black-bound address book. Scattered across four pages, and not in sequence, were the sets of digits that made up two telephone numbers— Carver's home number and the number of a French public phone box. Doyle committed the home number to memory.

He left the house and walked to the phone box at the end of the road. He dialled the number he had memorised from the book. It rang twice and then Carver's voice answered.

'Is Nancy there?' Doyle asked.

'What number were you calling?'

Doyle read out the number of the phone he held in his hand.

'That's not my number.'

'I'm sorry to have troubled you.'

Doyle replaced the handset. Nearly five minutes later, the phone rang and he picked it up. 'Doyle.'

'Carver.'

'This is like something out of a Bond movie.'

'I know, I know. Listen, do you know someone called Buggy?'

'Ah, yes. Mister and Missus Head had a son and they called him Richard. Not a gorm in sight. He's the clown set up the job I've just done.'

'He's here trying to set up another. With me.'

'Didn't I give satisfaction?'

'You couldn't do this job. You're the mark.'

Doyle stood in silence.

'Doyle? You there?'

'I'm here. Are you serious?'

'Sure am. Buggy works for a guy called Jim Cameron?'

'I don't know him.'

'He knows you. Apparently you have some extra-curricular activities he doesn't like. He thinks you're a danger.'

'And this Buggy clown goes along with this?'

'He's a messenger boy, Doyle.'

'He'll be a dead messenger boy when I'm through with him. What have you told him?'

'To wait here a few days while I decide. You want to come down?'

'Sure.'

'OK. Look, I've thought out a little scheme.'

Britain has never had a central police force equivalent to the American FBI or the French Police Nationale, and still hasn't, even after the passing into law of the Serious and Organised Crime Act. There are those who say this lack of a national force is the cornerstone of a free democracy. And there are those who say it inhibits successful policing, and that British democracy is a chimera anyway. Whatever the rights and wrongs of the argument, Essex Police dealt with the golf course murder of Matt Burns while the neighbouring Hertfordshire force were called out to the wreck of a Ford Mondeo, once white but blackened in a fierce fire when it was dumped on the edge of Northaw Great Wood.

Joy-riders was the first thought of the two Hertfordshire constables—a thought that did not outlast the discovery in the boot of two bodies, burned beyond all hope of recognition. Both PCs spent some time retching into the undergrowth before setting in train the long and difficult investigation that might eventually establish who the dead had once been.

The Essex police had, at least initially, the easier job. It did not take long to establish who Matt Burns was, which meant that it did not take long to throw up ideas about why his death might have been ordered. That the murder was a paid execution was hardly in doubt. Inquiries made it clear that Burns had been suffering from desperate boredom. Since he had made his name in London, and London was presumably where he would have wished to resume his career, the Met's Serious Crime unit was informed of his death. DI Hiden asked DS Forrest, one of Anne Milton's colleagues, to rattle the cage of Burns's one-time protégé, Jim Cameron. Neither Hiden nor Forrest thought they were likely to profit from the exercise. It was merely an example of the relentless following up of leads, most of them going nowhere, that constitutes routine police work.

Back in Cardiff, John Cooper had put in hand the DNA analysis of saliva in the Disque Bleu found at the site of Julie Been's murder. Anne Milton had arranged for the DNA profile of Stacy Teasdale's rapist to be sent for comparison to the same laboratory. This was another example of what is now becoming routine police work, and Cooper was confident that it, too, would produce no worthwhile result. Then Cooper had driven

Milton to the place where Julie Been had been done to death. He was happy to do this because it kept him out of his DI's presence and away from the pile of uncompleted paperwork; and she was happy to go along because she was enjoying Cooper's company.

'Are you staying over tonight?' Cooper asked. Yes, Anne replied with a stirring of hope for the evening, she was.

'Dinner?'

'That would be lovely.'

'Good. I'll call Bethan and tell her you'll be joining us.'

'Bethan?'

'My wife.'

'Oh, right. That'll be great, John.'

CHAPTER 19

Mitchell and Buggy breakfasted on croissants, baguettes and café au lait, then walked out to the Normandie's front garden and lit up.

On the other side of the boulevard was a tree-lined parking area. A maroon Renault came down from the right, bumped over the kerb and reversed into the space between two cars.

'Here's our man,' Mitchell said.

Carver got out of the Renault, locked the door and looked across the road towards the hotel. He strolled left towards a pedestrian crossing.

'Looks just like a frog, don't he?' said Mitchell.

Carver ambled past them without a word, paying them no more attention than he gave the big glazed pots of red geraniums. He mounted the steps to the hotel and spoke to the man behind the reception desk. He came back, selected a table with some shelter from the breeze and sat down. A waitress bustled down the stairs and placed before him a paper mat, knife, spoon and large cup. Mitchell sat down beside Carver. Buggy remained where he was, staring at the traffic on the boulevard. The man's rudeness was unbelievable. He had not said a word to either of them. Buggy was here to offer him work, well paid work, and Carver hadn't the courtesy even to acknowledge his presence.

The waitress returned. She set down a basket of croissants, bowls of jam, a large jug of coffee and another of hot milk. Carver said, 'Merci, madame.'

He lit a cigarette and poured his café au lait. He and Mitchell began to talk. Buggy let them. If Mitchell wanted to overlook

160

Carver's behaviour, that was his business. Really, he should find out how to use a French phone and call Sharon. Had she been home last night? Buggy smiled bitterly to himself. It wasn't likely, was it? He wondered who she had given herself to while he'd been here, earning money to take her up west. His eyes misted. He felt inexpressibly lonely.

'Buggy!' It was Mitchell, calling him to the table. He went, sat down, refused to look at Carver.

'Don wants some help from us, Buggy.'

Does he, Buggy thought. So what?

Mitchell grinned at Carver. 'Don't go pouty on us, Buggy.'

'It's a package,' Carver said. 'You want something from me, I want something from you.'

'So if we do whatever it is you want,' Buggy said, 'You'll do the job for us?'

'The moment we get through here, I'll be on a train to London.'

Buggy couldn't help the relief that flooded through him. 'What is it you want?'

'I've got to move a boat. There are locks on the canal, so it takes two people.'

'Boat? I don't know anything about boats. I've never been on a boat in my life.'

'Relax, Buggy,' Carver said. 'It's not the Americas Cup. This is a little motor boat. It never leaves the canal. It's like driving a car. I'll steer it. All I need you to do is get off at each lock, open the gates and close them again after me. Then I pick you up again on the other side.'

'I don't want to be on a boat. If you've got Mitchell, you don't need me.'

'I've got to get home, Buggy,' Mitchell said. 'My job here's done anyway. Don will make sure you get on the train.'

'I don't even know what a lock looks like.'

'It's a piece of cake—like opening a gate at home. Trust me.'

'Bloody hell. A boat.'

'Two days, Buggy. That's all it'll take. And you'll have no hotel room to pay for. We'll sleep on board. Then it's off to London and do your job.'

'I'll come along for the first day,' Mitchell said. 'Show you the ropes. Can you can drop me somewhere, Don?'

'Mailly-la-Ville,' Carver said. 'There's a station there. You can take the train back to Laroche-Migennes. But before we go anywhere, you'd better contact whoever it is you have to contact and get the money sent over here. Two and a half grand, sterling, or I top no-one.'

DS Duncan Forrest was a humourless Scot with a straightforward attitude to criminals—he didn't like them. It was a black and white approach with the law on one side and crooks on the other. He especially didn't like criminals who treated the law as a joke and its practitioners as obstacles to be bought, sidelined or lied to. No meeting between him and Cameron that did not end with the latter in a cell was ever going to bring him joy.

Cameron shook his head. 'I heard this morning, Inspector. A terrible thing. If I find out who did it...'

'It's Sergeant, Cameron. As you well know.'

'Only a matter of time, I'm sure.'

'Don't take the piss, Cameron. And if there's any revenge to be taken, we'll do it. You leave that to the police.'

Cameron inclined his head. 'Of course, Sergeant. If there's anything I can do to help...'

'You could start by telling me what you were doing yesterday afternoon?'

Cameron's expression moved effortlessly from bewilderment through shock to anger. 'Matt Burns was like a father to me. I hope you're not suggesting I had anything to do with his death?'

'Like a father, was he? Burns was a piece of...whatever nastiness went on around here, Burns had a hand in it.'

Cameron looked at Walker, silent in a chair against the wall. 'Nastiness? Did you ever hear that, Johnnie?'

Walker shook his head. 'Dead less than a day and bad-mouthed already. It's disgusting. Did Matt have a record, Sergeant?'

'You know as well as I do...'

'What I know, Mister Forrest,' Cameron said, 'Is that no-one ever hung anything on Matt Burns. He never stood trial for speeding, let alone anything else.'

'Much like yourself, Jim,' Walker said.

'That's right, Johnnie. Tell me, Mister Forrest, haven't you got anything better to do than come round here asking law-abiding people what they were doing when a pillar of the community got shot? Shouldn't you be out there looking for the killer?'

'Looks like police harassment to me,' said Walker.

'That's right.' Cameron took a long cigar from his desk and began to trim the end. 'Maybe we should get a brief here. Make an official complaint. That look good on your record, Mister Forrest?'

'I'd wear it like a medal,' Forrest said. 'Get this in your head. We know you had Burns knocked off. We're not sorry he's dead, but we're the law—not you. We've got some good leads on the killer and when we get him, you'll be right behind.'

Cameron took time to light the cigar, staring at the tip as he held it in the flame of an oversized match. When he was satisfied, he blew out a reflective cloud of grey smoke. He stared at Forrest in silence. Suddenly, his face burst into a smile. He laughed, loudly and boisterously. 'Go and chase your leads, you piece of Jock shit. I'm running a legitimate transport business here. I've got work to do.'

Forrest stood up. 'It's going to give me great pleasure to feel your collar, Cameron.'

'No doubt. But don't hold your breath.'

When Forrest had gone, Cameron handed the cigar to Walker. 'You want to finish that?'

'Why do you light them?'

'Because they're expensive. It drives coppers like Forrest round the bend.'

Cameron's secretary put her head round the door. 'Sharon Wright was here to see you.'

'Shazza? Buggy's old lady? What did she want?'

'She wouldn't say. Just it was something about her husband. He hasn't been home. She thought you might know when he was coming back?'

The laughter had drained out of Cameron's voice. 'She said that?'

'I told her I'd call her if you could tell her anything.'

'OK, Peggy. Thanks.' When she had gone he said, 'That stupid little bugger's told her he's doing something for me. D'you know where she lives?'

Walker nodded.

'Get round there and see what she knows. And tell her to keep her mouth shut.'

Burgundy is networked by waterways. As well as the navigable River Saône, there are at least five canals in excellent working order. Cut to transport logs, farm produce, wine and manufactured goods, they now mostly carry tourists. The river Yonne that flows through Auxerre has been canalised to form part of the Canal du Nivernais—the Canal of the Land of Nevers. And you, Buggy, Carver thought. You, mon ami, will nevers go 'ome. He laughed quietly.

The boat was tied up at the southern end of the Quai de la République, just before the bridge that carries traffic from the nondescript east bank onto the boulevards that skirt the old town. 'Three cabins,' Carver said. 'One each. They're doubles, Buggy, so feel free to bring back some petite fille for a feel—a poule if you pull.'

'It isn't funny,' Buggy said when Mitchell sniggered.

'Cooking facilities,' said Carver, opening cupboards in the saloon. 'Although there are auberges all down the canal. We've got baguettes and saucisson and fromage, Buggy, in case we get hungry between meals.' He looked in another cupboard. 'Ham we have, and eggs and beer. You like Kronenbourg? And wine. But cigarettes, only my own Disque Bleu. We're going on a voyage, Buggy. Do you have enough of your Marlboro red devils?'

In silence, Buggy took a red and white carton from his bag and laid it on the table.

'You are prepared,' Carver said. 'A true Boy Scout. So now I take the wheel and set us on the road for Mailly. Mitch, will you and Monsieur le Bug cast off? And then one of you could make du café?'

The engine started with a single turn of the key. 'Why is he talking like that?' Buggy asked as he and Mitchell untied the ropes from the low iron bollards.

'Because he's happy. Don't mind him, Buggy. He lives in France most of the time. The people he talks to are French. I don't think he likes the English much. Sometimes he pretends to be a Frog speaking English. And he's excited. This is a sort of holiday for him.'

'He's a moron.'

'Even if that were true, which it isn't, he'd still be a moron you need more than he needs you. Don't forget that, Buggy. I'll make the coffee. You go and talk to him.'

The boat had two driving stations, each with steering wheel and throttle—one under cover and the other on the open deck at the stern. The sun was shining, the day was warm and Carver was at the back. Buggy took the seat beside him and lit a cigarette.

'It isn't a quick way to travel,' Carver said. 'They control speeds on the canal. But I love it. You could go all the way into Germany from here. Or up to the Dutch coast. Take you a while, of course. You should do it some time, for a holiday. Is there a Mrs Buggy?'

Buggy nodded.

'Take her with you. Cast aside her drawers in the cabin of love. Take her to the gentle rocking of the boat. You think she'd like that?'

'If it involves fucking, she'd like it.'

'Ah, Buggy. Do I detect a sadness there? Is it not only with her husband that the Madame Bug fucks?'

'Can we talk about something else?'

'Of course.' Carver pointed to the white track that ran beside the canal. 'That's the route de halage. Tow-path in English. When this canal was built, they'd have used horses to pull the barges.' He pointed to a bicycle in the corner of the rear deck.

'Sometimes I stop and cycle to a village for bread or whatever. Tow-paths are good for cycling. They're flat.'

Mitchell brought three mugs of coffee aft. As the boat moved further from the town, the trees on each side came closer to the canal. The throttled-back engine gurgled quietly. Buggy was no birdsong expert, but he knew he hadn't heard these birds in England. 'If we're lucky,' Carver said, 'We'll see a kingfisher. Ever see a kingfisher?'

Buggy shook his head.

They approached the first lock. Carver pulled the boat into the bank and Mitchell and Buggy tied it to a bollard before approaching the lock gates.

Mitchell showed Buggy how to open the gate. They walked back and untied the boat. Carver drove it into the lock and Mitchell closed the gate behind it.

He pointed past the second gate. 'The canal there is higher than it is here, see?'

Buggy nodded.

'When we open the next gate, water will flow into the lock and the boat will come up. When it's the same level as the canal, Don drives the boat out and off we go.'

'How do you know all this?'

Mitchell shrugged. 'I'm a Black Country boy, Buggy. I grew up around the cut. Used to get a tanner from the bargemen for working the locks for them.'

Back on the boat, Mitchell said he was going to make a sandwich. 'I thought there'd be a lot of boats moving,' Buggy said.

'In summer there'll be queues for the locks,' said Carver. 'But right now the kids are in school and it's quiet. This is my best time on the canals.'

'Why are you moving the boat?'

'There's a yard near Nevers looks after it for me. I want to leave it with them, have them check the hull.'

'How long will it take to get to Nevers?' Buggy pronounced it "Never".

'Nevers, Buggy.' Carver shrugged. 'Three, four days.'

'You said two.'

'Relax, Buggy. I was just starting to warm to you. Were you ever on a French canal boat before? You're on your holidays, man.'

Mitchell stuck his head out of the door. 'You guys want mustard in your sandwich? Tomato? Lettuce?'

Carver waved a negligent hand. 'Whatever seems right to you, Mitch. And a glass of Chablis?' To Buggy he said, 'You know Chablis comes from Burgundy? Very near here, as a matter of fact.'

'I don't even know what Chablis is.'

Carver sighed. 'You'll like it, Buggy. I promise.'

CHAPTER 20

DS Cooper's confidence that the DNA analysis of the Disque Bleu stub would yield nothing was misplaced. DI Hiden's Serious Crime Squad now knew that the man who had raped Stacy Teasdale was also the man who had killed Julie Been. Anne Milton could hardly contain her excitement when five squad members gathered in front of the whiteboards in Hiden's office.

'I don't get it,' said DC Porter. 'Julie Been's killing was a pro job. An execution. Had to be. What's that got to do with a rapist in Richmond?'

'What are the odds against a random DNA match?' asked Hiden.

'260 billion to one,' Milton said.

Porter whistled. 'Worse than winning the Lottery. He's not on the French DNA register, I suppose?'

'"Fraid not,' said Hiden. 'Anyway, Anne doesn't see him coming from France to Richmond just for a woman.'

'Suppose he doesn't?' said Milton. 'Come for a woman, I mean? Suppose he comes to do his day job, which is assassination, and puts in a bit of off-duty rape while he's here?'

Hiden stared at her without expression. 'If he does, he's on tape. Ferry, plane, train—doesn't matter how he gets here, he's still on tape.'

'How does that help?' said Forrest. 'We don't know what he looks like.'

'Nevertheless,' said Hiden. 'Nevertheless.' He looked at Milton. 'They re-use those tapes on a two week cycle, Anne.

Commandeer all there are before Stacy Teasdale was raped and copy them. Just in case we ever want to take a look.'

'Looking through them would take one DC a fortnight,' Milton said.

'Do it anyway.'

She nodded. 'If you say so.'

The other DC said, 'France is popular today. Buggy's supposed to be over there.' He laughed.

'Who the hell's Buggy?' asked Hiden.

'John Wright,' Milton said, 'Nothing to do with us. A small time villain. Never been nicked, I don't think. Runs messages for bigger fish. Married to a right tart called Sharon.'

DS Forrest's eyes flickered. 'Describe her.'

Milton looked at the DC. 'Shazza?', he said. 'A tart, as DS Milton says. Bottle blonde, cut long, big knockers, short skirts, too much make-up. Has a fetish for gold blouses. Go with anybody.'

'And you know that because...?' said Milton.

'Word of mouth, Sarge. Scout's honour.'

'I think I saw her this morning,' Forrest said.

'Where?'

'Just a minute,' said Hiden. 'Before we go any further down this road, let's establish if it takes us anywhere.' He looked at the DC. 'How do you know this man Wright is in France?'

'A snout told me this morning. It's all over the manor. They think it's hilarious.'

'A snout. Are we talking registered informant here?'

'Er...well, no, guv. Just a guy I know.'

'A guy you know. Nothing we could ever use in evidence, then?'

'Guv,' said Milton, 'you told us to stay close to the ground.

Hear everything there was to hear.'

Hiden nodded. 'I know that. So, Constable Wylie, what's so funny about Buggy Wright being in France?'

'You'd have to know him, guv. He'd be out of place down Shepherd's Bush, never mind across the Channel.'

'And what's he doing there?'

The laughter went from DC Wylie's face. 'My informant didn't know, guv. But he was in the Black Bear a couple of days before he went, waving a thick wad of twenties around. By his standards, a very thick wad. And he talked to Jackie Gough.'

Hiden raised his eyebrows in Anne Milton's direction. 'Another small-timer, guv. Fixes things for bigger fish. Did a stretch for dealing a while ago, but I think he's out of that scene now. He was never a user. Interestingly in this context, he might be the guy you'd go to if you needed a funny passport.'

'Check whether Wright has one of his own, Anne.'

'Sure. And, er...Gough's done a bit of freelancing for us. For me, that is.'

'He's a registered snout?'

Milton's brow wrinkled. 'Not exactly, guv. But he's given us information. For money and to stay out of trouble.'

Hiden shook his head. He looked at Forrest. 'You saw his wife this morning?'

'I've never met her, guv, but it sounds like the woman I saw at Cameron's place, wanting to see him. She left in a hurry when I came out of his office. Cameron's secretary called her Sharon.'

Hiden looked thoughtful. 'So. We have a professional killer who may come from France to work. Work in this case means going to Cardiff and killing someone who may have been a drugs courier. He rapes Stacy Teasdale while he's here, but we don't know that that has anything to do with the drug killing. We have a messenger boy called Buggy who suddenly has a lot of money. He meets someone called Jackie Gough, who could have got him a passport if he happened to need one and then he goes to France. While he's there, his wife goes to see Jim Cameron, who we're as sure as we need be hired someone to kill a retired crook called Matt Burns. Right so far?'

There were grunts of confirmation. 'What are you saying, guv?', asked DC Wylie. 'That whoever killed Julie Been and raped Stacy Teasdale also topped Matt Burns?'

'It's a possibility,' Hiden said.

'He'd have had to get from Cardiff to Essex in eighteen hours,' said Forrest.

'Piece of cake,' Hiden answered. 'I think maybe we'd like to talk to Sharon Wright and Jackie Gough. You can do that, Duncan.'

'There's something else, guv,' Milton said. 'You remember we asked for details of rapes like ours?'

'Good job we did,' said Hiden, 'Or we'd never have tagged the Teasdale rapist as the Been killer. That was good thinking, Anne.'

'Thanks, guv. Well, another one's come up. A woman called Marie Trimnor was raped in Ashford fourteen months ago.'

'Ashford's miles from our three.'

'Yes, guv. It's a stop on the Eurostar line, though. The point is that there are lots of similarities in MO. Except for knickers being stolen—we don't know about that. And...' She reached into the manila folder she was holding with the air of a conjuror producing a rabbit from a hat. 'Marie Trimnor thought she'd been watched for a week beforehand. By someone looking like this.' She placed the photo-fit likeness on Hiden's desk.

'This could be our rapist?'

'Looks that way, guv.'

'OK. Let's not get ahead of ourselves. Trimnor saw a man looking like this. She doesn't know for sure he attacked her. We don't know for sure the man who attacked her did our rapes. We're a long way from putting this picture into a court room and saying "Here's Julie Been's killer".'

'Yes we are,' Milton said. 'A long way. But Marie Trimnor says she spotted this guy staring at her in a café near her home. There's a café almost opposite Stacy Teasdale's home. And guess what?'

'Amaze me. There are cafés near the homes of Torton and Bolan.'

'Bullseye. What I'd like to do is take this picture and show it to the staff in those cafés.'

'Do it.' Hiden pushed back from his desk. 'All right, guys and gal, you've got lots to do. Go and do it.'

Routine, not inspiration, solves crimes. While Hiden's team were de-briefing and mapping out their next moves, two DCs belonging to Hertfordshire CID were in a viewing room watching video tapes from the airport car park.

The charred bodies had not yet been identified, but the white Mondeo had been traced to a Malcolm Hayes. Hayes was a product development manager with a software company and, according to his wife, was in Bangalore visiting the company's Indian programming sub-contractors. When they contacted him there, after expressing outrage at the destruction of his vehicle, Hayes had read over the phone the floor and aisle numbers of the bay in which he had left his car, that information having been written on his ticket by him before he left the car park.

Between the time Hayes said he had parked his car and the

time police thought it had been torched, eighteen hours had elapsed. Even allowing for the minimum time it would have been on the road, there was a possible window of sixteen hours during which it might have been stolen. The two policemen returned to Hatfield police station with five four hour videotapes of the car park exit and heavy hearts.

They cheered up very quickly. Hayes's Mondeo had been driven out of the car park forty-two minutes after he had left it there. The front licence plate was clearly visible. Unfortunately, the face of the driver was not.

'Watching, wasn't he?', said the first DC.

'Looks that way,' said the second. 'Followed Hayes down to the check-in desks, made sure he went straight through, then back to the car and off.'

They returned to the airport and asked about camera surveillance of Floor 3, the deck from which the Mondeo had been stolen. Yes, the manager said, there were three cameras on that floor, but no, none of them was near that particular bay. This was as the policemen expected; no professional car thief would steal a motor parked next to a video camera, and a professional was clearly what they were dealing with. However, said the manager, the cameras moved according to a computer program designed to ensure that all areas of the deck were swept every two minutes. He opened a grey storage cupboard and produced the three Deck 3 tapes for the time at which Hayes's Mondeo had been driven away.

'Do you really want to take these all the way back to Hatfield?' he asked. 'We have a monitor right here.'

The time stamp on the video was five minutes earlier than the one showing the Mondeo's exit. The thief stood by the driver's door, head lowered and unidentifiable.

'Got a bunch of keys', said one DC.

'Trying them all,' agreed the other. Then the camera swung away. The two constables stared fixedly at the screen, willing the driver to be still there—with head raised—in two minutes.

'Bastard,' said the first DC as the camera swung back at last. The door was unopened. The thief's head was still lowered.

Again the camera moved away. Neither constable was in any doubt that the next sweep would be their last chance. By the one after that, the car had already left the car park.

Truth to tell, they did not expect much. Experienced officers, they knew that results were usually wrong; that evidence, more often than not, was inadequate for a prosecution; that the villain usually got away with it. The numbers incarcerated in British prisons rose year by year—but the increase represented the hapless amateur. The sort of professional criminal who barbecued people in the boot of a car rarely made a mistake that ended in a prison sentence.

The two minutes ended, the camera swung back—and there, for less than one glorious second, was the face of the thief staring straight into the lens. They stopped the tape.

'Do you know her?', asked the first constable as he stared at the image on the screen.

'Never seen her in my life,' said the other. 'No need to rush back to the Station, though. This job could have taken hours. Fancy a bacon buttie?'

CHAPTER 21

They had food, wine, cigarettes and coffee. The boat travelled slowly and the locks arrived only after long stretches of nothing to do but smoke, eat, drink and watch the passing woods and farmland. Once in a while, a cyclist passed on the route de halage, outpacing the boat and leaving it behind. Sometimes, the canal bent far enough to the west to be in earshot of cars on the N5 or, more rarely, a passing train. Mostly it was quiet. Buggy was content.

'What made you move to France?'

Carver drew on his Disque Bleu. 'A lot of things, really. I came here on holiday first. Well, sort of a holiday. I'd done a job, made some money.' He glanced towards Mitchell, who was reading a Dick Francis paperback. 'I had a tip-off. Someone suggested I should get out of the way for a while. So I drove onto a ferry in Dover, drove off again in Calais and kept going. Ended up in Dijon.'

'Did you speak French then?'

Carver laughed. 'Not a word. But I could point. And I'm a fast learner. Anyway, I liked it, so I stayed.'

'Don't you miss England?'

'What's to miss? The food? I don't think so. The climate? The railway? The lack of service? It's a funny thing, Buggy. The French don't have any manners. They're formal and polite, but they're nosy and they can be as rude as hell. But they know how to look after you. The English have manners up the ying-yang. And getting service out of them...

'But the real reason I live here is that it isn't England. I don't belong. I'll never be French, so I'll never have to treat French problems as though they were mine. They have terrible politicians, but they're not my politicians. They have outrageous taxes, but I don't...well, never mind that. Living here, I'm an outsider. And I like being an outsider.'

Mitchell looked up from his book. 'Sounds like you've given this a lot of thought.'

'Some,' Carver said.

'Haven't you got anybody in England?' asked Buggy.

'My parents are dead. I was an only child. There were cousins...' He shrugged. 'Families make demands.'

Buggy went to the back of the boat to urinate into the canal. Mitchell spoke quietly to Carver. 'You're a piece of work, you are. Even more than I knew.' He held his hand up. 'Don't get me wrong. I say that in total admiration. You've got Buggy eating out of your hand. He thinks you've come round to liking him.'

'No need to make his last hours on earth unpleasant, is there?'

'Very humane of you. Nothing to do with a man who isn't on his guard being easier to kill?'

Carver smiled.

'I hope to God I never get on the wrong side of you, Donny boy.'

The eyes, behind brown contact lenses today, came up and fixed Mitchell in a calm stare. 'So do I, Mitch. Seriously, so do I.'

'I need some exercise,' Mitchell said when Buggy came back. 'Put me ashore with that bike.'

Carver headed in towards the left hand bank. 'There's a guy I need to see in Accolay,' he said. 'Cravant is up ahead. You can't see it from the tow-path but you'll know you've reached it when the main road crosses to the east bank. A bit after that, there's a spur due east off the canal. There's an iron railway bridge right over the junction. If you're still on the bike when you get there, take the spur and wait for us.'

Mitchell cycled off, moving leisurely but still leaving them behind. Buggy went into the galley to make coffee.

'Wash your hands first,' shouted Carver. 'You've just taken a piss.'

Buggy brought two mugs out onto the warm rear deck and made himself comfortable. Feeling companionable, he told Carver about his conversation with the Frenchman on the train.

'It's Luton,' said Carver. 'Not Swindon. But he's right. Scottish and Newcastle should be banned from buying European brands. They're a menace. There'll be a lock when we turn into the Canal d'Accolay. You'll manage it fine.'

'Pas de problème,' said Buggy, waving his cigarette negligently.

Carver roared with laughter. 'Buggy, you're a linguist. Why didn't you say?'

Buggy grinned. He felt utterly relaxed. 'A guy called Jackie Gough says it. He's a college boy, Jackie. Did you go to college?'

Carver paused to watch a swan and its mate moving towards the bank, out of the boat's way. He sipped his coffee. 'Buggy, I'm going to say something and I hope you're not going to do one of your pouting jobs on me. But you ask a lot of questions. Do you know that? A lot of questions. And people like me, people who do what I do for a living, we don't necessarily like being asked lots of questions. Makes us nervous, you know?'

Buggy was too mellow to be offended. He held up a hand. 'Hey, no offence. I'm sorry.' Being drunk on wine felt different from being drunk on beer or scotch. In fact, he might prefer it.

He had begun to pick out the canal's various styles. Where it was really the river, it curved to one side or the other, often spreading into a wide expanse of sun-dappled, tree-lined water and sometimes dotted with small islands. Buoys marked the navigation channel. But where the river had been inadequate for navigation, or the navigators had seen the need for a lock, a real canal had been built and the canal sections were narrow and straight.

'You don't look like a killer,' Buggy said.

'Well, Buggy, I don't know what you think a killer looks like. But you just place your trust in me, OK? I kill people, all right.'

Before setting off for Sharon Wright's maisonette, Duncan Forrest told the Desk Sergeant he would like Jackie Gough brought in for questioning. Had he not spent the eight minutes it took to find the Desk Sergeant, who as usual was anywhere but at the desk, he and DC Porter might have been in time to see Walker leaving Sharon's place. But he did, and so they weren't. Which meant that they were unable to draw the correct conclusions from Sharon's damaged eye and split lip.

'You're going to have a real shiner there, Shazza,' Porter said. 'Want to tell us who did it?'

'I walked into a door.'

'Mhm? The door tore your blouse as well, did it?'

'Mind your own business.'

'Not Buggy's usual line, is it? Beating up his old lady?'

'I told you. I walked into a door.'

'Course you did,' said Forrest. 'Where is Buggy, anyway?'

Sharon rested her elbow on the kitchen table, her hand over her damaged eye. The other hand pulled a cigarette packet towards her and shook one out. Forrest picked up her lighter and held it to the end of the cigarette. 'Where is Buggy?' he repeated.

Sharon blew smoke downwards. 'Why do you want him?'

Porter said, 'You don't seem to have mastered this police thing, Shazza. How it works is, we ask questions and you answer them. Not the other way round.'

Sharon shrugged.

'You went to see Cameron this morning,' Forrest said.

'Who?'

'Don't be stupid, Sharon. I saw you there.'

'Oh, him.'

'What did you want him for?'

'It's private.'

'We've heard that Buggy's doing a job for Cameron.'

'News to me.'

'In France.'

Sharon smiled but said nothing.

'If Buggy's in France,' Porter said, 'who knocked you about?'

'You said he was in France. I didn't.'

'Sharon,' Forrest said. 'Has someone been round to put the frighteners on you? Have you been told to shut up?'

Sharon picked up her lighter and began to tap it on the table.

'Does the name Matt Burns mean anything to you, Sharon?' Forrest said.

She shook her head, still tapping the lighter.

'He's dead, Sharon. Murdered. We know Cameron had it done.'

'You'll arrest him, then?'

'Sharon, I'm trying to make you see what Buggy's involved with.'

Sharon shook another cigarette free from the packet. The bruised skin around her eye was darkening rapidly. She lifted the lighter, then began tapping it again. Forrest wrested it from her hand and threw it across the room. Sharon stared at him, wide-eyed.

'Cameron's a killer, Sharon. Buggy's at risk. You are at risk. You have to tell us what you know.'

Sharon lowered her eyes to the table. Forrest waited. Then he said, 'Come on, constable. There's nothing for us here.'

Sharon waited till they were gone. She walked over to the wall and picked up her lighter. Then she went into the bathroom and began to repair her ravaged face.

Because the attack on Stacy Teasdale was the most recent, Anne Milton and DC Wylie went there first with the Ashford photofit. The café was a Richmond place and might not have been at home in most other parts of Britain. It had clearly once been a shop with living accommodation behind and above. Outside were the metal tables that Carver had avoided in order, the weather being cold, not to stand out. The centre of what had once been the shop part was occupied by a long counter filled with ready-made salads; cut garlic sausages, hams, mortadella and beef in many guises; cheeses; jars of olives, capers and artichoke hearts; tarts filled with fruit; samosas and pasties; and filled rolls, baps and ciabattas. Uncut hams, sausages and sides of corned and salt beef and pastramis hung from the ceiling. To the left as Milton looked at the counter was a window under which were baskets of white, brown and rye breads in rolls, plaits, tins and bloomers, seeded, plain or topped with egg wash. Behind the counter were an espresso machine, a filter coffee machine, a microwave oven, a gas ring, a sink and surfaces for preparing food.

Opposite the counter was a long window with a shelf on which customers on bar stools placed their coffee, roll or tart while watching the passing scene. The two rooms behind the shop had been knocked into one and contained tables where customers could eat snacks of scrambled eggs and ham or salads, or merely have more space to put their coffee. Around the walls were racks stacked with jars of every imaginable thing that had ever been pickled or otherwise preserved; wines; bottles and cans of every grade of olive oil; plain vinegars and vinegars flavoured by herbs and spices; spaghetti, pasta, semolina, flour and other processed grains; peppers and mustards; and Italian cakes and almond biscuits. The chairs were wrought iron and every time a customer moved one it scraped the floor with agonising shrillness.

The man Milton took to be the manager was, in fact, the owner. He took the photofit picture from her. 'Yes,' he said. 'he looks familiar.' He called over his two waitresses. 'This lady is from the police,' he said. 'She wants to know if we've seen this man.'

'Oh, yes,' the first waitress said. The second waitress nodded. 'He won't be in for a while,' she said. 'He's gone back to France.'

Forrest and Porter's next move was back to the station, where Jackie Gough was waiting for them in an interview room. Porter put two tapes into the recording device and dictated the date, time and names of the three men present.

'Mister Gough,' Forrest began. 'You were seen in the Black Bear a few evenings ago, drinking with John Wright.'

'John Wright?'

'Don't get smart, Gough,' Porter said.

'Do you mean Buggy? It's years since I heard him called John Wright.'

'How long have you known him?' asked Forrest.

'We were at school together.'

'Buggy had a lot of money with him.'

Gough's face was a picture of helpful interest. He watched Forrest expectantly.

'Well?' Forrest said.

Gough sat up even straighter. His eyes turned to Porter, then back to Forrest. 'Did you ask me a question, Sergeant Forrest? I must have missed it.'

Forrest glared at him. 'Did Buggy have a lot of money with him?'

'I don't know how much he had. He was certainly waving a wad around. I didn't count it.'

'He was drunk,' Forrest said. 'Shouting his mouth off. There was something about a business proposition you had for him?'

'A business proposition?' Gough raised his eyebrows, pursed his lips and shook his head. 'No, Sergeant. I'm afraid you've been misinformed. Like Bogart.'

'What?'

'It's my favourite line from Casablanca. Most people think of "Play it again, Sam," which, of course, was never said in the movie, but I prefer when Bogart says "I was misinformed." What he really said was "I was mishinformed", but you know what he meant. Are you into movies, Sergeant?'

'This isn't a comedy theatre, Gough.'

Gough sat back, raising his hands. 'No offence, Sergeant. That was my degree, see? Film Studies.'

'Really? Mine was in Third Degree Questioning.'

'I didn't know you could do that.'

'Oh, yes. For my Masters I did a dissertation on effective use of the rubber truncheon. Still, we mustn't sit here reminiscing about student days, must we, Mister Gough? We'll be boring Constable Porter. So, let's talk about this business proposition. What would it have been, now? How do you earn your living?'

Gough shrugged. 'I'm on the dole, sergeant. One of those unemployed graduates you hear about.'

'There's been some mention of dodgy passports.'

'Not in connection with me, I hope. Believe me, sergeant, I learned my lesson when they hung that dope charge on me. "Nothing criminal from now on," I said. "Stay clean, stay free."'

'Buggy went to France,' Porter said.

'Did he?'

'With a passport you got for him.'

Gough smiled. 'Not me. Listen, I came here of my own free will to help with your inquiries. And now you're throwing funny passports at me. Do I need a brief?'

'You know your rights, Gough. Do you want us to call a lawyer for you?'

'Am I free to leave?'

'If that's what you want to do.'

'Then I don't need a brief. What else do you want to know?'

Forrest raised his eyebrows. 'You haven't told us anything yet. Jim Cameron.'

'No, sergeant, it's Jackie Gough.'

'My patience isn't unlimited, Gough. You know a man called Jim Cameron.'

'Me? I know who he is, of course. He owns that transport business off London Road. He's a successful businessman, far as I can judge. I don't move in those circles, Sergeant.'

'Jim Cameron is a crook.'

'He is? Surely not. I think you must be wrong there, Sergeant. Though, as I say, I don't know the man.'

'Buggy is doing something for him. In France.'

'Did Cameron tell you that?'

'And you got the passport for Buggy to go to France in the first place.'

'Not me, sergeant. I don't know where you get your information, but you want to check it a bit better. I don't know anything about Buggy's passport. Or France.'

'You do sleep with his wife, though?' Porter said.

'When I get the chance,' said Gough. 'She'll shag anyone, Sharon. Go round there if you fancy it. I'm sure she'll fit you in.'

Forrest frowned at Porter. 'All right, Gough. That'll be all. We'll likely want to see you again.'

'Any time, Sergeant Forrest. I'm always ready to help the police. I'll take the tape, shall I?'

Forrest took it from the machine and handed it to him. 'You're going to use this to ingratiate yourself with Cameron?'

Gough smiled, but said nothing.

'Just remember we're waiting, Gough. Sergeant Milton will expect to hear from you.'

Gough's smile didn't budge. He looked at the now empty tape machine. 'Sergeant Milton can smack my bottom and send me back to jail, Mister Forrest.'

'Where some nasty men might want to do other things to it.'

'True. But Jim Cameron, now. He can kill me.'

Hiden picked up the phone. 'DI Hiden.'

'DI Hiden here, too.'

'Hello, Muriel. How are things?'

'I thought they were OK when I came in this morning. Have you seen a fax Hertfordshire have sent to all forces?'

'No. Should I?'

'It might be an idea. There's a video capture of a woman wanted for car theft and murder.'

Anxiety gnawed coldly at Hiden's stomach. 'Not Sara?'

''Fraid so.'

'Shit.'

They don't know she's our daughter yet. But someone will tell them. I suggest one of us. I tossed a coin and you lost. I'll leave it with you, shall I?'

The phone went dead. Hiden stared at the cream painted wall. He tried to shout to a passing constable, but it came out a croak.

'Yes, sir?'

'Check the fax traffic, will you? There should be a fax from Hertfordshire police. A woman's picture.'

'All right, sir. Sir? Are you all right?'

CHAPTER 22

They picked Mitchell up on the Canal d'Accolay which was, in fact, a spur off the main Canal du Nivernais. It had a handsomeness that belied its apparent insignificance. The route de halage was wide and poplars lined the other side of the canal. An increase in the number of cyclists marked the nearness to a town.

After a short while they came to a place where the towpath was cobbled and edged with tall iron bollards. Behind the paved area were buildings. It was the first village they had encountered since leaving Auxerre that was on the canal, rather than standing back a mile or so.

'Welcome to Accolay,' Carver said. 'You may as well come with me. Stretch your legs.'

The stone houses turned in on each other. The few men they saw were dressed in thick woollen check shirts and woollen trousers belted high on the stomach, the women in black dresses and headscarves. Closed, weather-beaten faces glanced away as they passed.

They turned into the Rue de Reigny. An inn stood back from the road, forming a sort of courtyard—to the right, a small hedged garden; to the left an old, low-slung single storey building with more roof than wall; and, at the back, the modern inn itself, white walled with a pale biscuit coloured roof and shutters. A number of cars and vans were parked in the courtyard.

'This place is amazing,' Carver said. 'It just doesn't belong in Accolay. The food's good and the patron and his wife are civilised people. They have an excellent wine list. The restaurant is in the old wine cellar—it's like eating in a barrel-vaulted crypt. I don't suppose anyone's hungry?'

Buggy shook his head.

'Don't keep staring at the cars, Mitch,' said Carver. 'You're retired, remember?' He led the way to the half-glazed door at the right of the inn. It gave onto a stone-floored passageway and then to another door, beyond which was a lawn around a large bed of red roses. To the right, the spreading shade of trees; ahead, climbing bushes Buggy did not recognise spilling over a painted wall; to the left, a high brick wall beyond which was a road.

Carver sat down at a white plastic table and indicated that the others should do the same. A young man came from the inn and looked at them without expression.

'Bonjour monsieur,' said Carver. 'Trois bières, s'il vous plaît.'

The waiter nodded and turned back to the inn.

'Is this where you're meeting your mate?' Buggy said.

Carver nodded.

'Have you got a mobile phone?'

'Not sure you can get a signal here,' said Carver.

'Well, how will he know you're here?'

Carver turned to look at him. 'This is Accolay, Buggy. La France profonde. Auxerre and Dijon may not be far in miles, but they're a huge distance in spirit. About three hundred years. Commuters move into places like this from time to time. And they move out again. The people here are peasants. They won't trust you and they won't like you. On the other hand, they won't tell the police about you, either.'

'Bit like Stepney,' Mitchell said.

'The food's better,' said Carver. 'And revenge is bloodier. You don't need a mobile phone to let someone in Accolay know you're here. Everyone will know, and that includes my hunting friend, Monsieur Arbot.'

'What do you hunt?'

'All sorts of things, Buggy.'

They smoked and drank their beers. Occasional cars moved on the road outside. Bees nuzzled among the roses. From time to time, a wizened brown face peered at them through a kitchen window.

After about twenty minutes, the outer door scraped open. Buggy heard the sound of heavy boots on the passageway. A tall man appeared in the doorway and glanced at them. He disappeared for a moment and Buggy heard his raised voice calling to someone inside. Then he returned and walked towards them. 'Bonjour, Messieurs.'

Carver said, 'Bonjour, Monsieur Arbot.' Mitchell said, 'Bonjour, Monsieur.' The stranger looked at Buggy, then at Carver. Carver said something in French that was quite incomprehensible to Buggy, who found the man's eyes on him again.

'Manners are so important here, Buggy,' Carver said. 'I've explained that you're foreign to their ways, but...'

Buggy stood up. He bent his head in salute and said, 'Bonjour, Monsieur,' as he had heard the others say it. Carver and Mitchell laughed. The tall Frenchman bowed in return, held his arms wide, then seized Buggy by the hand, a smile creasing his brown, leathery face. 'Bravo, Monsieur.'

The waiter had appeared with four bottles of beer and a glass on a tray. The newcomer sat. He lit a cigarette and sank his beer in two quick draughts. He looked expectantly at Carver. 'Eh bien, Monsieur?'

'Will you two excuse me for a minute?' Carver stood up and walked towards the back wall, the Frenchman following. Buggy leaned back and stared at the balcony on the second floor of the inn. It was approached by an outside staircase and there appeared to be bedrooms up there. A woman had come out and was staring at the sky, as if to judge what the weather would do. She called to someone behind her in a language that meant nothing to Buggy.

'German,' Mitchell explained. 'Tourists. Get everywhere.'

DI Hiden assembled his staff in his office. 'Before we get to our own business,' he said, 'there's something I need to tell you. People are going to talk and I'd rather you heard it from me. Most people know I'm divorced.'

Heads nodded uncertainly.

'Most people know my ex-wife is also a DI, though not in the Met. As a matter of fact, I don't think either of us would have made Inspector if we'd stayed locked together. There's a bit of career counselling for you.'

'Guv,' said DS Milton, 'You don't have to tell us your personal business.'

'If that's all it was, Anne, I wouldn't. But it's gone a bit further than that. Muriel and I have two daughters. Joanna is married to a banker, never gives anyone any trouble, she's a joy to us. And Sara...Sara's been trouble since the day she was born. I don't know where we went wrong, but... I know Joanna's in touch with her, but neither Muriel nor I have seen Sara for years.

'Until this morning, when we saw her on this.' He held up the Hertfordshire fax. 'Sara is wanted for car theft. She stole a white Mondeo and it was set on fire with two women, so far unidentified, in the boot.'

He looked around at the horrified faces.

'If this were my case, I'd have to step aside. But it isn't. It's something we can safely leave to Hertfordshire to sort out. But there are plenty of people who know that Sara is my daughter. They'll talk and you'll hear it. So you've heard it from me first. Now. To business. Duncan, you start.'

'Sharon Wright is too scared to talk to us,' Forrest said. 'Someone had given her a smack before we got there.'

'Cameron? One of his men?'

'Who knows? She says she walked into a door. She admits she went to see Cameron, but only because I saw her there. She says she doesn't know where Buggy is. She says she knows nothing about any job for Cameron or whether he's in France. Although she seemed to find that idea amusing. She says she's never heard of Matt Burns. Apart from that, she couldn't have been more co-operative.

'Jackie Gough. Admits he saw Buggy in the Black Bear. Says they were at school together. Admits he saw Buggy waving money around—says he doesn't know how much, or what for. Denies having mentioned a business proposition to Buggy. Says he knows nothing about dodgy passports. Claims not to know where Buggy is, but he didn't look surprised when we mentioned France. Not a flicker. Admits he sleeps with Sharon Wright when he gets the chance, but says everyone else does, too. And on the record he doesn't know Jim Cameron as anything but a successful legitimate business man. Although off the record he admitted Cameron could kill him for speaking out of turn. I let him know Anne would be expecting to hear from him. He wasn't giving anything away.'

Hiden sighed. 'Well, it's no worse than I expected. These people aren't exactly famous for helping the police. Anne? What did you get?'

'Well, guv, first off I checked with the Passport Office. No legitimate passport has ever been issued to John Wright. So, if he has gone to France, he's using someone else's.

'The photofit was a hit. The Twickenham café weren't sure but they thought they'd probably seen him; the Barnes café were

191

sure they'd seen him but not for a while and they couldn't remember when; but the Richmond café have seen him a lot, last week being the most recent. *And* he told them he was going to France and probably wouldn't be coming back.'

Forrest let out a low whistle. 'What are we going to do about the French angle, guv?'

'I'm meeting someone from Interpol Liaison this afternoon. We're going to send the photofit across. But we have no idea what he calls himself or where he lives. My experience with the French police isn't good. If he isn't known to them, don't expect them to go looking for him.'

'I had those videos collected, guv,' Milton said.

'You also pointed out how long it would take to go through them.'

'We don't need to go through all of them. Ashford suggests he travels by Eurostar, so we can forget airports and ferry terminals. He told the waitress in Richmond he was going back the day Stacy Teasdale was attacked.'

'If he had,' Hiden said, 'He couldn't have killed Julie Been. So that was a lie.' He turned to DC Wylie. 'You and Sammy Porter get down to St Pancras. Work out the earliest train to Paris he could have been on if he went straight there from Cardiff. Keep looking for twenty-four hours after that. See if you can get uniform to lend you some bodies. Six people could get it done in four hours. If you don't find him, go to Ashford and start again.'

The meeting began to break up. On the way out, Anne Milton stopped for a word with Hiden. 'I'm sorry to hear about your troubles, guv.'

'Thanks, Anne. Let's just be grateful she's on someone else's manor.'

CHAPTER 23

The Shepherd's Crook was a rustic name for a far from rural pub less than a quarter of a mile from Jim Cameron's place of business. Jackie Gough had too much sense to go straight to Cameron at a time when the police were likely to be watching him. Walker was likely to stop in here for a drink during the evening. Cameron owned the pub and Walker kept it trouble-free.

Walker arrived alone and ordered a scotch at the bar. Gough got up from his seat against the wall, ostensibly to order a drink, and positioned himself next to Walker. 'I've got something Mister Cameron should hear,' he said as if to no-one in particular.

Speaking in the same undirected way, Walker said, 'What is it?'

'A tape. Of an interview I had with the police today. Mister Cameron is mentioned.'

'Not by you, I hope?'

'You're joking.'

'Good.' Walker turned and casually surveyed the bar. Gough ordered a sparkling mineral water from the barman. 'No-one's watching,' Walker said. 'Put it on the bar when you pay for your drink.'

Gough did as he was told. As he walked away with his glass, Walker said, 'Be here in the morning. If we don't come for you by eleven, you're in the clear.'

Sharon's cousin was alarmed by the state of her face when she arrived to collect her money. 'What the hell have you done to yourself? Kafteem isn't going to want to go with someone looking like that.'

'I need the money, Wayne.'

'Shit. What happened?'

'You don't want to know.'

'If I didn't want to know, I wouldn't have asked.'

'Well, I don't want to tell you. All right?'

Wayne took his wallet out of his trouser pocket and extracted five twenties. 'I'll get someone else for Friday. You owe me. When your face has mended. Okay?'

'Thanks, Wayne. You're a pal.'

Wayne's shock was as nothing compared with Adrian's.

'Now do you understand why you couldn't come to my place?'

'Your husband did that to you?'

'Who else?'

'But I thought you were divorced.'

'I didn't say that. I said we'd split up. I'm still wearing my ring, aren't I?'

He put his hand on hers where it lay on the white cloth. 'Why did he hit you?'

'I wouldn't tell him where I'd been.'

'But you've split up.'

'That doesn't stop him banging on my door at four in the morning. Doesn't stop him wanting to know why I wasn't there when he came round at nine o'clock the night before. Like I'm supposed to stay in and wait, in case he decides to show up.'

'Can't you get an injunction against him?'

'An injunction. Like a court order.'

'Yes.'

'Go to court against Buggy. Ask a court to tell him not to bother me any more.'

'Yes.'

She shook her head, said nothing.

'Why not?'

She looked up as the waiter offered menus. 'Something to drink?' he asked.

Adrian looked at Sharon. Sharon returned the look, hands turned outwards in a "You choose" gesture.

'Bottle of pinot grigio, please,' said Adrian.

'Pinot grigio. Yes sir.'

'And some water, please.'

'Yes, sir. Sparkling or still?'

'Out of a tap,' said Adrian. 'In a jug.'

The waiter sniffed. 'Yes sir.'

'So,' Adrian said when the waiter had gone. 'Why not?'

'Oh, Adrian. You don't know Buggy.' She picked up the menu. 'What shall I eat?'

'Is that it? Is that all I'm going to get?'

She laid the menu down again. 'Adrian. What do you know about me?'

His face turned pink. 'I know you're a...a lovely girl.'

'Woman.'

'Woman. I know I feel very strongly about you. I know...'

'Adrian. We met in a book shop. Once. I've been to your place. Once. I've met two of your friends. Once. You cooked me a lovely meal. Once. We slept together. Once.'

Pink had turned to bright red. 'I can think of something we did more than once.'

Sharon couldn't prevent herself from laughing. 'So can I, my sweet, and it was lovely.' She reached across and touched his cheek. 'I hope we'll do it again.'

Adrian was saved from the need to reply by the arrival of the waiter, fussing with ice bucket, bottle and corkscrew. When he'd swirled and sniffed the wine and the waiter had filled both glasses, they were faced with the need to order their meal which, as they hadn't looked at the menu, gave more time for Adrian's blushes to fade.

'What I'm trying to say to you,' Sharon said, 'is that you don't know me and you don't know anything about me.'

Adrian snapped a bread stick. 'That's what Lizzie says.'

'Oh. You've discussed me with Lizzie, have you?'

'I didn't get to do much of the discussing.'

'No, I don't suppose you do with Lizzie. But if she says you don't know anything about me, she's right.'

'She says I'm letting myself be led by my...you know.'

Sharon laughed. 'So what? Better be led by your cock than her horrible head.'

'Sharon!'

'What? I shouldn't say cock?' She leaned across the table. 'You've got a lovely cock.'

'Sharon! May I eat my antipasto?'

'Be my guest.'

The main course was a veal dish in a garlicky, tomatoey sauce. Eating it, Adrian said, 'I've brought the access course stuff.'

'Good. Can I take it away and study it?'

'Of course. What do you think you'll do?'

'Can't say till I've read it.'

'But what do you want to do?'

'I want to be someone else. No, I don't. I want to be me. The me I've never been able to be. Remember when you said that about the butterfly coming out of the chrysalis and soaring close to the sun?'

'Mhm.'

'I want to be that butterfly. I want to make up for the waste. I was clever, you know.'

'You are clever.'

'Thank you. What I meant was, I could have done well at school. If I'd let myself. And now I'm going to let myself.'

'What will your husband say?'

'He won't know anything about it. I'm going to find a course somewhere away from home. I'm going to go there and do my course, and I'm not going to tell him where I am. Then I'm going to go to university and I won't tell him where that is, either. I'm never going to go home. And I'll divorce him. Why are you looking like that?'

'If you go away, I won't see you again.'

'I'll tell *you* where I am, silly.'

'So you do want to see me again.'

'Of course I do.' She put her hand on his. 'I wouldn't be doing this without you. You told me how to do it.'

'Maybe we could get a flat together.'

She smiled. 'One thing at a time, my love. Maybe you could come for a weekend first. See how we go.'

'What are we going to do tonight?'

'Well, you can't come to mine, can you? And I'm not going to go to yours and let *her* see me like this.'

'So when will I see you?'

'In a few days. Okay?'

The following morning, Gough presented himself at the Shepherd's Crook shortly after the ten o'clock opening time. The barman waved his head silently towards the door behind him. Gough passed behind the bar, knocked once on the door and went through.

Although Gough couldn't know it, this was the same room as the one in which Buggy had been ordered to hire Carver for Doyle's murder. Cameron sat alone behind the table. He signalled Gough to sit down and pushed the tape across to him. 'You may need that again.'

Gough slipped it into his pocket.

'You did well,' Cameron said. 'Why do you suppose they called you in?'

'I'd guess some grass saw me and Buggy in the Black Bear. Buggy was waving a wad around. He said he got it from you. For a job he was doing.'

'If he told you...'

'...he could have told anyone,' Gough finished. 'We're not what you'd call good mates, Buggy and me.'

'Bit different with his wife, is it?'

'Shazza? She's anybody's. Always has been, since we were kids.'

Cameron took a roll of twenties from his pocket and peeled ten off the top. He passed them across the table. They disappeared into Gough's pocket.

'Buggy has his uses,' Cameron said. 'But we need someone better. Think of that as a retainer. The first thing I want you to do for me is stay close to Sharon. Anything she hears from Buggy, I want to know.'

'No problem.'

Cameron tapped on the table with his fingertips. 'What was this business proposition? The one you wanted to offer Buggy?'

Gough felt his heart beat suddenly faster. He tried to swallow, but his mouth was suddenly dry. 'Just a little drugs thing,' he said. 'I needed a mule. Buggy's a donkey—seemed like the next best thing.' He attempted a smile.

'You don't want to work drugs on your own,' Cameron said. 'That's how people get killed. See Johnnie. Give him all the details. We'll take it from here. You'll be cut in, of course.'

Gough forced a pleased expression onto his face. 'Thanks, Mister Cameron.'

Cameron smiled. 'Call me Jim, Jackie. You were wrong about that film, by the way.'

'Film?'

'Casablanca. Of course he says "Play it again, Sam." Everyone knows that.'

'Oh. Right, Jim.'

The smile on Cameron's face was almost paternal. 'Universities,' he said. He shook his head.

Gough left the pub. Buggy still owed him five hundred pounds for the passport, but as he'd paid only one fifty for it himself, he was ahead already. He'd lost his chance at the drug business, but Cameron knew he hadn't grassed him up when he'd had the chance. He now had Cameron's protection and there would be future earnings opportunities there. And—if he'd needed it—he had a reason to see Sharon again.

All told, a good morning's work.

Buggy sat on the stern deck while Carver drove the boat back along the Canal d'Accolay and into the Canal du Nivernais. A hundred years of scrubby tree growth lined the waterway on both sides. The route de halage was reduced to two pink clay ruts showing through the grass bank. Cyclists would find them treacherous when it rained. Buggy had never known such contentment. Why he'd ever found Carver obnoxious, he couldn't have said.

'How long to Mailly?', Mitchell asked.

199

'Hour and a half,' said Carver. 'We'll be there by six. That gives you an hour before the last train.'

'You've checked the train times?'

'I check everything. It's the secret of my success. This is Prégilbert coming up. I could drop you here but you'd have to wait three hours for a train and there's nothing there. Mailly's quite a little burg. And it has a good auberge, where I might eat tonight. You can look after the boat while I do that, Buggy?'

'Sure. I'll make myself something to eat.'

'There's a nice little tourist spot with picnic tables. You'll be right at home.'

Muriel Hiden hated answering machines, but she had to leave a message. She prayed that Joanna would know where to find Sara.

It was a wasted prayer, as Joanna explained when she returned her mother's call. 'She always rings me. She never says where she's living. She dodges the question. Presumably there's some man we wouldn't approve of.'

'How often does she call, Joanna?'

'Mother, what's this about? You sound dreadful.'

'I can't tell you. We need to speak to Sara. But if she calls you mustn't tell her that.'

'Oh, God, she's in trouble, isn't she? Real trouble?'

'Joanna, listen to me. If Sara calls you, you must not sound worried and you must not let her know that your father and I are looking for her.'

'Mother, will you please tell me what she's...'

'Tell her you're going out and ask her to call back in a couple of hours. Ring your father or me...'

'Mother...'

'...so we can have the call monitored.'

'Oh, mother!'

'Then dial 1471 and check the number she's calling from. Will you do that, Joanna?'

'Not unless you tell me...'

'I can't do that, Joanna, and you don't want to know. Trust me. Will you do what I ask?'

There was a long silence and then the young woman said, 'Yes, mother. If it's as bad as that, of course I will.'

Muriel Hiden breathed a sigh of relief. She need not have bothered. At the very moment one of her daughters was caving in and agreeing to try to find the other, two patrol cops in Hounslow recognised the woman they had seen on the Hertfordshire Police's fax going into a convenience store. After parking the car two hundred yards away, one went to the back door to prevent escape before the other entered by the front door.

They, too, need not have bothered. Sara Hiden had no reason to suppose the police to be searching for her and looked up in only mild interest when the young constable entered the shop. When he asked her to identify herself, it was too late to run.

'You don't smell too good. Do you know that?' he asked as he put her in the car.

They drove her to Hounslow police station where she was processed and put in a cell. Hounslow rang Hatfield, who sent two officers in a car to collect her. Hatfield also, as a courtesy, rang the Met's Serious Crime Squad and told DI Hiden his daughter was in custody. Hiden thanked them and asked to be kept informed. He rang his wife to give her the news. Then he told the desk sergeant he would be out for a while and drove to his one bedroom flat in Hammersmith. He switched off his radio, unplugged the telephone and lay down on his bed to rest.

Muriel Hiden rang her other daughter and warned her that the press could not be kept in the dark for ever. If they knocked on her door, Joanna should refuse to speak to them.

Doyle got off the TGV from Paris at Laroche-Migennes and waited ten minutes for the slow train to Avallon. He paid little attention when the train passed through Auxerre, other than to count it off on his mental list of stations. The train stopped again at Augy, Charnos-sur-Yonne, Vincelles and Cravant before leaving the main line south at the very point where the Canal d'Accolay branched off the Canal du Nivernais. Doyle left the train at Accolay.

He approached a Renault van in the road outside the station. The driver's window was rolled down. 'Monsieur Arbot?' asked Doyle.

'Bonsoir, Monsieur Doyle,' replied Arbot.

Doyle walked round to the passenger seat and got in. As he moved the van away from the kerb, Arbot jerked a thumb towards the space behind the seats. Doyle placed a hand down into the well and picked up a parcel wrapped in white cloth. Arbot held out a pair of gloves. Doyle put them on before unwrapping the parcel. He weighed the gun in his hand, checked that it was loaded, slid the safety catch off and then on again. He slipped the gun into his inside pocket.

CHAPTER 24

There was no response when DS Milton called her boss's radio. She tried his home phone. After seven rings, a woman's voice said, "This is BT Callminder." Milton waited for the tone, then recorded her message. 'Guv, this is Anne. Wylie and Porter found our man's picture on the video at Waterloo. They've shown it to porters and ticket staff—I'm afraid no-one remembers him. It'll be shown to every train crew member as they come on duty, but that could take a week. If anyone can place him in a seat, we'll have the name he travelled under. Guv, he could not have travelled to France on that train and killed Burns. We're dealing with two killers. Sorry, but that's how it is.' She thought for a moment, then said, 'I hope you're OK, guv. If you want someone to have a beer with, call me.'

Ninety minutes later, another message was recorded on Hiden's phone. 'Inspector Hiden, this is DS Longer at Hatfield. I've been asked to keep you up to date with our inquiries here. Your daughter's story is that she stole a car to order for some unknown person she met in a pub. She delivered it to him, collected fifty quid and left. Who are we to say different? There's no physical evidence to place her at the spot where the car was burned. In fact, there's no physical evidence to place her in the car anywhere after it left the car park. She's given us a wonderful description of the man and co-operated in a photofit. We'll circulate it, but I'd be very surprised if it had any foundation in reality. She's been charged with Taking and Driving Away, but we're going to have to bail her shortly. The CPS won't wear a more serious charge on what we've got so far. If anything changes, we'll let you know.'

At ten minutes to six, Buggy opened the lock just to the north of Mailly-la-Ville. While they waited for it to fill, Carver left Mitchell to hold the rope and strolled through into the saloon and galley to clear a few things away and wash some plates, mugs and glasses. Ten minutes later, they tied up near to a little park where tarmac paths meandered through the trees. There were Edwardian lamp standards and picnic tables, and a cluster of buildings beside a string of small, half hidden parking areas. Except for the public lavatories, the buildings were closed.

'Civilisation!' said Mitchell.

'It doesn't really open up till the season starts again,' Carver said. 'We'll pretty well have it to ourselves tonight.'

Mitchell went into the saloon and came out carrying his bag. He put out his hand. 'Buggy, it's been good to spend time with you. I won't deny I thought you were a dickhead. You've grown on this trip. Look after yourself. And give my best to Jim Cameron when you get back.'

Buggy shook the offered hand. 'See you around sometime.'

'Sure thing, Buggy. Now you've discovered travel, come down to Spain. I'll show you a good time.' He nudged Buggy in the ribs. 'Leave the wife at home and I'll show you a really good time.'

Buggy grinned uncomfortably.

'I'll walk Mitch over the bridge to the station,' said Carver. 'Then I'll come back to this side and stroll up to the auberge. It's up the hill on the road to Avigny if you need me—but I'd really rather you didn't leave the boat unless you have to.'

'I'll be fine. Have a good meal.'

Carver nodded. He looked carefully at Buggy, then turned away.

It took ten minutes to reach the station. 'Change at Laroche-Migennes,' Carver said. 'You'll be in Paris by ten.'

'I was thinking of staying another night in Auxerre and getting the morning train,' said Mitchell.

'Go to Paris tonight. You don't want to be in Auxerre. Trust me.'

'The police?'

'They might have questions you don't want to answer. Like why you're here, who you came to see. Go to Paris tonight, Mitch. Leave for Spain first thing in the morning.'

Mitchell nodded.

Carver said, 'You know Cameron. What's he going to do when Buggy goes missing?'

'Call me, I guess. You want me to take a holiday?'

'No, I don't. I want you to be there when he calls. You've no idea what happened. Buggy was okay when you left here. He and I were getting on fine. I'd promised to be in London by the end of the week to do the job for them.'

'No problem. You have to do this, I suppose?'

'Call it a debt of honour.'

'I've never understood much about honour.'

'No? I suppose I can count on you to get on the train?'

'Don, I wouldn't stay here and mess with what you're going to do for a big clock.'

'That's good.' Carver raised his hand in salute, then turned away. 'I'll see you some time.'

He left the station, walked back over the bridge and up the slope towards the village. The sun had almost sunk behind the wooded hillside, but the air was still pleasantly warm. A Renault van with two men in it was parked facing him. Carver's nod would have looked to a casual observer like nothing more than a meaningless movement of the head. The van moved forward. Carver reached the main road, crossed it and entered the auberge. 'Bonsoir, Madame,' he said. He passed through the bar and took a seat at one of the tables in the dining room beyond. The patronne bustled in, smiled and handed him a menu.

Buggy went into the saloon and poured himself a glass of red burgundy. Three empty bottles already stood on the central table. He opened a cupboard and took out a plate and a knife. From another he took a baguette, a length of garlic sausage, tomatoes, mustard and lettuce. It was a long way from a Big Mac. His eating habits would change when he got home. You must be able to get this stuff in London.

He split the baguette, spread mustard on both halves and laid slices of sausage on one. He sliced a ripe tomato and put that, with lettuce, on top of the sausage. Then he pressed the other half of the baguette into place. Sandwich in one hand and glass of wine in the other, he strolled out onto the stern deck.

Buggy sat down and took a bite from his sandwich. Somewhere near, tyres rolled on packed earth. He looked towards the trees. A van was moving from right to left across his line of vision about forty yards away. Without its headlights, it would have been hard to see in the gathering dusk. When it turned left into a parking space, the headlights focused directly on Buggy. They were on full beam. He waited for the driver to douse the lights, but it did not happen. Two lovers, perhaps, looking for privacy and disappointed to find someone here.

The door on the right of the van opened. Someone got out and looked this way. Buggy took another bite from his sandwich. Whoever it was had moved away from the van now and was coming in leisurely fashion towards the boat. Buggy was not sure he was up to conducting a conversation with a French visitor. He would have to make do with smiles and uncomprehending gestures.

The visitor was closer now. It was a man. Even in the dark, there was something familiar about him. Buggy shielded his eyes against the blinding headlights. The man was very close. He held up his left arm and the headlights were extinguished. Buggy blinked in the sudden darkness. The man stepped onto the boat and down onto the rear deck. Buggy stared at him. His sandwich dropped to the deck.

'Now, Buggy,' Doyle said. 'Let's go inside and you can tell me about these people who want me killed.'

Hertfordshire police got lucky in the way that people who work hard at routine tasks sometimes do. One of the DCs who had found Sara Hiden's picture on the car park video had returned with a print, asking that it be shown to all the staff as they came on duty. He expected nothing—but you never knew. Now, following a phone call, he was back at the car park and interviewing a woman who worked on the exits.

'You're sure it was her?' he asked.

'Positive. She's been in here before.'

'Often?'

'Often enough. This is a long stay park and she only leaves her car a few hours. She'll drive a car away at seven in the morning and yet she only brought it in an hour before.'

'How do you know that?'

'It's on her ticket, isn't it? That's why it's me that sees her. I work early shift, three days a week. She'd be better off in the short stay. Not that I tell her that, of course. And she can't be flying anywhere. She must be working night shift locally. But not at the airport or she'd have staff parking.'

'Does she always drive the same car?'

'Oh, we don't notice cars here. Not unless it's a Jag or a Porsche. A Roller, something like that. All we see is an open window and a face.'

'So you don't know what she was driving last time she was in?'

'No idea. Sorry. But it was Thursday, because I haven't been on since, and it was just after seven.'

'Thank you. You've been very helpful.'

Now that they knew what the woman looked like, it was fairly easy to spot her on the tape at the wheel of a dark blue Vauxhall Vectra. The DC noted down the licence number and called in a vehicle registration check. He then drove eighteen miles to the owner's home. Parked outside was a dark blue Vauxhall Vectra. The constable took out his notebook and compared the registration number with that of the car Sara Hiden had been seen driving away from the car park. They were the same.

Some time later, a third message joined the other two on DI Hiden's telephone. 'Inspector, this is DS Longer from Hatfield again. A curious addition to our story. The day after your daughter stole the white Mondeo, she drove another car away from the same place. A Vauxhall Vectra, dark blue. We know she did because we have it on tape. The strange thing is that the car was returned at some time, possibly by your daughter, possibly by someone else.

'We can't do her for car theft, because the car wasn't stolen. The owner has it back and never knew it was gone. Your daughter denies all knowledge. She knows we aren't going to charge her for the Vectra. The assumption has to be that it was used for something while it was away, but who knows what? My guvnor has asked me to let you know that we're working on the assumption that the Mondeo would also have been returned, but something happened that caused it to be used as a do-it-yourself crematorium. Once again, possibly by your daughter, possibly by someone else.

'We'll let you know if we come up with anything else. And if you think of anything that might help us, we'll be delighted to hear from you.'

Buggy sat with his head on his chest. Even sober, he would have struggled to understand this reversal—and he was far from sober. Buggy had known shifts of fortune, betrayals, plots before, but they had always involved heat and anger. The coolness, the casualness with which Carver had hung him out to dry robbed him of breath. Carver had seemed to have become a friend. Buggy had few enough friends. His gratitude for this new one had been almost puppy-like.

'I've told you everything I know. Now can I have a cigarette?'

'Go ahead, Buggy.' The gun lay gently in Doyle's hand.

'How did you find out?'

'That doesn't matter, Buggy.'

Buggy's eyes were misty with tears. 'Carver told you, didn't he? He's been so nice to me this last couple of days.' He dragged on his cigarette. 'What are you going to do to me?'

'That depends on you.'

'Me? What can I do?'

'I need someone to lead me to Cameron. Will you do that?'

'Of course I will. I didn't want him to do anything to you, Doyle. I said I could vouch for you.'

'That was kind of you, Buggy. I appreciate it.'

Fear had loosened Buggy's tongue. 'Really. I never thought you deserved to be killed. Not after you'd done what Cameron wanted.'

'Makes you wonder, doesn't it? Me this time, who next? Could be you, Buggy.'

'I wouldn't trust Cameron.'

'Very wise. Course, if I let you live, I'm going to have to watch you. Never let you out of my sight until I've done Cameron. Which creates a problem for me.'

'You can trust me, Doyle.'

'Can I, Buggy? I'd like to. Right now I need to go up, tell Carver what I've decided. What do I do about you while I'm doing that?'

'I could come with you?'

'You could. Or...tell you what. Let's get Arbot down here to sit with you.'

'Arbot?'

'He's driving the van, Buggy. You don't think I know my way around here, do you? Let's go out on the deck there.'

Buggy stood up and walked out onto the stern deck. If he could talk his way out of this one, he'd never deceive anyone again as long as he lived. He'd get a job, even if it was cleaning public urinals.

A shadowy figure stood among the trees.

'Monsieur Arbot!,' called Doyle. 'Will you come down here, please?'

'I don't think he speaks English,' said Buggy.

'Don't worry. I'm sure he'll get the drift.'

Arbot stepped onto the boat. Doyle said, 'I want him to check you for weapons, Buggy.'

'I'm not carrying. I never carry.'

'Even so, Buggy, we'll just check. Better safe than sorry, eh? Just turn round and face down river, will you?'

It cost Buggy an enormous effort of will to turn his back on the two men. He felt Arbot come close on his left, Doyle on his right. There was a sudden movement and he was seized by the ankles, each man heaving upwards as Buggy went over the rail. He let out a yell as his face hit the water.

His struggle was brief. Unable to shake the firm grip of two strong hands on each ankle, he could neither kick himself free nor raise his head from the water. Whether his life flashed before his eyes, whether he saw a vision of Sharon coupling where she would, whether he repented at the very last of the sinfulness or waste of his short life, neither Doyle nor Arbot was able to tell. What they did know was that he died. Unable to hold his breath for ever, he had to let it go; and when his lungs filled again, it was with water, and he drowned.

They let go of his ankles and watched as he slipped into the canal. Moving rapidly, they went to the van where Arbot opened the back doors and pulled out a bicycle. He clicked the gnurled wheel of the lighting dynamo onto the rear tyre and pushed the bike into Doyle's hands. 'Allez, monsieur. Vite, vite!'

Arbot watched Doyle's rear light move up the hill from the picnic site and turn left towards the road for Séry and Prégilbert. Then he got into his van and drove up the slope, turning right for the town. He parked at a careless angle to the kerb, left the engine running and the door open and ran into the auberge. Standing in the middle of the bar, he shouted, 'Vite un téléphone! Faites le dix-sept! Quelqu'un s'est noyé dans le canal!'

Lingering over his coffee in the dining room, Carver lit a cigarette. He allowed himself a small smile. There was one fewer traitor in the world.

CHAPTER 25

In larger towns and cities in France, policing is the business of the civil police or Police Judiciaire. This being the countryside, the Gendarmerie, a branch of the Army, is responsible. And, this being the fairly remote countryside and the hour being late, it took them some time to arrive.

Captain Duroc was an officer of some experience, approaching retirement, who had seen pretty much everything that was to be seen in rural French policing. The Procureur de la République in Dijon would have to be called and asked to appoint a Juge d'Instruction to oversee the investigation into the drowning and decide whether foul play was a possibility. Duroc, who had already made up his mind on that question, did not intend to trouble the Procureur this late in the evening.

It was fairly clear that the Englishman, this Jim Patterson, had been drinking a good deal of red Burgundy, to which he was no doubt unaccustomed. It was also clear that he had been doing so alone, since the owner of the boat, this Monsieur Carver, had been dining at the auberge. Again, it was clear that, had this Pierre Arbot from Accolay not stopped to relieve himself in the convenience he knew to be here, Patterson would have lain in the water rather longer than he had done. Since Arbot had heard the body go into the water, they could fix the time of death with some precision. And since Patterson still had his passport and a few hundred sodden Euros in his pockets, and since Monsieur Carver confirmed that nothing seemed—at any rate at first sight—to have been stolen from the boat it was clear that Arbot had not drowned the unfortunate English drunk for gain.

No, Duroc knew an accidental death when he saw one. He told Arbot to go home and to make himself available for interview the following morning. A more conscientious, energetic or interested officer might have wished to examine Arbot's van, in which case the presence of a gun would have raised interesting questions. But Duroc was none of those things.

Duroc was at first reluctant to allow Carver to sleep on the boat but agreed to do so when no alternative offered. The auberge had no rooms. Three or four kilometres away, in Mailly-le-Chateau, was an eating establishment granted two knives and forks by the Michelin Guide—but that, too, provided no sleeping accommodation. Carver could hardly be expected to hire a taxi to take him the thirty kilometres back to Auxerre and the next train would not run until six-thirty the following morning. Duroc's approval was subject to Carver accepting the presence of a young gendarme to ensure that no evidence was interfered with.

'Perhaps, Monsieur Carver,' said Duroc, 'You will join me in coffee and a fine while we wait for the officer who will spend the night on your boat.'

Carver indicated that it would be his pleasure. They sat in the dining room behind the bar, away from prying ears. 'This Monsieur Patterson,' Duroc said. 'You have known him long?'

'Since yesterday only.'

Duroc raised bushy eyebrows. 'How can this be, Monsieur?'

Carver shrugged. 'He attached himself to me in Auxerre. I assume he realised I was English. He said he was a visitor here; he said he had run out of money.'

'But, Monsieur! We found money in his pocket. A lot of money.'

'Really? You astound me. I assumed he was what he said—an English tourist who needed cash to buy a train ticket back to London. At any rate, he asked me if I would lend him fifty Euros.'

'A man you had never met? Impertinence.'

'Indeed. Anyway, I needed to move my boat to Nevers, so I asked if he knew anything about canals and locks. He said he was expert. So, I offered him the money and his keep to help me move the boat.'

'And was he expert?'

'Useless. But I taught him to open a lock.'

'So then, this evening, you left him on the boat while you went to eat at the auberge.'

'D'accord. When I offered him his keep, I didn't mean I'd pay for him to eat in restaurants. I laid in food for the trip.'

'And wine, I think.'

'And wine.' Carver shrugged. 'Not enough, as it turned out. I was going to buy more tomorrow. A bottle of local rouge is hardly expensive, Capitaine, and he was drinking steadily all day.'

'You did not join him?'

'I live here, monsieur. I have too much respect for my liver to treat it like that.'

'Of course. Would you say Monsieur Patterson was drunk when you left the boat last evening?'

'Not drunk, exactly. He seemed able to hold his liquor. But if your people examine his stomach, I think they will find he'd had a good deal to drink.'

'Eh bien. Our people will, as you say, examine his stomach, so we shall see. And his state of mind, Monsieur. How did he seem while you were on the boat together?'

Carver finished his fine and called for two more. He offered Duroc a cigarette and lit one for himself. 'You're wondering whether he threw himself in the canal? We spoke only of the generalities, Monsieur. His wife, his job. He asked why I chose to live in France. He had a great interest in football, but I'm afraid I'm a rugby man. But, no, I would not have taken him for someone who was thinking of ending his life.'

'What was his job, exactly?'

'Something to do with the chemical trade. I didn't pay much attention. To speak honestly, I took very little interest in him. He was one more Englishman who finds himself in Burgundy and wonders why it isn't more like Carlisle.'

A car pulled up outside. 'Eh, bien, Monsieur,' said Duroc, 'There is the officer who will pass the night with you. I shall have a few words with him and then I will see you tomorrow.'

When DI Hiden appeared for his morning team briefing, his first action was to ask for confirmation of the make and colour of car the golfers had seen driving away as they raced down the hill after Matt Burns's shooting. His second was to explain why.

'Guv,' Anne Milton said. 'How many dark blue Vectras do you suppose there are in the south-east? Don't you think it would be an amazing coincidence if your daughter was the driver on the Burns murder?'

'Perhaps. But I'd like you to pass the information on to Essex. Suggest they have her in and give her a hard time. And they might want to do a forensic check on the Vectra she nicked. See if they can place it at the shooting.'

'Do they know she's your daughter?'

'Of course. Why else would we have taken an interest? You can remind them the fact buys her nothing.'

CHAPTER 26

Milton was delayed in making her call to Essex police by an excited message from St Pancras station. The photograph of Carver taken from the videotape of travellers joining the train had been shown methodically to every Eurostar attendant as they reported for duty. One of them had recognised it. Milton and Wylie got there as fast as London's creaking transport system would allow.

'We had to let her go,' the personnel officer said. 'She's French, Paris-based and she was rostered out this morning. It plays havoc with the Working Time Directive if we try to hold someone back. But she was adamant it was him. She's seen him before. Mademoiselle Lafontaine is a smoker herself, so she used to ask for one of the smoking carriages. There were never many—most of our Business Premier class accommodation has always been non-smoking. Now there are none. But when there were, Mister Carver always booked a smoking seat.'

'How do you know his name is Carver?'

'You haven't travelled with us, Sergeant? You should. Customers don't just rush for their places, you know. Your seat is assigned by name when you book. Mister Carver almost always sat at the very end of one of the smoking carriages, when we had them. That's how Mademoiselle Lafontaine could be so certain about where he was. I think he must be a bit of a charmer, Sergeant. She's obviously exchanged more than a few words with him since he began to travel.'

'I suppose he's never mentioned where he lives?'

'If he did, Mademoiselle Lafontaine didn't say so. But we can help you find out.' She pushed a photocopy of a credit card voucher across the desk. 'I'm sure American Express will have his address.'

DS Milton felt she was floating out of the station on the way to apply for a warrant requiring American Express to divulge Carver's home address. 'If you weren't so ugly, Constable,' she told Wylie, 'I'd kiss you.'

'If I weren't your junior, you mean.'

'That too,' Milton affirmed. Her mobile rang.

'Anne?', said the lilting voice at the other end. 'John Cooper here. In Cardiff.'

'John! How are you?'

'I'm fine, thanks. It's Clive Jones I'm calling about. He's disappeared.'

'Do you mind? I mean, is that a loss to South Wales?'

'No, it isn't. And for all we know, he's sleeping the sleep of the blessed at the foot of some disused mine shaft. We've enough of those, Heaven knows. But the word on the street is he knows who topped his cousin and he's looking for revenge.'

'He knows who did it? Are you sure about that?'

'Anne, what does sure mean in our business? People are saying Jones had been buying from Spain. They're saying the Spanish suppliers didn't like being cut out and they would have wanted to prevent it. But you know what we mean when we say "the word on the street." You know what kind of people pass this stuff on. Sell their grannies, they would, for the price of a fix. Sure? No-one's sure of anything. But, for what it's worth, there it is.'

'OK, John. And thanks. Let me know if you get anything else, won't you. Love to Bethan.'

'She sends her regards. Says give us more notice next time you come down and she'll do you proud.'

'It isn't like him,' Sharon said. 'He hasn't even called. It's like he's disappeared off the face of the earth.'

Jackie Gough nuzzled her ear. This was the third morning in a row he'd woken with Sharon beside him. He wondered whether she'd ever shown that degree of faithfulness to anyone. Even her husband.

'He might be home already,' he said. Maybe you should pop round and check.'

'If he was home he'd answer the phone. Something's happened.'

'He'll turn up,' Gough whispered, his hands pushing up her short nightdress. 'He probably can't work out how to use a French telephone.'

Sharon lifted herself slightly to make things easier for him. 'Oh, Jackie,' she breathed. 'You're dead good at this. I am worried about him, though. I'm going to have to talk to Jim Cameron, see what he knows.'

Gough raised himself into position. 'Would you like me to do that for you?'

'Oh, yes, please, Jackie. I don't like that Johnnie Walker. He hurt me. Oh, Jackie. Oh, that feels good. Oh, yes.'

It was not until midday that the Procureur de la République had appointed Madame Hurette to be Juge d'Instruction in the matter of Buggy's drowning. Since Duroc was still making his inquiries several miles down the Canal du Nivernais, Madame Hurette had to decide whether to demand his immediate return or to order his attendance next day. From what she could gather, it was a straightforward matter of a drunk falling overboard with no-one on hand to rescue him—and she did have other things to do. She chose the second option.

She was glad that she had done so since, when the interview began at ten the following morning, she had received from London a piece of information she could use to wrong foot the Captain. 'What do you make of this Englishman, Carver?', she asked.

Duroc shrugged. 'Amiable enough for a *rosbif*. A good judge of food and wine. Independent means. Has no need to work to support himself. Unfortunate to have got mixed up in a drowning.'

'Not a suspect?'

'Suspect? But Madame la Juge, a suspect in what? The dead man was drunk and alone when he fell into the canal. Monsieur Carver is a local resident of good reputation with a cast-iron alibi. How can you have a suspect where no crime has been committed? You can ease the workload of each of us by finding that the man Patterson died accidentally while drunk. Forgive me, Madame; I am no longer in the first flush of youth and sometimes it falls to me to offer advice to those younger than myself.'

The Judge eyed her target affectionately. She accorded him a little smile. 'Younger and, perhaps, less experienced, Capitaine?'

Duroc bowed his head for a moment. 'Experience is a strange thing, Madame la Juge. There is only one way to get it.'

'Indeed. A local resident of good reputation—I believe those were the words you used of Monsieur Carver?'

'They were, Madame.'

'And that is how your great experience leads you to see him?'

'It is, Madame.'

The judge's smile was broader now. She picked a piece of paper from her desk and made ostentatious show of reading it from head to tail. 'A local resident of good reputation,' she repeated. 'Then please tell me, Capitaine, why it is that Scotland Yard—you are familiar with Scotland Yard, Capitaine? Why it is, I say, that Scotland Yard have advised us that they would like to converse with this local resident of good reputation concerning matters of multiple rape and murder? Do your years of experience enable you to offer a suggestion on this matter, Capitaine?'

Madame Hurette sat back, the very picture of contentment. Duroc's face went pink, then red. His mouth opened and closed in silence. His fists clenched and unclenched. The Judge's air of goodwill waxed. 'Monsieur, I have a suggestion that may help us work together effectively. One that will make the best use of my talents and of yours. Would you like to hear it?'

Duroc nodded mutely.

'Well, Monsieur, what I propose is that I do the thinking for both of us. And that you do the doing for both of us. Your doing to be in strict accordance with the results of my thinking. There, Monsieur. Does that strike you as a good suggestion?'

Duroc nodded again.

'I'm sorry, Monsieur. I seem unable to hear you. Does my suggestion strike you as good?'

Duroc gritted his teeth. 'Yes, Madame. It does.'

'Thank you, Capitaine.'

'Do you wish me to have Carver sent under guard to London?'

Madame Hurette leaned back in her chair and stared at Duroc. 'Monsieur, you have just agreed to a method of proceeding and here you are, breaking it already. Send Carver under guard to London? For what? Where is their warrant? If they had strong evidence against him, their mandat d'arrêt and request for extradition would be in our hands. I said they wish to converse with him—nothing more. And so do we—do we not, Capitaine?'

Duroc nodded.

'I think, Monsieur, that we have first call on the conversational resources of a French resident on French soil in relation to an extremely interesting drowning in a French canal. Would you not agree?'

'Yes, Madame la Juge.'

'You will wish to see to it, Monsieur. Without saying a word to him of the English police's interest.'

'Yes, Madame la Juge. Shall we, at least, inform Europol that we are interviewing Carver?'

'Pourquoi?'

'Madame, we are under strict instructions to collaborate wherever possible with our European colleagues. Monsieur de Baynast de Septfontaines himself commanded...'

'Allow me, Monsieur, to know what a chef de service in the Ministry of Justice commanded. We are, as you say, to collaborate with our European colleagues. Colleagues, Monsieur. Are you familiar with the state of European collaboration in fighting crime?'

'No, Madame la Juge.'

'Then let me tell you, Monsieur. The countries of Europe have agreed to place magistrats de liaison in each other's judiciaries. Do you know how many such functionaries are in place right now? In Paris, monsieur, we have two—an Italian and a Dutchman. We ourselves have been permitted to place one in each of those countries and another in Spain. Do we have a magistrat de liaison in London? Non. Is there a British magistrat de liaison in Paris? Non. Do not speak to me of collaboration with Scotland Yard, Monsieur.'

'What, then, shall I tell them, Madame la Juge?'

You will tell no-one anything, Monsieur. *I* shall ask Europol to inform Scotland Yard that Monsieur Carver is not presently at home—which is the case, is it not?—and that we will be in touch again in due course, when we have more information. Understood?'

'Perfectly, Madame la Juge.'

'Good.'

'So let me be clear. You wish me to interview Monsieur Carver again?'

'I do. But not yet. What would you ask him? Whether he is implicated in the drowning of Monsieur Patterson? I think I can tell you his answer. No; first you must work on this Arbot from Accolay. Who is he, how does he earn his living, what questionable friends does he have, has he ever been in trouble with the law? Then see if you can establish beyond doubt what took him into that picnic stop.'

'But, Madame, we already know...'

'Monsieur, does it not strike you as odd that Monsieur Arbot did nothing to try to save the unfortunate Patterson? If you were present when a man fell off a boat, what would you do? Try to fish him out? Or drive to an auberge a mile away and call the gendarmerie?

'And note that, Monsieur—he called the police. According to your report, he burst in upon innocent people eating and drinking and cried out, "Faites le dix-sept! Quelqu'un s'est noyé dans le canal!" Call the police, someone has drowned in the canal! Why not "Faites le quinze"? Eh, monsieur? Why did this public-spirited Monsieur Arbot not call the Fire Brigade to rescue Monsieur Patterson? Was it because he already knew that he was dead?

'And why a picnic stop? Because he was caught short and needed a urinal? Monsieur, the men of Accolay would micturate without remorse from the top of the Tour d'Eiffel on an August afternoon before the Président de la République and his lady wife. I use the word "lady" in this context for reasons of form only, you understand.'

'Perhaps, Madame, he needed the public utility for something more, let us say, substantial...'

'Perhaps he did. You will check that out.'

'Eh? Madame...'

'Capitaine, the season will not begin for another six weeks at least. Very few people use the facilities in that picnic stop at this time of year. If anyone has moved his bowels there during the past twenty-four hours, the fact should be obvious. And if they have not...'

Duroc coughed apologetically. 'I'm afraid I know that they have. My men...I myself...'

Madame Hurette assumed an attitude of astonishment. 'Capitaine. You have assured me of your incomparable experience. Do you now tell me that you have allowed the adulteration of a possible crime scene?'

Duroc hung his head in silence. The judge allowed time to tick away. Then she said, 'What's done is done. Go to Accolay. Say and do nothing to alert Carver's suspicions. I shall send Monsieur Patterson's details to Europol and ask them to examine what sort of man Monsieur James Patterson was, and why he might really have been on a boat in the Nivernais with a fellow Englishmen wanted for interview in relation to rape and murder.'

'Do you at least wish me to mount a watch on Carver's home?'

'And warn him? Leave Monsieur Carver alone, Duroc. That is an order.'

Duroc turned to go. The judge had a further thought. 'This boat of Carver's. Its progress will have been leisurely and the Nivernais is, after all, the Nivernais. It will have been noticed. Find the people who noticed it, Monsieur. Learn what it was they noticed. And report back to me. But take care you do not arouse suspicion!'

CHAPTER 27

The standard approach in the case of a drowned citizen of another country, at least where foul play is not suspected, is to contact the dead person's embassy. If Madame Hurette had really wanted to keep the British police ignorant of her investigation, this might have been a better ploy than sending Patterson's details to Europol.

That was not the judge's primary concern, however. Having smelt a rat in Patterson's death, she saw a chance to enhance her own career. She did not want Carver whisked away to London before she had had time to establish whether there was French limelight to be enjoyed. Making a monkey of Captain Duroc had been a bonus. Her most urgent need was to establish what kind of man James Patterson was. When her own mark was securely on the case, she would hand it graciously to London. There was no need to go through all the tedium of an investigation here if the British would do it elsewhere.

She spent some time in wording the enquiry. It made no reference to Carver or the fact that the British police had made contact about him. Using the best equipment the French judiciary could command, she procured a stunningly good photocopy of the back page of Patterson's passport. This showed the number, issue date and expiry date. It gave Patterson's full name and date of birth and affirmed that he was a British citizen. It said when the passport had been issued and when it would expire. And it showed a picture of Buggy as clear as the ones that had dropped out of the machine in the post office five days before.

Within three hours, she had received a fax containing information that did not surprise her. James Robert Patterson had had a stroke some time ago. He claimed not to have looked for his passport for months because he was not likely to be travelling anywhere.

Perhaps it had been stolen. Perhaps, being no longer needed, it had been sold—by Patterson himself or some relative—to raise a little cash. Madame Hurette could make only three assumptions at this point. That the passport had passed into the pool of nefarious credentials in which criminals swim. That the drowned man was not James Patterson. And that the British police would be circulating his passport photograph in an attempt to find out who he really was.

When Sara Hiden was brought into Romford police station, she handed the custody sergeant a piece of paper with a name and telephone number. 'This your brief?' the sergeant asked.

Sara nodded.

'Will you agree to be interviewed before he gets here? It's going to take a while.'

'I'll wait for Mister Thompson.'

The sergeant sighed. 'You'll have to wait in the cells. Empty your pockets and your handbag, please.'

Upstairs, DS Longer made another call to DI Martin Hiden. "Just to keep him in the picture."

Hiden called Anne Milton into his office. 'Do we know someone called Owen Thompson?'

'Brief, isn't he? Unsavoury client list.'

'Thank you, Anne. He's representing my daughter.'

Milton sat down. 'Sara? Where does she get money for someone like him?'

'Beats me. Presumably someone else is paying. Get Wylie to

put together a list of everyone we know Thompson has represented. Let's see if there's a pattern.'

As Milton stood up to go, Wylie's head appeared around the door. 'Thought you'd be interested in this, Sarge.'

She studied the fax, then passed it wordlessly to Hiden. 'Someone we know?' Hiden asked.

'He's been calling himself Jim Patterson,' said Milton. 'Sharon Wright calls him Darling. Meet Buggy. Dead in France. Accidental drowning. About twenty miles from where Donald Carver lives.'

She turned to Wylie. 'Let's go and see what Shazza makes of the news.'

'Send Sammy Porter in,' said Hiden. 'He can make the list of Thompson's clients.'

It took two hours for Owen Thompson to arrive at Romford. If DS Longer and his guvnor, DI Smart, had hoped that the delay would test Sara Hiden's defences, they were disappointed. Her eyes, when not dead, looked amused.

'Miss Hiden,' said Longer. 'I wonder if you'd mind telling us where you were last Thursday?'

'Thursday,' said Sara. 'What day is it today?'

'Today is Monday, Miss Hiden. I'm asking you to cast your mind back four days.'

'Monday. No, I can't remember anything special about Thursday. I'm sorry.'

'Miss Hiden,' Smart said, 'Is it not true that at seven o'clock last Thursday morning, you drove a dark blue Vauxhall Vectra away from a Heathrow car park without the owner's consent?'

Owen Thompson put his hand on Sara Hiden's sleeve. 'I understand you have already asked my client about that car,

Inspector. I also understand that there is no evidence that the car was ever stolen.'

'We have video tape evidence showing your client at the wheel of the car when it left the car park.'

'You have video tape evidence showing a woman who looks not completely unlike my client at the wheel of the car.' He looked at Hiden. 'For the record and for the tape, Sara—did you steal a car last Thursday morning?'

The woman's voice was firm. 'No. I did not.'

'We have forensic evidence placing that car at the site of a fatal shooting some three hours after it was stolen,' said Longer.

'What evidence, Sergeant?'

'We're not at liberty to disclose the nature of our evidence at this stage.'

Thompson smiled. 'You'd disclose it fast enough if it would stand up in court. If you interviewed my client without disclosing it to me, you would have serious difficulty in any case you attempted to bring. This is a try-on, Inspector. And even if you did place the car near this supposed shooting, do you have any evidence to put my client in it at the time? No? I thought not. May we go now?'

Longer said, 'Miss Hiden. You cannot remember what you did last Thursday. Can you remember what you did on Wednesday—the day before?'

'In the morning, I... '

'You've already charged my client with an offence on that day, Sergeant. She has done everything possible to assist you.'

'That was in the morning, and the offence was the theft of a white Ford Mondeo from the same car park. What I'm interested in, Miss Hiden, was what you did after you stole the car. What did you do on Wednesday afternoon and evening?'

'I can't remember.'

'You can't remember. That Mondeo was later found burned out, Miss Hiden. There were two dead women in the boot.'

'Have you charged my client with complicity in their deaths, Sergeant?'

'Not yet, but...'

'My client would be very happy to assist you in finding the real culprits. I understand she has given you a very clear description of the man she delivered the Mondeo to. Do you not feel your time might be better spent in looking for him, instead of harassing my client about a crime she very clearly had nothing to do with?'

'Miss Hiden, it is something of a coincidence, is it not, that you were involved in the theft of two cars on successive days, both of which were used in murders?'

Sara Hiden looked at her lawyer. He sighed. 'Sergeant Longer. My client did not steal a Vauxhall Vectra on Thursday. Despite what you say, you have no evidence that would satisfy a court placing the car you refer to anywhere near a murder site. Nor do you have any evidence connecting my client with any murder victims. I think we have wasted enough time on this transparent fishing expedition. My client is on bail on the Mondeo charge. Do you intend to charge her now with the theft of a Vauxhall Vectra that is currently in the possession of its owner and was demonstrably never stolen?'

'Not at this stage.'

'Do you intend to charge her in connection with any deaths, whether on Wednesday or on Thursday?'

'Not at this stage.'

'Then may I ask what we are doing here? Let me make you this offer, Sergeant. I will drive Miss Hiden home and we will tour the streets of Hounslow in an attempt to jog her memory as to what she was doing last Wednesday afternoon and Thursday. As soon as she has remembered, I will write to you with a full account of her actions.'

'I've got to hand it to you,' said Longer. 'You're telling me you're going to help her cook up an alibi.'

Smart reached out a hand to the recording machine. 'Interview terminated at eleven fourteen.' He pressed the button that stopped the recording.

Thompson grinned at Longer. 'That was a most improper remark, Sergeant. I'm sure counsel will have a field day with the transcript, should anyone be stupid enough to bring this heap of shit to court.'

'She took it far worse than I'd thought she might,' said Milton. 'I mean, to say she's a total slut, she really did seem stricken with grief that he was gone. Jackie Gough was with her, by the way.'

'I've asked the Frogs to send us the fingerprints they find on the passport. Let's hope Gough's are on there.'

'It had been in the water, hadn't it?' said Milton.

Hiden shrugged. 'Let's lay it out. What do we know? An ex-gangster called Matt Burns is murdered. We're pretty sure Jim Cameron ordered the hit. The killer escaped in a car of the same make and colour as one stolen from a car park that morning and subsequently returned. Forensic tests show traces in various parts of the car's underbody of seeding grasses similar in type to grasses at the place where the murderer's car is known to have lain in wait.

'The previous day, the woman believed to have taken that car is known to have stolen another from the same place. This car was found burned out, with two bodies in the boot. Both victims were women. They were so badly burned that identification may still be a long way off. There is nothing to tie the car thief to the women's deaths. However, what is interesting about this woman, apart from the fact that she's my daughter, is her brief, Owen Thompson. Thompson is an expensive advocate who can get away with his level of fees because most of his clients walk. DC Potter has produced a list of the clients he has represented over the past two years. Five of those people are known or suspected associates of Jim Cameron.

'A man called Don Carver lives in Auxerre, in France. There is very strong evidence linking him to the murder of a drug courier in South Wales, which was a professional hit, and three rapes and a murder in north-west London, which seem to have been on his own account. We can find no link between Carver and Cameron, but Cameron may have sent John Wright, alias Buggy, to France and Buggy has turned up dead very near Auxerre in possession of a fake passport.

'We don't know who killed Matt Burns, but we do know that it wasn't Carver.

'How much of this can we prove? Not a lot, at present. Cameron ordering the hit on Burns is surmise—he had the motive, he could find the means and he'd certainly be willing to do it. The same grasses as we found in the Vectra grow wild all over England south of the Severn and we don't have a single letter from the licence plate of the car seen at the golf course. Cameron denies sending Buggy to France and the only judge who's going to hear Buggy's side of the story is Saint Peter. The evidence of rape against Carver is purely circumstantial until we can get a DNA sample from him. Likewise the killing of Julie Been—and, in that case, even a DNA sample would only prove that he'd been in the same place at some fairly recent time.'

'Surely a jury would convict on that?' said Milton.

'Who knows what a jury will do? Unless we can get a confession out of someone, the CPS isn't going to wear charges on what we have here. No charges, no warrant, no extradition request. Ideas, anyone?'

'Get Cameron in and ask him to explain his involvement?' said Potter.

'He'd laugh at us.'

'Lean on your daughter?' Wylie offered.

'Essex have done that. She's got a good brief, no doubt paid for by Cameron, and she knows exactly what to say.'

'He's right, though, guv,' Milton said. 'You can only crack a case by sticking the crowbar in at the weakest point. How many times do we catch professional hitmen?'

'Not often.'

'The weakest point has to be Sara. But if Cameron thinks she might grass him up...'

'...her life is over,' Hiden finished. 'Thank you, Anne.'

'I'm sorry, guv. Do you think Cameron knows she's your daughter?'

Behind the eyes Hiden turned to her she caught a sudden glimpse of agony. 'I don't know, Anne. And if he doesn't, I don't know what will happen when he finds out.'

CHAPTER 28

It was a question that came up again at lunchtime. Martin and Muriel Hiden rarely met now. Since their divorce, their life together had receded into another existence and they had little to say to each other.

'Does he know she's our daughter?' asked Muriel.

'We've got to assume he does now. What we can't know is: did he know before? If not, will he see her as a threat?'

'How do you suppose she got into this?'

Hiden shrugged. 'Muriel, face facts. There was never a time when Sara wasn't trouble. She was lying from the moment she could speak. She was shop-lifting at seven. She was bunking off school at twelve. In her last three years, I don't suppose she was there more than one day in three. The only thing she's ever bothered to do well is drive. Did you think she'd take a job on the buses?'

'I keep asking myself where we went wrong.'

'Do you? I've stopped that. Every time a kid goes bad, you can ask what the parents could have done differently. Some people are just wrong 'uns, Muriel. And we raised one.'

Muriel looked at him. 'It can't have been easy, though, can it? Having two coppers for parents.'

'Joanna did all right.'

'And it still can't have been easy. We both put our career first. We put it before each other, never mind the kids. We were never there. They had higher standards to live up to than other kids, just so they wouldn't mess things up for us.'

Hiden was silent for a while. Then he said, 'OK. So maybe that's all true. But she's still in trouble and there's still nothing we can do to get her out. All we can do is dig her further in.'

Muriel lit a cigarette. Hiden sighed. 'Are you still doing that?'

She ignored him. 'Why do you think Cameron sent this guy Buggy to France?'

'It's fairly obvious he sent him to meet Carver. My working assumption would be that Cameron had arranged for Carver to top Buggy over there. Why?'

'Cameron wanted Burns dead. He needed a hitman and he needed a driver. From what you've said, it sounds to me as though Buggy was some kind of middle-man for Cameron. A fixer. If that's right, it could have been Buggy who arranged the hit on Burns.'

'And Buggy who got Sara to drive the car.'

'Right. Assuming that Sara drove the killer to the golf course.'

'I'd forgotten how good a detective you are, Muriel.'

'Did you think I made DI on the back of being married to you?'

'Please don't start.'

'It's ten times harder for a woman to reach senior rank. Do you know that? If I'd had my brains and your testicles, I'd have been a Chief Super by now.'

'I'd no idea you were so bitter.'

'I'm not bitter. I'm a realist. And I think your working assumption is wrong.'

'How so?'

'This man Carver lives in France, but he's unknown to the police there. My guess is that he lives there but works here. If Cameron had wanted him to wipe Buggy, Carver would have come here to do it. If he did kill Buggy in France, it was because of something that happened there. And when you get the story from France...'

'Which I think is going to take a little while. The Frogs don't seem in any hurry to give us information.'

'...but when you do, I'd bet Carver will have a cast-iron alibi.'

'If you're right about Buggy being the man in the middle, Sara would know him.'

'She won't tell us that.'

'She might be interested to learn that Cameron had him killed for knowing too much.'

'That's devious, Marty. You should have been a woman.'

Madame Hurette read the Europol communication with interest. So James Patterson was really John Wright, also known as Buggy, an Englishman with no convictions but known criminal connections. She pondered whether Captain Duroc should have this information. On balance, she thought not. She herself would dearly like to know whether Carver knew the drowned man's real identity. Once let Duroc blurt it out and the chance of surprise would be lost.

Duroc had fed—and watered—his humiliation in private. To have been so treated at this stage in his career! And by a woman! And a younger woman, at that! Who was only able to take the high ground because she had information from which she had deliberately excluded him until he had committed himself beyond hope of extrication.

"I will do the thinking for both of us. And you will do the doing for both of us. Your doing to be in strict accordance with the results of my thinking." A captain of his experience to be spoken to like this! He threw back his third marc. Duroc never drank before lunch, at which time a half bottle of blanc would normally be his ration, yet here he was with three glasses of the rough, fiery spirit inside him and lunch still an hour or more away! Mon Dieu, but the woman would pay for what she had done to him.

He took his notebook from his pocket. Who is Arbot? What does he do? Who are his friends? Has he a record? And, most ludicrous of all, why did he stop at a public convenience to relieve himself?

Duroc had already interviewed Arbot, amiably at the man's home over a glass or two of something better than the vinegar he was forcing between his lips in this second rate whore's tavern. He was damned if he was now going to ask the man these ludicrous questions. He stood up, somewhat shakily, to make his way to the commissariat and rapidly thought better of it. Young Martin could come to him. When Martin had been briefed, he himself would begin the tour of the Canal, finding out who had seen what during the doubtless stately passage of Monsieur Carver's boat. He took the radio from his pocket.

Jackie Gough arrived at the Shepherd's Crook just before the appointed time. As before, the barman nodded him through into the back room. When Walker entered, it was from a door concealed in the panelling at the other end.

Walker grinned at Gough's surprise. 'You said it was urgent?'

'Did you know Buggy was dead?'

The smile drained from Walker's face. 'You didn't,' said Gough.

Walker sat down and threw his cigarette packet onto the table. 'How did it happen?'

'Sharon's had the police round. Apparently Buggy drowned in a canal. In France.'

'What was he...I don't understand. He should have been back by now.'

Gough raised a hand before him. 'Johnnie, please. Don't tell me anything about what Buggy was doing in France. I don't want to know. All I need is a story to tell Sharon. One that'll stick.'

'You telling me she gives a toss?'

'Sharon's a funny girl. For all the way she treated him, he was her husband and she cared about him. She could go to the police, Johnnie.'

Putting a cigarette to his lips, Walker focused directly on Gough. 'And tell them what? OK, you want a story for Shazza, I'll give you one. You say you've talked to Jim and he's told you, on his mother's life, whatever Buggy was doing in France it was nothing to do with us.'

'But she knows...'

'She knows what Buggy told her. It won't be the first time she found out he lied to her.'

'So where did he get the thousand quid?'

'How do we know where he got the thousand quid? He wasn't there for us. In fact, you can tell the lovely Sharon that Jim Cameron is thoroughly pissed off to have his name connected to a criminal deadbeat like Buggy and he might ask me to do something about it.'

'Johnnie, she knows Buggy did some stuff for you.'

'No, Jackie, she doesn't. She knows he said he did. He was making himself look big. She doesn't *know* anything. Jackie, it's no good sitting there looking worried. You wanted to play in the big league. Now you're here, you'd better play big league style. You know what Diego Costa has that someone playing on the Common doesn't? He gives himself time on the ball, Jackie. He has the confidence to know he's better than the next man. He trusts his own ideas on where he's going.'

Walker grinned. 'And he has a good coach, Jackie boy. Who

tells him what he needs to hear. And you need to hear two things. The first is that no-one with a good brief ever got sent down on hearsay evidence. Which is all it is when Shazza says Buggy worked for us.'

Gough nodded. 'What's the second thing I need to hear?'

Walker's grin became even wider. 'Remember this, Jackie. Sharon's got a nice body and she's good in bed. But there are lots of nice bodies around. There's only one Jim Cameron. Shazza can't have you crippled for life, Jackie. Know what I mean?' He winked.

Gough shivered.

'There's something you're wondering,' said Walker. 'You'd be very stupid to ask it. But I'll tell you, anyway. No, we did not plan to have Buggy killed. In fact, him being dead makes life very difficult for us. Is that what you wanted to know?'

Gough nodded.

'Is there any way that passport can be traced back to you?'

'The guy I got it from would never grass. And he bought it from a druggy in a pub in Colchester.'

Walker spread his arms wide. 'So you're in the clear. And we're in the clear. And you know what to tell Sharon. Come on. I'll buy you a drink.'

Walker was a little less laid back when he reported to Cameron.

'What the hell was he doing near a canal?' asked Cameron.

'Beats me.'

'Was it an accident?'

'Sharon can't have the body back yet. The French police are investigating.'

'They'd do that anyway, though. Wouldn't they? Like an inquest.'

Walker shrugged. 'I guess so.'

'Will Gough keep Sharon under control?'

'Gough'll be OK. Don't worry. He's gonna be a good guy, Jackie. And coming through this will make him stronger.'

'What about Carver? Who's gonna point him at Doyle when he gets here?'

'I dunno. What about the driver? The Hiden woman? Does she know where to find him?'

'Ask her. And get on to Mitchell. See what he knows.'

'OK, Jim. Jim? You know this Sara Hiden has the same name as the copper? Coincidence? Isn't it?'

'Not according to Owen Thompson.'

'Shit. Should we be worried about that?'

'Nah. She knows Buggy. And Buggy's dead. What does she know about us? Nothing.'

'So we let her be?'

'So we let her be. Much less risky than offing her. And who knows when we'll need a bit of leverage on a Detective Chief Inspector?'

The Canal, the road and the railway run south together—which is how Carver had been able to go so easily from the picnic site in Mailly-la-Ville to the station and then to the auberge. When Duroc told his wife he planned to cycle down the canal to make his enquiries, she looked at him as though he were mad. 'Drive, idiot,' she said. 'There isn't a building on the canal that doesn't also have road access.'

'Of course,' Duroc said. 'Drive. That is what I meant.'

'On the road,' said his wife.

'Of course on the road. Where else?'

Madame Hurette knew her people. You can't travel slowly down a Burgundy canal without someone watching every move.

They may not seem to look at you, but they see you all right.

Duroc was relatively sober by the time he met the judge again. Or, at least, he had got enough food into his stomach to offset most of the alcohol.

'So,' Madame Hurette said. 'There were three of them. Three men in a boat.' She looked at Duroc expectantly, but the reference had passed him by. The judge sighed. 'Carver. Mister...Patterson. And a Third Man. It's terribly literary, isn't it?' Once again, her questioning eye was met with a blank gaze.

'So who was the third man, Capitaine? And where did he go?'

'He was on board when the boat left Auxerre. He was still on board when it passed through the lock at Mailly.'

'And he was gone when you arrived later that evening.'

Duroc flourished his ace. 'The boat arrived at Mailly at six. The last train north left Mailly at seven. It was joined by one passenger. An English male. His description matches those of the man seen as the boat passed through the locks.' He placed a computerised photo-fit picture on the judge's desk with a triumphant gesture. 'This man, Madame la Juge.'

Madame Hurette laughed. 'Well done, Capitaine. A triumph of detection.'

Duroc, somewhat placated, waved a hand in a negligent gesture.

'And Arbot. What of him?'

Duroc looked at the floor. 'A petty criminal, Madame la Juge. Never brought to trial, but... He lives on his wits. Some poaching, some theft. Girls, occasionally—strictly amateur, you understand. A young wife, husband out of work; a mother, deserted by the father of her children. They offer supply, Arbot arranges demand. All amicable, no violence that we know of. A social service, you might say.'

'So. And this man turns up where a suspicious drowning takes place. Interesting, would you not say?'

'I fear so. Madame la Juge, I must apologise...'

'No need, Monsieur. I had information you had not. You were patronising towards me. I took my revenge. I think you will not patronise me again?'

'Madame, I have learned the greatest respect for you.'

The judge smiled. 'Then we shall do splendidly. Do we know where the man Carver is?'

'No, Madame. You ordered me...'

'...to stay away from him. Quite so. I should like you now to see whether Monsieur Carver is at home. Do so quietly. If he is not home, I may be minded to grant you a mandat de perquisition in respect of his house.'

'A search warrant? But what would I be looking for?'

'That I do not know, monsieur. But if there is anything there, you will find it. And you will know that you have found it.'

She stared at the ceiling, fingers steepled in contemplation. 'And I think it might be time to inform the police in Britain of the place we have reached.'

241

The observational powers that had so pleased Madame Hurette worked both ways. Carver, Buggy and Mitchell had travelled down the canal and been watched. Duroc had travelled the same stretch, asking questions as he went—and he had been watched, too. Eric Arbot learned before Madame Hurette did that the captain of gendarmes had a photo-fit picture of Mitchell.

It was not long before Carver knew it, too.

'Where have you stashed Monsieur Doyle?' asked Carver.

'He is in the *Ibis,* Monsieur. On the Dijon road just outside Tonnerre. Would you like me to fetch him?'

'No. We may be watched. Can you arrange for someone to drive him to a meeting place?'

'But of course. May I suggest?'

'Go ahead, Monsieur.'

'Tonnerre is in the valley of the Armançon. To the north, across the river, the hillside is very steep. On the Coussegrey road is a crossroads for Dannemoine. It is at the very top of the hill. You can see for miles. If anyone watches you, or follows, you will see them.'

Hiden threw the faxed photo-fit across his desk. 'Anyone recognise this man?'

Anne Milton and Duncan Forrest shook their heads.

'No good showing it to you DCs,' Hiden said. 'You're too young to remember him.'

'You know who it is, guv?' asked Milton.

'Oh, yes. This is Malcolm Mitchell. Once Detective Sergeant Mitchell, since defrocked. Mitch and I are old friends.'

'Was he bent?' Forrest asked.

'As a wire coat-hanger,' Hiden said. 'But an amiable colleague, a good drinking companion and a skilled detective—when he hadn't been bought. I wasn't working with him when the wheels came off, so I didn't know what happened. But I've been talking to the man who was his guvnor then. A sometime DI called Gornal.

'It seems Mitch was selling information. If you could afford to pay, Mitch would let you know who the witnesses were, what they were saying—and where they lived. A few people got seriously hurt by Mitch's activities. One or two ended in wheelchairs. Some may even have died—who knows?

'Some people may have suspected him, but so what? He wasn't the only person doing it.' Hiden looked at his colleagues. 'Let's face it, some people in this building are still doing it. And we've got the CPS now, which we didn't have then, and some of them are doing it, too. Information is power. When you've got information in one set of hands and money in another, there'll always be middlemen to bring the two together.

'Then, it seems, Mitchell got really lucky. Who remembers the Longshaw robbery?'

Anne Milton nodded. 'I was a probationer, so it was, what— fifteen years ago?'

'All of that. A gang of blaggers got away with more than five million quid. That isn't peanuts now and it was worth a lot more then. They were clean gone. It was uncanny. There wasn't even a whisper on the street. No-one knew who'd done the job. Of course, someone always knows, but whoever it was was either well rewarded or terrified.

'Then we got a lead. I say "we" but I wasn't involved. Mitchell was, though. Gornal's team had three men in their sights, including the shootist. Did I mention that? Two security guards had died in the heist. And it wasn't the usual blasting away with sawn-off shotguns; they had a marksman. The killings were planned. They were meant to intimidate and they did.

'We had an armed squad closing in. And when it got there...'

'The birds had flown,' said Forrest.

'And so had the evidence. When the inquest started, all the forensics were missing. Mitchell's guvnor carried the can. He was broken to Constable and he never made it back to DI. When he retired it was on a reduced pension. He's a very bitter man. And he's convinced Mitchell was responsible.

'More than a year later, another villain was nicked. It was for something trivial, but his wife was playing around on him and he knew, if he went down, he'd lose her. He offered information in return for walking. The gist was that he'd been involved in getting half a million quid to an account Mitchell had in Switzerland. He had the account details and everything. Naturally, they talked to Mitchell, but he wasn't coughing and how could you force him? The Swiss wouldn't confirm or deny anything. Then, you'll be amazed to know, the informant was shot dead—but this time the gunman made a mistake. He was seen in his car moments before the killing. Except that we couldn't prove the driver was the killer and the child who'd seen it hadn't seen the driver's face anyway and probably wouldn't have been allowed to testify if he had. He was seven and he was collecting car numbers.'

'I didn't know anyone still did that,' said Forrest.

'Well, there you go. But before anyone can get to the owner, he walks into his nearest police station...'

'And reports his car stolen?' suggested Milton.

'You have it in one. By one of those coincidences that make life so fascinating, it had disappeared about three hours before the witness was shot. The assumption is that Mitchell called him and told him we had the registration number. And *then*—and you're not going to believe this—the car turned up on a patch of waste land. Burned out.'

'So we had nothing,' said Forrest.

'So we had nothing. But still the saga continues. Gornal, who used to be a DI and is now a constable, hasn't given up chasing Mitchell, whom now he has to call "Sarge". He thinks he can put a dent in the owner's alibi for the time the witness was shot. Of course, he isn't a detective now, he's a beat copper, and he wouldn't be on this case anyhow, but he pursues it and gets some information that Mitch's new guvnor thinks isn't worth even putting to the owner. But he tells Mitchell he thinks it is.'

'And Mitchell tells the owner, and the owner scarpers,' said Milton.

'Spot on. And this is the point where the Met says to Mitchell, "Sergeant, we have nothing on you we can bring to court, but we'd like you to go and never come back. And we're not too keen on warming your days of ease with a pension." And Mitchell laughs in their faces and says, in effect, that they can stuff their pension where it's always dark and often malodorous. And off he goes. To Spain. Where he has many friends from his earlier days. But where had the car owner scarpered to, I hear you ask?'

'Where had the car owner scarpered to, guv?' asked Wylie.

'Good question, Constable. You'll go far. He had scarpered...'

'...to France,' said Forrest.

'How *did* you guess?'

'It was Carver?' asked Milton.

'That wasn't the name he went under at the time, Anne. But, yes. After speaking to Gornal, I think we have to believe it was Carver.'

'What's the story, then, guv?' asked Wylie. 'Buggy, Mitchell, Carver. All in France. Why? And now Buggy's dead. What's that about?'

'Well, for a start, I think I got it wrong. I thought Cameron had sent Buggy to Carver to be killed. I told Muriel that and she said No. She said Carver lives in France and kills in Britain and if he was going to kill Buggy he'd have come here. I think she must be right. Because, if Cameron sent Buggy to be killed, he'd only have needed to tell Carver what Buggy looked like. He wouldn't have needed to involve Mitchell.

'The way it looks now is that Cameron didn't know Carver. Mitchell knew Carver and Cameron knew Mitchell. Mitchell would also have known Buggy, because he was a sergeant when Buggy was at school and learning to be the kind of naughty boy sergeants have to get acquainted with. So Cameron gets Mitchell to travel from Spain to France, meet Buggy and vouch for him to Carver. How does that look?'

'It looks good so far,' said Forrest. 'And it means that Cameron has a job he wants Carver to do. But why does he need a new hitman? He got someone to top Burns and we haven't a clue who it was. Why not use the same man?'

'Pass,' said Hiden.

'And why send Buggy at all?' asked Milton. 'Why not just get Mitchell to travel to Auxerre and say, "Go to England and shoot this guy for us"?'

'That I can answer. Hitmen are deeply suspicious by nature. They take a lot of risks and they like to know what they're getting into. Whoever shot Burns was guided to the spot, and had Burns pointed out to him, by someone. Possibly my daughter. Whoever Carver was going to shoot, Buggy would have taken him there. But now Buggy's dead.'

'So will the hit still take place? And who is the target?'

'I don't know the answer to either of those questions, Anne. Cameron could probably answer at least one of them. And so could Mitchell.'

'But neither of them will.'

'We have no levers. Even if we did, Mitchell won't grass. It isn't his style. And Cameron would be putting his own head on the block. We're not completely without resources, however. We know how Carver travels to England—he comes by Eurostar. I've asked for a watch for him. And let's remember he's still wanted here for questioning on three rapes and two murders.'

'None of which we can be sure will stick to him without a confession,' said Forrest.

'Well, we won't get a confession. So when he gets here, there's no point in picking him up. We'd gain nothing and he'd know we were onto him. We'll have to follow him wherever he goes. We'll have to catch him in the act. Whatever the act turns out to be.'

The landlord opened the door of a small flat in Archway, then stood back to allow the policeman who had called him to enter first. 'I hope this is going to be all right,' he said.

'The neighbour says there's been no-one here since last Wednesday.'

'It's only Monday today.'

'I know. But the neighbour says they never went away without telling her.'

'Well,' the landlord repeated, 'I just hope this is going to be all right. If there are any complaints, you'll have to deal with them.'

The policeman nodded. In a large glazed pot, white lilies had died. He moved into the bedroom. In the centre of the bedspread was a note. The policeman picked it up.

> Caroline
> You can trust the person who brings
> this. Please come to me. Say nothing to
> anyone or we may never see each other
> again
> Love
> Mel

'Well, I dunno,' the policeman said. 'I'll take this with me. If you hear anything, let me know?'

The landlord nodded. The policeman knocked at the next door flat to give the neighbour the same message.

High above Tonnerre, Doyle and Carver stared down into the valley of the River Armançon. The wind blew fresh over the upland fields. They were sure no-one was watching them.

'Mitchell's safely back in Spain?' asked Doyle.

'Must be by now.'

'And the police have no way of knowing he lives there, unless we tell them.'

'Or the British police do.'

'I hadn't realised they knew him. But that isn't why we're here, is it? You're concerned this Duroc guy isn't as happy as you thought he was.'

'Arbot thought he'd bull-shitted him fine. I thought I had. And yet he's asking who was on the boat. And now he knows there was a passenger I didn't mention. He's bound to see that as suspicious.'

'So what do we do?'

'Nobody's seen you. Go back to England as soon as possible. Now, in fact. The driver who brought you here will take you to get your bag, then to Laroche-Migennes. Go straight to Paris and take the Eurostar. I'll follow in a couple of days.'

'How will we meet up?'

'Buy one of those mobile phones you fill up as you go along. You don't need an account for them. Give a false name. As soon as you've got a number, leave it on my answering machine.'

'Will you be safe here?'

'What am I wanted for? I was in an auberge, eating in front of witnesses, when Wright died. They can ask me questions but they'll have to let me go.'

'You want me to meet you at St Pancras?'

Carver shook his head. 'Make it Heathrow. I'll let you know the flight number. I always go by train. We don't know how much they know, but maybe they know that.'

CHAPTER 30

Hiden was out of the office when Sharon Wright walked in. Anne Milton and Forrest saw her together.

The young woman lit a cigarette and stared at the table. 'You're not recording this, are you?'

Milton decided to ignore the illegal cigarette. 'No, Sharon,' she said. 'It's just between us three.'

Sharon looked at Forrest. 'Can we make it between us two?' she asked. 'Does she have to be here?'

'We could get a WPC?' said Milton.

'I'd rather not have a woman here.'

'We have to have a woman when a woman is interviewed,' said Forrest. 'Make up your mind about that. And whatever you have against successful women, try to forget about it.'

Sharon stared mutinously at Milton. Gently, the DS said, 'What did you want to tell us, Sharon?'

The young woman dragged hard on her cigarette. 'I don't want to get Jackie in trouble.'

'Jackie Gough?'

Sharon nodded. 'Been good to me, Jackie has.' Forrest glanced the ghost of a smile in Anne's direction. 'Yes, yes,' Sharon snapped, 'He's good in bed and all that. But he's looked after me over Buggy.'

She looked on the verge of tears.

'Why did Buggy go to France, Sharon?'

'He had a job to do for Cameron. He wouldn't tell me what it was. Cameron gave him a grand up front.'

'Cameron denies that,' said Forrest. 'Cameron says he hardly knew Buggy.'

'That's rubbish. Buggy was always doing things for Cameron.'

'Like what, Sharon?'

The woman shrugged. 'Buggy was a messenger boy. Whatever Cameron needed, he'd send Walker to tell Buggy what to do and pay him.'

'Yes, Sharon, but what sort of things? What might Cameron send Johnnie Walker to tell Buggy to do?'

Sharon squirmed on her seat. She lit another cigarette, which Milton again ignored. For all Sharon's distress, she noted, she was still immaculately made up, her lips still burnished red, the fading bruise around her eye carefully powdered over. The DS scolded herself for intolerance. Sharon was merely acting in character. She was distressed, all right. Buggy's death had hit her hard.

'Cars,' she said. 'Drivers.'

'What?'

'Say Cameron needed something taken from one place to another. Or some person. Buggy would find a driver. And he'd arrange to have a car nicked. Or he'd find a driver who nicked her own cars.' She caught herself.

'Her own cars?' said Milton. 'Buggy used a woman?'

'Her cars, his cars,' Sharon shrugged. 'You know. I was just talking in general.'

'No, you weren't, Sharon. You were talking very much in particular. Buggy knew a woman driver who could steal cars to order.'

Sharon said nothing.

'Did you know her name, Sharon?'

'No, I never...'

'Was her name Sara, Sharon?'

The young woman's eyes flicked desperately from one DS to the other. 'This isn't about Buggy. Buggy's dead. You can't touch him now. And I don't want him fitted up with everything just because he's not here to defend himself.'

'OK, Sharon,' said Forrest. 'Let's talk about Cameron. Did Cameron ever send Walker to ask Buggy to find a hitman? A killer?'

'A killer? Buggy?' Sharon laughed. 'That would be a bit out of Buggy's league, you know? Buggy was cars and drivers. Deliveries. Messages. Buggy wouldn't know a hitman.' She smiled fondly at Forrest. 'You didn't know my Buggy, Mister Forrest.'

'Ever seen this man, Sharon?'

Sharon glanced at the video still of Carver that Anne Milton pushed across the table. 'Nah. Never seen him.'

'How about this one?'

Sharon looked at Mitchell's picture with more interest. There was a touch of wistfulness in her smile. 'Oh, yeah. I remember him. Sergeant Mitchell. He's lost a lot of hair.'

'When did you last see Sergeant Mitchell, Sharon?'

She laughed. 'Years ago. When he...you know.'

'No, Sharon, we don't know. When he what?'

'Well, when he...it wasn't just with me. All the girls...you must know.'

Anne knew she didn't want to deal with this one. She looked at Forrest. Forrest said, 'Sharon. Are you saying that Mitchell had sex with you?'

'Not sex, no. Not proper sex. He just...he'd get you to do things to him. If your boyfriend was in trouble. You know.'

'To do things.'

'Yes. You know. Do I have to go into all of this?'

Forrest sighed. 'No, Sharon, you probably don't.'

'I was about fourteen, Mister Forrest. Buggy got into trouble. Mister Mitchell could have had him sent away.'

'Unless you did things to him.'

'Yeah. So I did. It didn't bother me. He wasn't nasty or nothing. He was always clean, which is more than you can say for some people. He was a bit of a gent, Mister Mitchell.'

'Sharon,' Anne Milton said. 'Have you seen Sergeant Mitchell again? With Buggy, maybe?'

'Nah. I haven't seen him since I was at school. Why?'

'Sharon. Would you be surprised to know that Sergeant Mitchell was on the boat Buggy fell off?'

Sharon's eyes grew large. 'Surprised? I'd be bloody amazed.'

Milton put her finger on the picture of Carver. 'And this man owned the boat. Are you sure you've never seen him?'

Sharon shook her head. 'No. Sorry. Never saw him in my life. He got a name?'

'The name he goes under is Carver,' Milton said. 'We know that Mitchell and Carver know each other. We think that Cameron knew Mitchell. What we desperately need to know is whether Cameron and this man Carver knew each other, or whether Mitchell had gone to France to introduce Buggy to Carver.'

'Why would Buggy want to meet him?'

'Carver is a hitman, Sharon. He kills people for money. We think Cameron wanted Buggy to hire Carver to kill someone over here. But something went wrong and Buggy died. Maybe accidentally. Maybe not. But there was a killer on that boat, Sharon.'

Sharon stared at each of them in turn.

'You said you didn't want to get Jackie Gough into trouble,' said Forrest. 'What do you know that might do that?'

'Nothing. There isn't anything.'

'It's off the record, Sharon.'

'Nothing's off the record with you lot.'

'Sharon. There are two killers running around.'

'Two? But...'

'Two. One of them almost certainly killed Buggy. Someone else killed a man called Matt Burns last week. We know Cameron is planning at least one more murder. If Jackie Gough is involved in that, we can't help. But we can ignore a little naughtiness on the side, if it helps us catch a killer.'

Sharon's brow furrowed miserably.

'Buggy would have needed a passport to go to France,' Milton said. 'He didn't have one. I know, because I checked with the Passport Office. Jackie Gough has done passports before. Did he do this one?'

Sharon nodded. Tears squeezed out of the corners of her eyes.

'How do you know, Sharon?'

'I was there, wasn't I? When Jackie brought it round.' She looked up, glaring at the two police officers. 'But he didn't know what Buggy was doing in France. I asked him and he didn't. Said if it was for Cameron he didn't want to know.'

The grieving look remained on Sharon's face all the way out of the police station and onto the street. She was still wearing it as she reached the pedestrian crossing on the corner. It was not until she was safely on the other side and had passed out of sight of anyone watching from the station's upper windows that she allowed a smile to touch her lips.

Buggy's death was sad, of course it was, and some of the tears she'd shed for him had been real. But it did slacken the hold on her of this life she so much wanted to leave behind. Jackie would know soon the extent of the trouble he was in. Within a few hours, she should be able to get him to take the step that would release her from what few chains remained.

A cruising police car scooped Jackie Gough off the pavement and drove him to the police station. DC Wylie put two new cassettes into the machine, started recording and dictated the date and time and the names of the three people present.

Anne Milton said, 'Thanks for coming in, Jackie.'

'I didn't know I had a choice.'

Wylie said, 'Mister Gough, let me get straight to the point. You've been spending a lot of time recently at the Shepherd's Crook. It doesn't seem to have been one of your traditional watering holes. The Shepherd's Crook belongs to Jim Cameron. When we met recently, you denied knowing that Jim Cameron had criminal interests.'

Gough looked from Wylie to Anne Milton. 'What's this about?'

'We understand from Sharon Wright that you have been acting as an intermediary between her and Mister Cameron. Would you care to comment on that?'

Gough licked his lips. 'I don't know what you're talking about.'

'No? For the tape, do you want to deny acting as intermediary between Sharon Wright and Jim Cameron?'

'Until you tell me where this is going, I'm not confirming or denying anything.'

'Perhaps you'd like us to get a brief for you, Jackie?' said Milton. 'Who would you like? Owen Thompson?'

'What are you up to?'

'Did you hear Mad Dan Ablett is back on the street?'

'You bastard.'

'Poor old Dan,' Milton went on. 'Went out on a job. Just a routine blag. Only, when he got there, the police were waiting for him. Ten years he went down for. Think of the time he must have spent banged up, wondering who'd grassed. What do you think he'd say if he knew it was you, Jackie?'

'Why are you doing this?'

'And what did you get out of it? Twenty quid. Twenty pounds, for ten years of a human being's life. Well, five, after remission.'

'Why are you doing this?'

Milton leaned forward. 'This tape is useless to us, Jackie. If we tried to use it against you, any decent brief would get it thrown out, on account of what it would tell the jury about you. But think what would happen if it came into Ablett's hands.' She turned to Wylie. 'Do you know why they call him Mad Dan?'

'Didn't he bite someone's balls off?'

'I think they made that up, to be fair,' Milton said. She looked at Gough. 'But he did throw his best mate off a tower block because he thought he'd messed with Dan's sister. Jackie, you're looking pale. Would you like a cup of tea?'

'Turn the tape off.'

'We handle snouts differently now, Jackie.'

'Turn the tape off.'

'Registered informants, that's what we have. Conversations have to be in the presence of two officers. And if we hope to use them in evidence, we have to record them.'

'Turn the tape off.'

'It's the Police and Criminal Evidence Act, Jackie. No-one trusts a copper's word any more.'

'Turn the tape off.'

Milton nodded at Wylie, who pressed a button on the recording machine.

'What do you want?' said Gough.

'You are acting as Sharon's go-between with Cameron?'

'I've talked to him a couple of times.'

'And if Cameron accepts you as go-between, you're working for him. You've taken Buggy's place. Right, Jackie?'

'No comment.'

'So what we want, Jackie, is for you to be our inside line to Cameron. Whatever he knows, whatever he plans to do, you will tell us.'

'You must be barmy.'

'Because, if we don't have your complete co-operation, we will see to it that Mad Dan Ablett gets that tape. We'll also make copies of it and give them to Cameron and various other people you and I can both think of with no effort at all.'

'You disgust me.'

'It's mutual, Jackie.'

CHAPTER 31

The following day was Tuesday—eight days since Stacy Teasdale had opened the door to Carver, seven days since he had ended Julie Been's life in Cardiff and six days since Caroline and Melanie had perished in a burning Mondeo. In the afternoon, Duroc reported to Madame Hurette that Carver's house appeared to be empty and that his car, whose licence number had been circulated throughout the local gendarmerie on an observation-only basis, was parked at Laroche-Migennes station. Showing his picture to the booking clerks had produced the information that Monsieur Carver had taken a train for Paris that morning. He was carrying a bag substantial enough for a trip of several days.

'I shall give you a mandat de perquisition,' said the judge. 'Let us see what we can find in Monsieur Carver's home.'

Duroc arrived at Carver's house with the people and the equipment he would need to force an entry. They were unnecessary. The house may have been empty when Duroc's men had checked it at lunchtime, but Madame Poitou was now in place, duster in hand. Duroc showed her his search warrant and ushered his men inside. Madame Poitou's face was unperturbed, her expression unreadable. Casually, she draped a heavy embroidered cloth over a large wooden box and sat on it. She leaned over, took an ashtray from the table and set it down on the box beside her. From her handbag she took a packet of cigarettes and a lighter. Duroc watched her. 'What do you think you're doing?'

'You don't expect me to try to clean the place while your goons are throwing everything around, do you? Get on with your work, and then I'll get on with mine.'

There was nothing. They looked upstairs and down. They tried the bedrooms, bathrooms and living rooms. They tested floorboards, peered into cisterns, emptied drawers, ransacked pockets, dug deep into tins of flour and sugar. Nothing.

Duroc, who had not known what to expect, nonetheless felt cheated that two hours effort had produced no result. He looked at Madame Poitou. How he would have liked to wipe that smug smile from her face. 'If you have any way of contacting Monsieur Carver, you will not do so. Is that understood?'

Madame Poitou shrugged. She stubbed her cigarette into the ashtray. 'Are you going now? May I proceed with the work I am paid for?'

Duroc stared at her. 'What is that you are sitting on?'

'Pardon?'

'I said...just get up. All right?'

Madame Poitou remained glued to the embroidered rug. 'Do not speak like that to me, Monsieur.'

'Madame, if you do not rise this moment, I shall have you arrested for obstruction. Now *get up*.'

Madame Poitou remained where she was. 'I am sitting on a seat, Monsieur. What do you suppose I am sitting on?'

Duroc turned to the gendarme beside him. 'Remove her.'

He swept the embroidered covering to the floor. 'Seat? This is not a seat, Madame.' To the gendarme, he said, 'The breaking equipment. In the van. Bring me an axe.'

Madame Poitou sighed. 'There is no need for that.' Removing the hairpin from her wispy grey head, she knelt before the chest. There was a soft click. She stood back. Duroc raised the lid.

Madame Hurette picked up one of the books and flicked through it. 'I hope, Capitaine, that you have not been reading this material. I would not like to see you corrupted on official duty.'

'My English would not allow it, Madame. But the pictures...'

'Ah, yes. The pictures. Monsieur Carver is a man of, let us say, exotic tastes. A cruel man, in fact.' She turned her attention to the small pile of underwear. 'Each of these has its own index slip? A person's name, and a date?'

'Just so, Madame la Juge.'

'Remarkable. And you say the woman, this...'

'...Madame Poitou, Madame la Juge.'

'...quite, this Madame Poitou, she knew what was in the box?'

'She did, Madame.'

'Incroyable. She did not care what sort of man she worked for?'

'She described Monsieur Carver as a perfect gentleman.'

'A perfect gentleman. It might be interesting to meet Monsieur Poitou.'

'Just so, Madame. She said also that it takes all sorts to make a world.'

'Pah. It does not take all sorts, Capitaine. We merely have all sorts. And one of these index slips was found without its garment?'

'Indeed so. The name on the slip is Stacy Teasdale. The date is this month.'

'But there was also a garment without a slip?'

'Old, Madame la Juge, and faded. It was not from this month. Not even this decade.'

'I suppose we shall have to send a list of these names and dates to London. Before I do so, arrange to check with all the carriers. Airlines, ferries, rail. Has anyone taken Monsieur Carver to England? Or anywhere else, for that matter.'

'I shall see to it, Madame. There is one other thing...'

'Yes?'

'While we were checking the box, Monsieur Carver's telephone rang. I allowed his answering machine to take the message. A man called Smith. In English. With a telephone number.'

He placed his open notebook on the judge's desk. 'I don't recognise that format,' she said.

'I have already spoken to France Telecom, Madame. It is an English mobile phone number. They contacted their opposite numbers in London. This number was allocated this morning to a Mister Smith.'

Clive Jones would have done better to stick to thieving. His Spanish suppliers were not pleased when they found out he was dumping them in favour of his uncle. Drug supply is not about family loyalties; it is about money, power and fear. To scare Clive back into the fold they had contacted Been on Clive's behalf, arranging a delivery he knew nothing about. Then they had sent Carver to kill the courier on a lonely Welsh hillside.

Instead of getting the point, Clive had thrashed around trying to find out who had topped his cousin. Never imagining it might have been his erstwhile partners, he asked for their help. Cutting their losses, they supplied him with a name. And an address.

Clive came off the aircraft in Orlando and made straight for the Hertz desk. He drove to the place where the Spaniards had said he would receive help. 'I'm Clive Jones,' he said in an accent the two Floridians had never heard before. 'You have a gun for me.'

'Indeed we do, Mister Jones,' said the older of the two men. 'Here it is.' And raising the Smith & Wesson, he placed a bullet exactly midway between Clive's eyebrows.

Later, as darkness fell, the men tied a heavy coil of steel wire securely to Clive's legs and carried him out of the back of the building to where a boat waited. Eleven hours after leaving Wales for only the third time in his life, Clive went over the side into half a mile of water bluer and warmer than a Welshman could dream of.

John Cooper left the file open for a year or two, and the death of Julie Been and disappearance of her cousin entered Welsh CID folklore. But all memories fade. The Spanish suppliers found other outlets. Someone else began to steal to order for the East European car export trade. And John and Bethan Cooper raised three children, not one of whom even thought of a career with the police.

French time is an hour ahead of English, and Madame Hurette had in any case been in no special hurry to pass her information to Europol. It was early Wednesday afternoon before DI Hiden was able to report to his troops.

'I don't believe this,' said Forrest. 'Every time Carver takes a pair of knickers, he records who he stole them from?'

'And when,' Hiden confirmed. 'There are thirty-eight names and dates. I want Wylie and Porter to check them against known incidents.'

'Are the ones we know there?' asked Milton.

Hiden picked up the list. 'Teasdale. Torton. Bolan. Trimnor. All there.'

'That's a case the CPS can't deny,' said Milton. 'Are we watching the Eurostar terminal?'

'We were,' Hiden said. 'Thanks to the frogs, we know that Carver passed through Heathrow at four o'clock yesterday afternoon. He's here, children.'

The two Detective Sergeants stared at him.

'He could be anywhere,' Forrest said.

'I've faxed his picture to Heathrow. We know what terminal he came through. They've got wall-to-wall video down there. I want to know if anyone met him and how they left the airport.'

'What will that tell us?' asked Milton.

'It'll tell us if anyone met him and how they left the airport. Look, how do I know what it'll tell us? It's routine, all right? I'm after facts, detail, links in the chain.'

'What's this telephone number the French picked up?'

'Now that could be quite useful. It was registered by a dealer at Waterloo. One of those phones where you pay in advance, so they don't need to do credit checks or take identification. We got a description of "Mister Smith". I'll circulate it—it doesn't sound like anyone I know.'

'How traceable are the calls?'

'Very, given time. We know he only made one call on it yesterday and that was to Carver's home in France.'

'The call the gendarmes intercepted.'

'Presumably. He made that call from Heston Service Station on the M4. We've served an order requiring the phone company to inform us whenever a call is made to or from that number and to tell us where it is. I've talked to the supervisor so she knows what's at stake. We'll get co-operation.'

'No action today, I suppose?' asked Milton.

'Not so far.'

CHAPTER *32*

Carver looked with distaste at his cup. 'Why can't you get decent coffee in England?'

'This is a pub, Don,' Doyle said. 'It cost us thirty quid to stay here last night.'

'For thirty quid in France...'

'You're not in France. You're in England. You pay more here, for less. That's how it is. Now finish your breakfast and let's get moving.'

'I'm finished.'

'Fine. So what's first?'

'Cameron's first. He's expecting to hear from me. Does he know Buggy's dead? Who knows? But he's paid me to come over here and top you. So I'll get in touch. Tell him I'm here. And then you and I will deal with him.'

'Do you think the French police will have been in contact?'

'We'd better take it that the British police know Buggy is dead. Whether that means they're looking for me, we can't know. If you can't be sure the police don't know something, assume they do.'

'Where will you go when we've done Cameron?'

Carver shrugged. 'Back to Auxerre. Why not? What have they got on me? They'll never get anything out of Arbot. Buggy isn't going to make a statement. '

Doyle said, 'OK. So while we're doing Cameron, we have to make sure the police think you're somewhere else—if they know you're over here at all.' He picked up the mobile. 'You know these things are traceable?'

264

'No more so than any other phone, surely?'

'No more, but no less. Give the law time, they can tell exactly where you are.'

'So how does that help? The police don't know about this phone.'

'We'll let them know.'

'How?'

Doyle grinned at Carver. 'The driver who took me on my job for Cameron was a woman. You want to know who her father is?'

They met in a Costa Coffee outlet off Oxford Street. Doyle smiled quietly when Carver stared into his cup, drank it empty and went to the counter for a second double macchiato. 'More shit English coffee?'

'When did this place open?'

Doyle shrugged. 'There's a chain of them. They've been around a while now.'

Sara Hiden said, 'I just want to say there are people who know where I am.'

Carver said, 'This is good coffee.'

'You don't say?'

Sara began, 'I just want to say there are people who know...'

'As you said,' Doyle said. 'You don't trust anyone.'

'Why are we here?'

Carver leaned across the table, speaking quietly, his eyes constantly checking the people at other tables. 'A man called Buggy hired you to take my friend here...'

'Doyle. She knows my name is Doyle.'

'...OK, to take Mister Doyle here on a job.'

'Did he?'

Doyle said, 'Buggy's dead, Sara.'

She stared at him in silence.

'He was killed by a man called Cameron,' Carver said. 'That name ring any bells?'

'Should it?'

'I've no idea. Look, Sara, we're on your side. Cameron...you tell her, Doyle.'

'It was Cameron who arranged for the hit on Matt Burns. But you know that. I remember you explaining why Burns had to die.'

'The police have already asked me about this. They know I was nowhere near Burns when he died.'

Carver said, 'Sara. Three people were involved in the hit on Burns. Buggy—and he's dead. Doyle here—and Cameron has contracted me to kill him.'

Sara raised an eyebrow.

'If Doyle and I didn't happen to be friends, he'd be on the slab by now. Which leaves you, Sara.'

Sara remained silent.

'Perhaps we're wasting our time,' Carver said.

Doyle said, 'Sara, I know you don't trust anyone. But you have to listen to us. Cameron wants everyone on the Burns job iced. Buggy. Me. You. If you sit around and do nothing, you're toast.'

Slowly, Sara fished a cigarette pack from the pocket of her denim jacket. She took her time over extracting a cigarette, placing it in her mouth and lighting it. 'So,' she said at last. 'If I did know what you were talking about, what should I do?'

'Simple,' Carver said. 'Draw the police away so we can get to Cameron before he gets to you.'

A young man in a black and red uniform top and pants came to the table. 'I'm sorry, Miss,' he said. 'You can't smoke here.'

Doyle looked up at him and smiled. 'Go fuck yourself, pal. Okay?'

The young man stared at him. Doyle went on smiling his smile of great sweetness.

'Only doing my job,' muttered the young man as he walked back behind the counter.

Hiden's telephone rang. 'Marty, I've just had Joanna on the phone. Sara called her.'

'Go on.'

'Something's scared her. She wants to meet us.'

'Sara is involved in an investigation by another force into a very serious offence. They're the people she has to talk to.'

'Marty, this is our daughter.'

'Muriel, I spent part of this morning talking to an ex-DI who lost everything. And it wasn't even him that broke the rules.'

'I'm going to meet her. Whether you join me is up to you. But you have got an interest. She might have been driving the car when Burns was killed. And that is your case.'

Hiden sighed. 'All right. But Hatfield have to host the meeting. We'll be there at their invitation.'

'However you want to arrange it, Marty. But Joanna thinks it needs to be soon. Sara's calling her back in an hour and Joanna says she sounds very scared.'

When Hiden reached Joanna's house, Muriel was already there. So was DS Longer from Hatfield. Joanna came in from the kitchen with a tray of coffee and biscuits.

'Sara?' asked Hiden.

'With me in the kitchen. Mum said you'd want to talk to each other first. Give me a call when you're ready.'

'No special treatment,' Hiden said. 'Bring her in now.'

When Sara was seated with them around the dining table, her sister left the room.

'This is a police interview, Sara,' Hiden said. 'It is not an opportunity for you to get off the hook. It's to enable you to tell us what you want to tell us, and us to ask you what we want to ask you. If you've committed a crime, you'll be charged. Do you understand?'

Sara glanced up for a moment, then down. 'I understand.'

Hiden looked at Muriel. 'Has she been read her rights?'

Muriel nodded.

'Sergeant Longer,' Hiden said. 'This is your case and your interview. Would you like to start?'

Longer cleared his throat. 'Sara. You telephoned your sister and said you wanted to talk to the police. Joanna says you were frightened. Were you frightened, Sara?'

Again the nod of the head.

'What of?'

She took a pack of cigarettes and a lighter from her shirt pocket. 'Will you ask Joanna if I can smoke? She doesn't like it, but I need one.'

'It'll be all right, Sara,' said Muriel. 'Use your saucer as an ash tray. Matter of fact, I think I'll have one myself.'

Sara blew smoke down her nose. 'A man called Walker came to see me.'

Longer looked inquiringly at Hiden. 'Johnnie Walker,' Hiden said. 'He works for Jim Cameron.'

'The man who inherited Matt Burns's empire?'

'That's right. What did he want, Sara?'

'He said he worked for Cameron. He said I'd worked for Cameron before.'

'Doing what?' asked Longer.

'Borrowing cars. Driving them places.'

'How was that usually arranged?'

'Buggy would come to see me. He'd tell me what wanted doing and drop me a few quid.'

'By "Buggy" you mean John Wright?'

'I've no idea what his name was. I knew him as Buggy.'

'And Buggy was definitely working for Cameron?'

'So this man Walker said. And he said Cameron had paid for Owen Thompson. My brief.'

'Where did you think Thompson came from?'

'I didn't know. He contacted me, said he'd been paid to represent me.'

'You didn't ask who by?'

Sara shrugged. 'I thought it might have been my father.'

Hiden clenched his fists but said nothing.

'How did you first meet Buggy?' Longer asked.

For the first time since Hiden had arrived, Sara smiled. 'He was trying to nick a car. God, he was hopeless. And you could see he was on the verge of tears. He was so bound up in it, he didn't even know I was there. I spoke to him and he nearly dropped dead. I told him he'd never make a car thief as long as he had a hole in his arse.'

'What did he say?'

'Nothing. Just stared at me like I was going to shop him. There were about thirty cars parked in a row. I asked him to choose one. You know—pick a car. Any car.' She laughed, cutting the laugh off abruptly and reaching for another cigarette. 'He chose a white Escort. Forty seconds later, we were driving off in it.'

'Did you get paid for stealing that car?'

'Borrowing it. I got twenty quid. He said it was all he could afford. But he was so relieved. If he hadn't come up with a car, he reckoned he was dead. And he said there'd be more next time.'

'How many next times have there been?'

Sara shrugged. 'Who knows? None. Look, can I tell the story I want to tell? About Walker? I'm not planning to list my T I Cs.'

'All right,' Longer said. 'So Walker came to see you and he told you the man you'd really been working for was Cameron.'

'Yes. And he said Cameron wanted something special done.'

'What did you say?'

'I asked him how I knew he wasn't a copper. I asked him why Buggy hadn't come. I said I wasn't doing anything till Buggy told me it was on the level.'

'And?'

Her voice came in a whisper. 'He said Buggy was dead. He said death was easy to arrange. He said if I didn't do what he told me, I'd be dead, too.'

'What did you say to that?'

'What do you think I said? I said I'd do what I was told. I said I wanted some money.'

'Did he give you any?'

'Two hundred quid.'

'And what was the something special you had to do?'

'Meet a man at Heathrow. Give him a mobile phone.'

'A mobile phone. And have you done it?'

She nodded. Taking a piece of paper from her pocket, she placed it on the table. 'That was the number.'

Hiden picked up the paper and examined it without expression before copying the number into his notebook and handing the paper to Longer.

'The man's name?'

'I don't know. He approached me.'

Hiden said, 'Why are you telling us this, Sara?'

'I'm scared. Nicking cars is a game. Getting killed isn't.'

'This man at Heathrow,' Longer said. 'If you gave us a description, would it be any more reliable than the one of the man you delivered the Mondeo to?'

Sara eyed him calmly. 'I'm sorry?'

'That Mondeo was burned. There were two people in the boot. Were you there when the car was burned?'

'No.'

'I don't believe you,' her father said.

'I wasn't there.'

'Did Buggy ask you to steal the car, darling?' asked her mother.

'Yes.'

'Did you deliver it to Buggy?'

'No.'

'Who did you deliver it to?'

'A man.'

'What man?' shouted Hiden.

'A man. I don't know. Buggy said there'd be a man in a yellow canvas jacket behind Marks & Spencer at Tolworth. There was. I gave the car to him. Then I went home.'

There was silence. Then Longer said, 'You invented that, Sara. Matt Burns was wearing a yellow canvas jacket when he got hit. You were there, weren't you?'

'How many times do I have to tell you? I wasn't there.'

'Sara,' Muriel Hiden said. 'You asked Joanna to arrange this meeting because you were frightened. Frightened for your life, it seems now. You've given us this information...'

'What information?' said Hiden. 'She's told us nothing.'

Muriel raised her voice over her ex-husband's. 'You've given us this information about the mobile phone number. What are you asking in return?'

'I'm not asking for anything. I just wanted you to know, if anything happens to me, I was threatened by Walker.'

Hiden looked away. 'OK. So we know. Sergeant Longer, are there any other questions you want to put to the suspect?'

Longer shook his head. 'What's the point? She isn't going to tell me anything.'

'Are you going to arrest her?'

'I'd love to. If I had anything I thought would stick.'

'Right. Sara, the three of us need to talk. We can't do that with you here, so you'd better go.'

'I haven't finished yet.'

Hiden sighed heavily. 'Always the game player.'

'What else is there, Sara?' asked Muriel.

'They'll be getting in touch again.'

'How?' said Hiden.

'What for?' said Muriel.

'How, I don't know. When they make contact, they'll tell me to go somewhere and be ready to pick them up.'

'And you don't know when this will happen?' asked Hiden. 'Or where you'll be going? Or what they'll have been doing before you pick them up?'

Sara shook her head and got to her feet. 'Somewhere near the M5. That's all they said.'

'Before you step out on us,' said Hiden, 'tell me how you knew the number of Smith's mobile.'

'Simple. I rang my own from it. The number was there on my screen.'

Muriel Hiden took her daughter into her arms and hugged her fiercely. 'Be careful, darling. And if anything happens to make you scared, call me. OK? Wherever you are. Whatever time it is. Call me.'

CHAPTER 33

Sara walked a quarter of a mile to a phone box. The number she rang was a payphone in the Ealing Broadway Centre. When Doyle picked it up on the second ring, she could hear the crowds of shoppers walking around him.

'Hook, line and sinker,' she said.

'Well done, baby. You know what to do now?'

'I'm on my way.'

'And it's a rental car? You're not going to be picked up with that mobile on you?'

'Relax.'

'OK. Sara, if you have to ring the emergency number, don't do it on the mobile.'

'I said, relax.'

Doyle hung up.

'How much do you think we can trust her?' said Carver.

'About as much as you'd trust any other woman you'd just met and knew nothing about.'

'That's what I thought.'

'So,' said DS Longer. 'What are we to make of that?'

'She told us nothing,' said Hiden. 'And most of that was lies.'

'Marty,' Muriel protested. 'She told us about the M5. Whoever Cameron wants them to kill isn't around here.'

'And you believe that, do you?'

'Why would she make it up?'

'Because she'd been told to, of course. To put us off the scent.'

Muriel shook her head. 'You're so distrusting. Maybe if you'd been less suspicious, we'd still have two daughters. And a marriage.'

Hiden turned away.

'At least she gave us the mobile number,' Muriel said.

'We already had it.'

'From where?'

'That phone was bought from a dealer near Waterloo on Tuesday by someone calling himself Smith. We're monitoring it already. So far, it's been used for one call—from Heston services to Carver's home in France. That's how we got the number—Smith or whoever he really is left it on Carver's answering machine. It has *not* been used to call Sara's mobile. Now do you believe she was lying?'

'Oh.'

'And we've got a description of Mister Smith, but no-one we can match it to.'

'Not Walker?' said Muriel.

'Nothing like him.'

'So your theory is—what?' said Muriel. 'That Cameron provided Carver with a phone so they could liaise over whatever job it is Carver's here to do?'

'Unless anyone comes up with a better idea, that's what we're going with. Yes.'

'It makes no sense. If you ring Carver and give him a phone number, you do it so he can call you. But he hasn't called it, and now he has the phone.'

'So your better idea is...?'

Muriel sighed. 'I've no idea, Marty. But your theory can't be right.'

Hiden stood up. 'Well, thanks for that input, Muriel. I'll treasure it. And now I must say goodbye to Joanna.'

A rental car! The man must be mad. To rent a car you need a driving licence and a credit card. Sara could lay hands on both of those things, as it happened. But not in the same name. "Hello, Mister Avis. I want to rent a car as Gloria Mellon. But I'm going to pay for it in my capacity as Mary Soper." No, Sara didn't think she'd care to play that scene.

Much better to pocket the hundred quid Doyle had given her to pay for the rental along with the two hundred for doing the job and borrow this nice blue Mercedes in the usual way. Having watched the owner check in for a flight to Rio, she felt fairly confident no-one would be reporting the car stolen for a few days.

She drove out of the airport car park and turned left. Had she looked in her rear view mirror as she came down the ramp, she might have seen the attendant staring after her. She might have noticed her write down the Mercedes registration. But she was focussed at the time on edging past a Lexus that had stalled while exiting the car park, and so she didn't.

Twenty minutes later, Hiden took a call from DS Longer. 'My guvnor thought you'd like to know your daughter's nicked another car, sir.'

'What are you going to do about it?'

'We're in two minds. She's heading west along the M4. We've got her under surveillance from an unmarked car. My guvnor was all for pulling her in, but I've persuaded him to let her run for a while.'

'Your thinking being?'

'She isn't a joyrider. She doesn't steal cars for fun. So where is she taking this one? And who for? I'd like to know. Maybe it gets us nowhere, in which case we've still got her for TDA. And maybe she leads us to whoever shot Matt Burns and torched two people in the boot of a Mondeo.'

Hiden couldn't fault Longer's thinking.

'I'll keep you in touch, sir.'

'I'd appreciate it.'

As soon as Hiden put down his phone, it buzzed again. The Chief Superintendent wanted to see him in his office. Hiden had been expecting this invitation for some time.

Marshall was known for not beating about the bush, and he didn't now.

'I've let you run with this one, Martin, even though your daughter was involved, because we could at least hope that hers was one case and yours was another. We can't do that any more. The two cases aren't just linked. They're one and the same.'

'Yes sir.'

'I'm taking you off the case and I'm putting Mary Prutton on it.'

'Yes sir.'

'I know I don't have to tell you why you can't be involved, so I won't. I probably also don't have to tell you to stay right away from the case from now on. But I will.' He looked up at Hiden. 'Have you heard me?'

'Yes sir.'

'You'll hear things, because you won't be able not to. You'll be interested, because it's your daughter, and she could be in danger. That's natural. But this is not *The Bill*, Martin. This is not *Morse*. My name is not Endeavour and you're not Lewis. You do nothing on your own. If you have any ideas, any insights, any advice, you discuss them with me. Not Hertfordshire, or any other force. And not Mary. Me.'

'Yes sir.'

'Good. I'm sure you have lots of things to do.'

Sara was not a complacent driver. She watched everything, in front, behind, to the sides, overhead. All the time. Melanie and Caroline had died because Sara spotted Mel's taxi tailing her and Doyle in their Mondeo. Now she picked up the BMW before she had passed Ealing. Whatever she did, the Beemer stayed five cars behind her. She went through minutes of consternation. If this was one of Cameron's men...

Then she relaxed. She smiled. She began to laugh. An unmarked car driven by uniformed policemen. What sort of gibbering incompetent would do that? Her parents would have been fuming.

The driver was no doubt well trained—for what he was normally expected to do. She didn't doubt he would be able to chase her safely at speeds of a hundred and fifty miles per hour. But follow her without her knowledge? Not a chance.

She slowed down, just a little. So did the Beemer. She accelerated, just a little. So did the Beemer. She passed two cars. So did the Beemer. She allowed a car to pass her. So did the Beemer.

She pushed in the Merc's cigarette lighter and fished out a cigarette. She pressed the button to crack open the driver's side window and allow smoke to drift out. She felt totally calm. Clearly, the police driver's instructions were to follow her but not to stop her. If she were caught with the mobile in her possession, she would not find it easy to wriggle out of any connection with Carver and Doyle, for the police had already placed that phone number in Doyle's possession—though they knew Doyle only as Smith. But once unload the mobile and the worst they could get her for was car theft. That was a risk she ran every week.

She thought ahead. There was no shortage of service stations on the M4. Junction 12 at Reading. Chieveley, right after it. Then

Junction 15, Membury. Leigh Delamere at Junction 17. Sara began to visualise each of these in turn, looking for the one best suited to the plan she was hatching.

Gough did not recognise the messenger. A young boy of about sixteen, one of Cameron's foot soldiers, knowing nothing about his errand and easily deniable if caught. 'Johnny Walker wants to see you. Usual place, he says.'

When he reached the Shepherd's Crook, Gough passed straight into the back room. It didn't take Walker long to tell him what he wanted. There was no sign of Cameron.

Gough had been back on the street about three minutes when the marked police car pulled up beside him. The colour drained from Gough's face.

'Get in,' said the uniformed driver.

'Are you mad?'

'I said, get in. Mrs Prutton wants to see you.'

At the police station, they made no attempt to give him cover. Instead of taking him into the yard and straight to the custody suite, they walked him in through the front door like a friend of the police attending the station voluntarily. Then they left him sitting in the reception area for fifteen minutes where any casual passer-by could see him. By the time DI Prutton and DC Wylie joined him, Gough was almost in tears. He leapt to his feet.

'Are you trying to get me killed?' he asked Prutton.

'It's not top of my list of things to do,' she said. 'But it wouldn't break my heart.' She pointed towards a door. 'You want to talk here? Or shall we use an interview room?'

Once inside, Wylie unwrapped two fresh tapes and put them into the recording machine.

'I'm not being taped,' Gough said.

Wylie started the recorder and dictated the date, time and names of those present.

'I'm not being taped,' Gough repeated.

'Sit down, Mister Gough,' said DI Prutton.

Gough sat. 'I'm not being taped.'

'It's the law, Mister Gough. Upholding the law is what we do here. Would you like a cup of tea? Coffee?'

Gough crossed his hands over his chest. Mary Prutton looked at Wylie, who went to the door and spoke to a uniformed constable passing in the corridor. 'Tea's on its way,' he said as he returned. Then he read Gough's rights to him.

'Do you want a lawyer present?' asked Prutton.

Gough shook his head.

'For the tape, please, Mister Gough.'

'No, thank you, I do not want a lawyer.'

'You do understand it's your right?'

Gough remained silent.

'For the tape, please, Mister Gough.'

'Yes. Yes, I understand. I don't want a lawyer, okay?'

'You people usually have Owen Thompson, don't you? Shall we call him for you? Perhaps we should.'

Gough kicked the table leg savagely as a uniformed constable brought in a tray with three plastic cups of tea. 'Which bit of "No" don't you understand? I don't want a lawyer here.'

'Well, as long as we're clear. I'm sorry it's only machine tea.' She placed one of the cups carefully in front of Gough and took another for herself.

'So, Mister Gough,' she went on. 'This morning you visited the Shepherd's Crook, a public house owned by a man called Jim Cameron. What happened there?'

Gough stared at the ceiling.

'For the tape, please, Mister Gough.'

'I've nothing to say.'

'Nothing to say? Why would that be, Mister Gough? If you made an innocent visit to a pub, why wouldn't you want to say anything about it?'

'It's a police state now, is it? Honest citizens have to answer questions about what they've been doing?'

'Do you know any honest citizens?'

'Very funny. If you've got anything to put to me, put it. Otherwise I'm going home.'

Prutton turned to Wylie. 'I think Mister Gough needs some time to reflect, Constable.'

Wylie pronounced the time at which the interview was suspended and stopped the tape machine. Mary Prutton smiled at Gough.

'Jackie, I'm not sure you realise how serious your situation is.'

Gough snorted. 'What? What? What do you think you can do to me? Send me to jail? I've been there.' He leaned forward. 'Have you any idea what Cameron would do to me if I grassed him up?'

'How about Dannie Ablett, Jackie?'

'You wouldn't dare.'

'You can take a chance on that if you like. It's your life you're gambling with.'

'That's immoral.'

'Yes? You think so? Give me a couple of minutes, would you, Constable?'

She waited till Wylie had left the room. Then she said, 'This isn't a game, Gough. That's where so many of you little douchebags go wrong. You think you can do what you want and we have to play by the rules. Well, you're right, Jackie—as long as that tape machine's playing, we do. But it isn't playing now.' She drained her tea and stood up.

'Don't be in any doubt, Gough. If you don't give me Cameron on a plate, I'll throw you to Mad Dan.'

'He'll kill me.'

'Probably. You think I'll have it on my conscience? Think again. I'm going for a sandwich. You want me to send you something?'

Gough shook his head.

'Use the time to think about your position, Jackie. When I come back, I want to know what Cameron told you to do.'

When Stacy Teasdale slept, the boning knife was under her pillow. Right now she was out on the street and it was in her handbag.

She would have to make a move soon. She knew that. Next week, probably. Go back to work. Resign and take the croupier's job on the cruise boats. Something. She was desperately anxious to get her life back to normal and put behind her the horrible thing that had been done to her. So far, she couldn't do it.

There was a play at the Richmond Theatre, but not till the evening and she didn't want to see it anyway. There were films at the Odeon and the Film House and she didn't want to see those, either. She could take the tube to Kew and walk in the gardens, but it didn't appeal. There was a lovely walk down to the river and along to Ham and Hampton Wick, but she was alone and the path could be solitary. In the past, she hadn't minded walking alone. Now...she wasn't sure. In fact, she was sure. She didn't want to do it. She wouldn't feel safe. Even with the knife in her handbag.

She could ring a friend, but her friends were at work. As she should really be.

All that was left was window shopping and coffee and a slice of carrot cake in the Bentall Centre. So that is what she did.

Stacy couldn't know what had made Carver pick her out as a victim. It might have helped her if she could, for she would have known how far she really was from Carver's picture of her. Carver saw a woman in a short skirt and knew she must be a whore. Carver saw a woman with attractive underwear and knew she must be a whore. Carver saw a woman who kept drink in her flat and knew she must be a whore. Stacy's friends saw a bright and bubbly young woman who cared about people.

The irony was that Stacy would have forgiven Carver, if only she could have listened to what he thought and why he thought it. But she couldn't do that. Instead, she carried the knife wherever she went.

Sara settled on Chieveley. Leigh Delamere had the tree-sheltered bays that might have hidden her while she executed her plan, but Chievely had something better—it was off the motorway itself, so you could go north or south as well as east or west.

At Junction 13 she turned south on the A34 and immediately left into the service station. She drove to the furthest end of the car park and parked in the row nearest the front. The BMW followed her in and came to a halt five rows behind her.

Sara took the cigarettes, lighter and mobile phone from her denim jacket and slipped them into her handbag. She left the jacket draped over the back of the front passenger seat. "I'm here," it said. "So my owner's coming back."

Two smokers stood just outside the entrance to the buildings. Sara stopped near them and lit a cigarette. She leaned against the pillar, smoking, a young car thief without a care in the world. The two coppers in the BMW pored ostentatiously over a map. Well to Sara's left, and as far as it could be from the Beemer's sightlines, a laden Mondeo parked. The driver, a woman of about forty, got out and helped a much older woman out of the passenger seat. Three girls aged from about eight to fifteen emerged from the back seat. They gazed enviously at a busload of teenage girls in school uniform who seemed to be everywhere.

The mother gave the old woman a walking stick and steadied her with one hand. 'Don't rush, Samantha,' Sara heard her say. 'Grandma needs something to eat and a cup of tea.'

Sara flicked away her cigarette and walked without haste to the Ladies. Inside were three of the schoolgirls in short navy blue skirts, white ankle socks, white blouses with striped ties and navy blue jumpers. Sara approached the most sullen looking one. 'Excuse me. Would you help me?'

The girl looked at her without comment.

Sara gestured back over her shoulder. 'There's a guy out there. Friend of a friend. I hitched a lift with him. He thinks that gives him special rights.'

All three girls' faces took on the same look of disgust. 'Bloody men,' said the sullen one in a strong Black Country accent.

'I thought I could handle him,' said Sara. 'Now I'm not so sure.'

'What do you want us to do?'

'Will you make a back for me so I can go out through that window?'

'Yeah!' The girls nodded, all traces of sullenness gone.

'And don't say anything about it out there?'

'Course not. That scumbag.'

Sara turned towards the window. As if on an afterthought she turned back, pulling the mobile from her bag. 'This is his,' she said.

'You want us to give it back to him?'

'Well, you could. But then he'd know I'd done a runner. And he's been a real creep.'

The sullen girl's face shone. 'We could use it!'

'Why not? It's got a few quid left on it.'

'Cool. What if he reports it to the police?'

'Don't be seen using it. If it rings, don't answer. Don't make any call that lasts so long they can trace where you are. When it stops working, sling it.'

'Oh. That is so cool.'

'Where are you going, by the way?'

'Home. Dudley.'

Sara waited for a middle-aged woman to wash her hands and leave. 'Now,' she said. 'Who's going to lift me out of here?'

Three willing pairs of hands came forward.

Outside, Sara moved swiftly to the edge of the building and peered round. The BMW hadn't moved, and neither had its occupants.

She took her key collection from her bag and walked confidently towards the Mondeo. Less than a minute later, she was out of the car park, under the motorway and heading north on the A4. When she reached Abingdon she turned off through Marcham and Frilford for Witney. There she picked up the A40 and pointed the Mondeo west.

At about the time Sara was passing Burford, two increasingly anxious policemen had left their unmarked BMW and were moving stealthily closer to a Mercedes with a girl's denim jacket draped over the passenger seat. They were approached by a furious woman. Some distance behind her, a stooped old lady supported by a stick was surrounded by three white-faced girls.

'Someone's stolen my car,' shouted the angry woman.

The two policemen looked at each other.

'Oh, bloody hell,' said one.

DI Prutton and DC Wylie returned to the interview room. Wylie pressed the button and dictated the date, time of interview resumption and names of those present.

'So, Mister Gough,' said Prutton. 'Are you ready to tell me the details of your meeting with Jim Cameron at the Shepherd's Crook pub today?'

Gough blinked. 'Cameron wasn't there.'

'Excuse me?'

'I said, Cameron wasn't there. I met Johnny Walker.'

Prutton smiled at Gough. The young constable standing beside the door had never seen anything that chilled the blood quite as much as that smile. The DI took a pack of Marlboro and a lighter from her jacket pocket and passed them across the table to Gough. Gough, who hadn't smoked for ten years, lit one and nodded his thanks.

'Who is Johnny Walker?' asked Prutton.

'He's a friend of Jim Cameron.'

'A friend?'

'Business associate.'

'Right hand man?'

Gough nodded.

'For the tape, please, Mister Gough.'

Gough cleared his throat. 'Yes.'

'And the business that these business associates associate for. How would you describe it?'

Gough moved uneasily in his chair.

'For the benefit of the tape, Mister Gough has made a gesture that can perhaps best be described as a shrug. Let me expand the question, Mister Gough. Would you describe the business activities of James Cameron and Johnny Walker as legitimate or criminal?'

Gough raised his eyes to look into the DI's face. She was smiling. The bloody woman was smiling at him as she turned him on the spit. He stared at her. Still smiling, she raised her eyebrows in silent interrogation. Gough looked at his feet.

'Criminal,' he said. 'Cameron and Walker are a pair of crooks.'

'And the matter you met Walker to discuss this morning? Was that a criminal matter?'

Gough nodded.

'For the tape, please, Mister Gough.'

'Yes. Yes, for God's sake. I met him to discuss a criminal matter. All right?'

'Mister Gough. I feel very bad about allowing you to incriminate yourself without a brief being present to protect your interests. Can I please, for your own sake, urge you to consider asking for the presence here of your lawyer, Mister Owen Thompson?'

Slowly, Gough raised his head. He stared into the face counterfeiting concern opposite him. 'You pitiless cow,' he said.

'For the benefit of the tape, will you please explain your reluctance to be represented by Owen Thompson?'

'Owen Thompson is Jim Cameron's lawyer. As you well know.'

'Are you suggesting Mister Thompson might not represent you as you would wish?'

'Owen Thompson is as bent as a nine bob note.'

'I see. Well, can we get you the duty lawyer?'

'Don't be ridiculous.'

'On your own head be it, Mister Gough. If the CPS decides to bring this before a court, I don't want anyone suggesting you were denied proper representation. Now. The criminal matter you discussed this morning with Johnny Walker. Was Walker speaking on behalf of James Cameron?'

Gough nodded.

'For the tape, please, Mister Gough.'

'Yes.'

'Yes what?'

'Yes, Walker was speaking on behalf of James Cameron.'

'I see. Please describe the contents of the conversation. In your own words.'

Gough took another cigarette from Prutton's pack. 'Buggy's dead.'

'Buggy?'

'John Wright. Used to fetch and carry for Cameron. He's dead. Walker says Buggy has the keys to some lock-ups. He stored stolen gear in them.'

'For Cameron?'

'Yes. Sort of.'

'What do you mean, sort of? It was for Cameron or it wasn't.'

'Cameron doesn't steal stuff, for God's sake. Other people do that.'

'He's a fence?'

'No. Other people do that, too.'

'Cameron puts up the money?'

'Cameron provides protection. You want to do anything on this manor, you need Cameron's permission. Whatever you get, he takes a share.'

'And what does he give in return?'

'You don't get the shit beaten out of you, for a start. And you might get the police kept off your back.'

Prutton leaned forward. 'Be very careful what you say, Mister Gough. How would Cameron arrange to keep the police off your back?'

'I really have no idea, Missus Prutton. But I'm sure there are people in this building who could tell you.' He stared defiantly at her, but it was he who broke first. He looked away, lit another cigarette.

'Tell me about these lock-ups. How many are there?'

'Walker doesn't know. Doesn't know where they are, either.'

'How is that possible?'

'Buggy rented them. Walker gave him the cash every month, and Buggy signed the forms and paid the rent. Anything goes wrong, you can't connect what's in the lock-ups to Cameron.'

'Clever.'

'But now Buggy's dead. And Cameron and Walker don't know where the lock-ups are.'

'Not so clever.'

'Guys want to sell what they've blagged, see. And they can't, 'cos Buggy took it away and stored it for them and now they can't ask him where it is. And what happens if the rent doesn't get paid? That's what Cameron's worried about. Landlords start opening lock-ups, what are they gonna find? See what I mean?'

'I do, Jackie, I really do. So what does Walker want you to do about it?'

'He wants me to see if Shazza knows where the keys and the rent books are.'

'Shazza?'

'Sharon Wright. Buggy's wife. Sharon Levitt before. We grew up together.'

'Why doesn't Walker ask her himself?'

'He gave her a black eye a couple of days ago.'

'What for?'

'A warning. I dunno. Stop her talking.'

'What would she have talked about?'

'Buggy told her he was going to France to do a job for Cameron. Cameron didn't want her repeating that.'

'Was it true?'

'I have no idea. He told me the same thing. But...Buggy tells you something...it might be true, might not.'

'And why would Walker think you might have some special power over Sharon Wright?'

Gough looked at her without replying.

'Is there a special relationship between you and Sharon?'

'I told you. We grew up together.'

'And that's all?'

Gough sighed. 'No. That isn't all.'

'You've been intimate with her?'

'I've fu... I've slept with her, if that's what you mean.'

'Often?'

'Yes, often.'

'Before her husband died?'

'Yes.'

'And after?'

'Yes.'

'Mister Gough, let me get this straight. You were carrying on an affair with John Wright's wife, and now he's dead in suspicious circumstances. And you're still carrying on an affair with his wife.'

'Now just a minute...'

'Do you know that's the commonest motive there is for murder?'

'You've no chance of pinning that on me, so forget it. Buggy died in France. I was here.'

'Ah, yes. There was some question over that, wasn't there? No passport has ever been issued to John Wright, but he got to France. Interestingly, with a passport in the name of James Robert Patterson. Can you explain why that passport has your fingerprints on it?'

Gough was jolted upright. 'I don't believe...you can't have...'

'Want to take a chance on it? You want to lie in the hope that the passport does not have your fingerprints on it?'

Gough stared at her in silence.

'The passport, Mister Gough. How did it come into John Wright's possession?'

The silence continued. Then: 'I got it for him. But if he was murdered, that's nothing to do with me.'

'I think we have enough for now.' She nodded to Wylie, who dictated the time of interview suspension and turned off the tape machine.

'Now what?' asked Gough.

'Now? Now, Jackie, you carry out Johnny Walker's instructions. You go to Sharon Wright and you exercise whatever wiles you must to get hold of those keys and rent books.'

'You want me to bring them to you?'

'That's right, Jackie.'

'What do I tell Walker?'

'I'll tell you that nearer the time, Jackie.'

'He'll kill me.'

'You'll have to stay on my good side, won't you? Give me the will to stop him.'

'Is that enough, guv?', Wylie asked when Gough had reluctantly departed.

'Nothing like enough, I'm afraid. We've got Gough for procuring a false passport. Everything else is Gough's word against someone else's. But we do have Gough, constable. Let that tape out and he's a goner. I have Jackie Gough in the palm of my hand. He's my snout till the end of time. If I tell him to lick me clean after I've taken my morning dump, he'll get down on his knees and stick out his tongue.'

She moved close to Wylie and stared into his eyes. 'I like that in a man.'

Wylie stood by the reception desk and watched DI Mary Prutton walk across the car park towards her little MG. 'Interesting woman,' he said to the desk sergeant.

'Out of your league,' said the sergeant. 'Forget about it. Whatever you're thinking.'

'Is she real, do you think? Does she mean the stuff she says?'

DS Milton had come silently up behind him. 'More experienced men than you have wondered that,' she said.

CHAPTER 34

Sara parked the Mondeo behind a supermarket in Tewkesbury and walked away. Parking was free here; with luck it could be days before anyone took an interest in it or a passing copper checked the licence plate against a list of stolen cars.

She stopped at a charity shop and spent five pounds on a new jacket—pale grey denim with pink flowers embroidered on the back. The friendly matron who took her money stood back a little as she told her where to catch the bus to Worcester.

Their landlord had given the names of Melanie and Caroline to the police. He had addresses for next of kin, but both proved false.

Their neighbours scarcely knew them—in the classic phrases loved by newspapers they were "quiet" people, "perfect neighbours" who "kept themselves to themselves." Melanie had a library card, but all the librarian knew about her was that she liked Georgian romances and Sapphic fiction.

'What's Sapphic fiction?' asked the police constable carrying out the enquiries.

'Stories about lesbians.'

'She rode the other bus?'

'That was certainly my impression.' The librarian smiled at him from behind her modish spectacles. 'I got the feeling she was selling tickets.'

'Ah. But you...'

'I'm a straight red double-decker woman, officer.' She ran her tongue between her lips. 'With a thing about men in uniform, if we're talking predilections.'

Later that evening, she persuaded the constable to keep most of his uniform on while he explored her predilections in detail. For her part, she retained only her sensible flat shoes and her glasses, through which she looked encouragingly back over her shoulder at him. Even later that evening, when she had finally allowed him to rid himself of the dark livery of the Law, they lay in each other's arms while she stroked his chest and wondered about the happy chance that had brought them together.

'Why were you looking for that woman?'

'She and the girl she shared with have disappeared.'

'Is it suspicious?'

'Routine. There was a note on their bed that raised some questions. But they could have dreamed that up themselves.'

'They shared a bed, then?'

'Mmm.'

'Will you go on looking for them?'

'That's not my decision. But I shouldn't think so. They're adults. They're entitled to disappear if that's what they want to do. If they wanted people to know where they were, they wouldn't have lied about their parents.'

'You could find their families, though?'

'Easily. But no crime's been committed, as far as we know. I think it'll be dropped.'

And so it was, the following day. Six years later, when Melanie Cantrell's unforgiving father had died, her mother began the search for the daughter she missed so much and who had so grievously offended her husband. Then it was that the teeth of one of the burned bodies were identified by the Cantrell family dentist and Mel's mother learned how, if not why, her daughter had died. But the constable never heard of it, for by then he was a sergeant in a rural force many miles away, where he and the librarian had moved to raise their three children far from the big city.

Melanie's mother had never known the name of her daughter's lover. No-one ever identified Caroline as the woman who had died with her.

Gough found Sharon moping in her kitchen. She watched in astonishment as he took out the DI's cigarettes and lit one.

'Jackie! You're smoking! You haven't smoked for years! You don't like it when people smoke.'

He puffed irritably at his cigarette.

Sharon made instant coffee in a mug and placed it on the table beside him. She kissed him on the cheek. 'Sharon needs cheering up, Jackie. She needs Jackie to be kind.'

Through the fog of despair, the old Adam raised itself. What would it take, Gough wondered, to get him to the point where Sharon couldn't turn him on?

'I've been waiting for you, Jackie. I'm ready.'

He looked up at her. 'What did you have in mind?'

Shy wasn't a word often used about Sharon, but it was with every sign of shyness that she raised her short skirt. Her legs were bare.

'Look at my knickers, Jackie.'

Gough moved furtively to prevent her seeing his sudden stiffness. He cleared his throat.

'Very nice,' he murmured.

'They're old, Jackie. That's the point. They're coming to bits. They'd tear easily. And I wouldn't miss them. If...'

Gough finished his cigarette and gulped his coffee. 'If what, Sharon?'

'Honestly, Jackie. Make me spell it out, why don't you? If I was lying on my bed, face down, sleeping. And someone crept into my bedroom and lifted up my skirt. Ripped off my knickers and did me.'

'That's what you want me to do?'

Sharon looked at the floor. 'Only if you want to.'

'Bloody hell, Sharon.' Gough pushed his chair away from the table. His excitement was all too visible.

'I wouldn't fight too hard, Jackie. I don't want you to hurt me. Just, like...pretend.'

'Pretend. Right. Who am I supposed to be while I'm doing this?'

'Do you remember Sergeant Mitchell?'

'Mitchell? Yeah, I remember Mitchell. Is this what he used to do?'

'He was a real gent, Sergeant Mitchell. Course, I was only a kid. He used to give me money to buy a new pair. My mother would've gone crazy.'

'What made you think of Mitchell?'

'Why don't you have another ciggie? While I go and get comfortable? Then you can come in and see what you find. Okay, Jackie?' She handed him the pack of Marlboro. 'Oh, and, Jackie?'

'Yeah?'

'You could make me use my mouth first. Before you...you know. Okay, Jackie?'

'Yeah.'

'And I'll be saying "No," and "Please don't." Like that. But you don't take any notice. Okay, Jackie?'

'Yeah. Yeah, okay, Sharon.'

Using the names Smith and Jones, Carver and Doyle checked into a cheap hotel near King's Cross. They paid cash.

'I need to take a credit card impression,' said the smart young Indian who booked them in.

'No, you don't,' said Doyle.

'It's a company rule.'

Carver pushed a twenty pound note across the counter. 'Don't be a silly boy,' he said.

The note disappeared. 'You won't be able to charge anything,' said the Indian.

'Like what?'

'Well. A meal, or a drink.'

'We'll pay cash,' Carver said.

'Okay, Mister Jones. Enjoy your stay.'

'As if I'd eat in a dump like this,' Carver said as they went to their rooms.

'This pub the girl mentioned.'

'The Shepherd's Crook? We won't be eating there, either.'

'But that's the place to start?'

'Has to be. It's the only place we've got. We can't go around Cameron's manor asking where he is.'

'So when do we start watching it?'

'As soon as she gets back here with a car.'

DS Anne Milton was surprised to be called to Mary Prutton's office. Since the DI had taken over from Hiden, Anne had pretty much been left out of the Cameron investigation.

'You and Marty have plenty to keep you busy?' asked Prutton.

'We've got a bit on.'

'And you know Marty's supposed to stay away from what I'm doing? Because of his daughter?'

'We all do.'

'This Smith and his mobile phone.'

'Yes, guv?'

'The phone's been making calls.' She looked at the sheet of paper in front of her. 'In Abingdon, in Oxford, in Birmingham and in Dudley.'

'So he's heading north west.'

'His phone certainly is.'

'Isn't that the same thing, guv?'

'Maybe. And maybe we're being led by the nose.'

'Someone wants us to believe he's heading north west?'

'It's a possibility. One I'd like you to bounce off your DI. At the same time as you tell him Hertfordshire have lost track of his daughter.'

'He's going to love that. What happened?'

'She dumped her stolen Merc in Berkshire. Left two dumb uniforms watching it while she drove off in someone else's Mondeo. There's been no sightings of that. It could be anywhere, and so could she.'

'You want me to tell the DI?'

'I think he'd want to know. Don't you? Just as I'd like to know if she makes any contact with him. Or his wife.'

'It's more likely to be with their daughter.'

'Whoever. I'd also like someone to drive by her gaff from time to time and tell me if she shows up.'

'You want her arrested?'

'I don't even want her to know she's been seen. I just want to know she's around. And if she's with anyone. She's gonna want to go home some time, if only to change her knicks and shave her armpits.'

'I don't get the feeling personal hygiene is high on her priorities, guv.'

'Maybe not. But if she's around, I want to know. Clear?'
'Clear.'

Jackie Gough lay on his back, staring at the ceiling and thinking that now he'd seen everything. Sharon nuzzled his side. The tattered remains of her torn knickers clung to one thigh. Neither of them had a stitch on otherwise.

'That was lovely, Jackie.'

'Yeah. Yeah it was.'

'Did you really like it?'

'The best, Sharon. The best I've ever had.'

'You don't think I'm funny?'

'I know you're funny, Sharon. That was still the best sex I've ever had.'

'You know what I liked best?'

'I daren't ask.'

'The way you'd gone to the bathroom and washed yourself. You know. Before you came in. Most men don't think about how they taste in a girl's mouth. You've gone red. Do I embarrass you?'

'You'd embarrass the Pope, sometimes.'

'You don't belong round here, Jackie. You're a gentleman.' She kissed him. 'Aren't you glad I'm not a lady?'

'You are a lady, Shazza. In your own way.'

'Funny, isn't it? How playing games makes it better.'

'Yeah.'

'We could play one of your games next time.'

'I don't know if I've got any games, Sharon. Of my own, I mean.'

'I'm sure you could think of one.' She doodled one-finger patterns on his shoulder. 'Jackie.'

'Yeah?'

'You know I'm a widow now?'

'Bloody hell. Yeah, I suppose you are. Bit of a merry widow, aren't you?'

'Jackie! I do care about Buggy being dead you know.'

'I know you do, petal.'

'That's why I've been wearing black knickers since he died.'

'He'd be deeply touched.'

'I loved Buggy.'

'Let's be fair, Sharon. You love a lot of people. Often at the same time.'

'Yes, well. That's because I loved Buggy, but I didn't respect him.'

'Oh.'

'Well, you couldn't, really, could you?'

'Couldn't you?'

'I respect you, Jackie.'

Gough raised himself on one elbow. 'Where are you going with this, Sharon? Shazza? Are you...why are you crying?'

'If I hadn't...if me and Buggy hadn't been...you know...do you think it might ever have been me and you instead?'

'Bloody hell, Sharon.'

'I always fancied you. But Buggy was Top Cat back then, wasn't he? And then, when I realised, we were married and it was too late. That's what happens. You realise something, and it's too late.'

'Life can only be understood backwards,' said Gough. 'But it has to be lived forwards.'

Sharon sat up, her eyes shining. 'Oh, Jackie,' she breathed. 'That's *brilliant*. Oh, I wish I'd gone to college, Jackie.'

'Yeah. Well. It'll be too late for me pretty soon. And then it won't matter whether it might ever have been me and you. Because there won't be any me to be part of it.'

'Jackie. Whatever do you mean?'

'I'm in the crap, Sharon. I've got the police on one side, Jim Cameron on another, and Mad Dan Ablett on the third.'

'Like a triangle. Why's Mad Dan cross with you?'

'He doesn't know he is, yet.'

She put her finger on his brow and ran it down his nose. 'It *was* you grassed him up.'

'Grass is a nasty word, Sharon. Don't use it. Even in fun.'

'Buggy said it was you.'

'Bloody hell. Who else did he tell?'

'No-one I shouldn't think. Buggy wouldn't shop a mate. Even one he thought was seeing to his wife.'

'He what?'

She sat cross-legged on the bed. 'Why don't you tell me the whole story? And don't look at me down there. You'll only get excited again.'

CHAPTER 35

Sara caught the 13.08 First Great Western from Worcester Foregate and arrived at Paddington five minutes early, at 15.20. Unaccustomedly flush with most of the three hundred pounds still in her pocket, she perched on a window stool at a Prêt A Manger for a poached salmon and rocket sandwich, a love bar and a blueberry yoghurt blender. The people on the stools to each side eased away from her. The same thing had happened on the train; it hadn't troubled her then, either. Satisfied, she went to look for an unattended car.

Sixty minutes later, she parked in the agreed place. After a few minutes, Doyle opened the passenger door and sat beside her. Carver got in the back.

Doyle stared at her. 'You don't smell too good.'

'I've been busy.'

'Too busy to shower?'

'Do you mind? Cheeky sod.'

Doyle opened the door. 'Come on. Out.'

'Where we going?'

'Back to the hotel so you can clean up.'

'I'm not taking my clothes off with you there. I saw what you did to those two girls.'

'We've got two rooms. And don't flatter yourself.'

They stopped on the way at a BhS for Sara to buy clean underwear and a T-shirt. 'What two girls were these?' asked Carver.

'It's not important. And let's make sure she washes her hair. She stinks.'

When Sara knocked on Carver's door, Doyle opened it. He inspected her, sniffed her hair and pronounced himself satisfied. They walked back to the car.

'Did you scout the pub?' asked Doyle.

Sara nodded. 'Plain clothes cop just down the road. Another on the other side, further up.'

'That's what you saw,' said Carver. 'If you spotted two, chances are there's more you didn't see.'

'What do we do now?' asked Doyle.

'Let me think about it. Does Cameron know you?' he asked Sara.

'No. But Walker does. And so do the coppers.'

'Well, we've got to get a message to Cameron. He's expecting me, after all. Put yourself in his position. He sent someone to bring me from France to do a job. The messenger was supposed to meet me here, but he's dead. He doesn't know I know that. What's he expecting?'

'You to wait to be met. Then, when you're not, to make contact.'

'How? I don't know him.' He scratched his chin. 'But I know someone who does.'

Sharon stroked Gough's head. 'Poor little cherub,' she murmured. 'You are in a mess and no mistake.'

'If I don't find those keys and rent books, I'm dead meat. On the slab. Cold.'

'You are, aren't you?' She kissed his forehead. 'Isn't it a good job I know where they are?'

'You? He told you?'

'Don't sound so surprised, Jackie. Of course he didn't tell me. But you knew Buggy. Do you think he could manage stuff like that without me knowing?'

'Well, where are they?'

'There are four of them. Four lock-ups. Four rent books. Four keys.'

'Sharon. Where *are* they?'

'Not so fast, Jackie Gough. After I've solved your problem, what do I get? Don't look like that. You know what I want. What have you got to trade?'

When Cameron went home that evening, the blue phone in what he liked to call his study rang. This was the line installed by a BT engineer on a foreigner, which meant a line the phone company knew nothing about. Installation had been paid for in cash. There were no rental or call charges.

Only a handful of people had this number. Mitchell was one of them.

'Where are you calling from?' asked Cameron.

'Spain.'

'I know that. I mean...'

'Not my own phone. Don't be so jumpy. I've had a call from Don Carver.'

'About bloody time.'

'I think you mean "Well done, Mitch." Carver's in London at your request. Buggy didn't meet him.'

'Buggy's dead.'

'Dead? Buggy?'

'Carver didn't know that?'

'How the hell would he?'

'Carver makes people dead, Mitch. I wondered...'

'Listen, Jim. Carver will be as amazed as I am. What d'you want him to do? He's talking about going back home.'

'Don't let him do that. He had the money, didn't he?'

'I didn't ask.'

'I still want the job done.'

'I don't know, Jim. He's going to be spooked when I tell him about Buggy.'

'So don't tell him. Say he's been picked up by the cops. For drugs or something.'

'You're not thinking, Jim. I tell him the cops have got Buggy, he's gonna run for the hills.'

'Well, invent something. I need that hit making.'

'He won't take it from me. You're going to have to meet him.'

'I never meet anyone, Mitch. You know that. There's always a cut-out between the guy and me.'

'I'll talk to him. But don't expect miracles.'

Mitchell hung up. He waited by the public phone overlooking the *playa*. After four minutes, it rang.

'How'd it go?' asked Carver.

'As expected.'

'Okay. Ring him back in an hour and read him the facts of life.'

Gough laid the documents on the table. 'Two passports, Mister and Missus Renton. Birth certificates, John Renton and Sharon Smith. Marriage certificate, John Renton and Sharon Smith.'

Sharon slipped her arm round his waist. 'Oh, Jackie. You're so clever.'

'It's nothing. It's what I do for a living.'

'It's still clever, Jackie.' She kissed him on the cheek. 'Won't it be great when it's not what you do for a living any more?'

'I dunno, Sharon. A B&B in Cornwall. That sounds a lot like work.'

Sharon put her hands on her hips and pouted. 'Jackie Gough, we agreed. You can't go back on me now.'

He put up his hand. 'Okay, okay.'

'I want you in honest work. Now there's a little one on the way.'

'There's a...you what?' He sat down suddenly, gazing at her in frank astonishment.

Sharon stepped forward, smiling down at Gough. Her eyes filmed over. She put her arms round his neck, pressing his face forward against her smooth belly. 'You're going to be a daddy, my love. You're pleased, aren't you?'

When the blue phone rang again, Cameron picked it up on the first ring.

'No deal,' Mitchell said. 'He meets you or he goes home. You'd better give me your address.'

'No-one gets this address, Mitch.'

'Your choice. You want the job done, or don't you?'

'Damn it to hell. All right. But it won't be at my place. Here's what you tell him.'

Gough handed the rent books and keys to Mary Prutton.

'Three?,' asked the DI. 'That's the lot? You're sure?'

'I turned the place upside down. There's nothing else.'

'Wait here.'

'How long?'

'Till I say you can go.' She turned back into the room. 'You're looking very pleased with yourself, Jackie. Is there something I should know?'

Gough looked down and said something too quietly for Prutton to hear.

'What?'

'I said, I'm going to be a father.'

Prutton stared at him. 'A father. You. Don't you think the police have enough trouble already? Without you spawning another petty crook?'

'That's not very nice, Missus Prutton.'

'Who's the mother? Who are you having this little bastard with?'

Real hurt showed in Gough's eyes. In a low voice he said, 'Sharon Wright.'

'Sharon Wright. Buggy's widow? The manor bicycle? Good God, man. How do you know the little bastard's your little bastard?'

Gough stood up. 'I don't have to listen to this shit.'

'That's really sweet. Sit down, Jackie. Or when you go out of here you'll find Mad Dan waiting to fry your balls as an appetiser. Before he eats your liver.'

Leaving Gough in the interview room, Prutton went to Marshall's office. 'Mind if I discuss something with you, sir?'

'Sit down, Mary.'

Prutton laid out the keys and rent books on the Chief Superintendent's desk. She explained where they came from.

'What do you want to do?'

'I thought I'd get the keys copied. Keep Gough till we've had a couple of DCs look in the lockups and tell us what's there. Then tell him to deliver the keys and the rent books to Cameron. Which is, after all, what Cameron is expecting to happen.'

'How does that help us?'

'We'll need to keep a round the clock watch on all three lockups.'

'That's a hell of a lot of manpower, Mary.'

'Sir, this station has been trying to get something on Cameron for years. This is the best chance we've ever had. Isn't it worth a bit of money?'

'The reason we've never pinned anything on him, Mary, is that he never does anything himself. What makes you think it'll be any different this time?'

There was no answer, and they both knew it.

'Send Gough to Cameron with the keys. If you don't, you'll have his blood on your hands. And by all means give the addresses to Uniform, and ask them to keep an eye out.'

'We're not going to catch Cameron like that, sir.'

'No, Mary, we're probably not. If you have any better ideas that won't cost an arm and a leg, by all means come and see me again.'

Prutton stood up. 'Thank you sir.'

'It's no good looking at me like that, Mary. I know you want Cameron. We all do. But I'm the one who'll answer for it if we go over budget.'

'Yes sir.'

'Johnny not here?'

'Johnny's gone to see someone.' Cameron looked at the keys without touching them. 'Three lockups.'

'That's it.'

'What's in them?'

'I dunno, Jim. I wasn't told to look.'

'That's right, Jackie. You weren't. You'd better do that next. Okay?'

'Whatever you say, Jim.'

Cameron used a pen to push the keys and rent books back to Gough. 'You'll need these.' He placed a bundle of bank notes on the table. 'And this. Pay the rent for me. Keep the rest for your wages. Get the name on the books changed. From Buggy to you.'

'Won't I need his signature?'

'Forge it, Jackie. You have any trouble getting these?'

'None at all.'

'What does Sharon know about it?'

'Nothing, Jim. I went through Buggy's stuff while she was asleep. She doesn't know a thing.'

'Best keep it like that, there's a good lad. You know Monty Green?'

'Everyone knows Monty, Jim. Best fence in the business.'

'Ever use him?'

Gough shook his head. 'Out of my league, Jim.'

Cameron smiled. 'Not any more, my son. You're working for me now. He'll expect a visit from you.'

'What do you want me to do?'

'Whatever's in those lockups, you deliver it where Monty tells you. He'll give you cash. You take that cash to the bank next to Wilson's Launderette.'

'That's a Paki bank, Jim.'

'Middle Eastern, Jackie. And very good people to deal with. Give the money to a guy called Muammar. Only to him, Jackie. If Muammar isn't there, take the cash away and go back when he is. Got it?'

'Only to Muammar. Got it.'

'Tell him Mister Reiver sent you. He'll give you the number of a bank account. It can be in Monte Carlo, Rome, Paris, Dubai. You choose. And you tell him what name you want the account to be in.'

'Not your name, Jim?'

'Nothing's ever in my name. When I want the money, you get it for me. If anything goes wrong, Jackie, what happened to Buggy will happen to you.'

Gough shivered. 'Did he do this stuff for you, Jim?'

'Don't be stupid. Buggy couldn't find his arse with both hands behind his back. This used to be Johnny Walker's job. But you're a bright boy. You're the first university man we've had on the team. I haven't got a son, Jackie. I have great hopes of you. Long as you don't do anything stupid. You follow me?'

'I follow you, Jim.'

'Monty pays out thirty per cent of the retail value of the goods. Watch out he doesn't stiff you for more. Remember, that's my money you're dealing with.'

'I'll watch him.'

'And Muammar gets ten per cent of the thirty per cent for washing the cash nice and clean. So we end up with how much?'

'Er. Ninety per cent of thirty per cent? Twenty-seven per cent?'

'Twenty-seven pence in the pound, Jackie. That's right.'

'It's not very much.'

Cameron looked pained. 'It's not like we paid for the stuff, Jackie.'

'Somebody took a hell of a risk nicking it.'

'They did, Jackie. For which they get two thirds of what I get. Less my expenses. You're one of my expenses.'

'I'm honoured, Jim.'

'You should be, my son.'

CHAPTER 36

'You're not really planning to visit those three lockups?'

'That's the plan, Sharon. Then I get Monty Green to buy what's in them.'

Sharon shook her head. 'Jackie. The police know about those lockups. You told them where they are. You even gave them the keys. What do you think's going to happen when you show up there?'

'It won't be like that. I'm DI Prutton's snout. She won't let them pick me up.'

'Put that in writing, has she?'

Gough looked uncertain. 'Well, how are we supposed to get the money? You're the one wants to go straight. You're the one wants a B&B in Cornwall. You're the one wants to change our name to Renton, disappear for ever. How are we supposed to do that if I don't get the money?'

'Jackie. How many lockups did you give the DI and Cameron? Three. How many lockups did I have keys for?'

'Oh.'

'Oh is right. Now I wonder which one of the four has about one and a half million quid's worth of nicked drink and cigarettes in it that would be a piece of piss to get rid of in a day? And which three are full of knock-off videos and jewellery and crap like that?'

'But we don't know what's in them.' He watched her face carefully. 'We do know what's in them.'

Sharon smiled.

'So the thing to do...the thing to do is to get Monty Green to buy the fags and booze and get Muammar to put the money in an account.'

Sharon went on smiling.

Gough's eyes lit up. 'John Renton's account, maybe?'

'John and Sharon Renton's would be better.'

'Same thing, isn't it?'

'Not quite. Suppose we need the money in a hurry...'

'...which we will...'

'...and you can't get away without making Cameron suspicious.'

'John and Sharon Renton, then.'

'Either to sign.'

'Either to sign. Bloody hell, Sharon. That's like two hundred and seventy and half of two hundred and seventy...that's four hundred thousand quid.'

'B&B in Cornwall. We'll need all of that.'

'I suppose. Sharon.'

'Yes, my petal.'

'How did you know that was the key to hold back?' He stared at her. 'I mean...how long have you...'

Sharon was still smiling.

'Sharon. When I came looking for the keys? Were you waiting for me to ask? Have you planned this all along?'

She moved forward and smoothed the collar of his shirt. She kissed him gently on the lips. 'Jackie. You know what I've learned? Started learning when I first went to school, and went on learning? Men need to think I'm dumb. Because I'm a woman, and I'm blonde, well, men think I'm blonde, and I like to spend a lot of time on my back with my legs in the air, and I like men for what they have that makes them men, I have to be

311

dumb. Well, I'm not dumb.'

Gough shook his head. 'You're not, are you?'

'I pretend to be, if that's the game the man needs me to play. You know, like we played the game where you ripped my knickers off and did me? I needed to play that game. If a man needs me to play the game where I'm dumb, I'll play that game for him.

'But what I really want is to play the game where we're both smart and we both know we're both smart. Think you can play that game with me, Jackie? Please?'

Gough nodded.

'I hope you can, Jackie. 'Cos we make a good team, you and me. There's stuff you can do that I can't. Getting those passports, for example. And there's stuff I can do that you can't.' She smiled. 'There's one very special thing I'm doing that you can never do, Jackie. I'm having your little boy. He's going to grow up to be just like his daddy. And he'll go to university, just like his daddy, but he'll be even smarter than his mummy and his daddy because he'll have gone to a private school first. And if I have a little girl, we'll do exactly the same thing. 'Cos girls can be as smart as boys, any day. Even blonde girls. You with me on this, Jackie?'

Gough nodded again. 'I am, Sharon. I really am.'

'I'm glad.' She took a key from her pocket and a sheet of paper from a drawer in the kitchen table. 'So now you're going to go see Monty Green and arrange to get rid of the booze and ciggies. You'll need this list, because Monty's going to want to know what's in there, isn't he? And I love you and I couldn't bear to lose you now, so you won't go anywhere near the other lockups. Will you?'

Gough shook his head. 'I won't.'

'Good. Jackie? Your copy of that PACE tape? The one that says you grassed up Dan Ablett? Where is it?'

'In my pocket.'

'Do you think it's a good idea to carry it around? Why don't you leave it with me? I'll find somewhere really safe for it.'

'Okay. Good idea.'

When Gough had left, Sharon put on a pair of kitchen gloves, took the tape out of its plastic box and washed the box. She dried it inside and out with a tea towel, carefully removing any possible trace of fingerprints. She put the tape back into the box. Then, still wearing the gloves, she extracted from the bottom of her underwear drawer an envelope on which was printed Dan Ablett's name and address. Already in the envelope was a printed note. It said:

```
Dear Mr Ablett
You may find the enclosed tape
interesting. It will tell you the name of
the person who grassed you up. If you
want him, he'll be on the westbound
platform at Ealing station on Wednesday
at midday.
Yours sincerely
A well wisher
```

She placed the tape, in its box, into the envelope, which she then returned to the bottom of her underwear drawer.

Monty Green, who a day earlier would not have deigned to notice Gough's presence, was the picture of affability.

'Mister Gough. Jackie. A pleasure to see you. You are well?'

'Er...yes, thanks, Monty. In the pink.'

'Splendid. And your young lady? The delightful Sharon? I believe you are comforting her after her sad loss?'

'Bloody hell, Monty. Does everybody know everything?'

'There are no private lives among friends, Jackie. Not among friends who need to trust each other. And we need to trust each other. So. What do you have for me?'

'Cigarettes and booze.'

'You have the inventory?'

Gough placed Sharon's sheet of paper on the table. Green studied it without laying a single finger on it. 'Yes. Yes, I see.' He took a calculator from a drawer and began pressing keys. 'Yes.'

Green looked up at Gough. 'Well. Good. You have a van?'

'I can get one.'

'You will rent it?'

'I guess so.'

'In your own name?'

'Oh, I don't think so, Monty. I've got a licence in the name of...'

'Thank you, Jackie, you need not tell me the name. As long as it is not yours. That's what I wanted to know.'

He leaned back in his chair. He lit a cigar, offering the case to Jackie, who refused.

'Wise. It is a filthy habit. Let me tell you how we work. Did you ever use SatNav?'

'SatNav?'

'You did not. When you leave here, Jackie, go to the High Street and buy a TomTom. It will cost you about three hundred pounds. Repeat that, please.'

'High Street. TomTom. Three hundred quid.'

'That's it. Now. An educated man like you won't have any trouble working out how to program the TomTom. It comes with instructions, and it's easy. When you get the first load into the van, drive to the Elephant. When you get there, program the TomTom to take you to the Southside Business Park in Egham. Then follow the instructions. Once in Egham, you're looking for the yellow warehouse with the maroon doors. Okay?'

'Yellow warehouse, maroon doors.'

'I've got your mobile number, Jackie. Carry the phone with you. Make sure the battery is charged. If, at any time, you receive a text with the message Happy Birthday, don't go near the warehouse. Don't even go to Egham.'

'Bloody hell. What do I do?'

'Anything you like, Jackie. Except approach the warehouse. "Happy Birthday" means you're being followed. Assuming you get to the warehouse, there'll be someone there to help you unload. Tell him how many trips it's going to take to move the full contents of the lockup. Go back to the lockup and do the whole thing again. Elephant, Southside Business Park, yellow warehouse, maroon doors. Don't miss a step each time. When you've made the last drop, you'll be paid. In full and in cash. Don't lose it, Jackie, because there won't be any more if you do.'

'Okay. Monty. Can I ask a question?'

Green made an expansive hand gesture.

'Well. Why do we have to do it this way? Why so complicated? Why can't I just deliver the gear where you tell me?'

'That's three questions, Jackie. But I'll be delighted to answer them. You've dealt with fences before, right?'

'Once or twice.'

'Think about the fences you've used. How many of them have never been to jail?'

'Well. None of them.'

'None of them. In fact, when Jimmy Nailor went down, he took you with him. You and a few others. Am I right?'

'You are, Monty.'

'You still bear the scars, I'll bet. Man like you doing time. Can't have been a lot of fun. I've never been to jail, Jackie. Never even been in court. Jim Cameron and Johnny Walker, Jackie. They've never been to jail either. They don't want to go. And neither do I.

'This lockup of yours, Jackie. I don't know where it is. And you know what? I don't want to know. That's why you're not setting the SatNav from there. Because I don't want to know where it is. So we start from the Elephant, because I do know where that is.

'There'll be other drivers, Jackie, setting the same route on their own NavMans. Might be one, might be three, you don't need to know how many. Their directions will come out the same as yours. "Left here, straight on, now turn right." That's how they'll know which way you're going. They'll be joining your journey at one point or another, and they'll be going the same way as you.'

'They'll be watching me?'

'No, Jackie. They'll be checking whether someone else is watching you. Someone you don't know about. Someone who did know where that lockup was. Someone who's been waiting for someone to turn up there in a van and drive off with some dodgy gear.'

'The police.'

'Just so, Jackie. The police. The police won't just want the van driver, Jackie. They'll want the address of the yellow warehouse with the maroon doors. And then they'll want to know who rented it. Are you with me?'

'Every inch of the way.'

'That's good. Let me tell you something else, Jackie. That warehouse is specific to you. That's how we work. One supplier, one warehouse. We rent them for a short time and then we go and rent another. Outside my organisation, the only person who knows where that warehouse is will be you. So, if a bunch of men in nice blue uniforms with flashing lights on their cars come knocking on the door, I'll be wondering who grassed us up. And there'll be one name in the frame. You know what that name will be?'

Gough licked his lips. 'Mine, Monty.'

'Yours, Jackie. And there's more than one cut-out between the name on the warehouse lease and me. So, whatever happens, I'll still be on the outside. And I'll be looking to settle scores. So that better not happen.'

Gough looked coolly at Green. 'I'm no grass, Monty.'

Green smiled, as though to himself. 'I'm pleased to hear that, Jackie. The arrangement with the SatNav is to make sure you don't give us away accidentally. Anything else you want to know?'

Gough shook his head. 'I don't think so.'

'Better be on your way, then. You're going to be a busy young man. It's midday. If you look sharp you can have it all done by six.'

'You want me to shift the gear in the daytime?'

'Jackie. Can you imagine anything more innocent than a van shifting goods from one warehouse to another in broad daylight? Or more suspicious than doing the same thing in the middle of the night? Oh, and Jackie. When it's all over, and *before* you go home, have a drink or whatever else you plan to do by way of celebration, put the SatNav on the road and drive over it. Destroy it utterly, Jackie.'

'Bloody hell, Monty. Three hundred quid's worth? Why?'

'SatNavs store the last few places they've been in their memory, Jackie. We don't want the police finding yours and asking it questions, now do we?'

'Where's the meeting?' asked Doyle.

'South Mimms.'

'Where the hell's that?'

'Service station on the M25. There's a motel.'

'Is it near where he lives?'

'Maybe. Does it matter?'

'I guess not. We gonna eat dinner tonight?'

Gough rang Sharon and told her, in elliptic phrasing they both believed would be impenetrable to anyone listening in, what he was up to and when he would be through. After she had hung up the phone, Sharon put on a pair of gloves, took the envelope addressed to Ablett from her underwear drawer, sealed and stamped it and went out to find a postbox. She carefully selected one some distance from home.

It was after nine when Gough finally got back to her place. Sharon's face glowed as she looked at the two sports bags. 'Is it all in there?'

'I haven't counted it.'

'Shall we count it now?'

When they had verified that the bags contained the thick end of four hundred and fifty thousand pounds, the two conspirators sat in silence.

'What are you thinking?' asked Sharon.

'I'm scared.'

'Go on?'

'That money's not ours, Sharon. It belongs to Jim Cameron.'

'Cameron stole it, Jackie.'

'Doesn't make any difference. He thinks of it as his. If we steal it, he's going to come looking for us.'

'But he won't find us, Jackie. Sharon Wright and Jackie Gough are going to disappear. John and Sharon Renton are going to be living in Cornwall with their little baby. We're never coming back here. Never going to make contact with anyone here, ever again.'

'But if he does find us...'

'He won't. Trust me. We can do this, Jackie.' She took his hand. 'But you have to be brave.'

'I want to be brave, Sharon. But I'm terrified.'

'Okay. Look. We won't do anything yet. We'll take that money to the bank tomorrow, Jackie. Get the account opened for John and Sharon Renton. We'll open it in Paris, 'cos I've always wanted to go to Paris. There's no harm in that, is there?'

'Not so far.'

'We're only doing what Jim Cameron wants, yes?'

'I suppose so.'

'The harm only starts if we clear off with the money. Right? Right, Jackie?'

'Right.'

'So we don't decide to do that yet. Okay?'

Gough was visibly brighter. 'Okay.'

'There's just one thing you have to promise me, Jackie. Promise you'll come to Cornwall with me tomorrow. Just to take a look.'

'But...'

'Just to take a look, Jackie. If you don't like it, we'll come straight back home and I'll never mention it again. We'll stay here. I'll have your baby. You can work for Cameron. And I promise you, Jackie, all the years we're together, I'll never once suggest you steal money from him and I'll never ever remind you we could have been rich. Is that a deal? Jackie?'

There were tears of gratitude in Gough's eyes. 'It's a deal. I've got to tell you, though, I don't think there's much chance I'll stay in Cornwall. Any chance at all, if I'm honest.'

'I understand. But you have to come and look. You promised me that. Tomorrow.'

'Tomorrow? I don't...'

'Tomorrow, Jackie. You *know* if you don't come tomorrow you won't come.'

'All right, Sharon. All right.'

'This is a crossroads for us, Jackie. You've made me a promise. Are you going to keep it?'

'I said all right.'

'Cos if you don't I don't think we've got much future, do you?'

Defeated, Gough raised his hands in the air.

'I saw this woman on the Oprah show. Do you ever watch the Oprah show?'

'No, Shaz. I never watch the Oprah show.'

'Well, I don't now because it isn't on any more. But I used to watch it and this woman said you can't have a relationship with someone you can't rely on to tell you the truth. Any kind of relationship. And she's right, Jackie.'

'Sharon. I've said yes.'

'Here's what we'll do. I'll go with you to the bank tomorrow.'

'Don't you trust me?'

'If the account's going to be either to sign, they'll need my signature, won't they? Then, after we've deposited the cash, we'll go to Cornwall. There's a train leaves Paddington at a quarter to twelve. I'll be on it. It stops at Ealing at five past. You get on there.'

'Why can't we both go from Paddington?'

'We don't want anyone seeing us together. Do we? In case we don't come back.'

'We probably will come back, Sharon. Almost certainly, in fact.'

'In case. All right?'

Gough sighed. 'All right.'

Sharon smiled. She kissed him on the cheek. 'Whatever you want, Jackie, that's what we'll do. But only after we've been to Cornwall and you've had a look. Now. I'm going to go and lie down. With just my nightie on. Why don't you pretend to be a burglar? A burglar who gets carried away by the sleeping woman he sees on the bed? A big strong burglar who has his way in spite of anything the poor weak girl can do?'

She picked up the two sports bags. 'Better have these in there with us, don't you think?'

Doyle drove the car he had rented in someone else's name into the South Mimms car park. He and Carver walked into separate cubicles of the men's toilets in the main services building, where each man checked his gun and attached a silencer. Both men preferred working at this time of year, when the overcoats that allowed weapons to pass unnoticed were not themselves conspicuous.

While Doyle returned to the car, Carver walked across the car park towards the Days Inn. As arranged, a man was standing just outside the entrance. He nodded as Carver approached. 'Don Carver?'

'Jim Cameron?'

'Jim isn't here. I'm Johnnie Walker.'

Carver ignored the proffered handshake. 'So where's Cameron?'

'He isn't here.'

'You said that. Where is he?'

'We thought you and I could...'

'You thought wrong. I told Mitch it was Cameron or no-one.'

Walker sighed. 'We were afraid you'd say that. All right, Don. I'll take you to him. You want to come with me? I'll bring you back for your car later.'

He was walking towards a silver Jag. As he pressed his key to open the doors, he took a mobile phone from his pocket. 'I have to let Jim know we're coming.'

'Go right ahead.'

Walker said a few words into his phone, then got into the driver's seat. Carver sat beside him. Walker turned the key and the car started smoothly forward.

'We going to Cameron's home?'

'You know something, Don? Even I don't know where Jim lives.'

'What is he? Paranoid?'

'Maybe. That or very careful.'

'So where are we going?'

'To a meeting place. You know, Don, you could be accused of paranoia yourself.'

'You think so? Sit where I'm sitting. Buggy comes to see me. I've never met the guy, but he's vouched for by Mitchell so I let him make his pitch. He arranges for me to get paid, and I do. I come here to do a job. Buggy's supposed to meet me, point me at the mark, but when I get here there's no sign of him. Mitch gives me some tale I simply don't believe about him having a sick mother.'

'You didn't believe that?'

'I'll tell you what I believe. I believe Buggy's been picked up by the cops for something and you didn't want to tell me that in case I wouldn't come.'

Walker didn't answer. He was looking hard at his rear view mirror. Carver said, 'You have any comment on what I just said?'

'We've got a tail,' said Walker.

'Yeah? You sure?'

'I'm sure.' He reached out a hand towards the phone.

'What are you doing?'

'I'm letting Jim know we're being followed.'

Carver slipped the silenced revolver from his pocket and pressed it into Walker's ribs. 'I don't think so, Johnnie.'

CHAPTER 37

At Carver's command, Walker pulled the Jag into the side of the road. Doyle parked immediately behind and got into the Jag's rear seat.

'Johnnie Walker,' said Carver. 'Meet Mister Smith.'

'I'm really pleased to meet you, Johnnie,' said Doyle. Walker said nothing.

'Mister Smith is my bodyguard,' said Carver. 'As I just pointed out to you, this is a paranoia-inducing situation. You didn't expect me to walk in unprotected, did you?'

Still Walker said nothing.

'Mister Smith,' said Carver. 'While I keep this little beauty trained on Johnnie's vital organs, why don't you find out if he's carrying?'

Doyle leaned over the back of the driver's seat and frisked Walker with every sign of practised expertise. He held up a snub-nosed Smith & Wesson for Carver to see.

'Well, well,' said Carver. 'And what exactly were we planning to do with that, Johnnie?'

There was no answer.

'Johnnie's the strong, silent type,' said Doyle.

'Let's review your options here, Johnnie,' Carver said. 'Because you do have them. Option number one is that you can drive Mister Smith and me to our meeting with Cameron. As you planned, except that you didn't know we'd have company. Cameron can tell me what he has to tell me, and I can decide whether or not I'm going to do what he wants. Whatever I decide, Mister Smith and I will go away afterwards. Your boss might be a bit angry with you for letting me and Mister Smith take your gun away, but what the hell? You're still alive. That's option number one.

'Option number two is that you can decide you don't want to take Mister Smith and me to meet Cameron. If you go for that one, Mister Smith and I will decide whether we still want to meet Cameron. If we don't, we'll both go home and Cameron will never get to tell me what he wants to tell me. If we do, we'll find him. Oh, yes. We'll find him. But either way it won't matter to you, Johnnie, because you'll be dead. You'll have died right here, by the side of this road. That's option number two.

'So why don't you tell us which option you favour, Johnnie? Because we haven't got all day. And my finger's getting itchy on this trigger.'

Walker turned to look straight into Carver's eyes. He was calm, his breathing normal, his gaze steady.

'I admire your courage, Johnnie,' said Carver. 'You ready to choose?'

Walker turned his attention back to the road. He turned the key and moved the car out into the carriageway. Doyle patted him on the shoulder.

'Good thinking,' said Doyle.

Carver kept the gun exactly where it had been. 'I want to know we're getting there before we get there. If Cameron sees Mister Smith before he's had a chance to drop down behind the seat, I'll pull this trigger.'

'Okay.'

Sharon and Jackie walked out of the bank together. 'Would you have believed it could be that easy?' asked Sharon.

Gough shook his head. 'These guys are on a different level.'

'How are you feeling, love?'

'I'm cool.'

'You know we won't do anything you don't want to do?'

Gough nodded.

'But a girl can dream. And you will be at Ealing station for midday?'

'Yes, Sharon. I said I would and I meant it. Just like I mean it when I say I'll be back home tomorrow.'

'That's okay, Jackie.'

'You're sure?'

She took his hand, hooking his arm round her own. She pressed herself against him like a cat asking its owner to feed it. 'I'm sure. As long as you do what you promised today, whatever you want to do tomorrow will be just fine.'

'So tell me, Johnnie,' said Carver. 'Why does Cameron want this Doyle guy iced?'

'Beats me,' said Walker.

'You don't know?'

'Oh, sure I know. But I don't understand.'

'So tell what you know.'

'Doyle did a job for us.'

'Doyle's a hitman.'

'I know that.'

'So when you say he did a job...'

'He killed someone Cameron wanted killed.'

'He killed him. He did the job.'

'Absolutely.'

'See, Johnnie,' said Carver, 'this makes me nervous. Cameron asks a hitman to kill someone, the hitman does the job, then

Cameron wants him killed. I'm a hitman, Johnnie, and Cameron wants me to off somebody. Like I say, that makes me nervous. You see how that could be?'

'I can see your point, yes.'

'So, why does he want this job done?'

'Buggy hired Doyle. We didn't know anything about the man. Then it just happened, Cameron was talking to a couple of guys from New Jersey. Gaming machines, stuff like that. Legitimate on the face of it. Only of course they're not. These guys want to put some of their machines into England. They talk to Jim. You know what Jim's like.'

'I don't. Why don't you tell me?'

'Jim's very big deal. You know? I mean, don't get me wrong, he's a good guy to work for, but he has to be the number one and he has to have people know that's what he is. He doesn't need to get machines from the US, he has a perfectly good supply from Nottingham, and those guys really are legit. As far as I know, anyway. But give him a chance to be able to let rumours spread he deals with organised hoods from New Jersey, he'll take it.'

'What's this have to do with killing Doyle?'

'So Jim gets talking to these guys, and maybe they threaten him a little. You know, what they'll do to him if he doesn't take their machines. Jim doesn't like being threatened. Wants to show them they're playing with fire. So he warns them he's got this American hitman who can follow them all the way home and off them in their own backyard.

'Naturally, they want to know who this mystery man is. And the bloody fool tells them.'

'Nice,' said Carver.

'I was surprised, I admit that. Jim's usually very discreet. Anyway, he tells them and they start to laugh, snigger really, and they tell Jim Doyle's a liability. A nutter, according to them. Kills people for fun. And he can't go back home because one of the people he killed was this woman, the wife of some gang leader. Doyle reckoned the guy had stiffed him out of some money, so he kidnapped the guy's wife. The guy paid out the ransom money, but when he got his wife back she was dead.'

'I'm still not hearing a reason Cameron would want him killed.'

'Like I say, it makes no sense to me. But you know what I think?'

'Tell us.'

'I think Jim wants to show off to the Yanks. You know? "You're the bigshot American bad guys. But you couldn't get to this guy. And I did. I wasted the man you couldn't touch, and if you threaten me again, I'll waste you." It's just a theory. We'll be there in three minutes.'

Doyle ducked down in the well between front and back seats.

There was a tremor in Walker's voice when he spoke again. 'So, when you've killed Cameron, what are you going to do to me?'

'Kill Cameron? Why should we kill Cameron?'

'That is Doyle back there, isn't it?'

'How long have you known?'

'Since now. I wondered when I heard his American accent. I didn't know till you said that.'

'Pull in.'

Walker did.

'Kill the engine.'

All became silent. Carver said, 'Tell me what we're going to find when we get where we're going.'

'A cricket field. With a pavilion in it. Cameron sponsors the club. Serious money by their standards. Sometimes he uses the pavilion for meetings. When he does, the club makes sure there's no-one there.'

'Cameron's in the pavilion?'

'Yup.'

'Armed?'

'I should think so, wouldn't you?'

'But he's not planning to shoot me?'

'That's not his plan, no.'

'Well, Johnnie. It's our plan to shoot him. And you. You got any better idea?'

'I don't much want to die.'

'Not many people do, Johnnie. I asked if you had a plan.'

'Suppose I kill him? I walk you right in there and then I kill him.'

'Go on.'

'You two go. I stay and take the rap. I say he threatened me. I'll pop off a couple from his gun into the wall, say he missed and I shot him in self-defence. Don't even mention you two. Owen Thompson's one of the best briefs in the business. Chances are I'll go down for manslaughter, mitigating circumstances, be on the street again in five years, max. You shoot me, I'll never see the street again.'

'What do you think, Doyle?'

'It could work. As long as he's covered every second.'

'We can manage that. How many shells in that little snubby?'

Doyle examined the Smith & Wesson. 'Four.'

'Four. This pavilion. Will Cameron be able to see us as we walk up to it?'

'No. He'll be in the back.'

'You're sure? Your life depends on this.'

'He won't be able to see us.'

'Okay. Here's what we do. We all walk up to the pavilion together. Doyle will be behind you and me. If there's the slightest sign of trouble, the first thing he does will be to shoot you. You understand?'

'I understand.'

'When we get inside, you empty four shots into Cameron. He has to be dead. You still understand?'

'I told you. I understand.'

'Then one of us will put two of his slugs into the wall. Not you. One of us.'

'Okay.'

'Then we walk away and leave you to take the consequences. You on for that?'

'I'm on.'

'Doyle?'

'Suits me.'

'Done deal. Gentlemen, you may start your engines.'

Stacy stared out of the window. Ordinary people going about their everyday business. But that's where HE'd been, when he watched her. Before what had happened to her.

She'd impressed herself, as well as everyone else, with the way she'd dealt with what had happened to her. She wanted to say, "her rape," but she couldn't bring herself to say that. She preferred to think about "what had happened to her." But she'd handled it. Or so it seemed.

There'd been casualties, sure. Her relationship with Mark had been one, and Mark himself felt that he'd been another.

She knew what he thought, how quietly proud he'd been of the way he was behaving. His woman, who should have been his alone, had had sex with another man. Her mouth had sucked another man's cock. Her thighs had opened for another man to lie between them. Her breasts had been rolled in another man's hands.

In another day and age, or even today in some countries you heard about, he'd have been able to put her righteously from him as damaged goods. She'd have killed herself because of the shame. If she hadn't, her family would have done it for her, and no jury in the land would have convicted.

Instead of which, he'd responded the way a new man should. Given her time and space. Sympathised. Cooked for her, changed the lock on her door. Gone with her to the police station. Talked on the phone to her friends in the kind of voice you might use to talk about an invalid miraculously recovering from cancer. He'd cuddled her at night, ostentatiously keeping his stiffie away from her back so she wouldn't know how he was suffering from this enforced celibacy, but letting her know anyway.

And he didn't understand when she decided he had to go.

Well, fuck him.

Stacy Teasdale wasn't into self harm. She wasn't going to kill herself for shame at what someone else had done.

She went into the kitchen. What did she want to eat? There were plenty of nice things she'd brought back from Waitrose. Things to tempt her appetite.

It wasn't, she realised, a question of what she wanted to eat but of how she wanted to eat. Which was: in the company of other people. Not alone.

Every once in a while, she used the café over the road. She hadn't been in since what had happened to her. Not because she hadn't wanted to, although she hadn't, particularly, but because she knew HE had been there. The Police had told her. It was from the café that HE had watched her. It was from that room that HE had plotted her degradation.

And the staff there, the waitresses and the manager, they would know that. They would know that she was the woman HE had schemed against.

Stacy sat for a while, making up her mind. She wanted to; she didn't want to. She was going to; she couldn't.

She walked back into the sitting room. She looked out of the window at the café. She picked up her coat.

Sharon entwined her arm more closely with Gough's.

'You'd better go, my love.'

'Everything's going to be all right, isn't it?'

She hugged his arm more tightly. 'Everything's going to be fine, darling. I'll see you at Ealing. We'll sleep together tonight in Penzance. Then, what will be will be.'

She kissed him. It was always she who kissed them. She'd noticed that. Men were delighted to get on top of her and do what they wanted to do, but if it was a matter of a kiss and a show of affection it was down to her. It had always been like that. Always would be, probably.

Maybe Adrian would be different. Was she going to see Adrian again? Probably. After she'd been to Paris, collected the money from the account Muammar had arranged there, and had a little bit of a good time. Then she'd come back, find a flat, do her access course, prepare for her future. There was no reason Adrian shouldn't be part of that future. Not long term, certainly. But for a little while.

She said, 'Go, my sweet. You to Ealing. Me to Paddington.'

He went. When he was out of sight, Sharon hailed a taxi and gave the driver her address. Once there, she packed a bag, showered and changed. There was no hurry. Her train wouldn't leave for another four hours, and when it did it wouldn't be from Paddington.

It took an effort of will to open the café door and pass inside. One of the waitresses looked at her, then the other did.

'Stacy!'

'Hi.'

They came towards her, one on each side. 'Oh, Stace, I'm so glad to see you. We've been talking about you. Haven't we?'

'Have you?'

Hands gentle on her arms. 'Hoping you'd come in. You know. After... Terrible thing, Stace. I'm so sorry.'

'We're so sorry.'

'Come in. Sit down. What are you going to have?'

'Oh. Um. Scrambled egg? Bacon?'

'Sure. Tomato? Toast?'

'Lovely.'

'To drink?'

'Um. Tea?'

'Comfort food, Stace. You're entitled. No-one more so.'

When she'd eaten, the two waitresses came back. 'You back at work now, Stace?'

She shook her head. 'Not going.'

'Oh?'

She could see their curiosity. Tact prevented them from asking, was she going back to her parents' home? Giving up? Crawling back into her burrow?

'Did you ever meet my mate Vanessa?'

'Don't think so. Did we?'

'Don't remember it.'

'She got a job on a cruise ship. As a croupier. I'm going to join them.'

Eyes shining. 'Oh, Stace. Oh, that's fantastic. What about...'

'Mark?'

The waitresses nodded in unison.

'He's gone.'

Faces poised to go either way. Sympathy, sadness, congratulations—waiting for their cue.

'I gave him his marching orders.'

She wished someone would ask when she'd made up her mind about the cruise ships. Because the answer would be: About thirty seconds ago.

Jackie arrived at Ealing with thirty minutes to spare. He went into Waitrose and bought a bottle of water and a sandwich for the journey. Before he reached the checkout, he went back and bought another bottle of water and another sandwich. There was no certainty Sharon, in her current state of excitement, would remember to provide for herself.

He walked to the station. Here a problem presented itself.

'The Penzance train doesn't stop here,' said the ticket seller.

'It must do.'

'Well, it doesn't. The 12.05 from Paddington gets to Penzance at five past five. But it doesn't stop here. If you want to go from here, you need the 12.33, change at Reading, arrive seven oh two. You want a ticket?'

'I don't understand.'

'You want me to say it again? Is that man looking for you?'

Gough turned round. Five yards behind him, grinning obscenely through a mostly toothless mouth, was the biggest, nastiest, craziest person of Gough's acquaintance.

'Jackie. Jackie Gough. Fancy seeing you here.'

The first intimations of disaster tinkled at the edge of Gough's fear-frozen mind. 'Dan. How...how are you?'

Ablett stepped forward and grabbed Gough's arm. Without apparent effort, he wheeled him away from the ticket office and towards the platform. 'I'm fine, Jackie boy. Considering. Considering I done five years I hadn't needed to do if some little shit hadn't grassed me up.'

'I...Dan...'

They were now on the edge of the platform.

'How could you do that, you little shit? How could you grass me up? What harm did I ever do you?'

'I...me? Dan, I don't know who's been talking to you, but...'

'No-one's been talking to me, Gough.' He pulled a tape from his pocket and waved it under Gough's nose. 'I've been listening to this.'

'I...oh, God. Oh, no. Dan, I...I didn't...I couldn't...Dan!'

'So why tell the bloody Bill you did? Eh?'

The track approaching Ealing station is straight for some distance. Trains that have eased and edged their way through the inner and outer reaches of west London hit their stride as they gather pace for the run to Reading. Fast trains to Wales and the west country, in particular, are closing on their top speed as they streak through Ealing. The 12.05 from Paddington to Penzance is a fast train to the west country. Gough had his back to it, but Ablett could see it clearly, still half a mile away but approaching rapidly.

'Dan, I swear to you. I said those things because that bloody Prutton woman told me to.'

'Liar.'

At that speed, it takes a train less than forty seconds to cover half a mile. The train was now two hundred yards away—a distance that would occupy it for nine seconds. Ablett leaned forward, heaved Gough's body over one shoulder, took his arm in one huge hand and his leg in the other. He swung the helpless graduate and failed criminal in a huge circle. At the top of the arc, he hurled Gough up and out into the path of the onrushing locomotive.

Gough screamed. He fell onto the tracks, turned, saw the train all but on top of him. He gathered all the strength he had for a desperate leap to safety before three hundred tonnes of accelerating steel hit him in the chest and threw him sideways. He fell on the track under the unforgiving wheels. As the train hurtled over him, his severed head and one hand were flung to one side. The rest disappeared below the speeding train.

There was silence on the platform. Then began a screaming that those who heard it swore they would never forget. The ticket seller rattled down the blind across his window and locked his door.

Mad Dan Ablett turned, grinned at his stunned audience and wandered forth into the street.

No-one made any attempt to stop him.

CHAPTER 38

The Jag eased its way onto the cricket field and up to the pavilion. Walker brought the car to a halt.

'You play this game?' asked Doyle.

'I used to.'

'I could never understand what the hell was going on. You can spend five days on one game and it ends in a draw.'

'Those are the most exciting matches.'

Doyle shook his head.

The three men got out and walked towards the pavilion, Doyle slightly to the rear. When they reached the door, Carver pushed Walker ahead of him.

Inside, Cameron was all amiability. He stepped forward, holding out his hand. 'Don Carver?' Then he stopped. 'Who is this?'

Carver said, 'Jim Cameron, meet Doyle.'

Cameron went for his inside pocket, but Doyle's gun was up and pointing at him. Cameron stopped his hand.

'I believe you want me dead, Cameron,' said Doyle.

'This is a joke, I think.'

'I did a job for you. And you decide to top me. Me. Who never ratted out a man in his life. You want to explain?'

'I...' Cameron looked at Walker. 'Johnnie? What's going on here?'

'I'm sorry, Jim.' Walker raised his Smith & Wesson and shot Cameron, once in the head and three times in the chest. He pressed the trigger again. It clicked emptily.

Doyle looked down at Cameron's lifeless body. Then he pointed his pistol at Walker.

Walker's body sagged. 'I won't beg, Mister Doyle. If you're going to kill me, get it done.'

Doyle sighted down the barrel at the centre of Walker's chest. Then he said, 'Me and Carver here, we have a thing about loyalty, Johnnie. About standing by your word. Old-fashioned stuff like trust. Honour. Whether people do what they say they're going to do. Including your boss here, two men are dead because of their disloyalty.'

Walker said, 'I did what I told you I'd do.'

'You did, Johnnie. You did.' He moved the gun slightly to the side. Then he put it in his pocket. Reaching down, he took a sleek automatic from Cameron's pocket. He wiped it clean with a tissue.

'You've been a stand up guy,' he said. 'You kept your word. But I'm going to have to shoot you. Bullets in the wall won't get you off. I'll pop you in the soft part of the arm. It'll hurt like hell when it starts to hurt, and you'll bleed. A lot. But you won't die.'

Walker nodded.

'Cameron picked you up at South Mimms,' Doyle went on. 'You left your car there. That's where it'll be when the police go looking for it. Tell them whatever you like about your argument with Cameron. But leave me and Carver here out of it. Or spend the rest of your life looking over your shoulder.'

'I'll leave you out.'

'Hold out your arm.'

The shot hurt even more than Doyle had said it would. Doyle wiped the gun again, then wrapped Cameron's hand around it. He squeezed Cameron's hand, firing a single bullet into the door frame behind Walker. 'Forensics can tell if a hand has fired a gun,' he explained. 'You got a mobile?'

Walker, clutching his injured arm and grimacing with pain, nodded.

'Give us fifteen. Then call an ambulance. Let them take care of the cops.'

'Okay.'

Driving back in the Jag to collect Doyle's rental car, Doyle asked, 'What you gonna do now?'

'Back to France. This afternoon.'

'Will that be safe?'

'I won't go straight home. I'll spend a couple of days in Paris. Ring Arbot, see what's what. If I have to, I'll abandon Burgundy.'

'Where will you go?'

'The Perigord Noir. I've fancied getting a place in Souillac for a while now. Even if I can't go back to Auxerre, they won't have been able to get their hands on my money. What about you?'

'I thought I'd go to Ireland.'

'No shortage of gunmen there.'

'I wasn't thinking of staying. It could be easier to fly out of. I think I might try Canada next.'

Carver nodded. 'Stay in touch.'

'Soon as I've got a new contact method, I'll let you know.'

'You think we did right letting Walker live?'

'He did right by us, we did right by him. Here's my car.'

'That stuff about the gang leader's wife. Was that true?'

'It didn't happen quite like they said. I don't kill people for fun. There has to be a good reason.'

'See you, Doyle.'

'Take care.'

Sharon settled into her comfortable Eurostar seat. She had all the magazines she wanted, and *In the Night Café* to finish. She'd been told they'd start serving a meal when they were through the tunnel.

At the end of the carriage, a man was watching her. Could he really have green eyes? Or were they coloured contact lenses? She thought they might be. Either way, he looked interesting. There was an attractive hint of violence beneath the civilised veneer. She wondered what it would be that turned him on. And what it would take to find out. Jackie had been so simple to fathom. Him with his university degree. It was like her mother used to say—some people had all the brains in the world and no common sense whatsoever. And fancy believing that poor old Sergeant Mitchell would ever rip a young girl's knicks off! To look and be touched, that was all Mitchell had ever asked.

The man with green eyes would want to do a bit more than look and be touched. You could see that. Although she didn't need to—she hadn't missed a day on the pill since she was thirteen and, whatever she may have told poor Jackie Gough, if there was one thing she knew she wasn't, it was pregnant— Sharon sauntered down the carriage towards the WC. The guy would either be interested or he wouldn't. If he was, he'd know what to do when they got to Paris. If he wasn't, she didn't think she'd have to wait too long before someone else stepped forward from the crowd.

As she passed the man's seat, she let her hips in the short skirt sway close to his face. When she got back to her seat he was staring straight at her. Oh, he was on the hook, all right.

As the train raced through its shimmering cocoon of time towards the City of Love, a shiver of anticipation ran through her.

And through Carver.

I hope you have enjoyed this book. If you have, and you'd like to know what else I've written, you could try these:

A Just and Upright Man. I published this as R J Lynch instead of John Lynch because historical fiction was a new direction for me. *AJAUM* is a crime/romance set in County Durham in northeast England in the 1760s. Here's what the Historical Novel Society Indie Review said about it: *Set against a background of the late 18th century threat of enclosure, and with numerous nice subplots running through it, A Just and Upright Man is a delightful read. An absolute gem, R.J Lynch's tale put me in mind of Winston Graham's Poldark, with its superb gamut of colourful characters, all of whom come alive on the page and capture your imagination. There are plenty of skeletons in cupboards here, as past actions catch up with many, including Blakiston, as he fights his attraction to the beautiful and spirited Kate Greener, a woman beneath his class but who he finds captivating. I thoroughly enjoyed this novel, not only an extremely well-constructed mix of historical, crime and romance but a tale of real people and village life that one felt fully absorbed in. The historical fact was extremely well researched and seemed flawless. I cannot praise this book highly enough, it was a novel I did not want to end...so I am delighted to see that it is the first of a planned series – I will be rushing out to purchase the sequel when it is published. A truly superb novel and indie publishing at its very best.*

Zappa's Mam's a Slapper. Billy McErlane wants to be the world's only recluse celeb. Having gone to jail at the age of fourteen for the murder of his stepfather doesn't make it easy and nor does having a harlot for a mother, but when he is reunited with his childhood sweetheart peace enters Billy's heart. Then fate deals a wrecking blow. The last thing Billy needs is Dillon, a four-year-old with a background as unpromising as his. A bittersweet story of love, loss and one young man's refusal to accept what life offers. The opening pages of *Zappa's Mam's a Slapper* begin on page 345 in order to give you the chance to decide whether it's your kind of book.

The International Sales Handbook. Something completely different! In more than 40 years as an international salesman I lived and worked on every continent except Antarctica. *The International Sales Handbook* distils everything I learned into the ultimate What to, How to and Why to guide for any company wanting to start or build their export business and for the salespeople who have to put it into practice.

JOHN LYNCH

ZAPPA'S MAM'S A SLAPPER

CHAPTER 1

All I'd said was, I wouldn't mind seeing her in her knickers. I wouldn't have thought, being honest, that that merited a showdown with her brothers.

I tried to explain. She's a bit on the chubby side, Kathleen, which I like. Not a grotesque fatty; just a bit of a plumper. Real fatties, I don't care for. I've got a pic I took of a thumper sitting on one chair when three would not have been too many. I took it from behind, which is the only way you could really bring yourself to look at her. Great blue denim bulges hanging down on each side. You'd wonder how anyone could let herself get like that.

Jessica made me leave that one out of the exhibition. 'It's an interesting eye you have, Billy,' she said, 'but it wouldn't please everyone.'

I said, 'That's not what the instructor told us in Young Offenders. He said you should nurture your own unique vision.'

Jessica's eye twitched. She didn't like being argued with, and she had this ambivalence towards my time inside – it was what made me a celeb but she said it was her job to publicise it and not mine. Which is all very well, but if I hadn't been in Young Offenders I'd never have got into taking pics. They'd run this course on digital photography (and how stupid is that? To do digital photography you need a digital camera and how did anyone think a Young Offender was going to get one of those once he was back on the street?) and I'd signed up to deal with the tension of not knowing whether I'd get out. I'd loved it.

No, with Kathleen I'd pictured her sitting on a bed in nothing but a pair of those knickers Marks & Sparks had in their adverts when they were going after the smart young people who wouldn't be seen dead in Marks, you might as well ask them to shop in Milletts. Everyone remembers those knickers. Every man, anyway. Lot of lezzies, too, I should think. The ones coming a couple of inches down the leg and cut square. Nice patterns, interesting colours and a dark edge to waist and leg. And the models they used hadn't exactly been short-changed in the upper body department.

Lovely. Kathleen would be sitting on the bed in these and nothing else, one leg pointing straight out in front and the other drawn up under her, arms crossed at the elbow and hands clasped so that you saw nothing more revealing than a bit of flesh squeezed each side of the arms. And she'd be looking straight at the camera and smiling. That's one of the things I liked about Kathleen – that she was always smiling. That and not being skinny. She had a lovely smile, Kathleen.

Jessica said I had a fantastic eye for a pic, 'a real intuitive grasp for composition,' which was exactly what the instructor at Young Offenders had said.

And that's all it was.

But I'd said it out loud and some mischief-making twat had told Kathleen's brothers and they were offended. Or pretended they were. They wanted me to explain myself. I suppose they thought, being two of them, they could take me on. Big mistake. I'd tried to leave my reputation behind when I'd been brought to this street. 'Make a new start,' the Education Officer had said. But you can't always do that. People won't always let you. It was 2004, I was sixteen years old and at the start of what I hoped was going to be a different life from the one I'd been living up to then, and here I was trying to talk myself out of trouble – a route I'd never taken in the past.

I told the brothers I'd just been thinking about a pic, didn't have any designs on their sister's luscious body. I suppose I can't keep calling them the brothers, you don't know who I'm talking about. Harry and Tommy Doyle, they were. First generation English, the father a copper who'd lived here since he was six but the Doyle boys still came on like they were born in Tipperary. My foster parents were called Howard, but PC Doyle knew I had an Irish surname so he'd stop me in the street and talk about Ireland, what a grand place it was and did I know where my family came from? Which I didn't. My grandparents were born here so if the call had ever come from Lansdowne Road I'd have had to say I wasn't qualified but if you've got an Irish name the Paddies always want to co-opt you. He was all right, Mister Doyle. He even asked the Howards if they wanted him to take me to Mass with his family when they went on Sundays. The Howards said they'd leave it to me, I didn't have to go but I could if I wanted to but if I didn't I needn't.

Which I didn't.

I've never been to Mass in my life.

Or any other kind of religious service, far as I know.

(Except in Young Offenders, of course, where you went to anything that was going just to get out of your cell.)

But I liked it that he'd thought enough of me to ask.

You'd wonder sometimes why, when the father's all right, the son has to be a dickhead.

(Another thing you'd sometimes wonder; if Ireland is such a grand place, why do so many Irish people come over here and never go back?)

Harry said, 'You keep your hands off our sister.' He stuck his finger in my chest as he said it. I've always hated it when people do that. Even then we could still all three of us have walked away, no harm done. That's certainly what I wanted. I said, 'I told you. I was just imagining a pic.' And then I told them the stuff about liking to see a girl who wasn't as thin as a rake, smiling. And about how I'd compose the pic.

Harry said, 'You calling our sister fat?' He had an English accent, same as I did, not a touch of the Paddy about him, but it takes at least a generation and usually two to get people to realise that they're English and not Irish. (If they're American, they never seem to grasp it.) We had about four Irish families in the street. They'd all troop off to Mass on Sundays and they didn't do their socialising locally but in the Hibernian Club downtown. Didn't have as much as they'd have liked but intended their children should have more. The aspirational working class, I learned to call them in Sociology. The English version has disappeared, apparently. Anyone who aspired has made it and those who are left have given up. Live off the State and what you can nick. Like my mother and the Creep. But there's still plenty of immigrants who aspire.

Christian Brothers did the teaching at Saint Simeon's, which is where the boys went, and they were known for their discipline. Maybe the treatment they handed out was what made the Catholic kids think they were so hard. It was a mistake, but most of them made it. Either that or it's just part of the Culture for Paddies to prance around pretending to be hard. They told us in Sociology never to underestimate the power of the Culture. Capital C.

'No,' I said. 'I'm not saying your sister is fat. I'm sayin' she'd make a lovely picture.'

I think I'd realised by now that Harry was determined to bring this to a fight and nothing I did was going to change that. But, I had to try. When you're in jail for an offence like mine, you never actually do your time. The best you can hope for, and this is what had happened to me, is that you're released on licence. What that means is that if you commit any kind of offence they can take you back inside to finish your original sentence. Even if the new offence is shoplifting a Snickers bar and the original sentence was life imprisonment, they can still take you back to serve it. And as it happens my original sentence was life imprisonment, because that's mandatory in this country for the offence I'd been found guilty of. Although, because of my age, they didn't call it that, they called it detention at the pleasure of Her Majesty. But life imprisonment is what that means, at least in my case. The judge made that clear when he sentenced me. And I wouldn't be going back to Young Offenders. I was an adult now, and it would be adult jail I went to, and I'd had some of that already and I hadn't liked it. At all. So I wanted to stay out of trouble if I could and if that meant seeming to back down in front of the Doyle boys, back down is what I'd have to do.

There are limits, though. Which Harry Doyle overstepped when he called my foster mother an ugly cow. I dropped him.

He went down with a satisfying thump and didn't move. I looked at Tommy. 'You can have one, too,' I said. 'But you don't have to. It's up to you.'

Tommy was younger than Harry, younger than me in fact, and was looking seriously nervous. All the bombast he'd got from standing beside his big and rather stupid brother had left him.

'Do you think he's all right?' he asked.

'He went down a bit hard.'

'Maybe we should get help.'

'Maybe *you* should get help,' I said. 'I didn't want this in the first place.'

'Me neither,' said Tommy. 'He makes me go along. If I don't do what he wants, he beats me up.'

'So,' I said. 'That's what they teach you at Catholic school, is it?'

Harry had started to make noises. He rolled over and tried to sit up. It took him three goes.

'Our dad likes you,' Tommy said. 'Our sister likes you, too.'

'Does she?'

'I doubt she'll let you see her in her knickers, though.' He grinned at me. 'That's not what they teach you at Catholic school.'

Mister Doyle stopped me in the street the next day. 'Harry's concussed,' he said. 'He's going to miss a few days' college.'

'I'm sorry. It wasn't my fault.'

'I know whose fault it was. I've heard the whole story. They won't trouble you again.' He looked as though he was going to move on, but didn't. 'They have a youth club,' he said. 'At the Hibernian. Dancing on Saturday nights.'

'Yes?'

'Kathleen goes there.' He looked at me closely. 'Well,' he said. 'Just a thought.' He looked back as he walked way. 'Harry told Kathleen you said she was fat.'

'I didn't say that.'

'I wouldn't be talking to you if I thought you had. Tommy told her what you said. I think she's flattered. You can forget glamour photos, though. Her mother would kill her. And then she'd kill you.'

* * *

6

He'd talked to my foster parents, too. Mister Howard asked me into their sitting room when I got home. You only got there by special invitation.

'Billy,' he said. 'Why do you always refer to us as your foster parents?'

I didn't answer.

'We're not your foster parents, Billy. And this isn't your foster home. This is a hostel, and Missus Howard and I are wardens.'

They had a wooden clock with a little plate on the front. There was an engraved message on it, but I couldn't read what the message said. I sat and listened to the tick.

'It's no good staring at your hands, Billy. We need to talk about this.'

As far as I could remember, we hadn't had a clock at home. There was a digital on the video, of course, and another on the microwave. The one on the video was always right because it came off the television signal. That clock ticking in a quiet room was the most comforting sound I could think of.

When they'd been doing their tests, I was asked to write down the three nicest words I could think of. I'd put "comforting" at the top.

Missus Howard made one of those little gestures at Mister Howard, and he shut up. 'Billy,' said Missus Howard. 'When ou first came here, you said you liked trees, and gardens, and rks. Do you remember saying that?'

I nodded.

There's an arboretum near here. Do you know what an etum is, Billy?'

hook my head.